Dvorak in Love

:C):C):C):C):C):C):C):C):C):C):C): C):C):C):C):C):C):C):C):

Dvorak in Love
A light-hearted dream

:C):C):C):C): C):C):C):C):C):C):C):C):C):C):C):C):C):C):

JOSEF SKVORECKY

Translated from the Czech by Paul Wilson

ALFRED A. KNOPF
New York 1987

THIS IS A BORZOI BOOK
PUBLISHED BY ALFRED A. KNOPF, INC.

Library of Congress Cataloging-in-Publication Data

Škvorecký, Josef.
    Dvorak in love.

    Translation of: Scherzo capriccioso.
    1. Dvořák, Antonín, 1841–1904—Fiction.
    I. Title.
PG5038.S527S313   1986   891.8'635   86-45466
ISBN 0-394-54681-4

Manufactured in the United States of America
FIRST AMERICAN EDITION

To my Josie

Man may embody truth,
but he cannot know it.

FRANZ KAFKA

TRANSLATOR'S ACKNOWLEDGEMENTS

The translator gratefully acknowledges the support of the Canada Council during his work on this translation. He also wishes to offer special thanks to John Reeves for reading a draft of the translation and giving comments and assistance in rendering the musical terminology; to Bobbie Bristol for her sensitive remarks on the text; and, as always, deepest gratitude to Louise Dennys and Gena Gorrell for their superb and invaluable help in the final stages of the work.

In memory of my brother Ted.

AUTHOR'S ACKNOWLEDGEMENTS

The author wishes to thank the John Simon Guggenheim Memorial Foundation for a grant which was most helpful in enabling him to write this novel.

My special thanks to Professor Mercer Cook for an interview and for the manuscript of his father's unfinished autobiography; to Josephine Harreld Love for information about Harry Burleigh; to the late Mary Klimesh and Lou Bernatz, ladies who knew Dvorak in Spillville, for interviews; to Cyril M. Klimesh for lending me his manuscript history of Spillville, since published under the title *They Came to This Place*; to Professor Michael Beckerman for musicological advice; to George Kovtun for help in the Library of Congress; to Charles Salaquarda for showing me Dvorak's New York; to Professor Zdenek Hruban for letting me peruse documents in the Czech archives in Chicago; to Miroslav Velek, M.D., for useful musicological hints; and to LeGrand Thurber for documents concerning his grandmother.

My thanks also to all those who helped me in any other way, especially Emma and William Barborka, Ruth Bernatz, Barbara Bristol, Lida Broder, John Clapham, Dominique-René de Lerma, Richard Drtina, Karl Gert zur Heide, D.W. Krummel, the late V. Laska, David Levering Lewis, Richard Liba, Professor Oskar Morawetz, John Novotney, Rosalyn Poshusta, Jana Prokop, Michaela Swinkels and Tillie Walsh.

Last but not least: with all my heart, to Louise Dennys, Gena Gorrell and Paul Wilson.

Dvorak in Love is my first attempt at writing a historical and biographical novel. It is not a scholarly life of Antonin Dvorak, and therefore I have used poetic licence where historical reality does not rule out historical possibility, and I have been inspired by many works which space does not allow me to acknowledge. To those interested in an exact factography, I would recommend the standard biographies of Dvorak, and in particular John Clapham's *Dvorak* (1979).

:C): CONTENTS

ANTONIN DVORAK'S COMPOSITIONS, AND MAIN EVENTS OF HIS LIFE,
that relate to the episodes described in this novel

1841	Sept. 8	born in Nelahozeves, Bohemia; son of village butcher and publican
1862		admitted to orchestra of Prague's National Theatre, as viola player
1865		begins teaching music to Josephine and Anna Cermakova, sometime early in year; composes Four Songs, dedicated to Josephine Cermakova; composes Cello Concerto in A Major
1871		composes the opera King and Collier
1873	March 9	has first significant success as composer when the Hlahol Choral Society performs The Heirs of the White Mountain
	Nov. 17	marries Anna Cermakova; she is 19
1874	April 4	birth of their first child, Otakar (died 1877)
1875	Sept. 19	birth of their daughter Josephine (died two days later)
1876	Sept. 18	birth of their daughter Rozarka (died ten months later)
1877		Josephine Cermakova marries Vaclav, Count Kounic
1878	June 6	birth of the Dvoraks' daughter Otylia composes Three Slavonic Rhapsodies; Slavonic Dances I
1880	Jan. 13	birth of daughter Anna composes Violin Concerto in A Minor
	Dec. 23	world première of Stabat Mater, in Prague
1881	Aug. 17	birth of daughter Magdalena
1883	March 7	birth of son Antonin composes Scherzo Capriccioso (symphonic poem in D-flat Major)
1885	Feb. 9	birth of son Otakar composes Symphony No. 2 in D Minor

1886		composes Slavonic Dances II
1888	*April 4*	birth of daughter Aloisia
1891	*June 6*	telegram from Jeannette Thurber offers him the post of Director of the National Conservatory in New York
	June 16	receives honorary doctorate from Cambridge University
	Oct. 9	world première of Requiem performed at Birmingham Festival
	autumn	signs contract with Mrs. Thurber
1892	*Sept. 27*	arrives in New York with his wife and two of the children, Otylia and Antonin
		composes Othello overture
1893	*May 24*	the rest of the children join the Dvoraks
	June 5	entire family arrives in Spillville, Iowa, for summer
	Aug. 12	conducts at the World Columbian Exhibition in Chicago
	Sept. 17	entire family returns to New York
	Dec. 16	world première of Symphony No. 5 in E Minor: From the New World
1894		composes Eight Humoresques (piano solos)
	May 30	entire family returns to Bohemia
		works on the final version of his opera Dimitri
	Sept. 8	plays new organ he has given to the church in Trebsko
	Oct. 26	returns with wife and son Otakar to New York
1895		composes Cello Concerto in B Minor, and American Suite in A minor
	April 27	returns with wife and son to Prague
	May 4	world première of the American Flag cantata in New York
	May 27	Josephine, Countess Kounic, dies at age 46
	June 17	visited by Adele Margulies, but she fails to persuade him to sign new contract with the National Conservatory in New York
	Aug. 17	resigns his post with the National Conservatory
1896	*March 19*	Leo Stern plays world première of Cello Concerto in B Minor, in London
	summer	Dvorak's American amanuensis, J.J. Kovarik, visits the Dvoraks in Bohemia
1898	*Nov. 17*	Otylia marries Josef Suk
1901	*March 31*	world première of Dvorak's opera Rusalka, in Prague
1904	*May 1*	death of Antonin Dvorak, at age 62; he is buried in Prague's Vysehrad cemetery May 5
1905	*July 5*	death of Otylia, at age 27
1931	*July 14*	death of Dvorak's wife, Anna, at age 77

Dvorak in Love

1   :C): THE MOOR

A FIELD OF GRAIN like an amber stiletto in the afternoon sun: she had to half close her eyes. A turquoise butterfly tottered up and out of the burning yellow, a blue reveller hovering unsteadily above the radiant ears of grain, as if it existed only to pose between the landscape and the sky, a fluttering sign of life. As Adele looked around, a wayward frond of hair fell across her eyes, casting a delicate mesh over the jubilant palette of colour. Dvorak is a devout man, she thought, that terrifying Gothic echo of Jacopone's Middle Ages resounds through his Stabat Mater.... God, the Devil, Christ, the thieves, their legs broken. Back then, they knew pain, they knew how real it was, were not distanced from it by the abstractions of this humanist century. His soul speaks from the music of the Stabat, a soul that can see, not as through a glass, darkly, but face to face. His music makes you feel like falling to your knees and then, pursued by devils and angels, fleeing to the nearest parish priest to be baptized. *"Inflammatus et accensus per te, Virgo, sim defensus...."* That absurd butterfly seemed to exist on earth only to serve as a radiant, ridiculous little spot set, like the clear ping of a musical triangle, against the pattern of angular amber fields, the rows of green sugar beets, the red bursting poppies and, driving their dark green wedges into the landscape, the romantic stands of spruce into which Will – insisting she stop the carriage, desperate to relieve his bladder – had vanished a short while ago.

The butterfly fluttered and danced in the sun. Suddenly a dark shadow swooped down and wiped the turquoise spot from the backdrop of the land. Adele glimpsed a tail, as forked as an adder's tongue. She tossed back her head, but the disturbing frond of hair still veiled the countryside. She had to brush it aside with her hand in order to see the brilliance of the profane world in its shadowless splendour. "*Quae maerebat et dolebat....*" It was as if someone had disrupted this pastorale in minor by strumming a dissonant major chord. The Master had for a moment closed his eyes to the world and opened the eyes of faith. A rock like Peter. *Tu es Petrus. Doctor angelicus.* Dvorak the Master. And about as educated as those fishermen from Galilee.

Except in music, of course. Adele closed her eyes, allowing the magical instrumentation to emerge with more clarity from the darkness behind her lids, from the first entry of the French horns to the coda's end, captivated by the mystery of music, the enigma of genius – the bewitching modulations of the waltz, dancing between harmonies that resolve into G major: Scherzo Capriccioso. A child of Weber. But what a child! A gorbelly, a Gargantua bursting with energy, regaling his audience with clever harmonies and astonishing tone-colours, briskly slapping them about. At times, the spirit rises to supreme bliss, then plunges back into its own helpless and uncertain ways, back to the heart of the mystery where even well-trained fingers may go astray.

Sibelius?

Back in New York, Adele recalled, Professor Door had advised Jeannette to consider Sibelius for the post of Director of the National Conservatory of Music. Sibelius was still a young man, but one upon whom the Muses had most passionately bestowed their favours. *Der beste Mann für das jüngste Land.* But – Jeannette had gone on to say – knowing you as well as I do, languid Adele, you will not heed the word of your teacher. Sibelius sits in fog-bound Helsinki, as far from Vienna as the village of Hannibal on the Mississippi (or some other God-forsaken outpost) is from civilized Manhattan. Knowing you as I do, Adele Margulies, you will betake your indolent body (iniquitous too – I know you!) first to Prague, and then – no need to go farther. That is, unless Dvorak is really such an incorrigible homebody and the allure of your gazelle-like eyes and my dollars falls upon the fertile, fallow rock of faith, virtue and music.

She opened her eyes. Jeannette Thurber, as usual, was wrong. She would have been quite happy to go to Helsinki. She had always been drawn to the exotic. What other young Viennese lady from a good family would, at the age of seventeen, have set out across the Atlantic into the musical wilderness of America where, as they say in Vienna (and though no one really believes it, she now knows it to be true), the audiences smoke cigars while listening to Beethoven?

After twelve years on that outsized continent, distances in Europe can hardly be daunting. As a matter of fact, I feel drawn to Finland ... a distant journey into the land of white nights.... But Sibelius's lacklustre little quintet? For a Jewish girl with the Devil in her body? Though of course an entirely different Devil from the terrifying diabolus of Jacopone! She closed her eyes again and danced several slow waltz steps in the dusty road. Dvorak's D major. Nice to listen to over a glass of beer – Brahms, the stuffed shirt, said that. Either he's ignorant, or jealous of the Master, the devout sorcerer who can conjure into his dances the whole history of garden restaurants, embroidered skirts flounced out by seven petticoats, romance beneath the smoking lanterns. Even the smoke of the cigars that show such disrespect for Beethoven. The apostate Brahms has never been able to cut a caper as this devout old Bohemian can. She pirouetted. And then – Sibelius is two years younger than I am.

She opened her eyes. A young man was emerging from the woods. He must have seen her pirouetting, for he was waltzing towards her, twisting his hips lasciviously as he did so. Will was elegantly dressed, as always. His black hair glistened in the sun, and he sported an ebony moustache above sensual lips. He waltzed across the meadow onto the road.

"Madame! Your kindness has preserved me from the sad fate of the great Tycho Brahe!" He spoke nasal but almost flawless Americanized German.

"Will," she said, "you are a blot on your race. I suppose even your Bible falls open at the least inspiring passages."

"My Bible, Miss Margulies, falls opens at the verse which goes: 'I am black, but comely....' "

She frowned, but he grinned, offered his arm and handed her back up into the carriage. Beyond his head, she could see patches of yellow, green, red and blue countryside, and the aroma of resin he had brought with him from the pinewoods tingled in her nostrils.

"*Weiterfahren!*" she commanded the driver. Will swung aboard behind her and casually slipped his arm around her waist. The heavenly, worldly landscape, the summer heat. When Mozart travelled this way more than a century ago, he may well have taken Constanza just as shamelessly in his arms. But she was his wife, and he wasn't a black man. And Will's so young, three years younger even than Sibelius! Almost six years younger than I. She made him put his hand back in his own lap, where she noticed a distinct bulge. Dear Lord!

"If you're going to be difficult, Will, I won't stop next time you ask."

"It was the Pilsener I had for breakfast," he said, with mock contrition. "A fundamental error. But I had to try it. Everyone knows it's Dvorak's favourite drink."

"That's no excuse," she replied. He laughed and leaned out the window, grinning at the dappled landscape. He started tapping his feet on the worn carpet and humming a song to an exotic countryside. "Joshua fit de battle of Jericho...."

How nicely the clip-clopping of the hoofs goes with the rhythm, she thought. The leather roof of the carriage flapped in the wind against the wooden frame, like a timpanist beating the drum-head with the flat of his hand. The carriage frame creaked: a subtle harmony of woodwinds. Occasionally, the driver would add to the pleasing cacophony by cracking his whip; the fields of grain sighed, a muted pianissimo of strings, and above it, Will's deep, carefree voice: "You may talk about your kings of Gideon...."

He stopped, then slid softly into Eine Kleine Nachtmusik.

Eine Kleine Negermusik.

She remembered Beethoven's Rondo Allegro in G Major. When they had played it together the day before yesterday, she felt as though she were hearing it for the first time in her life.

Door would no doubt have shaken his head. But I could hear America in it. The Negermusik continued quietly, while the toes of Will's polished shoes drummed out an exotic beat to the Mozart. The timpani of the leather roof, the charming cacophony of woodwinds. A bird flew past, screeching a provocative challenge to the passengers inside.

The red onion dome on the little white church was already visible in the distance. On top of a hill across the valley stood a château surrounded by a deer park. The landscape was ribboned with long, narrow fields of grain and sugar beets.

"He'll be in church, of course," she said.

They drove into the village square. Not a soul was about. Yes, they must all be at Sunday mass. She should have written to him. She began to feel discouraged. He's a homebody, and famous here, and the more famous he is, the less willing he'll be to budge. The thought of a long engagement across the Atlantic, far from his village shrine and no doubt from his pub as well.... Of course, Jeannette believes in the personal touch. She's a master of that herself. Getting old Belmont of Rothschild's bank to shell out for a quixotic venture like her Conservatory? I call that chutzpah. Even though it's in the stars now whether the Rothschild dollars will keep flowing. Well, if Rothschild won't come across, her husband will. All Jeannette has to do is say a few words to him in her cultivated French and her beloved goose will lay her another golden egg.

The personal touch, plus a fifteen-thousand-dollar offer – even the Master himself must yield to the magic of such grace notes. But had it been a good idea to bring Will along, as bait? Perhaps. There, lying in its case on the opposite seat, was Will's violin. If Will can play that well again.... (Look, Master! This is one of your future students at the New York Conservatory! He now wants to learn composition....) But I never dreamed he'd be so forward. Was it a good idea? Or pure selfishness?

The coachman brought the horses to a halt. Organ music was pouring out of the church. Will jumped down, and suddenly there he was in full sunlight, illuminated like a votive picture: a canary-yellow shirt front, brown face, snow-white shirt, pink vest, jacket of frog-green velvet, tight black trousers and patent-leather shoes of at least size thirteen – all this divine splendour displayed against a brilliant white wall on which a sundial with Roman numerals indicated that the time was past ten. He held out his hand. She gathered up her skirts and stepped to the ground.

"Wait here," she said to the coachman. "Or, if you prefer, you can come to church with us."

"If it's all the same to you, Miss, I'll wait in the tavern," and he pointed to a building with a sign that said FENCEL'S INN in florid lettering across the façade. Back in New York, when Antonin Dvorak was being considered as a possible candidate, Maretzek, taking a break from rehearsing his band, had laughed: "A religious people? Let me tell you, as soon as the Stars and Stripes are flying over their heads, the Czechs desert to the heathens in droves. The only Czechs who remain faithful to God in America, Madame, are we Jews."

"As you wish," she said. "But stay sober!" She turned to Will. "Shall we go?"

"You go, Miss Margulies. For a Congregationalist like myself, it would be sacrilege. Look at those idols!" And he pointed at the statues

of the saints on the church. Their haloes had recently been gilded
and their gowns glistened with fresh paint the colour of Will's jacket.

"All the pretty local girls are sure to be in church, Will," she said.

"I am not interested in *all* the pretty girls, Miss Margulies."

She ignored his emphasis.

"Don't you at least want to see the Master now that you've gone
to the trouble of coming this far?"

"Ah, but I will," he replied lightly. "Besides, I've seen him before."

"Oh? You mean in a picture?"

"No, in the flesh."

Where could that have been? Of course, the Master often went to
visit Joachim's conservatory in Berlin, where Will was studying now;
Joachim was well known to be somewhat daunted by the Master's
violin concerto.

"At Joachim's?"

"It wasn't at Joachim's. It would take too long to explain, Miss
Margulies; you'd miss the mass. And besides, I saw him in circumstances not entirely appropriate for a church-going man."

"Don't tell me you saw him eating meat on a Friday?" She smiled.

"Nothing quite so terrible."

"Oh, go to the Devil, Will."

She turned on her heel and walked into the temple of the Lord.

The ghastly blaring of a horn greeted her as she entered just in time
to see the organist in the choir gallery jump up, drop his pince-nez
and shout in a terrifying voice, "Silence, trombone! That's a bass line!"

At first, she thought she was imagining things. Could a black man,
a member of Will's race, be at the organ in this out-of-the-way village
in Central Europe? His nose was wide, his eyes deep, dark and pro-
truding, and his beard was short and bristly. With that complexion,
he might well have had trouble getting into some of the better restaurants in New York.

Again the voice boomed out, so startling the priest, who was about
to descend from the pulpit, that the congregation almost witnessed
their pastor tumble down the steps. "Don't just sit there, Suk!" roared
the voice. "Get up here and play! Girls don't need chaperoning in
church!"

She had picked up some Czech by listening to musicians in Vienna
and New York, and she could understand a little of what he was

saying. But the meaning was quite clear. As the priest scurried to the altar, she looked up and saw a haggard violinist rise to his feet beside the organ and gesture with his bow to one of the musicians huddled in the choir, their heads scarcely visible above the railing. In the pews below, a tall young man with a moustache slid quickly out past a fair-haired girl in a white blouse and hurried up the stairs to the choir. Meanwhile, in the choir, the trombonist, perhaps deafened by the din of his instrument, misread the violinist's cue and instead of stopping began playing louder still. The bass player followed suit, the two of them playing in unison, and under this barrage of bass thunder the thin-voiced violins, the viola and the clarinets wilted. The haggard violinist waved his bow in encouragement, his sheet music cascaded to the floor and the astonished string section stopped playing altogether, leaving the field to the bass and the trombone who, confused by the silence, went from fortissimo to double fortissimo. The ministrant at the altar dropped the burning censer.

Again the enormous voice boomed out. "Stop that trumpeting AT ONCE!"

The young man with the moustache appeared from behind the organ with his violin already under his chin, and as he started to play, an unexpectedly sweet, full tone flowed from his instrument. The first violinist stopped trying to gather up his music and began to conduct. The organist turned back to his console, and now the sonorous music rolled over her and swelled beneath the white-washed ceiling where a painted eye in a triangle with a faded grey dove at its apex stared down upon the believers. The priest, his composure restored, stepped up to the altar. The ministrant poured water from one of the ceremonial basins onto the smouldering carpet. The girl in the white blouse raised her eyes to the young man in the choir, who was now drawing his bow across the strings of his instrument with long sweeps, like a troubadour, then she boxed the ears of a little girl in the pew beside her who was kneeling on the seat, her back to the sanctuary, staring wide-eyed at the God of Wrath at the organ. Again the organist's mighty, resonant voice rang out, filled now with piety.

> *Ave, maris stella,*
> *Dei Mater alma,*
> *Atque semper Virgo,*
> *Felix caeli porta....*

The nave swelled with the sound of the congregation singing in unsteady harmony, all embarrassment forgotten.

She sat down in an empty place in the last row. The smell of the spilled incense reached her. The hands and feet that were drawing such heavenly sounds from the rickety organ were those of a sorcerer. Suk, the young man playing the violin, must be his apprentice, the other musicians – reformed and humble village spirits. The flushed trombonist, silent now and slumped at the edge of his row, was wiping the top of his bald head with a blue handkerchief. The nave of the little church pulsated with the music of the spheres. She thought again of the Scherzo Capriccioso. She thought, God knows why, of the music the godless Brahms constructed on rational principles in the Karlsgasse. But this was strange music, humorous and devout at the same time. Perhaps there was something in it of that false Messiah, the one who spent his time with scribes and prostitutes, rabbis and publicans.... She shook her head. Jewish mysticism, Adele.

She stood up as soon as the "*Ite missa est*" was pronounced and took up a position outside the church entrance. Will was already there, waiting. With the harsh noonday sun over her head, the magic of the sounds began to lose its power.

"You were right, Miss Margulies," Will said meekly. "But *all* the pretty girls are no longer in church."

Before she could think of a reply, two girls emerged from the door in folk costumes and stopped, transfixed, when they saw Will, black-skinned and as colourful as a sugar-plum in his bright suit. He bowed gallantly. The girls giggled.

Other girls were coming out of the church now, followed by young men. Will, exotic and strange, was swallowed up in an excited crowd. She looked back towards the door. People were dipping their fingers in the stoup as they left the church, making damp signs of the cross against the pitfalls of the coming Sunday afternoon. Will, surrounded by young people, was no longer visible from the entrance and now it was she who became the focus of attention. She felt conspicuous in her summer travelling ensemble purchased at Altman's on Fifth Avenue, her bird-of-paradise hat and her colourful gold Tiffany earrings. Middle-aged village men in black fedoras, and their wives in embroidered bonnets, stared at her openly. Old men getting ready to light up stood with their pipes halfway to their mouths, and their mouths were open.

She retreated a few steps. The villagers edged forward. She felt like a manikin in a shop window. Then they noticed the coach from Prague tied up in front of the inn. She tried to locate Will, but all she could see was a girl's arm, bare to the elbow, gingerly reaching out to touch a head of shiny black hair.

She turned back to the church. An elderly man carrying a trombone in a grey case slunk out the door and vanished swiftly around the corner; then two old men with clarinets under their arms came out and waited. Next came the viola player and two violinists. They began to argue excitedly, but their debate was cut short when the first violinist backed out into the harsh sun from the shadow of the entrance. Drops of perspiration sparkled on his bald head and a red handkerchief peered out from between the tails of an old-fashioned Kaiser jacket. He spread his arms and was standing there with them outstretched when into the glare of noonday stepped the organist. His grey hair accentuated his swarthy complexion, and the complexion accentuated his dark eyes. She heard the first violinist say in a flustered voice: "... he was upset, Dr. Dvorak, because Raiman hadn't written a part for the trombone, and he was looking forward to playing with you so much he decided to double the bass –"

"But my good fellow, can't you hear it? That bleating battlecry has no business in a piece by Raiman."

The voice was softer now, but still resonant. Along with the grey hair and the wild whiskers, the Creator had provided Dvorak with a strong body which in its youthfulness seemed almost arrogantly unsuited to the head. Beneath a bristling beard he wore an ostentatious necktie of emerald green, and his silk vest was contoured by the barely perceptible outline of an elegant paunch. As the sun struck his head, he donned a black homburg. She had to laugh, for he had cocked it at a raffish angle, just like a Fifth Avenue dandy.

"Yes, Master, of course I can hear it. But he's such a fine man I couldn't bring myself to spoil his pleasure. He plays at all the dances with us, and he's really quite good –"

"I'd be happy to hear him play in a tavern any day," said the God of Wrath Appeased. He took a huge cigar from a pocket in his jacket. "I've got nothing against brass-band music. But in church, sir? Only on Judgement Day – if at all. Come to think of it, they should hire him for that. The man can blow a trumpet, by Jove!"

"Dvorak!" a plump woman in a sober grey dress interrupted. "You still have one foot in the church."

"Then let's move," said the conciliated god. He put the big cigar in his mouth and stepped smartly away from the church. Behind him appeared the young man he had called Suk, and the girl in the white blouse leading the delinquent little girl by the hand.

Adele took a deep breath, walked up to Dvorak and addressed him in German: *"Hab ich die Ehre mit Herrn Doktor Dvorak zu sprechen?"*

His expression clouded. He glanced at the bird-of-paradise hat on its nest of dark red hair and brightened once again. The plump woman stared at the bird, and then at her.

"Das haben Sie," said the Master with a heavy accent. "And you are?"

"My name is Adele Margulies, from Vienna."

"Ah! From Vienna. *Wie geht es meinem geehrten Freund, dem grossen Brahms?"*

"Brahms weighs well over two hundred pounds and can't stop eating," she said. "For all I know, he may have got greater still." The scene she had witnessed in church had persuaded her that Dvorak, however godlike, was sitting on two stools, one in heaven and the other on earth, and she was encouraged to be impertinent. Still, there was a moment of uncertain silence; then a burst of Homeric laughter.

"How right you are, Miss Margulies: may have got greater still. Have you heard his latest? His Trio in A Minor?"

"Just a week ago, I played it with Professor Door and Mr. –"

"Ah, so you're a musician?" The deep dark eyes were suddenly friendly.

"I teach the pianoforte at the National Conservatory of Music," she said quickly.

"At the National...?"

"In New York. But each year, during the summer holidays, I come home to Vienna."

He grasped both her hands and squeezed them so hard she feared for her career. The bird-of-paradise slid down onto her forehead.

"Welcome to Vysoka! What brings you to Bohemia?"

She freed her hands, pushed the bird back into its nest, and said, "You, Master. I've come with an offer from Mrs. Jeannette Thurber, of New York."

But he was no longer listening. "Annie, come here!" he said, and took the plump woman by the hand. "My wife," he said, "and this" – pointing to the girl in the white blouse – "is my daughter Otylia, my daughter Aloisia, my...." But there was no one else there. He looked around. "Children! Where are you? By Jove – they're into mischief again." The voice thundered out, this time in a register of menace that frightened no one: "Annie! Magdalena! Tony! Otakar! Where are you?"

She looked around for Will, and glimpsed him being pulled and persuaded towards the inn, in a clutch of young men and women. Children of various sizes were cavorting around the edges of the crowd.

"Annie! Magdalena! Tony! Come here this instant. What in thunderation have you got there?"

"I'm afraid," she said, "it's my –" She stopped. How shall I describe him? My friend? Companion? Guide? He's not my student. The Master waited politely for an explanation. "– my colleague from Berlin. In any case, I believe you know him. He studies with Joachim. He's also in Vienna for the holidays."

"With Joachim, is he? He must know his instrument then. Suk, come over here."

With evident reluctance, the young man with the moustache left his place beside Dvorak's young daughter.

"This is Josef Suk, my amanuensis. He copies my scores."

"Adele Margulies," she said. "I heard you in church. You play wonderfully."

He bowed, took her hand, and kissed it.

"It's passable," admitted the Master. "I don't suppose he plays as well as your colleague, if Joachim has taken him on, but – you say I may know him? What is his name?"

Hidden from view by his retinue, Will had already reached the inn and was disappearing inside with the crowd pressing in behind him. The children, pushed to one side, were trying to get in as well. Once more the Master used the power of his voice to advantage:

"Anna! Magdalena! Tony! Otakar! DO YOU HEAR ME?"

They heard him and looked around, disappointment on their faces as the fairytale figure vanished through the gates of paradise. Reluctantly they shuffled back to their angry father – all except little Otakar who stood his ground, unwilling to accept such loss, and announced in a piercing voice: "Daddy, there's a real live blackamoor at the inn!"

"His name is Will Marion Cook," she said quickly. "He's an American Negro."

The trees smelled of apricots and honey. Dvorak's famous dovecote dominated the garden. While waiting for Will to join them, he showed her its wonders, and though she found the feathered creatures dull she tried to show a lively and informed interest anyway. When a grey and white bird responded to the Master's throaty cooing by flying up and perching on his outstretched arm, and as an expression of fondness, perhaps, deposited a liquid stool on his natty black boots, she asked whether it was the kind that could puff itself up. His gruff, monosyllabic reply made her feel she had dropped in his esteem. The bird was evidently not that kind. It was, however, interested in her hat, and fluttered onto her head to court the bird-of-paradise which promptly slipped down onto her nose again. To her relief, the Master laughed loudly and warmly. She straightened her hat and announced, ambiguously, that she had never seen a dove quite like this before.

The family were gathered together in the garden under a lush linden tree that smelled like the drugstores on Park Avenue, and the linden transformed the golden noon-hour into green and golden shade. Otylia, instructed to accompany Will back to the house, had been sent to the inn some time ago with an enormous jug for beer, and hadn't yet returned. Had she too fallen victim to his charms? Oh dear, the poor lovelorn amanuensis. Then Adele noticed that Mr. Suk was not there either. So that explained it. But the Master's suspicions were of a different nature.

"Tony!" said the Master to his eldest boy. "Your sister Otylia is lollygagging again and siphoning the foam off the beer, no doubt. Go and fetch her home."

The boy was eager to go, but his mother intervened. "Anton! Do you think that's wise?"

"Wise?" The wrinkle between his brows deepened into a canyon. "By Jove, Mother! You're right. It's like sending a goat to fetch vegetables from the garden. Tony, sit down. Otakar, you go instead."

And so the delighted six-year-old set off to look for Will and his sister, for whom – Adele guessed – the amanuensis was probably carrying the jug as slowly as his feet would carry him. But no sooner had the boy left than Suk slipped silently into the garden through a door behind the Master's back, coming from the interior of the house. A minute later, as though in a French farce, Otylia walked in through the garden gate. The Master, who was more interested in the state of the beer, failed to notice the timing. And Will was clearly not with them.

"The foam is almost gone, Otylia. You're sure you didn't drain some of it off?"

"No, Father." The girl's face was flushed, but she didn't look drunk. "I mean yes, I'm sure."

"Lying is a sin, you know that," said the Master. "And where is Mr.... Miss Margulies's friend? And we sent Otakar to fetch you. How in heaven's name could you have missed him?"

"I don't know," said the girl, turning poppy-red. "I told him and he said he was coming in a moment. The schoolmaster was going to bring him."

Wonderful Brahmsian aromas were drifting out from the kitchen. Pork, cabbage and dumplings. The beer was probably not from Pilsen. The smell, however, seemed to make the Master more impatient than ever.

"Now I suppose we'll have to send someone for Otakar. Who shall it be?"

He ran his wild eyes over the remaining children, and fastened on the ten-year-old. "Magda! –" and added something that Adele couldn't quite follow. From his wife's expression, she guessed that this time the tempestuous saint had taken the Lord's name in vain.

The girl shot out of the house.

There was an unreality to it all. Amid the aroma of dumplings and the throaty gurgling of the incontinent pigeons, little Aloisia's runny nose and the father's blindness to the seduction of innocence going on under his own roof, amid all this were born melodies that perhaps only Schubert could emulate, music from heaven. She glanced at this man blessed with the gift of song, dejectedly examining the sinking foam in his tankard. *Quando corpus morietur, fac ut animae donetur paradisi gloria.*

"*Paradisi gloria,*" she said to herself, without knowing why. Then she understood. *Quia turpe amo.* The Pope washing the smelly feet of twelve filthy old men, in memory of Christ's act of service. Heaven touching pigeon dung.

The Countess was beautiful. She didn't look forty. She had a high forehead, and dark shining hair twisted into ringlets that cascaded around her face to her shoulders. Her eyes were so melancholy that her face seemed no less than the framework of her soul. From the garden, they had all watched as she drove up in her carriage. The elegant man of forty who had been sitting next to the coachman, his legs crossed, was the Countess's husband. "My sister-in-law Josephine, Countess Kounic," the Master had said. So this creature out of an Andersen fairytale, and the plump woman labouring over her dumplings, were sisters. Later, back in New York, she learned that Dvorak's wife was the younger of the two sisters.

She thought she could see regret in the Countess's eyes. Her ringlets swayed as she fanned herself with a Venetian fan. She and Otylia looked like sisters. The girl – who could scarcely have been fourteen – had the same sad eyes as the Countess, that same glimmer of regret for something that would end too soon.

And Will, of course, was shirking his duty, for he knew very well that she had brought him along on this mission as bait. Will had chosen to lag behind at the inn, no doubt bewitching the local belles with his exotic charm. Do the girls in this backwater town speak German? But since when do girls have to know German to know what Will Marion wants of them? They would understand even if they were deaf.

"You ought to go, Anton, you really ought to go." They were discussing Jeannette Thurber's offer, and the Countess's voice was like a cello in the middle register. She had seldom heard a voice with such a distinctive timbre. When she asked if she sang, the Countess had laughed and said she was only an actress, a one-time actress at that, and anyway she had only played in farces and low comedies, and badly at that. Not even the notoriously kind Mr. Neruda had had a good word to say for her talent. Who Mr. Neruda was Adele had no idea, but she noticed that for a brief moment the light of a happier life flared up in the Countess's sad eyes.

"That's all very well, Josie," said the Master, "but America? That means crossing the Atlantic Ocean. We couldn't all go."

"Why not?" said the Count. "Fifteen thousand dollars...."

"You'd never make that kind of money in fifteen years in the conservatory in Prague, Anton," said Dvorak's wife.

She felt a tension creep into the idyllic Sunday calm. The children, except for Otylia, had gone off, ostensibly to play hide-and-seek though she knew what they were really up to. She felt uneasy, and to exorcize the tension she said quickly, "You are extremely popular in

America, Master. Not only do they play your music in New York, they play it in Baltimore, Cincinnati, Chicago –"

"Thomas, that's his name, isn't it, Theodore Thomas? They say he has his own orchestra. Imagine that, Annie, a private orchestra. Tell me, Miss Margulies, but honestly" – and from his glance she knew it wasn't the thought of crossing the ocean that was worrying him – "is his orchestra any good? I've heard he has Indians playing in it."

She laughed. "No, he doesn't, but it won't be long before he'll have Negroes. There are several students at the Conservatory already."

"How extraordinary."

Extraordinary? Yet when I first went there, Adele thought, I believed that Negroes were born and died as shoeshine boys. Now I know they only die that way.

Not all of them, though. "Wait till you meet Will Cook," she said. "If we can manage to get him out of the inn. But I'm afraid he's more interested in the local girls than he is in you. I hope you are not offended, Master. He tells me you've already met, in Berlin."

He shook his head. "I don't recall meeting any Negroes in Berlin."

"I suppose he only saw you at a concert somewhere and now he's bragging about it. He's a superb performer. We wanted to play some Beethoven for you so you'd see that Negroes don't just beat drums. Unfortunately," she sighed, "unless we can get him out of the tavern today, the concert is off."

The Master was growing restless. "You were saying you completed your studies under Door?"

"Magna cum laude."

He looked about him. The Countess smiled. Abruptly, he turned around, and just as abruptly the two people sitting on the bench behind him shifted apart.

"Suk!"

"Yes, sir?"

"Get your violin. We're going to play."

In the end, they performed the Rondo Allegro in a room on the second floor, where the piano was, and where the sharp aroma of the trees, the beehives and the nearby wood came through the open window. Technically Suk was Will's equal, but he played differently, differently. As with Will, however, the precise finger-work was informed by the kind of heaven-sent gift that distinguishes a real musician.

He played sweetly, though not exactly in the spirit of the score. It was not his fault, however; the girl on the chair behind the Master's back was staring down at the rug, and her ears were red.

They were applauded.

"You play nicely," the Master told her, and then, "Suk! You're putting too much into it! You make it sound like some kind of serenade!"

The amanuensis quickly slipped his violin back into the case. She noticed that his ears were burning too. Quickly, she made a bold request: "Master, could I ask you...? Your Slavonic Dances for four hands. If you'd be kind enough, I'd consider it a great honour...."

She saw uncertainty in his dark eyes; it told her he thought more of her playing than niggardly words could express. He waved his hands negatively. "I can't play like you. I'd spoil it. How about –" He turned to his wife. "Annie, would you like to try playing with the young lady from Vienna?"

His wife required no urging. Adele made room beside her on the piano bench.

"Which one?"

"The first," said his wife.

Five beats after the opening chord, she stopped wondering about the tensions in this family, about the surmised relationships that so interested her. Perhaps it was the music, but she was coming to believe that nothing and no one under this roof was quite as simple as the house, the garden, the smell of cooking, as the inn, from which music could be faintly heard in the distance, suggested. The energetic bass line put everything in the mundane world to flight and drove her thoughts into the cheerful abstraction of sounds. Dvorak writes light-hearted bass lines, original bass lines, Ehlert had said in his review – the heart of a true musician laughs in his body. The truth of the saying embraced her sweetly and she watched his wife's fingers, beautiful, nimble and so different from the wan face, the tightly pursed lips. She watched her fingers and forearms describing the swanlike arcs of the European virtuoso school before descending lightly to the ivory keys with the assurance that comes from the years of hard work on which this bliss is slowly built. With the sensation of happiness, her thoughts brought her back to this woman playing the bass line, and from there to her own carefree youth in the Prater, in Vienna. It was as though she could see herself there, skipping gaily in a circle of maids on their Sunday off, leaping up and down in a Viennese street dance, hitting the ground on the downbeat. One-two, one-two, one-two –

– but the street dance had passed through the prism of talent and been split into a seven-coloured rainbow of instrumentation. She could remember it vividly, but now it seemed to rise from the bass notes. Annie Dvorak was no ageing matron who had once, long ago, taken piano lessons. She was an energetic pianist, a true helpmate to the wild man who had charmed this music into existence.

They played and, in the slightly executed rhythms, the slight antipathy she had originally felt for Annie began to dissolve, and soon dissipated entirely.

They finished. Applause. Annie turned round to the Countess: "Jo, wouldn't you like to play?"

"Goodness no!" But the fan snapped shut. "You're the virtuoso in the family, Annie. In the last few years, I've got completely out of practice. No one should have to listen to my tinkling, least of all Miss Margulies."

The Count laughed. "The young lady teaches music. I'm sure she can bear it."

"And what about the composer? He shouldn't have to listen to bad playing."

"Don't be silly, Josie," said the Master. He seemed ill at ease.

"Anton will have to bear it too," the Count said. "He's teaching again, after all. Listening to pupils, good or bad, is part of his job."

The Countess laughed and glanced fondly at the Count. She stood up, placed her fan on the chair and approached the piano in her expensive white gown. The sweet scent of lily-of-the-valley surrounded her. Annie rose briskly and resumed her place beside her husband.

"But I'll have to play lead." She dipped her head and the ringlets tumbled over the high, pale forehead. A white hand swept the hair back where it belonged – her arm bare almost to the elbow – and then reached out towards the keyboard and touched it timidly. Mother-of-pearl nails. "I always play lead," she said, "and I'm not very good at sight-reading any more."

"Of course, as you wish." Adele made room for her. "Which one will it be?"

"The tenth," said the Countess.

Zigeunermusik. Silently, she gave the nod to start and the mother-of-pearl flowed across the keyboard. Now Adele could hear what she had first seen in the Countess's eyes. Time running out. And the sad tones, which could no longer succour the Countess, were like drops of glass in the upper register of the keyboard.

Adele, schooled in the tough, regimented ways of Door the disciplinarian, discovered she was learning something. She could suddenly hear another dimension. The Countess was no virtuoso. When she played the mazurka, notes were left out of chords but the tones were as close as they could be to heaven and the melody seemed to free itself from the short, choppy blows of the hammers, and began to sound like strings, like the amanuensis on the violin, except that his instrument sang of beginnings. She had gathered that the Countess had a weak heart. Observing her face, now in profile to her, comely and with an aura of purity, she understood that the Countess's spirit was ready for its journey.

She was oppressed by sadness. Music is like that, beyond meaning, untranslatable. She saw the girl, she saw Dvorak, his swarthy face, and saw that melancholy too sat in his large, deep, lively eyes. Next to him, his wife sat rigid once more, her mouth a tight, bitter line. The enormous Count, in a light grey vest with a gold watch-chain, was intently examining a signet ring on the middle finger of his left hand. A tiny silver pathway led through his brown hair, a pearly trace of that sadness.

Once again she turned around. The amanuensis was squatting like a stump by the young girl's side. The girl herself was lost inside the music.

She shuddered. Into the touching melody, from which entire chords were dropped, forgotten, like autumn leaves, there suddenly stole an alien rhythm. It was a while before she realized that it was coming from the inn, and that it was creeping through the open window. The acoustic joke of a sunny afternoon, the hay-wagon of a polka running headlong into the sadness of a swansong.

Dvorak heard it too. He stood up to close the window, then hesitated and turned, the body of an elegant gentleman with the head of a comic old man in black outline against a yellow-green tableau of trees and sunshine. The bleating of a trumpet marred their coda.

The Count, the wife, the girl and the lovelorn Suk all clapped politely as the Countess got up.

"That was so bad, so embarrassing! I wish I could just vanish."
And she turned to face the figure at the window. "Forgive me, Ton?"

A furrow as deep and straight as a duelling scar had appeared
between his eyebrows.

"You see?" murmured the Countess. "I've pained him, playing it
so poorly...."

But Dvorak had not heard her. He was listening intently. And
from an inner world, and then from the world beyond the window,
the eyes returned to the music room.

"Confound it, what are they playing over there?" he said gruffly,
bewildered. "Is that supposed to be a polka?" Adele listened atten-
tively to the distant trumpet.

It was a polka. But Will was toying with it; the pulse of his fortissimo did not coincide with the beat of the drum or the rhythmic
pulse of the clarinet. Indeed. Indeed.

She laughed. "I'm afraid, sir," she said, "that Will Marion is making free with one of your Slavonic Dances."

She glimpsed him through a shroud of smoke rising from a corner
table where a group of old men sat near the band. Will was standing
there in a white shirt soaked with perspiration, his skin against the
whiteness looking darker than it really was. Here in the pub, Dvorak's
music had transmigrated back to its beginnings. Tankards on oaken
tables, the smell of beer-soaked wood and tobacco, old men's faces
cross-hatched by their long-stemmed pipes. Girls in short skirts were
dancing up and down on the worn floorboards, their partners hoisting
them into the air while holding them firmly around the waist so they
would not fly away. The trombonist whose ambitions had been
thwarted in church that morning was thundering away on the right,
and the first violinist was earning his wages with gusto. In front of
the band, in that white shirt, Will Marion was slaughtering the polka.

The deep furrow divided Dvorak's forehead again. He appeared to
be grappling with the mystery encoded in Will's diminished thirds.
She knew them already. And the rhythm that appeared to elude the
bow-strokes of the desperate bass fiddler and throw the old clarinetist
into confusion....

Or was it driving him to ecstasy? She was witnessing the engagement of two worlds, both of them in fact unknown to her, a Viennese
girl from a good family. She had caught glimpses of them on Sunday

walks with her family in the Prater, or when Huneker, mildly in his cups, had taken her for a cab ride along the East River in New York and somewhere, from one of the Irish dives, the strains of a rough-hewn jig had flown out the door and struck her like a sudden slap in the face. The girls flew up and down while Will was grafting onto the polka sounds from – where, exactly, were they from? And where was Will from? And where had he learned that? Hardly at Joachim's Berlin conservatory.

The music ended. Will's fine teeth shone whiter than his shirt. He ejected a stream of saliva from the trumpet and handed the instrument back to its owner. The girls, back on their feet again, broke into applause. Will, as bandleader, his mouth a wide smile, bowed deeply.

Suddenly the smile vanished, and the trombonist jumped up, knocking a tankard of ale to the floor with his chair in what looked like an attempt to run away. But there was no way out; the inn was jammed with people. Panicked, the first violinist ran forward a few steps, but he didn't get far. The Master was pushing his way through the exhausted couples on the floor and heading straight for Will.

When they saw who it was they made way for him. Will was now surrounded by children, and in the sudden silence a child's face turned round, then several small bodies bolted for the safety of the crowd. In vain. Adele saw the Master's wife making straight for the smallest one.

Dvorak stopped in front of Will, who was almost standing at attention. Joachim's Prussian training.

"What in the world," said the Master in menacing German, "were you playing?"

Will turned ashen. "A polka – I think – sir."

"And is that how you play polkas in America?"

Adele's fine hearing had again detected a nuance: what sounded like menace could be eager curiosity. This man, who had made himself master of all tone-colours, rhythms, modulations and chord combinations, was overcome by his passion for collecting new sounds.

"Yes," Will swallowed. She had to laugh to herself – the handsome, self-confident young man suddenly become a diffident student. "Sometimes...."

"Hm." A sound that defied description resounded in the Master's chest. "All right," he commanded, "play!"

Will looked at him uncertainly. *"Ich habe – "* he said, and then his almost perfect German abandoned him and he made a grammatical mistake in gender: *"meine Geige in dem Kutsche – Herr Doktor –"*

"Then *leave* your violin in the coach!" commanded the Master. He looked terrifying. "My good fellow, you play like – I don't know.... " And he turned to her. "I've just remembered that when I was nine, I was afraid I'd have to spend the rest of my days in the butcher shop, so I wrote a polka out of sheer desperation."

He looked up at the ceiling, and she thought how unexpectedly negroid his features seemed – a white man with a minstrel-show black-face. "Even at the age of nine, I'm sure you couldn't have written anything bad," she said flatteringly.

"Well, it was a polka, Miss Margulies, and it was passable. And yet, I hadn't the slightest notion of instrumentation. I wrote the trumpet part in the same key as the violin. You can't imagine what it sounded like."

She laughed. "In any case, it must have been interesting."

"It sounded – by heaven! – it sounded odd, to put it politely. But never mind." He turned to Will. "So play, play, my good man. We're eager to hear you."

They made a place for him at one of the tables. The innkeeper, who wore an apron with a large greasy blotch shaped like a cow on it, set a tankard on the table. The Master blew aside the stiff foam and drank. His wife led away the delinquent children. The young girl pulled the infatuated amanuensis to a table. Terrified, Will licked his dry lips and got ready, and the band began to play.

Will stumbled over the first note. But he recovered. And, very cleverly, he understood what the Master wanted to hear. Through the sounds of a Viennese waltz he began to infiltrate the alien sounds of some other music, a kind of music she herself didn't know....

"My good fellow," Dvorak said as they finally sat down to lunch in the house. "You say we met in Berlin. But I've never seen you before in my life. And I'd certainly remember *you*."

Will let the remark go by. He had grown accustomed to being the first black man most people he met here had seen. And the Master was clearly an innocent. "I'm sorry, but I didn't say we'd met. I said I'd seen you."

"At Joachim's?"

"No, I saw you once in a restaurant."

"That's not surprising," said Anna, his wife, as she served the savoury dumplings and pork. "Wherever you find a pub, you'll find Anton inside."

"It was a concert café," said Will respectfully.

"I'm surprised," said his wife. "Dvorak goes to restaurants for the beer, not for the music." It seemed to Adele that he blushed. It wasn't until later that she understood why.

"What did you see in the concert café, Will?"

His arm was around her waist. She did not protest and her mind was teeming with thoughts inappropriate for a music teacher. Margulies! Even Jeannette, who tolerates all kinds of misbehaviour, would probably disapprove of this. But what of it? We're on holiday.

The carriage was rattling along the dusty road which divided the sweet-smelling countryside into two dark halves like a line of chalk. A moon hung over the landscape, almost as magic as its limelight imitation in one of Jeannette's operas.

"What did you see in that concert café, Will?"

"I don't remember," he murmured into her hair, and kissed her on the back of the neck.

"That's a lie. You were there with some fräulein."

"You didn't ask me that."

"Well, I'm asking now."

He slid his hand onto her breast. The bed in her room made terrible creaking noises, she thought. Should she go to his room? Maybe all the beds in the hotel creaked.

"Were you?"

"I was."

"And what did you see?"

A moth flew in through the open window of the carriage and flattened itself against the upholstery of the seat opposite them. "Wait!" she said, extricating herself from his embrace and leaning towards the creature. The theatrical moon stood directly overhead, and the first houses on the outskirts of Prague were beginning to appear, the pale glow from their windows providing a faint illumination inside the carriage. She shuddered. The creature's wings were convulsing slowly, helplessly, as though it was having trouble breathing. On its shaggy thorax she could make out the clear outline of a human skull.

She shuddered, remembering the momentary shadow that had wiped the butterfly from the air.

"I'll tell you some other time," she heard Will say as he drew her back into his embrace. But the death's-head moth drove thoughts of sin from her mind.

The lights of the city became brighter and the melodramatic moon grew proportionately pale. She was touched by an intimation of the brevity of time. The Countess with the ailing heart – a fleeting soul in a frame of black hair – the girl with her aunt's eyes, and the Master himself, irascible, imposing, elegant – but at the age of fifty with the head of an irritable old man. She remembered how Huneker, frequently tipsy, unpleasant but clever none the less, had once said to her in the staff room of the Conservatory: "Have you ever thought, my dear Adele, how short your life is? I mean your conscious life? You've got twenty active, working years and suddenly you have reached the grand climacteric. Before twenty-five or thirty, you are mentally pulp, without a face of your own; after fifty you regain the traits of your individual tribe or family. The harvest years are from thirty to fifty."

And this year, I'll be thirty. This thoughtless creature beside me, twenty-three years old and full of juices and hypothetical infinity. Dvorak – transformed, wondering, enthralled by Will's tricks. Soon, when his body catches up to his old man's head, he will vanish and with him all his enchantment, the *oeuvre* will be for ever closed, with nothing more to be added, nothing more. She was overcome by sorrow at the thought that such a fountain of music would eventually have to dry up.... *Quando corpus morietur....*

The carriage wheels began to clatter over bumpy cobblestones. From somewhere, she could hear a drunken chorus, and the door of a tavern slammed.

"Wait, Will! Not now!" She struggled out of his arms. "I have to look like a teacher, after all! Not like some –" Decorously, she set her hat straight and smoothed out her skirt.

Paradisi gloria....

2　:C): A LETTER FROM JEANNETTE

FRANCIS LOOKED DOWN from his high office into Hudson Street, where an exhausted horse had collapsed a short while before. The wagoner was trying to whip the animal to its feet, and he was going to open the window to reprimand him and order him to unharness the horse and take him to the stable, when he saw that a gentleman in a top hat and a grey overcoat, in the company of two ladies carrying parasols, had beaten him to it. Seen from his window, the whole affair became a pantomime. The gentleman waved a Spanish walking-stick with a yellow knob, the wagoner brandished his whip, but the first blow was struck by the elder of the two ladies, who cracked the driver over the head with her parasol. At that moment, a policeman intervened. Watching the scene as it unfolded, Francis was reminded of the farces in Brownwell's theatre, and the only upsetting thing was the sign on the side of the wagon, his sign, which clearly read: THURBER, WHYLAND & CO.

There was a knock on the door. Come in! he said, and an office boy stepped into the room with a letter from England. Eagerly, he took the envelope. The paper had the texture of birchbark, Jeannette's unmistakable trademark. His mood improved at once. He took the envelope to the writing desk where her photograph stood, bright and shining in an oval frame between the bronze inkwell and a marble bust of Abraham Lincoln. Hazel eyes, walnut hair gathered up pompadour-style, and a revealing décolletage. She could still make his head spin, and each time he had to remind himself that Jeannette was adept at almost everything but looking after money.

That's my job, he said to himself. He slit the envelope open with a bronze letter-opener.

Dear Francis,

Wonderful news! He's coming! At least I think he is. But it was not easy. He is rather different from Adele's description of him. He's not homespun at all. He looks very handsome in tails and I'm sure he must be a dandy at heart. Of all the candidates for honorary doctorates at Cambridge University – and there were certainly some swanky-looking gentlemen among them, like Dufferin, as well as some dowdy-looking louts like that Russian Machnikoff – he was by far the most elegant. He wore a black velvet cap with gold cording and a cape of golden brocade with a floral pattern, and when he shook hands with the Chancellor, you could see that it had a divine, a truly divine lining of black silk. I must try and find something like it in London for Marianna. He cuts a magnificent figure; Adele described that accurately enough – she has an eye for such details, doesn't she. His face is not especially handsome – except for the eyes, which are sparkling, large, gay and clever. His features don't seem Slavic – he has a broad nose and a dark complexion – but when I remarked on it he chuckled heartily and said, "I'm a hundred per cent Czech, Mrs. Thurber, except for the ten per cent of me that is Tartar, and for that I have Attila, the Scourge of God, to blame. And since you've mentioned it, I can't for the life of me remember whether the Tartars had black skin or white." Then he raised his finger and said, almost severely: "But I don't have a drop of German blood. Not a drop!" Still, his German is decidedly better than his English. I heard him speak with Rathenau at the banquet, but the moment I began speaking to him in that language, he said, "Please, Mrs. Thurber, let us speak in English. Or do you too think that we Czechs are really just Germans?"

He looked up from the letter to prolong the pleasure. A Hamburg-America liner was steaming proudly up the Hudson River, smoke pouring from its two black and yellow stacks. Lord, he thought, what have I done that You should have bestowed such a woman upon me? He looked at the photograph of his beautiful, educated wife, so full of energy, her elegant head teeming with ideas that had not exactly made her popular in New York society. For that matter, their husbands are not what you'd call kindly disposed towards me, either. He could hear her contralto voice reading her – and therefore his – favourite poems: Annabel Lee, Hiawatha.... Not Shakespeare, not Tennyson – but the wretched Poe and his Ulalume, The Conqueror

Worm, To Helen. Because for her Poe was the first great American poet, and she is an American first and last, though she occasionally converses with her ancient father in Danish, and when she does she sounds exotic and irrevocably a part of Europe.

But that's what America is – divided personalities. Partly from these shores, and partly from God knows where – the Congo basin perhaps. And a maestro, a former tenor with an Italian name, had sat in the salon by the fireplace and said, "Madame, I find your patriotism honourable. But the American language? Judge for yourself, I implore you." His chins wobbled, he shaped his lips into an "O" and in a voice that contained only a hint of its former glory yet with a gesture that retained the pomp of the grand opera, he began, "*La donna è mobile –*" Then he rolled his eyes, unpursed his lips and croaked in an offensive tone: "Ladies' fidelity sways like a melody, Tossed like a feather on every zephyr...." He closed his eyes and shuddered in theatrical disgust. "But Maestro," his wife had said, with an alluring movement of her partially bared shoulders, "that is simply a bad translation. If we'd been able to persuade one of our excellent American poets – someone like Lowell or Whittier – to write the libretto, the aria would have sounded as beautiful in English as in the original." But the maestro had gestured dismissively and, without so much as a glance at Jeannette's warm, white, persuasive shoulders, croaked in a voice more distressing still, "Waaay down upon the Swaaaneee Ribber...."

And so nothing changed in the Metropolitan Opera House, and evening after evening, Italian tenors, and tenors whose Italian was merely fractured, struck poses that resembled the wary stance of a wrestler more than the waiting embrace of a lover, and instead of singing their arias to the prima donnas, they turned to face the footlights so that the glow would enhance their sparkling eyes and well-fed, olive-hued features, and they sang magnificently to the public in words no one could understand. Could they not sing in English even once a week? Just once a week? She was unable to convince the gentlemen from the Met. In those precincts where night after night crystal chandeliers set fire to diamond tiaras, the only English to be heard was among the audience. One night, after a delightful day in the woods at the foot of Mount Onteora, in the Catskills, she came to him in a lace nightgown from Worth, for she always used what she had to good advantage, and always in a worthy cause: "Francis, I need a hundred thousand. Will my dear goose lay a golden egg for me?"

Willingly, willingly. And afterwards, under the influence of those eyes and that bronze hair, Belmont, Carnegie and others had provided a few more golden eggs.

He returned to the letter:

When he thawed towards me – and I'll tell you how that happened later – I understood why he'd had so many objections at first. "Do you have any children, Mrs. Thurber?" he asked. I told him we had two daughters and a son. He was silent for a moment, then he said sadly, "We had three children too. Our first, Otakar – he was born after the wedding; Josephine, who was born a year later; and Rozarka, a year after Josephine. And all three of them died. Otakar was three, Rozarka was only ten months, and poor little Josephine passed away two days after she was born. Fortunately we had her christened in time. But you know, Mrs. Thurber, we're believers. The Lord gives, and the Lord takes away, though we mortals seldom know the reason why." And tears were flowing down his cheeks! He wiped them away with the palms of his hands and said, "We tried to accept it with humility, but it still hurts, Mrs. Thurber. We were young and poor at the time, I was making a living as an organist – and we lost three children – one after the other." My heart went out to him. We were sitting on an ottoman, sheltered behind some fig plants, but I could see people looking at us curiously. Everyone would have loved to talk to Dvorak and here was I, a brassy American, monopolizing him. You can imagine the looks I got. "But Dr. Dvorak," I said, "that same Lord gave you six more beautiful children." He pulled out a white handkerchief and blew his nose loudly. "Yes, but that's just the point, Mrs. Thurber. How could I possibly take them all with me to America?" "Why not? Your income will be more than enough for that, and –" "But what if the ship sinks? What then?" It was certainly inappropriate of me to find his worry almost funny at that moment, but I couldn't help it. There was such terror in his eyes at the thought that another six innocent children might perish, and yet I don't think it had crossed his mind that in the event of such an improbable disaster, he and his wife would no doubt perish as well, so that the entire family would enter paradise together. And Francis – he believes literally in heaven. He imagines it to be a permanent feast with enough for everybody. He said, "You know, well as things are going for me now, I am still deeply troubled when I see others less fortunate. Sometimes it dampens my own pleasure, Mrs. Thurber, even the pleasure I get from the celebration of Christmas. When I see poor people – and there's nothing one can do to help them, one or two perhaps but look at how many there are in the world! If the socialists weren't such a godless lot, I'd join them at once. But what do we know of the Lord's design, Mrs. Thurber? Nothing. And we won't learn much in this life, either. Look!" And he pointed somewhere behind us, and when I turned around, I saw through a large window a beautiful view of the star-filled heavens. "You see that? The stars are enormous worlds, and who will ever explore them? How insignificant we are before the Creator! How can we dare to doubt? And that always eases my mind, Mrs. Thurber. God is just. Master or man, we have all entered the world with the same soul, and those who keep their soul pure will some day...." I'm sure you'll like him, Francis. You who give shares in your company to any drunken wagoner. Sometimes I'm surprised you haven't gone bankrupt long ago.

He laughed. Well, I generally know how to handle things, Jeannette. Still, you know how to handle me. If you like this maestro of yours, I certainly will.

The black and yellow steamer, an antediluvian dinosaur, blew its whistle. Never mind that hundred thousand. It gave me a glimpse of something like the Master's starry heavens. Lohengrin, The Flying Dutchman, Orpheus in the Underworld, Norma, Faust, Aida, The Magic Flute – a long line of expensive but fabulous miracles paraded through his mind. For the first time, with his cultivated and patriotic wife by his side, he had been able to understand those operas. A pity her American Opera Company had lasted only two years. If you hadn't been betrayed by your investors, dear Jeannette, the debits might have balanced the credits in the end. But Gould backed off, and I'm willing to bet it wasn't because he was afraid of losing money, but because he wanted to land me one below the belt. He'll never forgive me for that anti-monopoly legislation that passed through Congress. And that conspicuous churchgoer Carnegie? He'd rather buy three thousand harmoniums for three thousand Sunday Schools than foot the bill for a single Magic Flute. He knows that here in this land where we are still haunted by the Salem witches, it is a much better form of advertising.

He lit a cigar. Had America ever before seen such exquisite stage productions as his wife's extravagant follies? Not to mention such statuesque dancers, imported directly from Paris? But you should have known, Jeannette, that Carnegie and his spiritual advisors believe

God created woman for a single purpose, and even that purpose is less than dear to His heart. How upset she was! How she flushed, right to the depths of her famous décolletage. He puffed on his cigar, opened the bottom drawer of his desk and pulled out a book bound in velvet. Newspaper clippings were pasted onto the black pages. He leafed through it until he found what he was looking for. There it was – the philippic of an outraged minister.

"The entire history of the stage and, with few exceptions, the biographies of actors and actresses, have demonstrated the corrupt and demoralizing character and influence of the theatrical profession and performances. With regard to the ballet dances in connection with theatre or the operas performed by Mrs. Thurber's American Opera Company, I cannot understand the type of virtue that engages in it, that employs and manages it, or that can look upon it without a blush. A woman must have lost the grace of modesty to have become a ballet-dancer. A money-maker must have forgotten what he owes to the memory of his mother and have lost his chivalric honour for womanhood to employ girls for such sensual purposes."

Jeannette had been furious. The ballet within an opera had been her idea. Small improvements were one of her hobby-horses. She had run to Signor del Frino with the newspaper, and the usually sanguine Italian from Baltimore had sat down and with a quill pen – a stage prop from one of the operas – dashed off a caustic letter which Jeannette sent to the newspaper by personal courier. "The average cleric has as much appreciation of beauty as a mule," raged the pious Catholic *maître de ballet*. "His one horror is to see others happy. My only fear is that such people will become advocates of the ballet. If they do, they will make it a bore, a nuisance, a terror, as with everything they touch." His fears proved groundless, but Jeannette's magnificent vision ended on the auction block in a roller-skating rink in Jersey City Heights. The scenery, the costumes, the musical scores, the stage machinery and properties from fifteen operas – representing an investment of a good three hundred thousand dollars. In the end, the old money-lender Lawrence, who was the principal creditor, bought it all up for twenty-five thousand dollars. The auctioneer practically wept as he brought his gavel down on a magnificent cape from Aida, sparkling with cut-glass diamonds, sold for a pittance because no one offered more than the parsimonious Lawrence. Jeannette, understandably, did not show up. But he had to go, to witness the sad

demise of another American dream. Above the concrete ring where
the youth of New Jersey usually went roller-skating, the monstrous
voice of Mammon called out the absurd lots: "Lohengrin's boat with
one swan. Two Chinamen, ten caps, a hundred and nine people,
twenty-four green priests, five pairs of ballet slippers, three bootlegs,
one set of crown jewels." The final item, a sewing machine, went
for one dollar. Old Lawrence bought that too, clearly his best buy of
the day. By that time the sun had set and the small crowd of interested
people, most of them curious onlookers, had long since left, and old
Lawrence stood alone on the skating rink, surrounded by useless
possessions, scratching his head.

Francis returned to the letter:

*But he didn't confide his fears to me until after the ice was broken.
At first he looked sullen, he had his wife close by him and she examined me in exactly the way Adele had described. Fortunately she
spoke no English, although she did know German, so our conversations were trilingual – since they spoke Czech to each other. "Mrs.
Thurber," he said to me, "before deciding, I must know first of all
what it is, this conservatory of yours. And who exactly are you?"
Well, I thought, a genius has a right to plain talk, and I replied,
"Herr Dvorak," and he corrected me: "Please, call me Mister." "Maestro –" "No," and he was practically shouting at me. "I'm not German and I'm not Italian and you are an American, so to you I am
Mister, because you don't know Czech." Shortly after that, who
should appear but Francine de la Bellegarde, from the Opéra Co-
mique, who came gushing over, and in that shrill voice of hers she
said, "Jeannette darling, you must introduce me to Maestro Dvorak!"
Naturally she was speaking French, a language he doesn't understand. I reluctantly did so and for the next five minutes or so Francine
showered him with flatteries – in her English, which you've heard!
One unpleasant consequence was that the bystanders were encouraged to butt in. Giuseppe del Frino came waltzing up and requested
an audience, but of course he was speaking his opera-house Italian.
Dvorak's scowl deepened and he began looking at me as though I
were some kind of unnatural phenomenon. So I left him to Giuseppe
and took Mrs. Dvorak with me to freshen up. I spoke to her in German. I don't think she was happy about leaving him to the tender
mercies of the ladies who were beginning to crowd around him. But
I had scarcely managed to powder my nose when she came directly
to the point: "Madame Thurber, wasn't Miss Margulies mistaken*

when she talked about fifteen thousand?" So I knew where I was. She is obviously the senior partner, and chief accountant as well. I assured her that she had understood Miss Margulies correctly. And do you know what her response was? "Very well," she said, "but of course my husband couldn't possibly go for under twenty." I almost dropped my powder puff, and it was all I could do to reply, "Well, by all means there's no reason why we can't talk about it," as the woman began reciting a list of items: it would be considerable work for her husband, it would mean a two-year absence from the European concert scene, where the impresarios fight over him.... In short, she proved a very crafty agent indeed, and before I could recover my senses I had very nearly promised to meet her extortionate demands.

But fear not, my sweet keeper of the purse. I came to my senses in time. I reassured her, of course, that her husband's salary is open to future negotiations, but first I had to know what his decision was. Only then could I present her proposal to the Conservatory's backers.

Once more he set the letter aside and gazed out the window. So she has learned something from me, after all. And he remembered.... He remembered the uncovered cheques his enterprising wife had written; he recalled how they had turned up now and again, accompanied by the indignant complaints of disgruntled creditors, whose mouths, however, could always be stopped with a few hundred dollars. But slowly their numbers had increased until cheques and creditors began to rain down upon her. Some had even taken her to court. Indeed, one of them, Eloi Sylva, the celebrated tenor, took this minor economic setback as a gross personal insult. He appeared in police court before Judge Snell in his full majesty, his stomach encased in a velvet cummerbund, his plump shoulders in a velvet cape, his face a theatrical mask of pained disbelief.

"Would you care to tell the court," said the prosecuting attorney, "what transpired in Carson and Macartney's Bank?"

Eloi put his right foot forward towards the prosecutor as though he were getting ready to sing and, with theatrical exaggeration, declaimed: "I make a deposit in my bank of a cheque for nine hundred dollar. It was signed from Mrs. Thurber. It was not covered from Mrs. Thurber. It made me to be feeling like a cheat."

"Was that nine hundred dollars an amount owed to you by the National American Opera Company?"

"*Oui, oui!*" said the tenor indignantly. "For one appear in Norfolk and for one appear here in the city."

The somnolent judge perked up. "Do you mean, sir, that you got four hundred and fifty dollars for one performance?"

"*Oui!* I mean so."

"One man?"

"*Oui!*" said the tenor and now his reply was proud. "I am getting thirteen hundred and fifty dollar for one week, pay in advance. I do not sing on Friday. Friday is not a good day for my singing."

That took the judge's breath away. Thirteen hundred dollars was probably as much as he made in four months.

Francis chuckled at the memory. It is not surprising, dear Jeannette, that you had to go — for reasons of health, of course — to go into retreat in the Catskills. Nor was I entirely without blame in the matter. I should have negotiated like a street-pedlar, not like a love-struck dunce. But I would rather be a dunce, and the Devil take the money. The great pity of it was he took your opera too. I can't bear to see you cry.

He lowered his eyes to the letter.

When we returned to the salon, I could see at once how miserable Dvorak was. He was surrounded by university luminaries speaking Latin to him. I don't know if that is the custom in Cambridge, or whether these august gentlemen were only trying to show that they did not belong to the profanum vulgus. *But I noticed that rather than reply, he would only grunt noncommittally: his eyes were wandering, and I felt sorry for him. After all, the gentlemen wearing the gold chains must have known that he had once been a butcher's apprentice. Why, the Chancellor himself had mentioned it in his citation. So there he was, grunting his replies and rolling a huge cigar in his fingers till the ashes fell on that magnificent cape. I hurried to his rescue. "Excuse me,* spectabili," *I said sweetly. "If you don't mind, I'd like to steal Mr. Dvorak away from you. Business before pleasure, as we say." They stared at me, as only Cambridge dons can stare at an upstart Yankee woman, and I dragged him over to that ottoman behind the palms and the fig plants, by the window that gave us a view of the starry heavens outside, and I could see how grateful he felt. I had to proceed quickly before he seized up on me again. "Mr. Dvorak," I said, "you must be tired, and I am leaving for Paris in the morning. You've had a busy day: a concert, this party, the convocation ceremony. Everything was splendid, even the Chancellor's address, I'm sure. I must get a translation so I can read all the nice things he said about you — so useful in a publicity cam-*

paign." "You –" he interrupted me, as I'd hoped he would, and then he stopped. "Yes?" "You speak French beautifully," he said. "I don't know if it's beautiful or not, but I studied in Paris, you know –" and he interrupted again: "And you also speak Italian beautifully." "That's a sine qua non of producing operas." A shadow flitted across the furrow between his brow that Adele described, so I quickly added: "Without Italian – at least in America – it's impossible to get along in the world of opera." "And you know German as well," he said, but it was more like a statement. "You can blame that on my love for the German classics: Haydn, Mozart, Beethoven." The shadow vanished and he asked, "Do you know any other languages?" "A little Spanish, because many opera singers in America who can perform in Italian are really Latin Americans, and I picked up a few words of Danish from my father." He looked at me intently, but his frown had vanished. There was something like malicious gaiety in his eyes, and he huffed at me triumphantly, "But you don't know Latin!" "No, I don't," I lied. "It's nothing to worry about," he said. "I don't either, and here I am – a doctor!" And he laughed and laughed.

So the ice was broken – and then he told me those sad things about his children and how he was afraid they might all drown in a shipwreck. But by this time, he was mine! I even believe he was attracted to me, and that's something. They say that when he talks to someone, he pays no attention to whether it's a woman or not. But now he let his eyes wander over me the way men do, then he told me I had a beautiful dress. So that's something, at least! We agreed he would divide the family, so they wouldn't all drown at once, and that – if we could come to an agreement – he would come with his wife, his eldest daughter and one of his sons, depending on which one would behave himself best. Those were his own words. And just when his eyes began to wander again and I could see he was getting ready to pay another compliment, his wife unfortunately appeared. But by that time, I knew he would accept the offer of fifteen thousand – regardless of what his accountant tells him.

And so, dear Francis, I'm satisfied. And I now long more than anything else to be at home with you once more.

Jeannette

He folded the letter, lit a fresh cigar and gazed out at the Hudson River through a cloud of smoke. I miss her, I miss my wife, my expensive wife who is worth more to me than anything money can buy.

Down in Hudson Street, the cursing wagoner was leading his exhausted horse to the stable, followed by the reproachful glances of the gentleman in the top hat and the two ladies, one of whom clutched a broken parasol. The policeman was walking away.

And the letter, that little sun, slid – slowly at first, then more rapidly – behind a cloud of commercial cares.

3 :𝄢: SOLO FOR TUBA

"DON'T BELIEVE ME if you don't want to," said the little man. He measured somewhat under five feet and a long life had transformed his face into a relief map of a landscape furrowed with dried-up riverbeds, all converging on the delta of his mouth – which did not, however, resemble a sunken crater, as the tectonics of the surrounding countryside might have led one to expect. When he grinned, an unusually expensive set of dentures appeared. The frock coat, which might have served him well enough in the back row of an orchestra, from where the two patches mended with red and blue thread would have been invisible to an audience, cried out for an explanation here in the bar whenever his lips parted to reveal the luxurious investment in his mouth. But the explanation loomed behind him: on an unoccupied stool, leaning against the bar, rested an enormous Wagnerian bass tuba. Had the instrument had legs, it would have been two heads higher than its owner. "It was my doing," the little man was insisting. "Even though the whole thing began because Jim Huneker was such a lush."

"But there was never any love lost between Huneker and Dvorak," objected a man sitting beside the tuba player, drinking undiluted bourbon. He too wore a frock coat, although his was in better condition. Resting on the bar in front of him was a flute in its case.

"Indeed there wasn't, Mr. Zeckwer," said the little man. "Huneker couldn't stand being so close to immortality, for the simple reason that he has such an itch for it himself." He drained his beer mug and sent it sliding like a curling stone along the marble bar to the black barman.

"Seven," said the barman.

"Right you are," said the little man. "Trouble was, old Borax – that's what we called him, though not to his face, of course – believed everything Huneker said, and he never understood that Huneker couldn't have cared less whether God existed or not. Borax couldn't stand that. But Huneker felt good thumbing his nose at immortality. That's why he spread all that crap about Borax writing the New World Symphony long before he got to America. According to Huneker it was originally a ceremonial march written for the Emperor Franz Joseph, but Franz Joseph sent it back because none of his brass bands could play it."

The refilled beer mug slid down the bar towards the tuba player, and he caught it and drained it in a gulp.

"With all that beer you put away, by now you should be wider than you are tall," commented another drinker, who had a violin case leaning against his bar stool. "And anyway, I can't believe Huneker spread nonsense like that. The guy is a reputable critic, after all."

"Don't believe me if you don't want to," said the little man, reaching behind him to see if his instrument was still there. He sent the mug sliding back down the bar to the barman.

"Eight!" sang the barman. Carbide lights from the cabs moving along Broadway twinkled up and down on the rows of friendly bottles behind his back.

"All one's energy goes into the tuba," said the little man. "She uses up a lot, I'll tell you. That story about the march for Franz Joseph was nothing. Huneker spread a lot of other nonsense too. In the Old Vienna Café he would bore old Borax to tears with his know-it-all talk. That kind of thing really rubbed Borax the wrong way and Huneker, the son of a bitch, knew it. They'd be drinking champagne, and it went to Huneker's head far quicker than to Borax's. So every second word he used was Latin and he accused Borax of not knowing how to orchestrate. Borax! Music – sure, Huneker knew all there was to know about music. But Borax could *write* the damn stuff."

"How true," said a woman who had, so far, been silent. She was about forty years old, with dark red hair gathered up into a magnificent hairdo on top of which perched a small hat. On the bar in front of her stood a cup of coffee topped with foamy whipped cream.

"Right you are," nodded the little man. "And that same afternoon, in case any of you here think I'm making all this up, he was needling

Borax about piccolos. I remember that exactly, because I know exactly what it led to. Don't believe me if you don't want." A new mug sailed down the bar into his hand, but this time he didn't drain it right away. "He said Borax used piccolos only spasmodically. Those were his words. Well, the Master hadn't a clue what he was talking about and neither had I, at least not then – I asked about it later. The Master could tell Huneker was picking on him for something, so he said, kind of neutral, 'For example?' 'For example,' Huneker says, 'in your four symphonies there are, by my count, only twenty bars in all for the piccolo, and twelve of them are at the beginning of the Fourth, and they're tied D's to boot.' 'But it has to be that way,' says Borax. 'Why?' says Huneker, and he sneers. 'It must,' says Borax. 'What have you got against piccolos?' Huneker retorts. Fortunately, Borax's English was only so-so. If he were speaking Gypsy, he'd have probably told him to bugger off."

"Bohemian," the red-haired lady interrupted.

"What?"

"The Master spoke Bohemian," said the lady. "And mind your language."

"My apologies, Miss Margulies," said the little man. "In Bohemian, he'd have probably told him to get lost. But Huneker deserved plainer language." He took a drink. "I wanted to help Borax out, so I said, 'Sir, are you familiar with the Gran Sinfonia Apoplectica Atlantica?' "

"There's no such thing," said the violinist.

"Oh, yes there is," said the little man. "The name may be a bit different, but it's just as dumb. I knew what I was doing, though. Borax, you see, was a gypsy patriot."

"Bohemian," said the man with the flute.

"Maybe both," said the little man. "He used to browbeat his students something awful for massacring his name. Most people just couldn't get their tongues around that 'r' in the middle with the drunken accent over it. That's how he got the nickname Borax. It was probably Huneker who gave it to him. No good reason – it was just a hell of a lot easier to say. Not Mrs. Thurber, though. She made a real effort and learned to pronounce it beautifully. Rzh." The little man took a mouthful of beer and, with great effort, began to recite: "Dvorzhak – Dvorzhak – Dvorzhak –"

"She tried hard because she was sweet on him," said the flautist.

"That's utter nonsense, Mr. Zeckwer!" said the redhead.

"If she was, she couldn't have got very far," said the man with the violin. "Old Borax wasn't interested in women."

"I can't tell you about that side of him," said the little man. "But when I asked him about the symphony, he gave me a suspicious look, maybe thinking I was putting the rag on him, like Huneker. So I jumped right in and said, 'It's by a countryman of yours, Anton Philip Heinrich. Called Gran Sinfonia Apoplectica or something like that.' Well, Borax's eyes lit up and he said, 'Ah, this man I know! Once he gave a concert in Prague, it was just when they accepted me into organ school. Someone gave me a free ticket. It must have been the first concert I'd ever been to in Prague. But I tell you, it was strange music. Not very good, but the man had such ideas – sometimes they couldn't even be played.' 'That's exactly it,' I said. 'Ideas. I once got into a lot of shit over one of them.' "

The empty glass brushed by the flute and came to rest in the black bartender's hand.

"Such language," said the redhead.

"Nine!" sang the bartender.

"Right you are," said the little man. "My apologies, madam. 'Speaking of piccolos, sir,' I said, 'Heinrich wrote a duet for piccolo and tuba in that composition.' Borax's eyes lit up again and he said, 'A Charakterstück? I thought you said it was a symphony?' 'I did, but it was program music,' I said. 'The movement was called something like A Grizzly Talks to a Nightingale across the Grand Canyon of Yellowstone.' "

"How did a Yellowstone canyon get into an Atlantic symphony?" asked the woman.

"Or a nightingale into the wilderness of Wyoming?" asked the violinist.

"Heinrich never bothered himself with details," said the little man. "Anyway, that was the only movement in that apoplectic symphony that the great conductor Teddy Thomas chose, and we played it between The March of the New York Firemen and the first movement of the Unfinished. Teddy figured the lowbrows who came to the Terrace Garden on summer evenings to enjoy themselves would stop talking during a dramatic duet like that, and they'd stay quiet till at least halfway through the Unfinished, when they might possibly notice that the Unfinished had as much flash as The March of the New York Firemen. Yes, gentlemen – and lady – those were the days! Borax was fascinated by New York in those days! Sometimes

he'd invite me to go for a walk –and I tell you he was quite a walker
– and we'd hoof it around the Lower East Side and listen to the organ-
grinders." He drained the glass and sent it on its way along the bar.
The black barman grinned and refilled it. The clock above his head
stood at half-past eleven.

The little man sighed. "But that was back in '93, more than a
decade ago. And now poor old Borax is dead and gone to heaven.
Today's a dark day. Well, if there was no heaven before he died, then
I'll bet they made one specially for him. They couldn't have let him
die only to find out there was no God."

"Who?" asked the violinist.

"Ten!" sang the barman, pitching his voice higher.

"Right you are," said the little man. "Who what?"

"Who couldn't have let him die?"

"Oh, I don't know," said the little man. "Those above the Lord
God."

"Haven't all those apoplectic symphonies made you apoplectic
yourself?" asked the flautist.

"What if they have?" said the little man. "Borax was an odd stick
too, and yet, what a giant!" He took a drink. "But to get back to
Heinrich – he wrote a set of instructions on the score that went
something like this: 'In the following movement, let the conductor
place the tuba and the piccolo at the most extreme opposite ends of
the orchestra, in order to create the proper illusion of two creatures
conversing together across Yellowstone Canyon.' A stupid idea, but
Teddy got the notion of.improving upon it."

A saffron evening almost half a century ago, the little man remembered, downing his beer, *the podium surrounded by a green lawn
and Teddy in his frock coat, inspired perhaps by the lunatic moon
that hung low over the garden. Tables were laid, waiters with glasses
on trays hurried to and fro in the dusk like fireflies, the candles
flickered over young girls in straw hats with sky-blue ribbons reaching down their backs, boaters, top hats, dandies with walking sticks
and gold watch-chains draped across their waistcoats, monocles in
their eyes. The happy hum of excitement, the clinking of glasses,
and once in a while a girl shrieked as her bottom was pinched – an
evening crowd, determined to enjoy themselves, ready even to tol-
erate Teddy's occasional efforts to bring them European culture. A
thick cloud of smoke from cigars and pipes, accented by grey swirls
of cigarette smoke, drifted up towards the gas lamps and the lanterns*

strung on wires between the trees, and around those lamps swarmed mosquitoes and nocturnal insects of all kinds, while a magnificent fifty-piece orchestra performed The Firemen's March to break the ground for Schubert. They finished playing to enormous applause. Music was part of the formula of delight, which included girls, young men, alcohol, nicotine, conversations about politics. The applause was generous. And then, at a sign from Teddy, the piccoloist rose and wound his way among the tables to the edge of the enormous garden restaurant, where he climbed a tree. He himself, with his tuba, was more conspicuous. He had to force his way in the opposite direction through the throngs of waiters and young women and men whom the alcohol had carried to states of heightened immorality: they patted the full, female roundness of the huge instrument and offered him the kind of jocular advice one might expect. At last he reached some bushes at the far side of the garden. Beyond was a street leading to the city centre. He crawled into the bushes and made himself comfortable. Parting the leaves, he peered back and in the distance, above the straw hats, glimpsed Teddy's walrus moustache in the lights of the stage, and heard the drum-roll that always preceded the announcement of the next number. The hum of the crowd quietened and he heard Teddy's powerful voice: "You will now hear the second movement of a symphony by our own American composer Anton Philip Heinrich entitled" – and the conversation subsided, for the crowd was patriotic – "A Grizzly Talks to a Nightingale on a Moonlit Night across the Grand Canyon of Yellowstone." Teddy raised his baton, indicated the tempo, and the muted strings, with an echo of French horns, began to paint the natural beauties of Yellowstone. After six slow bars the nightingale sang out from the crown of a chestnut tree on the right, and top hats, boaters and bowlers all turned to look, for the effect had captivated them more than the most beautiful counterpoint. There was even applause from some of the tables, quickly hushed – they wanted to hear the nightingale. Its song was high-pitched, rather like the piping of a fledgeling, but the shrill sound, the fragrant, blossoming tree, the muted strings, suddenly seemed to take on a shaman-like power. Now, when the audience is entranced, he thought, is the time for Teddy to slide the orchestra into the first movement of the Unfinished. The audience, spellbound, would scarcely notice the transition and they would maintain that intense silence, thinking they were listening to an American composition celebrating the natural wonders of their land.

*Teddy might have been able to make it work. To further the sacred
cause of music, he would have been willing to stage a boxing match
in between the Allegro and the Adagio.*

So, seated on the ground in the bushes, he lifted his tuba, set it
on his lap, moistened his lips and waited for the bird to finish singing.
Then he took a deep breath and abruptly blared out, in his most
thunderous fortissimo, the grizzly's first tones.

He had just glimpsed the straw hats and bowlers turning suddenly
towards him, the faces beneath them beaming with anticipation,
when the leaves rustled and four strong arms grabbed him and raised
him and his tuba briskly in the air, whereupon the roar of the rutting
bear glissando'd to become the bleating of a suckling pig. The last
thing he saw was Teddy's bristling moustache. But by that time the
police were dragging him along the street. In a fit of professional
zeal one of them, after accusing him of disturbing the peace and
wilfully disrupting a public concert with his noise, struck him over
the head with a nightstick.

Later, when the world had been set to rights, he discovered that
Teddy had done his best to save the situation even though the sudden
intervention of the police had diminished the impact. With great
presence of mind the bass trombonist improvised the grizzly's part,
but he all but drowned out the nightingale. The audience's interest
waned and the final duet between a quavering trombone and an
unsteady piccolo was played once more to the clinking of glasses,
the shouts of the young men from Tammany Hall, and the shrieking
of young women.

"Old Borax loved stories like that," said the little man. "He'd laugh
so loud people would look round at him. So I struck while the iron
was hot. That's why there's a tuba in the New World Symphony."

"Eleven," said the barman, and the beer slid smoothly down the bar.

"Right you are," said the little man.

"So are you going to blow your horn about it, so to speak?" said
the flautist. "Do you really expect us to believe he wrote in a tuba
part because of you?"

"I sure as hell am," said the little man, slapping the bar with his
hand. "And I'm not bragging. I'm not saying he hammerlocked himself into it just because of me. But he sure got his inspiration from
me."

"How?" asked the man with the violin. "Just because you and
your tuba got arrested?"

"Don't believe me if you don't want to. The fact is, Papa Heinrich had something to do with it. What Borax did in the New World Symphony, Papa Heinrich had at least thought of long before him. We played them all: the Sinfonia Eratico Fantachia, The Indian Festival of Dreams – whatever the hell they were called. Compared to Borax's stuff, it was night and day, of course. But Papa Heinrich did use Indian music, like Borax wanted to do. Manitou Mysteries, or The Voice of the Great Spirit: Gran Sinfonia Mysteriosa Indiana – or some goddamn thing. It wouldn't have been the first time a real artist took a bank clerk's idea and turned it into a masterpiece. It was me who told Borax about Papa Heinrich, and that's a fact. Borax was interested in everything that had to do with his countrymen. Papa Heinrich was a gypsy born and bred too."

"Bohemian," said the red-haired lady, and the tuba player recalled how *tears came to the Master's eyes. "I know exactly what he must have gone through," Borax said. "The last thing I wanted to be was a butcher. The thought of spending the rest of my life cutting little piglets' throats was enough to make me despair." "It wasn't quite the same with Papa Heinrich, sir. He was happy enough when he was a banker. He'd settled in Philadelphia, played in the orchestra of an amateur theatre for fun, but then the bank went bust and he found himself at the age of forty without a livelihood. So he went to Kentucky, taught the violin to children and lived among the Indians for some time." "You see? The hand of God again," and Borax looked at him with those pious eyes. "You see? As a young banker, he buys himself a Cremona violin and teaches himself to play on it for his own amusement – and then suddenly – " "I suppose that's how it was, Master, if you say so," he said, and wondered why the Almighty hadn't arranged for Heinrich to receive, along with that Cremona violin, at least a fraction of the talent He had given the butcher's apprentice. He had been there when Papa Heinrich, in a threadbare coat with tails, looking like Liszt with his long, unwashed hair, the sharp smell of garlic heralding his arrival, had approached the piano with great pomp to play for Theodore Thomas – and to comment upon – a work with the pompous title of Rhapsodia Majestica ad Maiorem Gloriam Rei Publicae Americanae Transatlanticae. He sat down, spread the tails of his coat to reveal a large patch on the seat of his trousers, raised his bony fingers above the keyboard as though trying to inject it with a mesmeric fluidum, and plunged into the work. And the music? Beethoven in his wildest dreams couldn't have come up with more complicated harmonies. Stormy passages followed one another in rapid succession, like planets from another universe caroming and crashing into each other, unsullied by musical theory or culture – and buried within it all, some incomplete genius struggling to be born. He could still see him to this day, that distant, paradoxical figure in his threadbare coat, his trousers too short for his gangling legs, an Uncle Sam incarnate with dirty white socks disappearing into black lace-up boots with leather so cracked that the socks shone through where his enormous toes had worn holes in the leather. The tortured pianoforte groaned and his shrill voice occasionally broke through the outlandish clusters of sound to explain some especially obscure passage meant to conjure up Comanches hunting buffalo. Unlike old Borax, however, Heinrich had actually been there, he knew the smell of smoke rising from the tepees. The only time Borax had ever seen an Indian was when Jeannette Thurber had taken him to see Buffalo Bill's Wild West Show, and there he was more interested in the young lady who shot cigars out of her partner's mouth while galloping past him on horseback. Unlike Borax, Papa Heinrich had crisscrossed this enormous land, and was full of pride and love for it. An American Beethoven. Well, unquestionably American, something old Borax could never be. Yet all he had received from the Creator was that Cremona violin. The final majestic cluster of chords died away, Papa Heinrich stood up from the pianoforte and in his gaunt face, framed by a long beard stained with yellow tobacco juice, two triumphant eyes burned. "Have you ever heard anything like it, gentlemen?" And they, Theodore Thomas and he, shook their heads sincerely and in unison.*

Poor Heinrich. Teddy turned down that particular rhapsody, saying full justice could be done to it only by an orchestra of the gigantic proportions of Patrick Sarsfield Gilmore's, with a choir of ten thousand voices, and cannon and steam engines; and oddly enough Papa Heinrich was not disappointed, much less insulted. He accepted it as a compliment to his genius, transplanted to this wild continent from the heart of Europe to bear witness to a new country, a testimony that the country itself would only appreciate in the next century.

Rejection never offended him. He was too used to it. Yet in that soul of his there were sensitive spots – and he told Borax about how Heinrich had played his grandiose rhapsody before President Tyler himself, because he wanted to dedicate it to him and felt he should ask Tyler's permission to use his name. The President, his legs crossed in the pose of a great man appreciating art, watched Papa's life-and-death struggle with the pianoforte for a while, then uncrossed his legs, planted both feet firmly on the floor, lit a cigar and began to smoke with a look of dogged concentration on his face. When the rhapsody had made it halfway from Washington to San Francisco, Tyler got up, set his cigar on the edge of the piano, placed his hand gently on the agitated shoulders and declared in a statesmanlike voice: "A remarkable composition, sir! It is quite – in fact entirely – unusual. But couldn't you just play us a good old Virginia reel?"

An otherworldly chord hung in the air as Papa Heinrich rose from the stool, gathered up his sheets of music, rolled them into a tube, took his top hat from the floor, grasped the cane that was leaning against the stool and, without bowing, measured the uncomprehending President with eyes that burned with the contempt of an aristocrat who has just realized he has been casting pearls before swine. "No, sir," he said, "I cannot. I never play dance music."

And he walked proudly out of the room.

He walked proudly, but tripped as he was crossing the threshold.

Old Borax almost wept when he told him about it.

Another mug of beer came sailing down the bar. "Twelve!" cried the barman gleefully.

"Borax never shed a tear over us," said the man with the violin. "He could get into terrible fits of rage. He once ripped my Symphony in A Minor, Opus One to shreds."

"At twenty," said the red-haired woman, "a man needs to be rapped across the knuckles. At seventy, he needs praise. He doesn't need to be asked to play old favourites."

"Borax would play old favourites," said the flautist.

"When he was twenty," said the woman. A memory stirred in her mind of the tempestuous man listening eagerly to Will. What would he have thought of him today? Yet the Master was in a way responsible for what had become of Will. Will had just been dismissed in disgrace by the Master, for refusing to play in the school orchestra on the grounds that he was out of practice on the violin. She saw him through the glass doors of the reading room, sitting over the latest issue of the Musical Courier with an ironic smile on his lips, when suddenly the haughty grin faded. He took a pencil from his *pocket and underlined something. The pale light of New York flowed through the reading-room window onto his brown face. Now the mask of the Berlin heartbreaker had vanished, the pose dissolved in the passion, and the black eyes were intent on the lines of print. Quietly she entered the reading room and walked up to him.*

"What are you reading, Will?"

The mask went up once more. "The wisdom of an old philanderer,"
he said sarcastically. He closed the magazine and put it back in the shelves behind the glass.

Later, she returned and went through the whole issue. Only one passage was underlined. The wisdom of old Borax: "All great musicians have borrowed music from simple people. Beethoven's most charming scherzo is based on a motif which today we may consider as a skilfully adapted Negro melody." Her recollections flew ahead two – or was it three – years. A high yellow woman with the profile of Nefertiti sat stiffly in the wings, having been unable to get a seat among the white audience: the theatre was sold out. At the time, she wondered whether this woman's intelligent eyes would see through her, would recognize that Will had once been more than just her student. But not a muscle in the woman's smooth face moved as she watched the comedians going through their routines on stage. Clorindy, or The Origin of the Cakewalk. What would the Master have said about this music, written by one of his students? She knew what this black woman had said: "Will, oh Will! I sent you all over the world to study and become a great musician, and you've come back such a nigger!"

Another leap in time. Will was raging in her office. She had just given him the review to read, foolishly thinking it would please him. "Will Marion Cook," wrote the New York Magazine, "is in our opinion the best coloured concert violinist we have in America today." He was yelling at her as though she had written it herself. Awkwardly, to soothe him, she reminded him of the time Huneker had written that the Master was the best second-rate composer in the world. The Master had simply dismissed it with a wave of his hand. "That's exactly the point, Adele," he interrupted, taking her hand in his. "That's precisely what this review means. But he could afford it since he already had a worldwide reputation. I can't afford it, and I won't simply dismiss it, because I'll never be anything more than 'coloured' to these people and I'll always be right back where I started."

And that was the end of his concert career. He joined up with Harry T. Burleigh, Paul Laurence Dunbar, Bob Cole and James Weldon Johnson and, as if to confirm the most slanderous things people were saying about him, he married a girl who had danced in his musical. She was not yet fourteen. He turned his back on Joachim, and embraced the Cakewalk.

In the beginning, and in the end of course, was music: Joachim and the Cakewalk. But in between was the Master, who had introduced the B-flat clarinet into the Albert Hall. It was the only thing about him Will wanted to emulate. How some professors, like Henry Finck, turned their noses up at it! "Why does the savage prefer his monotonous drumming and ear-piercing war songs to a soft, beautiful, dreamy Chopin nocturne? Because he cannot understand the nocturne." She smiled. Will certainly had his wild ways. A thirteen-year-old memory – the moon rising over the tiled roofs outside the window of a hotel in which, as she had suspected, the bed creaked, until dawn rose over the baroque church, the sun touching the town that smelled of smoke from many chimneys, the light falling upon their naked bodies, on hers, the colour of cream, and on Will's warm brown skin, when Will told her what he had seen in the concert café in Berlin....

She licked at the whipped cream and concentrated her attention on events in the bar. Another glass slid by her, accompanied by the bartender's cheerful announcement: "Thirteen!"

"Right you are," said the little man. "And Borax did weep over Papa Heinrich's misfortunes, but at the same time, he could never get enough of those stories, like the one about the Gran Sinfonia Atlantica, or whatever it was called. And he was always astonished by them. 'Is that possible?' he'd say. 'You're pulling my leg!' 'Upon my soul, sir, I'm not,' I'd say. 'That could only happen in America,' he'd sigh. But the story he liked best was the one about Gilmore. Perhaps he envied him. Once he complained that if he could have had four double-basses in Prague, think of what he could have written for them. You know Gilmore – four double-basses? Ha!" The little man took a drink and closed his eyes. *He saw a gigantic colosseum, the great stadium in Boston where whole sections of instruments, rather than gladiators, were to clash in mortal combat with such vigour that Dwight, the famous music critic, fled the city to his summer-house in the country because he knew the ethereal muse*

Euterpe was about to become the fattest woman in the world. He stared in amazement at a hundred brand-new anvils especially imported from England, at the ten cannon deployed around the stage and connected by electric wires to the conductor's podium which towered above the stadium like an enormous lighthouse. At the other side of the orchestra pit was a larger-than-life orchestrion painted in carnival colours. Instead of the seventy serfs who once pumped the bellows of the famous Winchester organ, there was a steam engine ready to impel a gale of hurricane force into pipes as thick as the smoke-stacks of a trans-Atlantic liner.

But when he sat in a single row with eighty-two other tuba players (and where that row ended a phalanx of eighty-six trombones began), and when he looked around at the vanguard of three hundred and thirty strings and the formation of a hundred and nineteen woodwinds, all with sub-conductors in black dress coats – "Is that possible? A hundred and nineteen?" Borax was amazed. "Yes, sir, and seventy-five drums and timpani," he replied. "When I was waiting there with the tubas, each of them polished to parade standards, I tried to imagine the sound. Just think about it, eighty-three bass Ds...." "My good man, I would love to have heard it!" "Well, I did hear it," he said, and in his mind he saw, instead of the bottles neatly arranged in rows behind the bar, *a thousand men parading into the colosseum to play before an audience of fifty thousand. They marched around the field and with their instruments saluted President Grant, seated in the box of honour. Then they searched among the chairs, for the next half hour, until each musician had found his place. His own seat was very high up, and from this vantage point he could see, at the far side of the orchestra below, fifteen dolls sitting beside fifteen miniature harps, and farther still, a fly in a dress coat climbing up to sit among the registers of the colourful cathedral-like orchestrion. The wheels of the steam engine began to turn. At first only the enormous wheezing of the machine could be heard. Later that noise was drowned out by the sound of the tubas. Then, from the two opposite gates, a throng of ten thousand singers, men and women, paraded into the stadium, led by the choirmaster Zerrahn wrapped in a silver cloak. Three hundred firemen, in brilliant white uniforms and armed with hammers, marched into position at the anvils, and fifty gunners manned the cannon. It took an hour for everyone to get into position and there was constant applause. At last the creator* of this dream, Patrick Sarsfield Gilmore, dressed all in gold, came galloping in on a white horse. A one-man elevator raised him to the summit of the lighthouse, so high above the stadium that it seemed to touch the bright white clouds. Though reduced to the size of a pinhead, he had a baton with a crystal in the tip that reflected the rays of the sun. He surveyed the endless rows. The audience settled down, the applause died and the smoke from twenty thousand cigars rose to the clear sky. From his perch on high, Patrick Sarsfield Gilmore raised his flashing baton, brought it down abruptly and with his left hand pressed the first button. Smoke emerged from the barrel of the first cannon, followed a moment later by the boom of the explosion. But an instant before that he had seen the red-faced sub-conductors wave their batons, and the doll-like harpists had strummed the opening chord; as the puff of smoke appeared, the tubas began to play Yankee Doodle. "The second cannon went off before we had finished the opening bar, while the cannoneers swarmed around the first one, a fellow with a cleaning rod went to work, and they rammed a new charge down the barrel. And behind us, a choir ten thousand voices strong —" "Why, that must have been...." Borax shook his head and did not finish his sentence. "It was awful, sir. Delicate ladies fainted," he said. "But people were jubilant. They'd never heard anything like it before — as a matter of fact, we couldn't hear very much of it ourselves. We were sitting in the eye of the hurricane. The only thing I remember clearly is the cannonade, and then those three hundred firemen in the Anvil Chorus of Il Trovatore, trying to strike the anvils in unison and not managing it. On the whole it was — well, a sound," he said. "Ghastly. But there was something ... majestic about it too. Something. ... " "Like America," said Borax. "Such things could not be anywhere else!"

"Well, I guess they couldn't," said the little tuba player and tipped back his beer. "Though I've never been anywhere else. Folks that have say it's not worth it." He sent the empty glass down the counter to the black man behind the bar. They sat in silence together for a while, then the little man broke the silence: "Would you all excuse me for a moment, please? Make sure no one walks off with my tuba, okay?" He slid off his seat and disappeared, leaving the tuba enthroned on the bar stool like a legless monarch.

"I think he takes it to bed with him," the violinist said, nodding at the fat instrument. "In any case, his wife ran off on him. But do you think Borax would have actually acted on his advice? Borax only listened to God — and then maybe to Brahms."

"I think he's stringing us a line," said the flautist.

"He was always pestering Borax – I can believe that," said the violinist. He drained his glass and imitated the little man by sliding it down the bar to the barman. "Three," he said. The barman grinned.

The door leading to the basement opened and the tuba player returned to the bar. He swung onto his stool, checking to see his tuba was still there. The beer flew down the bar like a meteor.

"Fourteen!"

"Right you are. You don't have to believe me if you don't want to," said the little man. By now he was sitting somewhat askew on his stool. "Huneker, of course, tried to make a fool out of Borax. 'Ever since Wagner invented the foot-operated tuba,' he said, 'it's actually been possible to use it in a light song. But so far no one has done it, so the job is all yours, Doctor.' Borax said nothing, but sipped away at his champagne cocktail. It wasn't until Huneker fell nose first into a puddle of beer that he turned to me and said, 'My good man, you said you wouldn't trade your tuba for anything, is that right?' 'Not for anything, sir. Not even for a Stradivarius, assuming I could play it. After all, I've been playing the tuba for nigh on fifty years.' 'I'm fond of the tuba myself,' said Borax. 'Every instrument is beautiful. It's just that every instrument is good for something particular, and in the piece I'm working on now, I somehow don't hear....' Of course he was working on the New World Symphony, you know? 'Unless ...' and he stopped. I could see his fingers running up and down the edge of the table. 'Sir,' I said, 'I don't think I could live with myself if I never got to play a single note in your American symphony. A single blast. Me and my tuba, we've been everywhere something was happening. With Teddy Thomas in New York, in Cincinnati and in Mrs. Thurber's famous American Opera Company. I even played under Jullien. He brought me in when his own tuba player ran off with some Creole woman.' "

The old fellow is lying, making it all up, Adele thought. Would the Master have embroidered twelve bars of an esoteric bass joke into the fabric of his sonic wizardry just for this little tuba player? Absurd. The little man simply never stopped being a part of those New York musical fantasies *à la* Jullien....

He had been fourteen at the time, smaller than his tuba, but already able to make it sound like thunder in the Rockies. Jullien was directing The Firemen's Quadrille. First the ushers warned the audience that there was some danger attached to the piece, but then they heard a gentle nocturne-like melody on the flutes and oboes, and the violins joined in, and it was such a sweet, light piece of night music that the alarmed audience fell silent. Suddenly, trumpets sounded from without. Red Bengal fires exploded near the ceiling and three platoons of men in firemen's raincoats burst into the hall, real water pouring from real hoses. The orchestra quickly shifted from piano to mezzoforte and then to forte, the audience opened their umbrellas, women fainted away and the ushers in the panicking crowd roared at the top of their lungs: "Please remain in your seats! The fire is part of the concert!" Even so, many people fled from the hall in the teeth of a majestic fortissimo finale; and all the while, across the chaos, fell the shadow of the great Jullien, who was directing it all from his podium; the strings and the firemen, the brass, the streams of water and the general alarm.

When it was over he sank exhausted into his scarlet throne in the middle of the orchestra and wiped away his perspiration with an enormous scarlet handkerchief, while on each side of him a flunkey tried to revive him with a fan. Meanwhile, the ushers were slowly calming the terrified crowd and chasing the fainthearted back to their places. Slowly, slowly, the applause grew until at last Jullien rose from his throne, tottered, steadied himself, the applause swelled to a climax underscored by the brass and the tuba and then, ceremoniously and triumphantly, Jullien bowed....

"The main reason Jullien did it, Master," he said to Borax when he told him about it, "was to get people to come, and then come again, and then to start listening, and finally to listen, really listen to the music. He wanted to treat all those people, from all those improbable little countries all over the world, to Beethoven – "

Borax's eyes glowed. "Only in America!"

"But Jullien gave hints to the more observant about how to treat the music. He conducted trash with an ordinary baton. For Mendelssohn, he used a silver baton. For Mozart, he wore gloves and used a gold baton. And for Beethoven? That, sir, was quite a ceremony. We'd play a fanfare and down the centre aisle would come a flunkey all dressed in gold and purple holding up a red pillow, the kind they carry crown jewels on. He'd go up to the little statue of the muse Euterpe which Jullien had fixed to his music stand. Jullien would ceremoniously put on a pair of white gloves, lift a gold baton studded with diamonds from the cushion and cry out – and you could always hear him clearly because the biggest boors, the kind that wouldn't shut up during *The Battle Hymn of the Republic*, were silenced by this ceremony – he'd cry out, 'FALL TO YOUR KNEES!' And then he'd turn to the orchestra, raise his baton – and some people in the audience actually knelt, listened to the whole piece on their knees. That's how taken in they all were."

The last beer of the night slid by. The little man downed it as if it were the first.

"In the end, Borax even wrote a part for the piccolo into the New World Symphony. Spasmodically, of course," said the tuba player. "Only four bars' worth."

"And he did that all in memory of your arrest, is that right?" sneered the violinist.

"Don't believe me if you don't want to." The little man shrugged. "The Grizzly and the Nightingale. The score speaks for itself. I'm only telling you how it was. Old Borax would say, 'That is possible only in America.' "

He slipped dangerously to the edge of the stool, but caught hold of the tuba and regained his balance. "And he wrote it in America, didn't he? Or do you believe Huneker?"

The bar was emptying. They put on their coats and went out into the May night and the lights of Broadway. The flautist stopped a hansom, helped the little man inside, and disappeared after him into the dark interior. Then, into the glow of the night, two small, impatient hands reached out to them. They handed him the tuba. That too was swallowed up by the darkness.

Perhaps he was telling the truth, she thought, as she rode home in a hansom cab. Surely he wouldn't have dared to lie, on this day of all days, when they'd just received news that old Borax had died. *Back then*, the little man had told them in the bar, *when they left Huneker to his fate in that puddle of beer and went into the street arm in arm, the Master said, "You shall have it, my good man. But only spa– how did he put it?"*

"Spasmelodically," replied the little tuba player. "You mean to say, sir, that you ...?"

"*You shall have your tuba part,*" *repeated the Master, and set out bravely on the long walk from the thirst belt to his house on Seventeenth Street.*

4 :C): THE CONCERT CAFÉ

THROUGH THE WINDOW, mingling with a faint aroma of smoke from the chimneys that stood erect over rooftops of undulating red tile, a full yellow moon hanging above them, drifted the sound of bells. It was two o'clock: from the tower of the royal castle on the hill came a deep, resonant chime, the reverberation of a huge mass of bell-metal; then, from somewhere across the river to the south, rang out two strokes a fifth lower, and while these were still echoing in the air the same melody, but in a different key, sounded from the spire of the Church of the Knights of Malta, while from the north, bells in a third key interposed themselves between the first two. She felt as though she were inside a gigantic celesta on which an inebriated Johann Sebastian Bach was improvising a cacophonous counterpoint. More and more bells now entered the fugue in cruel, clashing couplets, a gigantic polyrhythm beating the air above a city submerged in sleep. It was as though the bell on the royal castle of Prague had pulled itself loose from its fittings and gone rolling down the slope to the river, and then careered on up the other bank, smashing into all the other bells in their towers on the way. A thirty-second Moonlight Sonata under the brilliant moon, an enormous gong struck by Chronos himself, its reverberation now dying out in a many-voiced echo.

"There's music for you!" Will murmured beside her on the bed.

"Forget the music, Will," she said, though she was still caught inside the resonating celesta. The panes of glass in the window were almost trembling in sympathy with the throbbing of the bells. "Was she white or black?"

"Now she's white. Then she was black."

The moonlight caught a reflection of white teeth.

"Isn't this just a Negro fairytale?"

"It's Negro reality, honey."

"Not even a touch of Negro fantasy?"

"A touch, maybe. To this day, Hattie is still passing."

She didn't understand. She said pedantically, " 'Passing' is a transitive verb. It requires an object."

"Not where I come from, it doesn't. Hattie is passing," Will repeated.

She was baffled. He laughed again. His damp body glistened darkly in the soft light of the night.

"She was thirteen when I first got to know her."

"And how old were you?"

"No more than two, maybe three years younger."

"Oh, my!"

"It happened at Grandfather Lewis's in Chattanooga," she heard Will's voice say, while she wondered whether he really had been so wicked at that age. "He was a wagon-maker," said Will, "and he had a reputation for being a hard man. Mother thought Grandfather Lewis could tame me, because I loved fighting and I was always getting into all kinds of trouble. Everyone else had given up on me – my uncles, my teachers, the ministers – but she was so determined to straighten me out she was willing to send me all the way back down across the Mason-Dixon line to do it. Anyway, my grandfather had an empty stockroom behind his workshop and no one ever went there after dark."

Ten years old! How old was I then? she wondered. I know very well how old I was. If you subtract his age from mine.... She would have been sixteen when he was ten, and she'd been away from home too, at her uncle's place in the Tyrolean Alps. And Johannes had been about ... well, about ten years older than her. He had sung her a Schubert serenade, accompanying himself on her uncle's old spinet:

> Hear my singing, hear my pleading
> Borne across the night;
> Now the woods are cool and quiet,
> Come, my heart's delight.

The spinet had tinkled pleasantly, she had caught the smell of clover from the open window – and here? Wood smoke from the chimneys. There hadn't been a nearby stockroom in the Tyrol. But there were barns....

"Hattie was a snob," she heard Will say. "It wasn't just that she had white blood in her veins – who doesn't? – but she thought hers was blue. Just like the Negroes in Washington who boast about being related to Thomas Jefferson on their mothers' side. Anyway, her father was a colonel in the Confederate army."

"A colonel! But surely, Will –" She knew at least that much about America. But she quickly discovered she didn't know enough.

"Did I say she was legitimate?"

The moon began to slip behind the castle tower. A black shadow fell across the crystal carafe of water on the night-table. The light in the water went out.

"Of course, it was a very respectable non-marriage," said Will. "By day, the colonel lived with his white family in an old plantation house. But as soon as the sun went down, he'd ride off to join his black family. He even built a small stable by their house so his horse wouldn't have to wait in the rain. In the morning, he'd swing into the saddle and gallop off to play with his white children. He spoiled Hattie. She was the only black kid in Chattanooga whose teeth were rotten from eating too much candy."

"But didn't his wife find out about it?"

"Oh, she knew about it all along. Everybody did. The colonel was always a correct and proper husband in both households," said Will. "Of course, they still wouldn't let Hattie go to any white church, so she went to the high-falutin' black Presbyterian church, where none of the congregation was any darker than your Master. But she was a pretty girl. So I stomached her snobbery and bought her a lollipop."

"A lollipop?"

"I was still a virgin."

"Of course."

"Of course," he repeated. "Hattie was playing the lady, but she could still roll her eyes like a minstrel. And she had eyes like – well, like the serpent of Eden. She was wearing a black silk blouse to make her look whiter, and she had a red ribbon in her hair to go with the colour of her lips. Anyway, I was willing to ignore her airs until she said" – and Will imitated the voice of that little black lady of long ago – " 'Do you have any trouble with the niggers in Washington, William?' Well, that did it. I shouted at her, 'You stupid goddamn little fool!' and I left her sitting in the garden with her lollipop, furious with myself for having wasted a whole nickel on such a dumbbell."

"A hot-tempered fellow even then."

"Aren't we all?" he said. "But most of us learn to control it and never step out of line. I was always stepping out of line. Negrocentric and egocentric, that's me. And I talked a mess." He laughed wryly. "In Oberlin, I got expelled from high school because of Hannibal." He mimicked a high-pitched voice. " 'What is it, William?' That was our Latin teacher. 'What was Hannibal, Miss?' I asked. 'I don't quite understand your question, William.' 'Was Hannibal white or coloured?' She put on this strict face. 'Hannibal was white.' But I knew she was lying. I'd read somewhere that Hannibal had Negro blood, and he almost destroyed Rome. They couldn't bring themselves to admit that an African almost brought low the flower of their genius. Anyway, next day I asked the same question. 'What was Hannibal, Miss Safford?' 'I told you, William, Hannibal was white.' The third day I tried again, and this time I half shouted: 'WHAT WAS HANNI-BAL?' And she replied, 'For the third and last time, William, I am telling you that Hannibal was white!' And I yelled back at her, 'MISS SAFFORD, YOU'RE A DAMN LIAR!' An hour later, Hannibal had one less descendant at Oberlin Public High School."

Will had actually shouted this and she was alarmed: "Will! Shh! What if they hear us next door?"

"Sorry, Professor," he said, and put his arms around her.

"So you never slept with Hattie, then?"

"Of course I did. As far as colour went, I was at the lower end of Hattie's threshold of acceptability. But I had a reputation for being a pretty tough customer – and with the German I'd picked up from my granddaddy, I could make love in two languages at once – and Hattie was curious."

The moon slid out from behind the tower and the carafe sparkled like a rainbow.

"Curious about what?"

"The same thing all girls are curious about. You too. Colour is not the only thing."

"Aren't you being a little insolent?"

"Maybe," he replied. "The fräuleins of Berlin have spoiled me. I'm on a solo gig in Berlin and I'm a great sensation."

"And colour, I take it, is not the only thing you're curious about either."

"As far as the fräuleins are concerned, I'm colour-blind."

"You're a model of your race." She said it somewhat stiffly, yet with a rush of sensual pleasure.

"And what would your race rather be doing, playing chess?"

"Oh, shut up!" she said. "And how did little Hattie fare then?"

"I've never met a finer virtuoso. Except for you, of course, Adele. A Cleopatra, raven-haired, lips as red as her ribbon, a master of this greatest and most ancient of arts. She knew all the answers, and most of the questions too."

"Were you ever with her again? After the storage room, I mean?"

"No. Shortly after that she went north and started passing."

"Passing?"

"Passing for white," he said. "And before long, she got married."

"But what if –?" She stopped as he pressed close to her. She turned on her side to face him directly. His back was arched, a bowman poised for action. "What if she had children? Wouldn't it have come out?"

He laughed, and pressed her to him with both arms. "Hattie wasn't that stupid. It only made her feel good to be taken for a white woman in Boston. Naturally, she married a black man. His colour was almost a perfect match for hers, but he'd never tried to pass and he was delighted to be able to marry into the master race. So if they had a kid who looked like yours truly, Hattie could blame it on her husband."

He ran his hand over her thigh and rose above her.

"Wait, my dear." She stopped him and reached beyond the carafe. A white hand in the moonlight. He watched her, and then lay back with a sigh. She found what she was looking for, turned towards him, and with her supple, pianist's fingers drew it over his upright shaft. "And who would *I* blame it on, my dear Moor?"

The bell on the castle tower rang out again, rolling down the hill to the river and up the opposite bank to the top of the hill, crashing into other bells on the way. The city reverberated like a giant celesta, and they were inside it, together.

The moon was now out of sight beyond the window but its light, still pouring into the room, was refracted into the seven colours of the rainbow as it passed through the carafe and through the tiny drops of sweat on her white skin, on his brown velvet.

"You haven't told me yet."

"What?"

"What you saw in the concert café."

"I'll tell you in the morning."

"No! Right now!"

"In the morn...." His voice died away. The power of youthful sleep. She lifted herself on one elbow and her breasts brushed against his damp chest. He was asleep. The beautiful brown face, the slightly Semitic features. Beautiful Will.

She lay next to him. She closed her eyes. She fell asleep. In her dream, she accompanied him on the Steinway in Mary Nalle's salon. *He was playing Wieniawski's Polonaise in the candlelight, in the presence of the important Negro leaders of Washington – including Frederick Douglass, Dick Thompkins, Henry Grant, Turner Layton Sr. and the Minister to Haiti. In the glow of the candles the brown and olive faces gathered in a semicircle around the piano were pursed in grave apprehension; then they brightened, smiles appeared, followed by expressions of delight and finally of pride. Will's fiddling was marred by that awful, uneven technique he had learned in Oberlin, and his phrasing was so chaotic that she was always outrunning him on the yellowing keyboard, or else having to catch up. But his tone was big and broad and it soared above the piano, above the candles and the heads, and flew through the open window into the Washington night. And the soul within it sang in that single common language of a people who once spoke many different languages. A majestic, urgent tone –*

And Will, in his dream, heard that great majestic tone: *and, a year after the candlelight recital, that tone saved him in Berlin, where his career was almost cut short by the technique he had learned from Professor Doolittle of the Oberlin conservatory, the world's worst violinist, who nevertheless, like Salieri, could recognize qualities that lay beyond technique, but unlike Salieri had said, "My boy, you've learned all I can teach you. Berlin's the place for you now, and Joachim's the man." So he went, and his lack of technique, aggravated by laziness and arrogance, met its come-uppance when in a moment of aggressive self-confidence he chose to play something by Bruch for the entrance exam to the Hochschule and he was so terrified that he fell out of step with Professor Kruse, the accompanist, went to pieces and finally tucked his violin under his arm and started walking off the podium in tears, whereupon from the semicircle of faces, not coloured but pale and bearded, lit not by candles but by the cold light of a winter's day coming through the large windows of the rehearsal hall, he heard a voice say, "Ask the young man if he can play anything else." It was spoken in literate German, the kind his Grandfather Lewis loved to speak, who was born free and therefore hated the language of slavery, who had had to buy his grandmother out of slavery before he could marry her; a proud, dom- ineering, surly wagon-maker who played clarinet and violin in his own orchestra, in which he was the only non-German....*

Tears of anger and pain flowed from his eyes. He said, "It's no use, I'm licked." But Professor Kruse, who – like Adele in her dream – had kept slipping behind and overtaking him on the bright white Bechstein keyboard, whispered sternly, "Master Joachim wants you to play something else!" It gradually dawned on him that the voice he had heard belonged to Joachim himself, that it was he who had spoken from the semicircle of bearded faces. He could not see him, but he felt his presence and the generous heart of the old virtuoso gave courage to his own angry and disappointed heart. "Beethoven's Melody in F," he whispered, and then began to play the simple, beautiful composition, and his great tone and soul came back, he suddenly felt at home in the music just as he had when once, out of laziness and joy, he had turned from those endless études to play instead an improvised, embellished version of Gimme Dat Ol' Time Religion. Professor Kruse no longer had to hurry to catch up to him. And the tears continued to flow, but they were tears of defiance now, weakened by hope. And when he had finished, an enormous hand twice the size of his own reached out towards him, swept aside his tears, and the hairy face of a huge man with an ominously black beard but kind eyes swam into view, and a melodic voice said, "You are a stranger in a strange land, young man. We are going to become friends. Come to my home for lunch this Sunday."

In her dream of the candlelight recital, the Polonaise came to an end and they all stood up as one man. "A second Ole Bull!" called out a huge white-haired black man, who reached the dizzying height of almost six and a half feet. It was Frederick Douglass, the great race leader and a friend of his widowed mother – who with her domestic seamstress's wages could not afford to send him overseas – and a friend of Mary Nalle who had convened this candlelight recital for the purpose of doing something about it. "A José White!" cried Major Fleetwood, trying to outdo him. "A de Salas Brindis!" declared Dick Thompkins, whereupon Henry Grant said to Will's mother: "They could all learn something, Belle, just by hearing our boy play!" Bravo! Bravissimo! The candle flames flickered in the excite- ment.

Suddenly, a man from Boston spoke up. Of all those present he was the greatest authority on music, and like Douglass he was almost a legend for he had written a thin book about Negro music and musicians. "The boy has a great talent," said this voice of sober reason, "but he has to study, study, study. He has a lot of faults: bowing, interpretation, stance, phrasing, everything except tone and rhythm –"

He didn't finish what he was saying. A dignified old man, the first person of his race chosen to represent the United States abroad – even though it was as Minister to Haiti – jumped up, and the blood rushed so swiftly into his black cheeks that Will was afraid his recital would end in a fight. "That is an outrage!" the old man thundered. "This boy is an artist, a genius of geniuses!" And he flew at the music critic, swinging his fists.

They rescued the critic. A week later, a benefit concert was held in the First Congregational Church in Washington, and this time the candlelight illuminated a spectrum of faces from coal black to the deathly white of abolitionist women laced into their corsets.

They collected two thousand dollars. Will went off to Berlin a well-to-do American. He may even have been the most affluent of Joachim's students – certainly more affluent than the daughter of Mrs. John Morgan, who borrowed three hundred marks from him on his first day in Berlin.

Borrowed? said Adele in her dream.

If those good benefactors of the First Congregational Church had known why Will ran through his money so fast that they had to take up another collection; if they had seen the procession of blonde fräuleins treated to Viennese coffee and cognac, the crowds of elegant friends touching him for small loans that would almost certainly not be returned within the week, the tailors' bills....

But talent, that he had. Though he had turned into a crusher of corsets and a breaker of hearts, into a bacchanalian child of the night, yet he graduated first in his class, earned a good living by playing and, thanks to his exotic charm and the absence of South Carolina traditions, lived very well and did not feel much like going home....

The bell crashed out of its tower and rolled away across the city, careering into other bells.

My God! Seven o'clock!

How was Will to get back to his own room?

. . .

With difficulty. At breakfast Adele found herself looking away every time the waiter stepped up to pour another cup of chocolate for the Madame from Vienna, or to light a cigar for her suntanned companion. For Madame knew that the waiter, taking breakfast to someone's room along the hall, had seen the gentleman – in entirely appropriate dress but at an entirely inappropriate hour – coming out of Madame's room and tiptoeing towards his own door.

The waiter, of course, was discreet. In fact, during breakfast he fairly radiated discretion. She glowered at Will. He sat there, obviously pleased, puffing on his cigar. I'm just another fräulein in his collection. Stuck on a needle in his box.... And what about your own collection, Adele? Isn't he a remarkable Admiral among your cabbage butterflies?

"Your cigar smells," she said.

Without taking it from his mouth, he replied through his teeth, "You don't understand cigars, Adele. This is an original Havana."

"It has a very original stench."

"You obviously don't know what bad cigars smell like. I wish you could have smelled the ones I used to smoke in Chattanooga."

"Thank God I was spared the pleasure. Would you mind putting it out?"

He took the cigar out of his mouth and looked regretfully at the long greenish roll. There was only about half an inch of grey ash at the end of it. As he was bracing himself to forgo this pleasure, the hot ash fell on his trousers, and he swore coarsely in English.

"Did you burn a hole?" she asked maliciously.

He shook his head. "Adele," he said, holding the greenish object under her nose so that she angrily jerked her head back, "I have a weakness for cigars. I connect them with the end of my innocence, to put it politely. I started smoking cigars in the train my Grandfather Lewis sent me back home on when he finally realized that trouble to me was sweet music, and I loved sweet music. He knew he'd have to kill me to knock the mischief out of me. And Grandfather Lewis wasn't a killer."

She stopped frowning. "Did Hattie give them to you instead of lollipops?" she asked.

"No, I bought them myself. A whole box."

"And you all of ten years old!"

"I was almost eleven, but I looked fourteen."

"And you wanted the cigars to make you look sixteen, so you could impress eighteen-year-olds, is that it?"

A man with a Kaiser moustache walked into the dining room. Unfortunately, she recognized him as a man from Vienna with whom she had a nodding acquaintance. Fortunately, the woman he was with was not his wife, whom she also knew from Vienna. The woman looked young enough to be his daughter – but she knew his daughter as well. This woman was wearing a gaudy green dress and carried a yellow parasol, and her Titian hair was gathered up in a beehive. She was, Adele had to admit, prettier than the man's daughter, not to mention his wife.

My goodness, she wondered. What sort of a hotel is this? This is the one Door himself recommended. Of course, what do I know about where Door stays when he's not in Vienna? Then she remembered that she had asked the rakish Door about a decent hotel in Prague in the presence of the dashing Will Marion.

The man from Vienna had obviously concluded that the presence of the unusual gentleman at her table so early in the morning meant that no danger threatened him from her quarter, and he waved to her jovially, sat down and pulled out a cigar. The woman with him wore a neutral expression.

Will had of course noticed. "Geraldine has hair like that."

"Who is Geraldine?"

"Geraldine Morgan, the daughter of the lady who found a room for me in Berlin. She translates German songs into English."

"She's the one who borrowed three hundred marks from you, isn't she? Did she ever pay you back?"

"No."

"I assume she made it up to you some other way. But don't tell me. I'm not interested. I've had enough of your Hatties and your Geraldines for one day."

"Adele, I may be a rambling man, but I wasn't rambling this time. It was Geraldine who took me to that concert café. Remember? You asked me about it last night, but I fell asleep."

She glowered at him. But she liked gossip, and Jeannette liked it even more. And since this particular piece of gossip had something to do with the Master.... "All right," she said, in what she hoped was a nonchalant tone. "Out with it!"

"Geraldine Morgan, who borrowed three hundred marks from me without returning them, without in fact paying me back in any way whatsoever," Will said slowly, putting his cigar down on the ashtray, "simply *had* to talk to her mother. I don't know why, but it seemed very important to her. I happened to know that Mrs. Morgan was meeting that afternoon with someone from Simrock's in the Beaux Jardins Konzertcafé, where her son Paul was making some extra cash playing cello. So I went to the café with Geraldine, and when we got there her mother hadn't arrived, so we sat down and ordered coffee."

Will glanced over at the Titian head at the table by the window. Smoke rings from the Viennese gentleman's cigar were floating lazily around it. He sighed, and returned to his story. "Are you familiar with the Beaux Jardins?" he asked.

She shook her head.

"It's a fancy old place with little boxes where you can sit and whisper *tête à tête*, look each other in the eye and listen to Viennese waltzes, all at once. The boxes are separated by panels of coloured glass, and it was in one of those boxes that I saw them."

"Saw whom?"

He took the cigar from the table, sniffed it hungrily, frowned, then regretfully put it down again. "My first thought was, Damn! I'm not playing solo any more, there are two of us sons of Ham here. Then I gave him the onceover and said to myself, Brother, you're not going to be much competition. You're getting on in years, and your face won't break any hearts in Berlin. But when I looked at the lady, my confidence wilted. What a beauty, Adele! Straight from a fairytale. Of course, a fairytale written by Bizet."

"Was she red-haired too?"

"She had dark brown hair, with ringlets on her forehead and curly hair bunched up behind and held by a jewelled clasp, and cascading out of the clasp and down her back. And her eyes, her eyes, Adele...." He paused dreamily, then added matter-of-factly, "Rather like yours."

"Enough description," she said, equally matter-of-fact. "Who was it?"

The cigar rose automatically to his mouth, then stopped. "At that moment," he continued, ignoring her question, "I noticed that Geraldine was staring at him, and whenever he turned his head, Geraldine would smile and nod as if to greet him. But the fellow was mesmerized by his companion and took no notice. 'Who is it?' I asked

Geraldine, and she looked at me as though such incredible ignorance was a personal insult. 'Don't be foolish! It's Antonin Dvorak.' "

He stopped to watch the impression this made.

Considerable. Her interest in the story had driven everything else from her mind. "And who was the woman?" she asked breathlessly.

"I don't know," he said, with an exasperated air. "And neither did Geraldine. Probably an extremely well-heeled Berliner, somebody von something-or-other."

"Couldn't you hear what they were talking about? Were they speaking German, or –"

"They never talked at all."

"They never talked?"

"To be honest, every once in a while she'd whisper something in his ear, but the Master never said a word. Maybe he was deaf too – he didn't even appear to notice how the house orchestra was making mincemeat of Strauss."

And suddenly it came to her. She could guess who the Master's Bizet fairy was. Will could not. He hadn't been there with them yesterday afternoon, under the linden tree. He had been charming the village girls with his trumpet at the local inn. But she remembered those eyes that told a story. The Master, it seemed, was a part of that story.

Her nose was struck by a horrid smell. Vice had triumphed over veto. Will was slouched back in his chair, the long green shaft of tobacco smoking victoriously in his mouth. "Can't you get along without a pacifier?" she said.

He took the malodorous object out of his mouth and frowned. "In this matter, you're mistaken, Adele. I didn't buy those stogies to make an impression on eighteen-year-olds – girls never travelled in the smoking car anyway. But our people never travelled in the non-smoking. In the smokers' car there were whites who wanted to smoke, and blacks who wanted to take the train."

She understood.

"And I was outraged, do you see? So I said, if they're going to put me in that smoking car, then by God I'll smoke. I thought it might make me feel less humiliated and angry."

He exhaled. The momentary anger disappeared from his eyes to be replaced by his irrepressible laughter. "And so I lit up a three-cent cigar and I smoked it. My stomach rebelled, but I went on smoking and smoking, and when I was done the first stogie, I used the butt to light another one. The conductor came by, punched my ticket, took a good look at me and said, 'Ain't you kinda young to be smokin', boy?' And I just blew some smoke into his face, like this...."

Will made a circle of his lips and puffed a perfect smoke-ring towards the ceiling. She watched it as it floated across the room and settled on a small set of antlers on the wall.

"Well, not exactly like that. You have to learn how to blow smoke-rings. I just blew the smoke right between his eyes. And you know what I told him?"

She shook her head. Something insolent, for sure.

"I told him, 'How about him? He's old enough to ride in the smoking car, right?' and I pointed to a kid sitting in the corner. He was all of two and a half, black as the ace of spades and he had a sign around his neck with a Washington address where he was to be delivered."

She looked at him a moment in perplexity. Then she put back her head and laughed.

"By the time we got to Washington," he went on, "I'd smoked my last stogie. I stumbled out of the car and lay down on the platform like a plank of wood and the boy with the sign around his neck had to take me by the ankles and drag me to the gate where my mother was waiting to pick me up."

5   :𝄐: JEANNETTE IN TROUBLE

WELL, I'VE ACCEPTED THE POSITION in Chicago. Starting all over again, Mr. Garrigue, is nothing new to me. New York has already had its fill of Theodore Thomas – it wants Anton Seidl, Seidl it shall have. Chicago wants Thomas, and Thomas it shall get. I am on my way.

Since you ask, Mrs. Garrigue, yes, I do mind. And I'd add to that that I'm not happy to be losing such fine neighbours as yourselves. But worse things have happened to me, and it can't be compared with what's befallen others. Look at poor old Hill – did you hear he took his own life? Yes, Ureli Corelli Hill. But he was seventy-two, and just between you and me, when he persuaded himself that he was no more than a relic tolerated only for what he'd once done for music in New York, he wasn't far from the truth. Even if he *was* only a fiddler, a gut-scraper, he knew good music when he heard it. I wasn't yet in this world, Mr. Garrigue, when old Ureli Corelli performed Handel's Messiah in New York. And he did Beethoven's Fifth here too – I was only seven at the time and something of a child prodigy, playing in my father's band in Esens on the other side of the ocean. The little Mozart of Friesenland, they called me. Musicians would give me music and take bets on my ability to sight-read it. I could always play whatever they gave me. *What* was I playing when old Ureli was serving up Beethoven to the public over here? I'd rather not talk about that. Fatuous trifles. People loved it. This was in Beethoven's own country! And in New York at the time there were no sewers; people kept pigs instead. No, Mr. Garrigue, it's no joke. The pigs ate the garbage people threw into the streets, otherwise New York would have choked on its own refuse. And just around the corner, there was Ureli, conducting Beethoven. How do you like that?

What kind of sound the poor man coaxed out of his fiddlers and hornblowers is another matter. I know what orchestras were like in those days. A quarter of a century later, I was playing in ones just like them myself. Take my first engagement: the conductor was Signor Lietti, and he didn't even own a baton. He conducted in the Viennese style, that is, he would play first violin standing up. His notion was that simply bearing down on the strings as hard as he could would be enough to keep the orchestra together. And so that the wind instruments could hear him too, he would stamp his feet on the floor as though marching. Problem was, the strings interpreted his stamping to mean they were to play forte – so they played forte, which in turn meant the winds couldn't hear him at all and Signor Lietti, in an effort to make himself heard, would scrape away with increasing vigour – so the strings scraped harder too, till the overture began to sound like a concerto for a sawmill. Be thankful you have never heard anything like it, Mr. Garrigue. The piccolo squealed like a newborn piglet, the wind instruments wailed an alarm, the trombones blared out a broadside in an attempt to rein in the strings, the harp tried to urge on the trombones – but nothing worked. Not even the kettledrum player was able to bring us back together, although he sounded like a cannonade. The overture just died out. The last instrument to finish was the ophicleide – we weren't using tubas at the time – and it played the bottom tone of the last chord two bars after the trombones and a good six after the violins. Signor Lietti himself was a bar ahead of them. That's what the music was like, Mr. Garrigue. So God knows how Beethoven turned out under Ureli. But the important thing is that Beethoven got performed here at all back then in the thirties, when pigs were still at large in the streets and most of the music-going public in New York still believed that cellists were impoverished double-bass players who couldn't afford a larger instrument. Here and there in all this, perhaps Ureli managed to create some flashes of beauty, and someone may even have noticed. I always say, Mr. Garrigue, that a man who has never heard Beethoven hasn't lived half his life. And I'm not merely trying to be witty, like Jim Huneker. Let me tell you something, Mr. Garrigue. Not so long ago we were on the way back from California with the orchestra and the train was held up for two hours in some backwater town in Nebraska while they repaired the tracks or something. I took a stroll through town, it was evening, and a German band was playing on the main street, the kind that have been forcing the hurdy-gurdy players and organ grinders in New York out of business these past few years. They had a trumpet, a bass flügelhorn, a B-flat clarinet, a trombone, and a tuba. Bewhiskered fellows in Tyrolean hats. The clarinetist was the spitting image of my father, who used to be town piper back home in Esens. Lord knows what brought them to a God-forsaken place like that. They were playing Strauss, and doing a rather decent job of it. Good, honest music. So I stopped to listen. These bands, to my mind, represent real progress over the barrel-organ players. They each have their own territory, and you never find more than one on a street. It often used to be you'd find five organ grinders crowded into a single block, all playing something different, but simultaneously of course, and only the deaf could stand it. So there I was, enjoying the music, and beside me stood an old man in a shabby suit-coat, a cloth cap on his head. Might have been clean-shaven about a week before. One of his shoes was bound with a piece of string – he seemed to be having trouble keeping the sole on – and his hands were stuffed in his pockets, but he never took his eyes off the musicians. You know how it is when you hear something you like and you want to share the experience with someone else. So the old fellow turned to me and said, "Sure can play, eh what?" "They're doing a fine job," I replied. "A fine job," said the old man, "but I tell you sir, this is nothing. I once heard a band – a big one – maybe a hundred people in it. Now there was music. Not waltzes – symponys, sir. Ever heard a sympony? My, it was lovely." "Where was that?" I asked. "Oh, it must be a good twenty years back, in New York," he said. "Friend of mine took me to Terrace Garden, that's where I heard it. A sympony. Ever hear a sympony? If you haven't, then you don't know what music is!" I swear to you, Mr. Garrigue, nothing, not even the finest review in the world, has given me such pleasure. Here I am, standing in a one-horse town in Nebraska, and a tattered old man tells me he heard my orchestra twenty years ago, and the experience stayed with him for the rest of his life. I've been waving the baton for a quarter of a century, and sometimes I wonder whether it's all in vain. But that old codger from Nebraska persuaded me it's worth it after all. Once in his entire lifetime he heard Beethoven, and he never forgot it. Perhaps there are more old codgers like him around.

That's why I think poor old Corelli's miserable end is such a scandal. They said he was crazy. Of course he must have been a little crazy. He was a stubborn Connecticut Yankee and they all seem a little touched. Perhaps he inherited it from his father. What kind of father, after all, would christen his child Ureli Corelli Hill? In the end, when he had lost everything, they might have tried to find him a sinecure, but no, they left the poor old man to stand in for a third violinist who happened to come up with a better engagement that night at the Vanderbilts' ball. And yet, were it not for his dogged perseverance, there would be no Philharmonic Society of New York. If they'd just paid him a few dollars to rummage around in the archives, he'd never have come to believe, in his old age, that he no longer meant anything to American music. How did he do it? An overdose of morphine, Mr. Garrigue.

Oh no, sir, there's no need to worry about me. Chicago has some magnificent musicians these days. I'll put together an orchestra that will be a delight to hear. I managed it here in New York when there was no surplus of good musicians, as there is today. And most important of all, they have money in Chicago.

That reminds me – how is your daughter Charlotte? Oh, she's had a son, has she? I'm glad to hear it. What's she calling him? Jan? Perhaps he'll turn out a musician too. Charlotte's a talented woman, could easily have been a female Rubinstein. Her husband's a Czech, is he not? Plays the violin rather well. What does he do? A professor? What was his name? Of course, Thomas Masaryk. I remember. A fine man.

I tell you I'll bid farewell to New York with a light heart except for one thing: I'll miss being able to slip across the street to your place whenever I hear the sounds of singing. You know, Mrs. Garrigue, I didn't see your daughters very often, but I heard them – I was always hearing them. It must have been like that at the Bachs' house: everyone making music.

Ah well, nothing lasts for ever. Only the past can seem like an eternity. Why, I've been in America for almost half a century. An eternity, Mrs. Garrigue. And the catastrophes!

But there's one thing you have to give this ungrateful country credit for: they always give you another chance – it's not like Europe: if you fall out with officialdom there, you're done for. Of course you mustn't be too far on in years, like poor old Ureli. And you have to be a man, though occasionally the man may wear a skirt, like Jeannette Thurber. I tell you, Mr. Garrigue, when I saw her hopes for her opera company dashed in Buffalo in '87, I said to myself, girl, this is a mess you've dragged me into, but I can't stand seeing you this way. Even so, maybe this will cure you so that next time, like other society ladies with musical aspirations, you'll limit yourself to holding musical soirées in your salon. At least it won't cost your poor husband an arm and a leg. And you see? I had her figured wrong, completely. At the time, she was just about in tears – now imagine that, if you can: Jeannette in tears? And she wasn't just putting on an act for Carnegie so he'd kick in more money. These were real tears, not business tears. What's she up to now? This may interest you, since your son-in-law's a Czech: I hear she's in Europe, spreading her net for Antonin Dvorak. You know, in Buffalo, I thought her husband Francis would certainly put an end to those expensive ideas of hers. But one shouldn't underestimate love. Thurber's another one of those Yankees, starts out with nothing, ends up a multimillionaire but he's still an eccentric. Look at that anti-monopoly league he founded! Why, the bastards will destroy him! But that's Francis. Jeannette, for him, is a goddess – he told me he feels uneducated beside her, yet half Jeannette's wild ideas come from him. Unfortunately, he understands the grocery business but not music. Take her new conservatory here in New York: she's offering free tuition, and then for three years after graduation, students are expected to give a fifth of their professional earnings as musicians back to the school. Sounds clever, doesn't it? Well, it's not. If Francis had asked my opinion first, I'd have told him to forget the socialism and charge a straight fee, tailored to the students' pockets if necessary. Everyone knows that music schools usually overflow with young girls, and what happens to your share of their professional earnings? They all get married as soon as they graduate, and the only time they ever practise music is in drawing-room recitals. And what are you supposed to do then, make their husbands give over a fifth of *their* earnings as professional businessmen? But Francis didn't agree with me, nor Jeannette.

Or take Jeannette's famous American Opera Company. When the first season was over, it was obvious the public liked us but the backers didn't, because the deficit was too enormous and all the glory couldn't balance it out. Then Jeannette came up with a brilliant idea: take a public company, with investors like Belmont, Morgan,

Carnegie, Gould and other financial heavyweights of that ilk, turn it into a co-operative venture and sell shares to the stagehands. You know Jeannette, Mr. Garrigue. She has a silver tongue in her head, and she even persuaded Eloi Sylva, a self-inflated Scrooge if ever there was one, to go along with it. And where do you suppose she got her economic ideas from? Francis, naturally. In his grocery enterprise, every cleaning-lady is a shareholder. I don't profess to understand business, Mr. Garrigue, but there are people who think Jeannette is a socialist. You must remember how she was attacked when she asked Congress for two hundred thousand for her conservatory? What was it the gutter press wrote? "The American people is not a sordid people, but it is averse to pouring money down a rathole." In Boston, they were more genteel. "Music is a luxury for the wealthy." That's what the Dial said. A fine sentiment, wouldn't you say? Oh, there's nothing like calling a spade a spade. Why didn't Jeannette turn to her millionaire friends to support her brain-child, they asked, or even reach into her own well-filled pockets? As if she hadn't done so already. Leave the public's money alone, they said. Let it be used for institutions like military academies that serve the common good, or for agricultural research. Very well, perhaps music isn't of benefit to everyone, Mr. Garrigue. After all, there are the deaf to consider. But I only wish that scribbler from the Dial could have listened to my old man in Nebraska.

This same sage also wrote that Mrs. Thurber stubbornly clung to her disasters with the American Opera Company, believing they had actually been triumphs. Well, if you measure by the box office, perhaps they were disasters. But what do you think, Mr. Garrigue? If you add up *all* the pluses and subtract all the minuses, was it such a calamity after all?

It's true that by the time we had hobbled all the way across the country from San Francisco to Buffalo, I was a nervous wreck and in a foul frame of mind. I felt like Napoleon retreating from Moscow. Jeannette, unlike Napoleon, stayed with her troops till the bitter end. I did not, Mr. Garrigue, and I admit that to this day I feel guilty about letting her down and leaving her to soldier on alone from Buffalo to Toronto. But I simply hadn't the strength to go on. Jeannette's millionaire backers had long since backed out, there was only money enough left to ship the scenery and the props. We had to buy food for the company from our own money, and both of us had to spend each night incognito in a different hotel, even in the same town, to avoid constables armed with writs.

By the end, however, I was furious with her, though I knew she meant well and wasn't in fact responsible for what happened. After all, she wasn't a businessman like Carnegie and Belmont and those birds. They pulled out in time. She has music in her, body and soul, I can vouch for that. It's something like fifteen years now since we put on concerts for children, and who financed them? She did, naturally. She also sent talented young girls to study at the Paris conservatory and paid all their expenses. And the American Opera Company was something so new most people couldn't understand it. But what can you do, Mr. Garrigue? She owed me half a year's wages. Not that she was trying to cheat me – she simply didn't have the money and in any case there were people in the company in line before me.

Yes, I was furious with her, why try to deny it? It was me the constables were after, because the creditors seemed to think a conductor is something like a bank manager, responsible not only for the orchestra, but for the bookkeeping as well. In Buffalo, I was fit to be tied. Then I saw her in that stinking hotel room – it was an awful place, Mr. Garrigue; we'd moved in because we felt certain no sheriff would ever come looking for the wife of Francis B. Thurber in a flop-house, if you'll pardon the expression – when I saw that pretty, upright lady in her tweed vest, with a bow-tie under her chin, in the dim light of the smoky gas lamp, and her little chin, always so firm and proud, suddenly trembling, and tears welling up into those lovely eyes – when I saw that, Mrs. Garrigue, I swallowed my pride and I felt my rage melting away. I pulled out my handkerchief and, well, I'm not sure how it happened, but suddenly Jeannette's tears were dripping onto my own vest.

So I conducted one last time in Buffalo that night. One scene was particularly beautiful, with a special effect that required the invention of a completely new machine. God knows how much that little detail cost her, but Jeannette wanted everything about the American Opera to be first class. "We'll be playing for people who have never seen opera before, and that's precisely why we must have everything they have at the Met," she said. "And it must be better!" Again, it brings to mind that old man in Nebraska. As I see it now, the American Opera Company couldn't have avoided going bankrupt because

Jeannette insisted on the very best for all those old men out there. Singers, scenery, costumes, props, the orchestra – everything had to be tip top. There were only two seasons, but what seasons they were! Really, Mr. Garrigue – wasn't the collapse worth it?

I conducted the overture, then the curtain rose to reveal a magnificent set, a shady grove and, visible through the trees, a romantic countryside at night. Then Jeannette's machine – that invisible machine – slowly raised a large red moon, just like a harvest moon, and as it rose it turned yellow, then white, until it was a beautiful silver – and you know, Mr. Garrigue, that ordinary stage moons can only rise to a certain height, well, Jeannette's moon kept on climbing, up among the tree-trunks, through the leaves, on and on until I forgot I was conducting, I no longer noticed the duet on the stage and stared only at the moon, sparkling high among the leaves. Finally it vanished into the flies, but its white light still poured down from the heights on Emma Juch and Candidus, flooding the romantic countryside with splendour, and suddenly I began to weep, Mr. Garrigue, because I knew it would all come to nothing, and I no longer felt any bitterness towards Jeannette, merely regret. She had invented this magnificent moon – but Belmont and Carnegie, of course, had done their arithmetic and the results told them the same money could buy them far greater glory in ecclesiastical charity. And that put paid to the moon.

Regret, Mr. Garrigue, and pangs of conscience for abandoning her, because next morning, after that performance and despite my feelings, I let her go off to Toronto alone. Of course Candidus told me about that later – he's a good egg with an eye for the funny side of everything. But Jeannette must have felt awful. The only fortunate thing about it was that the ultimate embarrassment took place on foreign soil.

The Toronto performance must have been worth seeing. Things went wrong from the start, beginning with the hall itself. The stage was too small. Some clever local impresario hadn't measured it properly and the stagehands didn't realize this until they started putting up the set. Next, the good clergymen of Toronto raised a moral ruckus over Don Juan, labelling it a godless piece of American decadence. They organized a boycott and the hall was half empty. As if that weren't enough, the first flautist had a fight with the tuba player, who knocked two of his teeth out, front teeth, naturally. The tuba player was practically a midget, smaller than his instrument, but a marvellous musician. He also had a terrible temper. He had played in my orchestra for as long as I can remember. They had to hire a local flautist at short notice, and the man they got was an organist who only played the flute occasionally, and to make matters worse he had a bad case of the jitters and sounded like a hissing serpent. On top of everything, Emma Juch came down with a cold. Ten bars into her first solo, she sounded like a street crier. Her nerves collapsed under the strain and in the end she and Jeannette had a terrible altercation. And they were such good friends!

The greatest catastrophe came at the end. The part of Don Juan was sung by Alonzo Stoddard, a good baritone but built like a double bass. In the final scene, the old reprobate is supposed to be swallowed up by hell for deflowering a thousand and three virgins in Spain alone. But the Canadians had not only been parsimonious about the size of their stage, they'd tried to save on everything, and their trap-door was built for dolls, not people. Stoddard was correctly positioned, the machinery worked and the sinner began his descent into hell. Right on cue, light from hell-fires blazed up from below. But suddenly the flames went out and there was Don Juan, stuck like a cork in the trap-door. Struggle as he might, the poor fellow couldn't budge. Frank Bellamy, who was conducting this mess, very cleverly got the orchestra to repeat the same five bars over and over again to give Stoddard time to work his way down to hell, but nothing helped. To top it all off, the fellow operating the curtain was drunk and had fallen asleep.

It was dreadful. And that wasn't all. Finally, when Stoddard had been stuck for so long that even the Canadian bumpkins realized something was wrong, some wag in the balcony shouted at the top of his voice: "Hurrah! No more vacancies in hell!"

And that brought the saga of Jeannette's American Opera Company to an end, and though hell may be overcrowded, I hope room can still be found for a few more. I would love to see Belmont there. And Carnegie. I sincerely hope his donation of ten thousand organs to ten thousand churches, instead of paying off Jeannette's debts, won't go down in his favour. It was wonderful advertising, of that I have no doubt. Certainly better than financing moon-machines. But I can't believe the Lord places much stock in self-promotion. He knows what He knows.

So was the entire undertaking really a catastrophe? Well, it cost Francis a million, Jeannette a few grey hairs and me half a year's salary and a few more thousand that I spent on food for our share-holders. The French consul paid the ballerinas' passage home to France. The musicians, the soloists, the chorus, the stagehands, all lost their shirts. And those beautiful machines, magnificent costumes, the wonderfully painted scenery – it was all bought up by some greedy jobber for peanuts. What he did with it all I have no idea and I don't care. But I doubt you could use the moon-machine to lift cases of sardines.

And now I hear our indefatigable Jeannette is training her sights on Dvorak. You wait and see, Mrs. Garrigue, she'll get him. And who knows, perhaps he'll write his own American Dances.

And I'm going to Chicago and I'll conduct them there. I premiered his Slavonic Rhapsody in Cincinnati, you know, barely half a year after Taubert conducted it in Berlin. And since then, hardly a year has gone by when I haven't included something by him in my program. He's a real musician, Mr. Garrigue. He knows what melody is. Perhaps only Schubert knew better.

I suppose if he does write his American Dances, Seidl will conduct – in New York. I'll do it in Chicago after that. You know, I feel a bit hurt that after all those years I – but never mind, Seidl is good. And of course there's a difference between spending seven years as secretary to the great Wagner, going through the Ring of the Nibelungen with him, measure by measure, as he did and doing what I did, wandering from town to town on horseback, putting up posters that said "Master Theodore Thomas, the Youngest Violin Virtuoso in the World", and then, the same evening, collecting money in front of the saloon and when there was enough money in the hat, pulling out my violin and playing Home, Sweet Home. But that, I suppose, is life. Seidl would never have waved the baton in a barn. For that you need a Ureli Corelli. And when he's brought those music-making cobblers to a state of perfection, it's time for a Seidl to take over. Seidl's talents would be wasted on breaking in new musicians.

That's how it is in America these days. No use crying over spilt milk. Well, I must go now. Give my regards to your daughters, Mrs. Garrigue. And say hello to Charlotte in Prague too. My congratulations on her new son. And on her husband, the professor, as well. Oh? He's in politics now? What was his –? Oh yes, Masaryk. A fine name. Please forgive an old bandmaster his fading memory. Farewell, friends. Goodbye. Tomorrow I'm off to Chicago.

6 :C): HUNEKER ON A CRAWL

THERE'S NOTHING PERSONAL in this, I assure you, sir. I only return public insult for public insult, and old Borax never wrote a word about me. "Jim Huneker is my American friend," he used to say. What he did write concerned his naive notions about American folk idiom, in which he notoriously confused Indian with Negro music. But he wrote about it in such glowing superlatives that today some of our young adepts in the art of composition seem to think that ragtime is music. He also publicly supported Jeannette – and who can blame him for that? – in her crusade to have Congress allocate public funds to keep the Conservatory afloat, and to that enterprise he lent his name, though of course no one could pronounce it.

Why don't I blame him for that? Only someone who never knew Jeannette could ask such a question, sir, for only such a man could have escaped her "personal touch", as she called it. Of course, as a teacher at the Conservatory I seldom experienced it – Jeannette almost never interfered with the staff – but as secretary to the Secretary of the National Conservatory of Music, I had the most pleasant duty of visiting her residence daily and sitting for an hour with her and admiring her beauty while she, in an extravagant peignoir, drank her morning coffee. In fact, it was my only duty. I don't mind admitting that her dark, eloquent eyes troubled my sleep more than once. But that was as far as my admiration took me, sir. Whether old Borax had more gumption than I did I don't know. I would occasionally see him in her office, sitting in a chair across from her and gazing at her the way I did every morning. Jeannette would certainly have been worth the sinning, even to someone as strait-laced as Borax. Of course, regardless of whether or not anything ever transpired between them, they were ultimately separated not by any ecclesiastical inhibitions Borax might have had, but by the root of all evil. Yes indeed, my friend – money. After the stock market panic of '93, Jeannette's sources in the wholesale grocery business began to dry up, and her troublesome eyes no longer had the same power over Borax. I suspect, though, it may have been old Mrs. Borax who put a stop to it. As long as the dollars flowed, she managed to turn a blind eye to the little meetings her husband had with Jeannette in her office instead of going to watch the trains at Penn Station – that famous habit of his. Be that as it may, I understand that Mrs. Borax had a lifetime of practice in turning a blind eye. Paterfamilias? He was certainly that. And yet – there are things that warm a man more than the family hearth, nor is their fire so quick to subside.

No, I insist, there is nothing personal in my opinion of his music. I genuinely disliked his Ninth Symphony, the so-called New World or From the New World Symphony. It was melodious, yes, but shallow and insincere. Impressionistic, as was everything he ever wrote, yet in this case the impressions were superficial, and he tried to give them a semblance of profundity by lacing his orchestration with special effects. The more I listen to it, the more its shallowness grates upon my ears. Very well – he quotes one spiritual and one minstrel song in it, tossing them both into the same pot. An American symphony? Look, Borax was always a bit of a musical pirate, and thematically it is a composite of Irish, Slavic, Scottish, Negro and German themes: the work of a successful man who is doing his best to execute an important commission but does so using too much generally accessible information. And masters like Schubert and Wagner should not be quoted without quotation marks, if you get my meaning. That's old Borax's Achilles' heel, and of course he's not alone. Art is always endangered by success. A successful artist loses his personality, and turns into the popular notion of himself. That is exactly what happened to old Borax.

You're right, of course. It only happened in his music, not in his personal life. Evening after evening, he would play cards with his secretary Kovarik – who was the one who persuaded him to make the journey halfway across America just to spend the summer in that odd little town of Spillville in the middle of nowhere – instead of putting in an appearance in the Fifth Avenue salons where they doubtless would have loved to show him off. He continued to live like a peasant though he no longer wrote peasant music. No more Slavonic Dances, in which he is absolutely authentic, though not the equal of Smetana. No more Scherzo Capriccioso, where my feeling is precisely the opposite to that for the New World Symphony: the more I listen to it, the more I long to hear it again. He never wrote another scherzo like it.

The music in the symphony is beautiful, I won't dispute that, and indeed, I wrote as much after the première in New York. Borax was a magnificent song-writer and his melodies are exquisite. Well, if anything, that symphony is perhaps a bit too beautiful.

No, there's absolutely nothing personal in this at all. Of course, I admit that at times I may have been unduly severe. Critics who spend a good deal of their time listening to third-rate music tend to feel annoyed at a composer who carries within him potential greatness and compromises his reputation merely to please. And who was he pleasing? Himself – or rather his notions of his own greatness which he accepted uncritically from his flatterers. This sort of thing happens most frequently to artists of Borax's stature, men of natural talent from whom the music flows in a manner beyond their comprehension yet who lack the mental capacity of a Brahms to regulate the meandering river of their own uncomprehended gift.

Perhaps I should begin at the beginning. I came to meet Borax, in fact, in my capacity as Jeannette Thurber's morning admirer. One day she said to me – in French, because she enjoyed speaking that language when she had the chance – "Perhaps you could show the Master around town. Of all the people at the Conservatory, you are undoubtedly the most qualified."

"But Madame," I protested, "I'm not even a native New Yorker. Why not ask –"

"The Master loves to drink beer," she interrupted, fixing her languid eyes on me. Well, her wish was my command. And so, on the boss's orders, I set out with Borax on a tour through most of the more picturesque corners of Manhattan.

We started out at Goerwitz's, where they served an excellent Budweiser from Milwaukee, but it turned out that Jeannette's intelligence concerning Borax's taste in alcohol was not quite accurate, because he said to me, *"Ich will etwas echt amerikanisch trinken. Bier hab ich zu Haus."* I should point out that we spoke German together, and I was encouraged since I have seldom come across anyone whose accent was worse and whose ignorance in matters of grammar was greater than mine.

"*Echt amerikanisch?*" I asked. "Okay." And so I ordered a double whisky cocktail for him and a Budweiser for myself.

Borax, as you know, had the features of an angry bulldog and fierce Slavic eyes. They placed a glass of golden liquid in front of him and he looked at it with those penetrating eyes, then did something so unexpected I was unable to prevent him from doing it. He raised the cocktail to his nose, flared his nostrils, inhaled deeply, muttered something, and abruptly tossed his head back as though he had been taken by a sudden seizure.

He had quite simply swallowed the entire cocktail at a single gulp. I was flabbergasted, but he turned those piercing eyes upon me and very calmly said, "*Nicht schlecht.*"

"Would you like another one, *Herr Doktor?*"

He looked around the room and his face grew glum. Goerwitz's was a favourite haunt of German student clubs and one of their potentates had obviously just been married, because a tipsy group were lounging around a huge table underneath a portrait of Kaiser Wilhelm. They were all got up in uniforms of some kind and at the head of the table sat the groom with mutton-chop whiskers and a rather hefty-looking bride. They were singing the wedding march from Lohengrin in alcoholic discord.

Either the sight of those Prussian uniforms – Borax was a passionate Bohemian chauvinist – or what they were doing to Lohengrin prompted Borax to give what was to become a standard response to my question: "*Ja, noch einmal, aber hier nicht zweimal.*"

I gathered from this that he was ready to move on.

In the next establishment, half a block to the south, he drank two more whisky cocktails and I had another beer. I cannot stand spirits, so I kept to my favourite mixture of malt, hops and cold spring water. Our thoughts were very quickly simplified by the alcohol and we established a plausible rapport despite our broken German. The evening, as you can appreciate, was not to be over after the first two bars. We were driven out of the second by a man from South Carolina who mistook Borax for a coloured person and singlehandedly tried to eject him from the bar. The man himself ended up in the gutter, and it wasn't the bouncer's doing. Borax was handy with his fists, though he was not one to seek out a fight, for despite his resemblance to that tenacious breed of pit bull he was a gentle and peaceful soul. At the next bar, he was quickly gripped by an urge to explore, so we needed no further excuses to change our locale regularly. Thus we traced a large arc through lower Manhattan's thirst belt. Borax continued to down his cocktails and he soon noticed that I was merely sipping my beer. It was in the fifth bar – Libby's on Eighteenth Street – that he began to teach me the technique of drinking at one go, or "ex", as he called it, and after my seventh beer and eighth bar, I had it down pat. At that point, Borax had consumed about nine whisky cocktails and three beers, which he drank to satisfy his curiosity, and in the ninth bar – a dive called Martin's on University Place – we bumped into Francis Neilson, a young man Jeannette had asked to write a libretto for Borax based on Longfellow's Hiawatha. Neilson was currently wrestling with the problem of how to square the circle, that is, how to turn Longfellow's tangled skein of legend into a coherent story. When we arrived, however, Neilson was struggling with a different problem: how to overcome the inhibitions of a pretty young lady sitting with him at the bar. Needless to say he was not particularly glad to see us. He knew only too well the tendency of some of the female students to seek my favour with the aid of approved horizontal methods. I assumed that Neilson's young lady was a student, for beside her glass on the bar lay a copy of Schubert's Lieder. Her glass – and this was surprising in a woman of such tender years – was brimming with undiluted whisky.

Borax at once asked Neilson how the libretto was progressing, and Neilson, in turn, tried to explain how difficult it was to convert Longfellow's nonsense into a comprehensible plot that would work on stage. They spoke English, and consequently Borax understood very little of what Neilson was saying.

Meanwhile I turned my attentions to Neilson's young lady. Her name was Rosemary McIntosh and she told me she had come to New York from Mammoth's Tooth, Colorado, to study singing. My first reaction was one of pity. She appeared well situated, living with an older sister who had married into money, but she was clearly suffering from shortness of breath, and perhaps anemia also. I had already had occasion – both at the Conservatory and elsewhere – to make the acquaintance of a number of young ladies from the Midwest who had made the pilgrimage to New York to become another Adelina Patti or at the very least another Emma Juch. Not all of them had an older sister to act as a *centrum securitatis* and yet that was precisely what they needed most, for like babes in the woods they fell prey to charlatans posing as singing instructors who had all, without exception, taught Liza Lehmann *and* the renowned de Reszke brothers how to sing. When the girls had thus been stripped of their savings, they could only – except for the handful who jumped into the Hudson River – take what little they had left, go back to Cooper's Ferry and marry the local druggist, exactly as their parents had wanted them to do all along.

Rosemary, however, had happened upon a teacher who was remarkable indeed. When I asked if the liquid in her glass was in fact straight whisky, she replied, "Yes, my singing instructor says whisky makes it easier to breathe and improves the intonation."

The words were scarcely out of her mouth when she turned pale and gasped for breath. Her modest décolletage displayed an elegant but hopelessly enthrottled bosom, though her chest indicated a generous capacity for resonance, suggesting that the young lady's dreams of a concert career may not have been mere wishful thinking. But her waist was fashionably wasplike and her hand trembled as she raised the glass to her lips and sipped the liquid.

"You seem to be having trouble breathing," I observed solicitously. She shook her head, and the ringlets on either side of her narrow face swung back and forth. "Are you wearing ...?" And I indicated her waist. I could have encircled it with both hands.

"Yes," she almost groaned.

"Tightly laced?"

She nodded, and the ringlets bobbed up and down.

"You oughtn't to wear those things, you know. Singers must be able to relax their chests to produce the proper resonance."

Once again the ringlets changed direction. "An old-fashioned idea," she gasped.

"Indeed?"

"My teacher says my singing is too forced. He says – he says that when I wear a tightly laced corset, the pressure on the diaphragm helps the voice to escape from the throat effort ... lessly."

She was a chalky white. I drank my tenth beer.

"Perhaps you should try another teacher," I suggested.

"But Maestro di Canopi is very famous. He taught Liza Lehmann and he advertised in the Mammoth's Tooth Courier."

"Very well, but since then his methods have become obsolete."

"He assured me it was the very latest thing."

"Last month, perhaps, but as you know, Miss McIntosh, this is the modern age and new discoveries are being made every day. An improved system has recently been developed by Madame Fursch-Madi. Have you heard of her?"

The ringlets once more swung gently back and forth around the pale face.

"She teaches at the National Conservatory where I work. She has discovered that while a tightly laced corset may indeed help the voice, it forces too much air from the lungs and can cause shortness of breath. I think this may be what has happened in your case. Signor di Canopi's method may be excellent, but it is obviously unsuited to you personally."

Her cornflower eyes looked at me with all the innocence of Mammoth's Tooth. "Do you think so?" she gasped, almost happily.

"Certainly. If you wish, I can arrange an introduction to Madame Fursch-Madi," I said, quietly so that Neilson couldn't hear me. But he and Borax were talking so intensely that I needn't have worried. To run ahead of my story, I actually did introduce Rosemary to Madame Fursch-Madi, who took her on as a student, but she remained faithful to Neilson, at least until she started studying music history under Finck. Finck dedicated the seventh edition of his famous manual on physical beauty to her, and they were married even before she graduated. I was rather surprised, because Finck was a man of the world, but the explanation turned out to be the usual one.

At the time, however, Rosemary looked helplessly around the room, squirmed uncomfortably and then blurted out, "If only I could...."

I beckoned to Reggie, the waitress, who was just passing by with an empty tray, and handed her a quarter. Soon the two of them were hurrying off to the powder room.

I turned my attention to Neilson and Borax – and Borax, whose complexion had darkened to such an extent that I ceased to wonder at the reaction of the man from South Carolina, was now beating the bar with the palms of his hands, staring with that radiant gaze of his into Neilson's thoughtful face. Dum-de-dum-de-de-de-dum.

"Trochees?" suggested Neilson.

"Is this it?" asked Borax, and tried again. "Dum-de-dum-de-dum-de-dum-de."

"I believe it is." Neilson began thumping the bar along with him and the effect was like nothing so much as aboriginal drumming. On top of it, Borax began singing a wordless tune that employed dimin-

ished sevenths. Despite being in a public place, he made no attempt
to keep his voice down. Over by the door, the bouncer looked sus-
piciously in our direction and began rolling up his sleeves.

But soon they desisted and Neilson said, "Fine, we shall use an-
apests and trochees. I'll have to trim Longfellow back somewhat, of
course, but that melody really does sound Indian."

Borax waved to the barman and soon two whisky cocktails stood
in front of them. They touched glasses, Neilson wet his lips and Borax
showed us once again how cocktails are consumed in Bohemia. If
my count was correct, it was his fourteenth such demonstration.

I ordered another beer.

A lovely young lady with a healthy prairie complexion walked
out of the powder room and came over to us. I saw that it was
Rosemary. She was carrying a paper bag with the name of the restaurant on it.

And she ordered a grenadine.

From that point on my memory fails me. I recall only that in a
certain bar on the East Side, where Borax celebrated the twentieth
anniversary of his first whisky cocktail and I drank my twentieth
beer in the Master's style, I was suddenly overcome with alcoholic
hunger.

"Master," I said thickly, "don't you think it's time we ate
something?"

"Eat?" he replied, his eyes widening as though he found the idea
astonishing. "Not me. But let us go to a bar on East Houston Street
where my secretary, Kovarik, took me my second night in town, and
you can have a drink of slivovice. You've had too much cold beer.
The slivovice will warm you up."

He was still standing as firm as an oak, not even leaning against
the bar, that last refuge of the tipsy. Not a sway or a wobble. He
seemed to be mocking me. Such a man is as dangerous to a moderate
drinker like myself, sir, as a false beacon to a sailor in a storm. So I
refused to follow him to his Bohemian dive, even though Jeannette
had entrusted me with his welfare. Recklessly, I left him to face his
fate and set out for home. It was almost midnight and the streets
were teeming with people, aggressively painted ladies of the night,
drunken Irish wenches singing of the mountains of Mourne, and
newspaper vendors shouting out reports of fresh murders.

But Borax knew how to look after himself, though he had been
in New York for scarcely a month. That same night, I must confess,

I fell victim to one of those butterflies of the night, or more precisely, to her pimp, for I was in no condition for horizontal activity. The following morning, I found myself stripped of my gold watch and diamond tie-pin. My wallet was not missing, but everything in it was.

Borax? He made it safely to East Houston Street where he played his Slavonic Dances for the local fermentarians until four in the morning. The subtleties of his music were so appreciated that when he finally set out for his home on Seventeenth Street, he was accompanied by an entourage of people who had to cling to the walls to stay upright. At home, he breakfasted on the dinner his wife had left in the oven for him the night before. He timed his arrival and subsequent departure for the Conservatory so that the children were up but had not yet left for school. I understand that old Mrs. Borax would never make a scene in front of the children.

She made quite a scene in Jeannette's office, however, and as a result I was through with piloting old Borax through New York. It was a relief, for my kidneys weren't up to the task.

That same morning, Borax taught his three classes as though nothing had happened – except that his students reported him to be unusually affable – then took the El to the 120th Street tunnel to watch the trains. And there our escapades of the night before finally caught up with him and he fell asleep on a patch of grass outside the tunnel. He was picked up by the police on their routine rounds. They intended to book him for vagrancy but the duty officer in the precinct station was a devotee of music and recognized Borax from a picture that had appeared in the newspapers. So Mrs. Borax was never the wiser.

As you can see, it's nothing personal. In fact, we were the best of friends. It's simply that I have never shared the general admiration for his New World Symphony, which is, to be precise, a medley, as they say in popular music.

It's melodious to listen to, I agree, but so much the worse. It will lead our composers astray. It won't be long before they're blowing the clarinet in Carnegie Hall like drunken Negroes in Chicago and calling it serious music.

7 :C): JESSIE IN THE OYSTER BAR

JESSIE HARPER was deeply dissatisfied with herself. The money in her purse only amounted to one dollar and ninety-three cents, not enough to get in to the opera. She'd known it from the moment she gave in to temptation and bought another apple tart. Jessie! she scolded herself, you'll end up like one of those fat sopranos the audiences listen to with their eyes closed because they can't imagine her as Madame Butterfly. A curse on my appetite! Malva says she can last the whole day on three glasses of orange juice. What a whopper. Why, that girl's waist is three inches thicker than mine! Still....

She was counting the money in her purse for the third time when she heard a voice with the timbre of an oboe: "Financial difficulties, young lady?"

She tried to look inaccessible, and older than her seventeen years, and then gave up and turned around. In the glare of the lights in the foyer of the Met stood a gentleman, perhaps in his seventies, with gold-rimmed glasses and a white, natty little moustache that contrasted elegantly with his smooth brown face. A felt homburg sat aslant his head, his suit was a dark blue pinstripe, and the polished tips of two shiny black shoes peered out from under a pair of old-fashioned, spotless white spats. Not a bad-looking old goat. She hoped that she was showing off her yellow hat and light-brown silk dress to advantage, and that her stocking-seams were straight. Mama warned me this might happen, she thought. Three old goats to every promising man in New York.

She smiled – haughtily, she hoped – and said, "If I were you, I'd mind my own business, mister."

The man laughed. The old boy *was* rather handsome, she thought. He had a nice baritone voice.

"I'm always delighted to see a young lady of our race taking an interest in classical music, not just in Dizzy Gillespie or in be-bop," he said. "Not that I mind Dizzy or be-bop, but there's more to the palace of music than the basement."

She didn't respond. Her purse cried out for the missing seven cents and Siegfried's powerful call tugged at her heart. If he offers me a ticket, should I take it? I'll bet it won't stop there. He'll want to take me out to supper afterwards ... and I've gone and had those two apple tarts today already.

"More than fifty years ago, young lady, I was a janitor in this establishment." He pointed towards the door to the auditorium. A swelling stream of men and women in evening gowns and tuxedos was flowing through it. "Sometimes I'd hide in nigger heaven and watch the show. I saw Carmen, The Magic Flute, The Ring of the Nibelungen – "

"Did they really call it nigger heaven?" she blurted out, then stopped herself. Don't give him an inch, she thought.

"Of course they did. The very top of the gods. You probably call it the peanut gallery now. Whatever you want to call it, it certainly suited us. That's just about all we had in our pockets – peanuts."

He laughed, white teeth flashing in his dark face, and pulled a ticket from a small pocket in his waistcoat. Here it comes. She noticed his thick gold ring, the gold watch-chain elegantly garlanding his stomach and – for the first time – a raffish walking-stick with a knob in the shape of a woman's head, carved in deep yellow ivory, the same colour as her skin.

"Your eyes are a dead giveaway, my dear. You are aching to hear the great Wagner and woefully short of means."

"I can't accept this," she said, trying to sound prim but only managing to sound sorry for herself.

"Why not? It comes without strings," he said. A sly old goat, he was.

"I was afraid you were going to ask me out to supper afterwards."

"Not unless you're hungry."

She shook her head.

"Does that mean you don't want to see Siegfried or you're not interested in supper? If you insist on missing the show, then allow me to invite you to The Barber of Seville next week."

"I still won't be interested in supper."

He laughed again and said, as though he were reading her mind, "I'll bet you have a very wise mother. I respect that. I had one too. If it hadn't been for her, I'd have spent my days in a minstrel show. But I don't suppose you can understand what that would have meant."

Uneasily, she felt her mistrust melting away. "You're a musician?"

"A musician, and a saintly one at that. I sing in a church choir and I never take young ladies out to supper." And something gleamed in his eyes. Was it lust? No, more like cunning. "How about breakfast at nine tomorrow morning in the Oyster Bar, the one in Grand Central Station?"

Well, and what a smooth old man, she thought, and reached out for the ticket. "My breakfast consists of orange juice."

He laughed. "Oysters are not fattening, Miss...?"

Shall I give him a false name? What shall it be? "Josephine Harper," she replied truthfully.

"I must say I'm delighted, Miss Harper," he said earnestly. "My name is Harry T. Burleigh."

She caught her breath and her hand flew involuntarily to her mouth.

The old man was flattered and laughed. "It's always a pleasure to see that word of my unimpeachable reputation has reached the ears of a younger generation. But on your way, Miss Josephine, or you'll miss the overture."

He took her by the shoulders and gently steered her towards the entrance to the auditorium. Damn these high heels! How can I look elegant if I wobble? Then she turned around again. "Aren't you coming, Mr. Burleigh?"

"Oho," he laughed. "The old man is happy not to have been entirely forgotten. No, I won't join you, Miss Harper. I've seen this show I don't know how many times. And besides, I tend to share old Dvorak's opinion of it. But you should hear it anyway. Go on now, enjoy yourself."

He turned and walked away. A youthful figure, a wreath of white hair between the brim of his grey felt hat and his brown neck. He gave his cane a little flourish and walked briskly into the crowd, his white spats making stylish arcs across the floor.

In a trance, she let herself be carried along by the crowd into the hall. The great Harry T.! She scarcely heard the tones of the overture, was scarcely aware of sitting in an expensive seat halfway to the stage where snow-white Siegfried in a golden wig would get down to business with Fafner, the slimy green dragon, spewing fireworks. Jessie, luck is with you after all. She felt her heart beat with excitement.

But she was too full of music. Of a seventeen-year-old's dreams of grandeur. And her delight at meeting the great Harry T. merged with her delight in the music, and slender, brown-skinned Jessie became one with a three-hundred-pound Brünnhilde deathly pale in a gold wig. I must never look like that! And I'll bet Harry T. is right. Oysters are probably no worse than orange juice, as far as calories go.

Next morning, along with the oysters, they were sipping white wine, a drink she'd only had on special occasions at home when her father, mother or ten grown-up brothers and sisters were celebrating a birthday, and certainly never at this time of day! Perhaps because of this, and perhaps because she had gone to bed last night without her usual apple, Harry T., in his light-blue tweed suit, was soon swimming in the yellow, beige and green lights of the Oyster Bar like a disembodied spirit. But he was a living, breathing Harry T. Burleigh and she, Jessie Harper from Detroit, Michigan, was drinking wine with him as though they were old friends.

Against her will, she glanced at the oysters the waiter had brought to the next table, and then with regret watched as the same waiter removed a plate of empty shells from their table. Why did I have to go and ask about his wife? I wanted to talk about music. Jessie, you're a fool! Just when he starts talking about Siegfried and how Antonin Dvorak left after Act One because it sounded to him like a blacksmith's shop, you have to interrupt him with such an idiotic question: Are you married?

I suppose you might say that I am, he had replied. But I don't think so any more. I don't understand, she said, and the conversation drifted hopelessly away from music. There was sadness in Harry T.'s voice, but it was a strange kind of sadness. It wasn't sentimental. She bust down, he said. Expressions like this were now beginning to dance through his normally refined speech. Wine at nine in the morning! She was three-quarters Cree, he said. She just bust down. Went back to the reservation to live with her people, to live like her people. She walked out, I was only thirty. Maybe you weren't treating her right, she ventured. Maybe I wasn't, he said. But – take a look at me – and he braced his arms against the edge of the table and ex-

panded his chest. A handsome, masculine fellow – oh no, Jessie! –
old man. What is he driving at? She never did enjoy it very much,
he went on, though when it happened it was beautiful with her, it
just didn't happen too often, that was all. He shook his head – com-
ically, Jessie thought. And for forty years now, every single weekend,
I've been singing in the synagogue on the sabbath and in St. George's
on Sunday, and rehearsing during the week with the cathedral choir.
And of course being black, I had to keep a cool head. All you had
to do was trip up once, and there were a lot of people just waiting
for that to happen. It was a miracle they took me at St. George's at
all. In '94 their choir was all white. But I applied anyway. At the
time, Josephine, you could sing like a soloist in a choir of angels and
most Christians would still.... Luckily for me, the Reverend Dr. Rainsford was an unusual Christian – like the Master was – and what was
more, he was a brave man. One of the elders – a very pious man,
owned half the tenement houses in the Lower East Side so he had
good reason to be pious – told everybody that if Dr. Rainsford was
planning on turning the cathedral choir into a minstrel show, he'd
hand in his resignation. So Dr. Rainsford looks at him over his glasses
and says: Yes, I've heard you prefer burlesque. Now that's what I
call a smart minister, wouldn't you say so, Josephine? Harry T. laughed.
That was a turning point in my life. One just man. He sighed. Now
things are starting to get a bit better for Negroes, but back then, if
it hadn't been for people like Dr. Rainsford, or Mrs. Thurber, or the
Master.... Anyway. It took a while but they finally got used to me,
and people respected me. The old man's rings flashed among the
yellow, beige and green lights of the Oyster Bar. The waiter winked
at her on his way past.... What does he mean by that, the jerk!

"Waiter!" Burleigh called. "I don't see any oysters."

"But Mr. Burleigh, I can't eat another one."

He placed a large, warm brown hand on her smooth arm, the one
holding the glass of yellow wine: "Oysters are actually good for taking
off weight," he said soothingly.

His remark alarmed her. I can't be that overweight, can I? But the
thought was fleeting because she didn't dare lose this once-in-a-
lifetime chance to talk about music with the great Harry T. So
as the oysters arrived she tried, nonchalantly, to prompt him.
"Well, these people, the Reverend What's-his-name and so on,
that must have been nice but weren't you working with Dvorak
then too?"

He swallowed another oyster. "Well, for one thing, I wasn't Dvorak's student. Willy Cook used to say I was just his pampered darling. When I'm dead and buried and no one remembers Harry T. Burleigh any more –"

"People will always remember Harry T. Burleigh," she said with deep conviction. "Our people will, at least."

He shook his head. "No, no they won't. In fifty years they won't give me three lines in the thickest encyclopedia. *Vanitas vanitatum*, Josephine. And yet, I will have left an indestructible monument behind."

He lifted his glass ceremoniously, as though about to propose a toast. The waiter winked at Josephine again and she made a face at him this time. Harry T. was gazing somewhere beyond her.

"I was the first person to sing him Swing Low," he said, almost dreamily. "He used it in his American symphony." He took a drink. "It's a fact, Josephine. I was never let into his class. According to his contract, he took only the best students, and I had barely made it through the entrance exams. But I earned some extra money as a caretaker at the school – just like my mother used to – and my grandfather. Anyway, we've all gone through those things."

She understood. He didn't need to say very much. It was as if she heard his rich voice recede, as if it faded out to be embellished by her own memories of childhood stories told to her, as if she entered his memories. In her mind's eye, the memories took shape –

... of how he used to sing while he worked. One day he was mopping up the winter filth the students tracked through the corridors with their boots. Everyone had long since gone home, the silence of evening reigned in the building and the acoustics were good. When he reached the corner of the first-floor corridor, he discovered a wonderful echo effect and began singing with verve, scrubbing and swinging the rag across the dirty tiles to the rhythm. "Swing low, sweet chariot...." The echo made it sound as though a second and third voice were singing in harmony with his own, and the old feeling returned: music lifts the burden of weariness, eases the nightmare of anxiety. "Comin' for to carry me home." Suddenly, a wedge of light shot across the dusky corridor. Someone had opened a door. Against the background of a golden oblong of light he saw a black head, the fuzzy hair in disarray, and a voice, speaking a strange kind of English, said:

"What is this singing?"

And so he met the Master. Half an hour later, the corridor un-mopped (but the Master had taken responsibility for that), he was sitting down to supper in the Master's apartment. The food he ate was good but strange, and it gave him heartburn later that night. The Master's ten-year-old boy stared at him. His plump wife tried bravely to make conversation, but the barrier of a foreign tongue was too much for her. The only one who ignored him was the Master's secretary, a young man who only had eyes for the Master's teenaged daughter.

"Did he end up marrying her?" asked Jessie.

"He sure looked like he wanted to. They were carrying on right under Dvorak's nose. But they were lucky. In that regard, the Master was blind. And besides that, we had sauerbraten for supper. His favourite food. His wife had made it for him because that day was their wedding anniversary. Their nineteenth wedding anniversary. I remember the date well – it was the seventeenth of November.

And right after supper he said in his strange English: "Now, please, go to piano and play. And sing too, please!"

So he sat down at the piano and sang: "I'm troubled, I'm troubled, I'm troubled in my mind. If Jesus don't save me, I surely will die...."

He had scarcely finished the first verse when the Master asked sharply, "They sing it like that? Like that?" Wordlessly, he hummed the melody, emphasizing the diminished thirds.

"Yes, Dr. Dvorak. They're all sung like that. Diminished thirds, sevenths...."

"Hmm. Like that ... " he said. "It is nice. Please, sing more."

He sang: "Lord Jesus, my Saviour, on Thee I will depend, when troubles am near me You'll be my true friend...."

"Where you know this from?" asked the Master. "About what is it?"

"It's a song my granddaddy used to sing, and he said – "

– he said it was a song he'd sung when they flogged him – "if Jesus don't save me, I surely will die." The Master did not understand: what does "flogged" mean? When they beat him. "Beat?" He knew only the musical meaning of the word. He got up, pulled a dictionary from a shelf on the wall and leafed through it, stopped, and his eyes opened wide. They beat them? Yes, he said. And for why? For lots of reasons. They tried to run away. Or the overseer thought they worked too slow. Or they stole a chicken. And they were badly beaten?

Sometimes till the blood flowed. Sometimes till they were dead. Oh, God, said the Master, and such a melody! Beethoven could not have written anything finer than that.

For the rest of the evening, he told stories. About the blind grand-father who was given his freedom because it didn't pay to keep him. His wife was pregnant and they wouldn't let her go because the owner wanted her child as compensation for the useless old blind man. But the old man was a natural rebel. That was how he came to be blind. He had talked back to the overseer – and a knot on the end of the bullwhip had taken out one of his eyes. He could still see with the other one, but before long his sight went cloudy, the world turned grey, then black and then it disappeared altogether. So he had become useless. He was given his freedom. Even for a useless man, freedom is of enormous value.

And his wife was young, strong and brave. At night, under their breath, they hatched a plan. When darkness fell next evening, they set off down an old, bloody trail through the swamps. His wife led him by the hand and together they waded two miles up the stream. They were not caught. They crossed the border dividing one set of Christians from another, the free from the useless. A stern, whiskery farmer, sitting motionless in a dark cabin over an enormous Bible printed in a foreign language, listened to their tale, looked at the woman's swelling womb, fed them cornmeal, let them sleep in the barn and next morning gave them a cart, an old mule and a sack of corn. They set off for a chimera called Canada, a land somewhere far to the north where it was said all subjects, both black and white, were ruled over by a kind queen. The journey was long, and when they arrived at a town by the name of Erie, the woman's time came. In the cart a little girl first saw the light of day. My mother, Dr. Dvorak.

The Master's eyes grew moist. His pretty daughter stopped flirting with the secretary, and the little boy clung to him with his eyes.

The old blind man was not useless. The birth of a child in the land of the Yankees awakened within him a Yankee sense of enter-prise. They settled in hospitable Erie among the Quakers, the Society of Friends, and Jesus was a friend once more. The blind man found work as the town lamplighter and drummer. His voice was resonant, but now he sang spirituals only on Sunday in church, and not because he was desperate but because he was happy. A beautiful melody is always a joy.

And he was enterprising. He opened an ironing shop. He could not see, but his sensitive fingers infallibly told him which way the crease went, the complex pattern of the pleats. Fine ladies' blouses yielded to his skilfully handled iron. He made enough money to send my mother to study to be a teacher.

So your mother was a teacher? the Master asked.

No. A caretaker. In the same school she'd applied to for a teaching post. Even in the land of the Friends, people could not imagine their ugly, freckle-faced children being educated by a beautiful, chocolate-coloured woman. So they made her caretaker. She was a gifted woman. She spoke French fluently. She knew Latin and Greek. But she was only allowed to teach at Sunday School, where she told black children the ancient story of a God who, in sorrow for what He had created, suffered Himself to die a slave's death.

Was she religious? asked the Master.

She was.

"The Master was a very religious man," said Harry T. Jessie was hungry again. Oysters were hardly more filling than orange juice and the carafe of wine, empty a short while ago, seemed to be full again. "Of course, he was Catholic, and I never saw him in our church on a Sunday. St. George's was Episcopalian. He went to church somewhere around First Avenue and Seventeenth Street. But once I saw him." *He was hurrying back to the Conservatory from a rehearsal at Temple Emanu-El, and walking past the Catholic church he saw candle flames through the open door and a man and woman kneeling before the altar, black against the shimmering background of tiny flickering flames. And he recognized the unkempt silhouette as belonging to the same man who, not long before, had asked him in that strange English: "What is this singing?" He stopped and stood by the open door, though it was almost time for school. He now worshipped the Master, the greatest person he had ever met. Great and ordinary. Happy, yet terribly sad.* Harry T. grinned. "Like the blues, Josephine." And he laughed.

He entered the church and knelt in the last row of pews. He was not religious, but the sight of the Master praying made him want to sink to his knees. He waited. At last the couple crossed themselves, rose and made their way to the exit. When they had walked past him, he stood up and waited until they had moistened their fingers in the stoup and crossed themselves again; then he went into the street behind them.

"Ah, Burleigh," said the Master with pleasure. "I did not know you were Catholic."

"I'm not, Dr. Dvorak," he said, "but I saw you at prayer. Well, I was moved, so I went in to pray as well."

"Yes, Burleigh. We all believe. But today is special. We have a sad anniversary."

His wife touched her eyes with the edge of her scarf.

"Our first son, Otakar, was born nineteen years ago today, Burleigh," said the Master. "We always light a candle for him. We believe he's in heaven. He was only three when he died." He sniffed loudly. But then he said almost gaily, "Well, he will be an angel, singing in the heavenly choir. One day – I hope – we will be there too, to sing with him."

"And now you pay close attention to what I say, Josephine," said Harry T. "That was on April the fourth, 1893. I remember the date because I'd just finished copying out the third movement of the New World Symphony that day. The Master got to be so fond of me that he entrusted me with that important work. Of course, I could write notes as well as they could be printed. Those six years I studied shorthand weren't for nothing. It's good training for the hand."

Look at all he's accomplished, thought Jessie. Our black life stories. She knew so many of them. Everyone knew them. Everyone had a story like that, as complicated as a novel. But they were all basically the same. The salon of Mrs. Russell in Erie, and hundreds, perhaps thousands, of others like it. *Tiffany windows, gold wallpaper, alabaster statues, expensive and worthless bric-à-brac. A huge pianoforte, and leaning against it, Rafael Joseffi, tugging at his shirt-cuffs that sparkle with sapphire studs. He takes a sip of sherry. Translucent silk fans stirring a gentle breeze, evening gowns from New York, perfume wafting from deep décolletages. Maestro Joseffi is talking with Mrs. Russell and the wife of Judge Douglas, and a charming black girl walks through the salon in a white apron and cap, offering liqueurs to the lawyer's wife and the banker's wife, to the colonel and his wife, to the druggist. The black girl speaks English and French, and can read Latin and Greek, but here she is silent and only smiles. Then the undertaker's wife begins to talk about Schubert but the tidbits of knowledge she has crammed into her mind for this evening's conversation have become scrambled, and only the black girl and Maestro Joseffi – but he is tactful and polite – know that she really means Schumann. The black girl, who has been hired for the evening, says nothing. Then Mrs. Russell claps her hands, Maestro Joseffi sits down at the pianoforte, pulls back his sleeves, the sapphires sparkle, and his short, strong hands gently but firmly engage the instrument's ivory keys. Liszt, Beethoven, Chopin, a zephyr from the fans mingles the warm air with the odour of sandalwood, Mrs. Russell surveys her guests with satisfaction and a touch of pride when suddenly, across a corsage of orchids that adorns the bare, lightly freckled shoulders of the colonel's wife, she sees outside the window, against a background of falling snow, an apparition. But her shock quickly subsides. The apparition is comic. A little black ear is flattened against the glass, a button nose seen in ridiculous profile, and beyond, the swirling snow. Applause. The fans cease their fanning, Maestro Joseffi rises from the piano and bare swan necks hung with necklaces of pearl and gold crowd around him. Mrs. Russell goes into the kitchen, where the black girl hired for the evening is putting small canapés on a tray.*

"Louise, there's a little black boy outside the window and he's staring at the guests. I expect he's hungry. Go and give him a couple of sandwiches and some money and tell him to go away. Some of the guests might notice."

The black girl hired for the evening stiffens, and the blood rushes to her cheeks.

"Mrs. Russell, that's my son Harry."

"Your son?" The woman is amazed, and then embarrassed. "But you have a job...."

"He's not hungry. He heard that Maestro Joseffi was going to play here tonight, and he wanted to hear him. My boy is very talented musically, madam."

"Louise!" says Mrs. Russell, distressed now. "Why didn't you — why, he'll catch his death of cold. Bring him inside. He can sit here in the kitchen and listen."

The black girl hired for the evening goes outside. Gently, she tugs the frozen ear from the window and leads the small, living black icicle into the kitchen, where he thaws out as soon as Rafael Joseffi sits down at the pianoforte again and sets it resounding like a symphony orchestra with his short, powerful hands. The little black boy has never heard such beautiful clusters of sound before. As the Mozart flows into his frozen ears, he wants to die of sheer delight. The kind Mrs. Russell puts a sandwich in his mouth, but the boy scarcely notices. At that moment, he is living through his ears alone.

So the lady appoints him to open doors, empty ashtrays, offer cigars and wipe up spilled wine. And when next the pianoforte resounds, and a famous golden voice soars above the sound of the metal strings, the little page-boy, in a beautiful livery that the good Mrs. Russell has had tailored especially for him, is allowed to stand by the salon door and listen. Never again will his ear be frozen to the window outside.

But there are many such stories, thought Jessie, and she looked at the handsome old man who was just lighting up a cigar with a gold band around it. Not a trace of his former rakishness remained, except for the old-fashioned elegance of those white spats covering his large shoes, those relics of turn-of-the-century fashion that Jessie knew only from photographs. His face displayed a passion she could recognize. She now understood this man, who for fifty years had shone as the bright light of black vocal art, now somewhat overshadowed by the stars of swing and Paul Robeson's operatic bass, but burning undisturbed for half a century in Temple Emanu-El, at St. George's, in his arrangements of the great spirituals. America can have its own beautiful music, born of those melodies. In them is the soul of America: the longing for freedom. She understood this man, his love, his uncritical admiration: for Dvorak had cared nothing for pigment, he heard only music, understood it, heard the cry emerging from it. "I'll never forget his words, Josephine. I read them in Harper's New Monthly Magazine. I know them by heart: 'In the Negro melodies of America I find all that is needed for a great and noble school of music.... There is nothing in the whole range of composition which cannot be supplied from this source.... I am satisfied that the future of music in this country must be founded on what are called Negro melodies.' "

The old man paused. "One day, Josephine," he said, urgently, bitterly, "you should read for yourself how they tried mighty hard to deny that any of that was in his New World Symphony. You can hear Swing Low in the first movement; the trombones carry it, clear as can be – and you know what they said? Who can say whether Dvorak even knew any spirituals! And when people with ears for music wouldn't listen, well, the debunkers started badmouthing him. They accused him of plagiarism. Huneker – Mr. James Gibbons Huneker, no less – he taught at the Conservatory too, always arguing with Dvorak about one thing or another – he claimed he heard Yankee Doodle in the last movement, but Miss Margulies tricked him by playing Yankee Doodle as a Beethoven rondo, complete with altered harmony, and they say he didn't even recognize it. To hear him, you'd think the New World Symphony was nothing more than a medley of popular melodies – Celtic, Scandinavian, Chinese – anything but Negro!"

Harry T. closed his eyes. She poured him a drink from the carafe. His hand, with its gold ring, was clenched into a fist. His defence of the Master had been an act of love and hate intermingled. His passion swept over her. Love and hate. She was young, like a tea-coloured rose. Love and hate mingled to become pride.

"Huneker claimed the Master himself said it was Czech music." Harry T. opened his eyes. "That when all was said and done it was just more Czech music. But that was because he was modest, he'd never have claimed to be a founder of American music. Yet if it hadn't been for America – and I heard the Master say this too – he never could have written it."

With excited fingers he put the cigar to his lips. There was an inch of ash on the tip and it dropped to his vest, scattering on the fine material. Harry T. drew deeply on it and regained his composure. Jessie could feel his anger stirring in her too. She had never read anything about the symphony, she had merely listened to it, always alert for the swing in it, always finding it there in the Kansas riff of that powerful trombone figure....

"And so, Josephine, I'll tell you the story about the second movement in the symphony, the Largo. My ticket to immortality. I told Huneker and Finck, and MacDowell knew it too, though they thought I was making things up. But they never saw the Master listening to those Negro kids singing over on the Lower East Side and making notations on his shirt-cuffs." Harry T. exhaled a contemptuous cloud of smoke, which assumed the shape of a grey bird, drifted across the Oyster Bar and faded away. "That time I saw them praying in the church, the Master invited me to go home with him after. I was on my way to school, but I skipped classes and went. He was at peace with himself, Josephine, but he was sad. He thought the world of his children and he'd lit that candle for his firstborn son. When we got home, he said, 'Sing me something, Burleigh, sing me something.' I sat down at the piano and racked my brains but I couldn't come up with a single cheerful song to sing. So I began with the song my blind granddaddy used to sing when they whipped him: 'I'm troubled, I'm troubled.' The Master listened, his head bowed to his chest, but all of a sudden he jumped to his feet, rushed to his writing desk and rummaged about for a pencil. But every one he found was worn right down. I could hear him over there snorting and complaining until Miss Otylia went to the table, pulled a jack-knife out of the drawer and sharpened a pencil for him. Well, the Master almost snatched it out of her hand, ran back to the writing table, took the unfinished score, stroked something out heavily, wrote something else in and rushed over to me, all aglow, the way he always was when he got an idea. 'Burleigh!' he cried in that powerful voice of his and I stopped singing – 'Eureka!' he shouted, and he stuck the score under my nose. It was the second movement, the Largo. I had given it back to him earlier, neatly copied out, but over the seventh bar, where the flute and clarinet duo began, he had boldly written in '*Corno inglese*.' 'The English horn, Burleigh!' he said. 'I knew those flutes didn't belong there. There has to be a voice there – something from the prairie – it needs a feeling of distance to contrast with that forlorn timbre – just like you, Burleigh.' And he laughed the way he did when something pleased him, like a child. Then he said that when he heard me sing, he suddenly realized my voice had the same timbre as an English horn and the English horn was just the thing to suggest a lonesome voice echoing across the prairie. That was the voice of my granddaddy, Josephine, who turned to Jesus when he was all alone."

He leaned towards her and she could smell the pleasant odour of tweed impregnated with cigar smoke. "Now people say that voice on the prairie is supposed to express Dvorak's longing for his home-land," he said. "But think about this, Josephine – whose voice is it, that English horn? The voice of my granddaddy. And what homeland was *he* longing for?" He stared hard at her, his eyes wide. "Fisher wrote words for it. Going Home. That naturally fits *their* interpretation. But the Master, back in Bohemia, personally approved when somebody wrote a Czech spiritual to the melody!"

"A spiritual? In Czech?" She was astonished.

"Yes! My blind granddaddy's music, Josephine!" And Harry T. expanded his chest in the handsome waistcoat, and without regard for the quiet atmosphere of the Oyster Bar he sang in his still beautiful voice, still majestic, lyrical, and no one in the bar complained.

Veliky Boze nas, shledni z vysin svych
ma verne ditky sve, dusi oddanych....

And when Harry T. finished singing, there was even some applause.

"Aren't you hungry?" asked Harry T. afterwards, prosaically.

"No!" she cried.

"Now that's a fib if ever I heard one, Josephine. When you're seventeen, you're always hungry."

"But I mustn't eat so much."

"I thought so. You are hungry. I have an excellent remedy for that: eat something."

"I can't."

"No? Then there's another method. Do you remember Dennett's Restaurant on Broadway? How could you? I used to watch the man baking his cakes right there in the window, but I could never afford them. When I got so hungry I couldn't stand it any longer, I'd take a toothpick out of my pocket and pick my teeth, like I'd just finished a huge meal. It's a psychological trick. Try it. But I'll bet it still won't stop your stomach from growling."

She laughed and looked around for the toothpicks. There were none to be seen. With the refinement of American civilization, toothpicks seemed to have disappeared from the restaurants. In the end, Harry T. cured her hunger in the traditional manner.

"You know, the Master always had terrible stage fright whenever he had to conduct," said Harry T. as he watched her eat. "Two days before a concert he would lose his appetite, and for two days afterwards he could never get enough to eat."

Three musicians – a pianist, a drummer and an alto saxophonist – walked onto the podium of the Oyster Bar. All of them were black and wore white jackets. They began to play. Perhaps the Master had arranged for this moment in heaven. In a swinging rhythm, they played Swing Low, Sweet Chariot. The handsome Harry T. straightened his shoulders and the shadow of a contented smile crossed his face. She noticed that the polished toes of his large shoes under those white spats were tapping up and down to the rhythm. "Comin' for to carry me home...."

He was waiting nervously in his best mended clothes, in his pocket a used train ticket from Erie to New York, bought by his mother with borrowed money. He knew he had sung badly, far worse than he usually sang in the church in Erie or in the synagogue of his home town. The door opened, and they summoned him in to hear the verdict. Inside he stood as steadily as he could in front of a table at which Maestro Joseffi sat. He remembered him well, but how could the maestro recognize in this twenty-six-year-old man the little head

that belonged to the frozen ear pressed to the window, or the gatherer
of cigar butts? Beside Joseffi sat a pretty red-haired lady and a fashionably dressed man with a large chin, who introduced himself
as James Huneker. When the man spoke, his breath reeked of the
barrel.

"Mr. Burleigh, we are giving you an ABA in sight reading and a
B for voice. Those are excellent grades. However...." He knew bad
news was coming and he stopped listening. With horror, he saw
instead the return journey to Erie by train; he saw his mother, her
eyes – full of anxious hope when she had seen him off – now full of
disappointment. She would say nothing, but her silence would be
harder to bear than open reproach. And how would he even pay for
the journey home? " ... your grades are just slightly below the minimum requirement."

"I went over Jordan and what did I see?..."

A corridor. Leading somewhere. He stumbles as though drunk. He
bumps into a woman.

"Is something wrong?"

I am dead, but there is nothing the matter with me, madam.
"Señora Carreño?"

"Are you sure you're all right?"

"Are you ... ?"

"Señora Carreño? No, I'm the registrar. Do you know Señora
Carreño?"

"You were with her in Erie, at Mrs. Russell's. It's a long time ago,
but...."

He had opened the door, announced the guests, emptied the ashtrays, and cleared away cigar butts hidden behind vases on the chif-
foniers. Then he stood by the doors like a pillar of salt while Señora
Carreño played Bach. The Well-Tempered Clavichord. He remembered the letter of recommendation that Mrs. Russell had written for
his trip to New York, just in case.

"Comin' for to carry me home...."

The lady reads it. She almost certainly does not remember him.
But the names – Mrs. Russell, Teresa Carreño. He watches, with faint
hope, as the expression on her face changes. She is thinking.

"Come the day after tomorrow. I'll try to arrange for you to have
another audition."

"Thank you! Thank you, Mrs...."

"MacDowell."

Once more stumbling like a drunk along avenues, streets, down alleyways, then drawn to the open back door of a building by the sound of singing, a banjo, violins, a small drum –
"A band of angels, coming after me...."
Mesmerized, he walks through the door. Black minstrels on a podium, their faces not smeared with grease paint because this is just a rehearsal. He sits down on a bench at the back.

> De Camptown ladies sing dis song,
>   Doodah, Doodah,
> De Camptown race-track five miles
>   long,
> Oh! Doodah-day!

The song ends. An argument starts up. The man with the violin curses loudly, turns around in disgust and walks to the edge of the podium to cool down. He sees the young man sitting at the back.
"Hey, you there! Know how to sing?"
He gets up, as though the teacher were calling on him in school. Earlier that day he would have replied, "Yes, I do!" Now he says, "A little."
"Like to earn a couple of bucks?"
For the trip home.... "Sure."
"Come on up here, then. You know Swanee?"
And so he sings, his beautiful voice echoing through the barnlike hall, soaring above the plunking of the banjo, in a duet with the violin –

> Way down upon de Swanee Ribber,
> Far, far away....

Why hadn't he sung that song in the audition? The others join him in the chorus, in broad sonorous harmony. Beside him is a steely bass voice, and when it sings low he can almost hear the throb of the man's vocal cords. He glances at him from the corner of his eye and sees a roly-poly fifty-year-old with white curly hair, a trembling double chin, an enormous stomach but a voice like a bell cast from black gold. How different the man's life would be if the gold were not black....

His despair slowly eases. Just as the despair his grandfather felt so long ago gradually vanished, the bleak future dissolves in the resounding chorus of minstrel harmony.

"You must be cracked, man. I mean you're pushing it so hard,"
the fat man tells him later in the bar. He has ordered him a whisky.

"So you don't think I can sing either?"

"You could sing opera on the spot, butterhead."

"That's exactly what I'd like to do."

"Butterhead."

"Why you calling me butterhead?"

"Because you're a nigger, butterhead."

His brain is already somewhat numbed by the alcohol, but he
understands that much and he swells with rage. "I'm going to try
again."

"Go ahead and try, butterhead. But you can have a solid gig here
till the end of the month. Then you can go on the road with us.
We'll be hitting Philly, Washington and on down south...."

Greasepaint on our black skin to make us look even blacker. Wide
lips as grotesque as a clown's. Come on, you black apes; you've got
your freedom, now entertain us!

"I'll try again!"

The pot-bellied bass singer shrugs his shoulders and says in a voice
that even in conversation sounds like a well-made bass viol: "Go
right ahead and try, butterhead. But come back this evening. You
don't look to me like no millionaire. A couple of bucks is a couple
of bucks."

He comes back that evening. He sings: "That's where my heart
is turning ever...."

And next day, at the audition, he sings: "There let me ever stay."

The words have no power to move him; he has chosen the song
only for the melody. His oboe voice rises and descends and he sees
that Rafael Joseffi, Adele Margulies and Jim Huneker are beginning
to pay attention.

He sings: "... Far from de old folks at home...."

"You were nervous last time, weren't you?" says Huneker. "Today
it was a hundred per cent better. You've been accepted."

Accepted.

Accepted!

The singers in the Oyster Bar were still playing Swing Low. The
pianist took the chorus and shaped the melody into a shadow picture,
underlining it with syncopated chords. I've never heard this group
before, she thought. There are so many, and nobody knows their
names –

"The Master chose it because of the melody too," said Harry T. "Of course, he couldn't understand what the words might mean to someone like me. He just loved melody. And he wrote a special arrangement for me. And for Sissieretta Jones. No memory gives me greater pleasure than that."

The shadow picture of the melody was passed to the alto sax. "Swing low, sweet sweet chariot...."

"And the daughter Otylia," she said, "did she marry the American secretary?"

This drove the smile from Harry T.'s face and once more he became the dapper and somewhat daunting ladies' man. "Kovarik? She wanted to marry him," he said and he licked his lips. "She came back to New York all full of tears from that village somewhere in Iowa where they spent the summer of '93. They packed her out of there practically overnight. But it may have been too late, for all I know."

"How do you mean that?"

"The way it's usually meant."

"She had a baby?"

"There doesn't always have to be a baby," he said, and winked at her. "I think Otylia took after her father."

"Now what is *that* supposed to mean?" she said.

"Ain't misbehavin'," wailed the sax.

"Sometimes the facts speak for themselves," said Harry T.

"What facts?"

"How did you do in arithmetic in school?"

"I got a B, why?"

"Because," said Harry T., and he slowly emerged from a cloud of grey smoke. A few moments before, he had nodded at the waiter again, but she had failed to notice. Out of the same cloud of smoke, the carafe emerged. It was full again. "Because in April of '93, they lit those candles for their firstborn son, who would have been nineteen that day. And the November before that, they celebrated their *nineteenth* wedding anniversary."

The lascivious eyes twinkled at her wickedly through the thinning cloud of smoke.

The sax wailed.

Ain't misbehavin'....

8   :(): THE COUNTESS ON THE TERRACE

THE CLOSER HER HOUR of death came, the calmer the Countess grew. Days that used to pass like ships on a stormy sea now flowed by like slow movements in a pastoral symphony, for it was summer and the Countess was recalling the happy moments of her life.

An odd thing. When she learned she was suffering from the condition that had killed her father, she was gripped by a fear of death. She was thirty-three, and the diagnosis had come only five years after the wedding. At the same time, the disease destroyed any hope of having a child with Vaclav. Before, she had worried about being unable to bear children; now she knew she must not. But as death drew nearer, the burden of fear made life so difficult that the fear, paradoxically, diminished. Life, her present, difficult life, gave way more and more to the life of the past and she would recall its happy moments.

She sat in a wicker armchair on the terrace of the manor house, near the sandstone balustrade. The sunlight glinted off the bottles of medicine on which her life now depended, irradiating them with amber light. It shone above the countryside beyond, with its swaths of green, yellow and blue, in which a splash of white, a building, marked the place where Ton was sitting in the garden, writing his scores.

A stork flapped over the valley.

Annie, in a cotton dress with cocoa spattered down the front, white lace knickers peeking out from under it. Annie, as yet with a child's flat chest, her blonde hair braided into two pigtails tied with blue ribbons. Annie, rolling her grey eyes like a frog, smiles mischievously and says, affecting a quavering voice: "Miss Josephine, I ... I ... " and then, with astonishing accuracy, mimicking her own alto voice: "Yes, Mr. Dvorak?" and her artfully half-closed eyes that she knew would make her swarthy teacher even more nervous. "I ... I ... Miss Jo ... Josephine.... " "Yes, Mr. Dvorak?" "Annie, stop that at once!" she shouts at her, but she laughs in spite of herself. The brat! She'll be a better actor than I am. "That son-sonatina ... you'll have to pra-practise it again." And once again, in a tone of eloquent disappointment, "Yes, Mr. Dvorak."

"Annie! You monkey!"

Eight years later: "And does Anton love you, Annie?"

The grey eyes of her younger sister, her reasonable, hard-headed sister, firmly hold her own.

"Not as much as he loves you, Jo – "

"Shush! That's long over with."

" – but we're going to have a baby."

Blessed Virgin!

Four years before that: "Fallen in love? That's wonderful, Annie. Who's the victim?"

"Me."

"I don't understand."

"I've fallen in love with Anton."

Mother of God!

My brave, wise, ambitious sister. And I was the barefoot muse of the family, she thought with a smile. "Miss Cermakova's talent is brilliantly suited to light French comedies and what it lacks in profundity, it makes up for in charm and grace." That piercing judgement of Neruda, whose poetry I so much admired. It was bitter.

"We're going to have a baby." She says it calmly, proudly, with dignity. As though it were four months after the wedding and not two months – let us hope – before.

Seven months later: "Josie! Josie! She's dying!"

"Who, Mother?"

"Anna! She's having contractions! In her fifth month! Josie!"

So we shall have to come out with the truth.

"She won't die, Mother. She's in her ninth month."

"But they were only married...."

Lord in heaven!

"What will people think?"

The musical world of Prague found it a source of amusement. The happy father was a new star in the patriotic heaven.

"You know, Josie, she did seem to me rather too – large – for five months...."

For a long time she savoured the memory of those happy moments of her life, and through a spyglass she observed a stork feeding its family on the chimney of an abandoned brick-works. A figure emerged from the white house. She pointed the spyglass in that direction. Otylia. In the glass's flat field of vision, she was making her way towards the wood. And she was sad. The reason was not difficult to fathom. Something must have happened in America – and whatever her sorrow was, she had brought it home with her. Though it was nearly July, and though Anton and his family had come to Vysoka less than a week after their return from America, Josef Suk, Anton's favorite amanuensis who had been so very attentive to Otylia before, had not yet put in even the briefest of appearances. The Countess smiled at the easy sadness of youth. Otylia walked along despondently in her pink and blue dress brought back from America. She was also wearing her hair differently. Before she left she had looked like a dark blonde mouse, and for the trip they had bought her that impossible cape – Anton had ignored her pleas and protests, saying they could expect foul weather on the ocean and she might catch a cold. The Countess looked at the sweet face through the glass. In her two years away from home, the child had vanished and a young woman had emerged. Her sick heart rejoiced with love. What, she wondered, would Josephina, Anton's firstborn daughter, have been like? Who could say? She was only in this world for two days. How old would she have been today? Eighteen? Nineteen? Perhaps, like Otylia, she would have inherited only her father's eyes, set alluringly far apart. She sighed. The Lord denied me that child, too. It would have been a memento, at least in name – the name of love.

"They say he's a genius, Josie. And he's only twenty-four. He's going to be a famous man, that's what Papa thinks." So said Helina Pstrosova, *eager as always to meet a young man her father was about to introduce to the family.*

"A genius – from Krc?"

"Why can't a genius come from the suburbs? And anyway, he doesn't live there. He was only there on a visit. Papa heard him playing in a tavern and invited him home at once. And Papa doesn't do that every day."

"I don't feel like coming," she said.

"Josie! You have to come! You can't let me down!" Helina put her arms around her. "Something tells me he's the one. I've always dreamed of marrying a great musician."

"And what am I supposed to do?"

"You must tell me what you think of him."

Well, she didn't think much. She wore a new dress of dark gold satin to go with her hair, in which she set a gold clasp, a gift for her sixteenth birthday. A cleverly designed clasp. She had set it on top of her head and it divided her hair into five strands, fringing her face with a dark curtain of hair. Helina too wore a new dress, but she had laced her corset too tight and it squeaked when she moved. They awaited the genius in the Pstros's piano room and the encounter was a considerable disappointment. He looked a little like a gypsy: rumpled, raven-black hair, eyes like a bullfrog, a deep furrow between his brows, a black moustache that wanted trimming. And his clothes! When he sat down, his black trousers turned pale where they stretched over his knees, so thin had the material become. When he turned his back on them to sit down at the piano, there was a patch on his left elbow. It was artfully, carefully sewn, but unmistakably a patch.

Besides, it was clear at once what had happened. As soon as he looked at Josephine, the bullfrog eyes froze and he could not take them off her, not even when Annie dropped a dish of ice-cream which fell first onto her lap – she too was wearing a new dress, a gift for her twelfth birthday – and from there to the Persian rug, and the conversation was interrupted while instructions were being given to the maid. It was embarrassing.

"I warned you, Helina," she said to her friend afterwards.

"I didn't invite you so you could ply your charms on him, you – you hussy!" said Helina indignantly. "I wanted you to tell me what you thought of him, not wiggle your bottom at him."

"I was sitting down the whole time!"

"But when you went home with Annie, I saw you!"

"Have you fallen in love with him, Helina?"

"He broke my heart. You broke it."

The Countess smiled at the happy moments of her life. Half a year later, Helina had become engaged to a manager of the Commercial Bank.

She had, she remembered, been impressed by his playing. She wasn't sure if she, at the age of sixteen, could recognize genius, but the bullfrog of the threads and patches played like a prince. Even Annie had ceased her whimpering over the soiled dress (she feared a scolding when she got home) and become entirely lost in his Moonlight Sonata.

"Miss Starkova is retiring," her father said. "She's going to live with her sister in Kralupy. I shall have to make inquiries about a new music teacher."

"How would it be if you engaged Mr. Dvorak, Father?" she said, but only because he played so beautifully.

"A man? To break your heart, Josie?"

Like a vine, she wound herself around her invalid father in his easy-chair. The old goldsmith was wearing thick, woolly slippers and smoking a foot-long pipe.

"But Father, you know my heart is broken already."

He smiled. "Are you fond of young Kounic?"

"Hmm," she replied, noncommittal.

To tell the truth, thought the Countess, smiling at the memory, I rather fancied myself in the role of a countess. The Countess Kounic. It sounds quite fine. Of course that would be the end of my career in the theatre. An acting countess seems inappropriate somehow. Well, what of it? Neruda thinks I'm wooden anyway. A joy for old bachelors like himself to look at, he obviously thought, but at her best when she speaks least on stage. And anyway, God knows if Kounic's ardour will last. The big, gangling Kounic – he looks thoroughly trapped, and he's not making the slightest effort to get free of it. But he was only eighteen then – and she had thought there was so much time, so much time.

"What if this gentleman – what is his name? Dvorak? " She nodded. "What if he appeals to you more?"

"He won't, Father. I've already seen him. He looks like a bullfrog."

"Ribbit ribbit," said Annie.

Father laughed, but he began to choke and she had to give him his drops.

"Then I have absolutely no idea why you want me to engage him," said her father, watching her slyly, when the attack had passed.

He was clever but so was she. She made no mention of how magnificently Dvorak had played The Moonlight Sonata but said, "Because von Pstros recommended him."

And so the young man recommended by the old aristocrat was engaged as an instructor in singing and the pianoforte.

Otylia continued her sad pilgrimage, alone. God knows what happened across the ocean. Ah, well, sighed the Countess, no need of an omniscient God to get to the bottom of this, just a good memory of what happened when you were sixteen yourself. Otylia walked towards Rusalka's pond. She will collapse on the pond's edge, weeping convulsively, the Countess decided. When she returns, her eyes will be as red as a turtledove's. The Countess turned the glass back to the storks. Both the parents had just lifted off the nest and flapped off to forage for food. The heads of the tiny storklets, etched against the blue sky, looked like open scissors. They vanished into the safety of the nest. She swept her telescope across the countryside and back again to the white building. Ton stepped out of the summer-house and began his ritual feeding of the pigeons. Poor Ton, he's aged in America, while Otylia has flowered. There must have been more to it than time alone, in those two brief years between fourteen and sixteen. I must ask her about it. She has always confided in me.

But Ton certainly hasn't turned into a venerable old gentleman like the poet Vrchlicky, his contemporary. He's become an irascible old codger. She smiled. With love, she watched her brilliant friend, whom the birds had converted into a walking pigeon roost. She put the spyglass down.

"Miss ... Miss Josephine, I ... I...."

"Yes, Mr. Dvorak?"

Oh, I'm wicked! Why, the poor man is burning like a church candle, all melting, and I address him in this unnatural voice, like a character in a French farce.

"I ... I'm...."

"Yes, Mr. Dvorak?"

Enough, you coquette! He's clearly such a good, poor man –

"I ... I took the liberty.... "

"Yes, Mr. Dvorak?"

Josephine! Unkind! A hussy indeed.

" ... the liberty ... of composing something – for you –"

That horrid handkerchief. It's red. And he's actually sweating as if it were June though it's only May, and rather chilly May at that –

"Oh!"

And must you pucker your lips, Josephine? And hang your head on one side to make the earrings your father gave you swing back and forth in your ears?

"What have I done to deserve this, Mr. Dvorak?"

"You – M-Miss Josephine – you deserve –"

A good slap in the face. She took the sheets of music from him and spread them out on the piano's music stand. My God, he's taken so much trouble with this. The calligraphy! I know his scrawl – and now look at this: "This work is dedicated, with deep respect, to the Esteemed Young Lady, Miss Josephine Cermakova" – a work of pure calligraphy!

She placed her hands on the keyboard and meticulously played the introduction. She sang in her muted alto:

> No balm is there, no sweet relief
> For this poor, smitten heart;
> For love denied is sad despair,
> And fortune's cruelest dart.

Annie walked into the piano room, chewing on a liquorice root. Out of the corner of her eye, Josephine saw her sit down on a chair and listen.

> A linden and a cairn of stone
> Stand near; the linden weeps,
> And on the stone these words inscribed:
> A broken heart here sleeps....

She finished playing, then sat silent for a moment. The song moved her. It was truly beautiful. You beast, she reprimanded herself, stop playing these games with him. What will I say to him?

"Did you write that yourself?" *Annie piped up.*

"Oh, no, Miss Annie. I only composed the music. I can't write lyrics. I don't know how."

The horrid handkerchief again. What shall I say? "Oh, who wrote the poem for you?"

"I ... it's by Gustav Pflegr-Moravsky. I took it from his collected works." *He turned from Annie to face her, swallowing deeply.* "Do ... do you like it?"

I must simply tell him the truth. She made very sure there wasn't a hint of artificial mannerism in her voice this time: "I like the music very much, Mr. Dvorak. The melody is enchanting."

She became a witness to complete happiness: I could never have played the scene as well as this on stage. She scolded herself at once for the thought.

"But Mr. Dvorak, I really don't deserve it –"

"Did he write it for you, Jo?"

"Annie – go back into the kitchen with that liquorice root. Your lesson doesn't start for another twenty minutes."

Annie slipped off the chair and stuck out her tongue at her sister. Then she got an idea and offered the partially chewed stick to the teacher.

"Would you like some? Take it."

The young man, distracted by his happiness, accepted the sticky gift and stuck the chewed end into his mouth. "Thank you."

"Annie, you're impossible!" she scolded angrily. "First you chew it yourself and then...."

The muddled admirer removed the piece of root from his mouth, turned it around and began chewing the other end.

"Let him give it back to me, then, and I'll give him a fresh one."

Once again he took the delicacy out of his mouth, and put it into her outstretched hand.

"Don't bring any more!" she shouted. Annie slammed the door behind her.

She turned to her teacher. A large drop of perspiration slipped down the deep furrow between his eyes.

"Miss ... Miss Josephine, I ... I love –"

"Shhh! Don't say it. You must never say it." Oh, Lord, a Labiche farce.

And she witnessed a complete metamorphosis: total happiness transformed into total despair. A single lonely word uttered in the tragic tones of disappointment: "Never?"

Mary, Mother of God, what am I going to do with him? And his song is so enchanting. For the first time in her life, the bottomless chasm of love opened up before her. "A rather shallow talent...." You don't deserve anything so beautiful.

"Not – not today, at least," she said weakly, and found herself, again, face to face with hope. "Now" – quickly – "sit down and accompany me. You must tell me how you think this should be sung."

He sat down and played. The pianoforte resounded like a chorus of flutes and panpipes.

And even counts suffer from that affliction.

Four years later Count Kounic – having reached the age of majority, as large as a lumberjack, wearing an immaculately tailored frock coat, trousers with knife-edge creases, and with an enormous *bouquet of roses in his hands but his brow likewise beaded with perspiration – suddenly began to behave like a character in a romantic novel, or perhaps he was merely observing the instructions found in Courting and Marriage: Precepts for Young Gentlemen. He had fulfilled the requirements of etiquette in her father's room the day before, she knew. Now he fell to one knee, the parquet flooring creaked – and now you're caught in a French farce all over again, Josephine.*

She smiled at the happy moments in her life. Dear, sweet Vaclav. Dear, sweet Ton.

"*I'm still young, sir. It's much too soon for me to get married. And then I have my stage career to consider.*"

"*I'd be happy to wait, Josephine – if only you won't reject me outright.*"

I couldn't do that. Father would have a fit. Josephine, you comedienne with the shallow talent, how do you get yourself out of this mess? Assuming, of course, you want out, which you don't. But who's to advise me if the heart won't? And I do so enjoy being nice to both of them. I'm an actress, dash it all!

Anna walked out of the white house with a cup of coffee for Dvorak. She was wearing a white summer dress, with vertical black stripes. That was from America too. *Ton had been in a good mood then. He had just come back from England – fêted, as always, by the English, awarded an honorary doctorate by Cambridge University – full of impressions, bubbling over with a rather suspect enthusiasm for that American woman Mrs. Thurber. But his innocence remained, even then. He simply liked handsome women, without pursuing the practical consequences of his inclination. They both knew it.* "Just imagine," he announced with ingenuous astonishment. "In Brighton, beautiful English ladies go bathing in public!" Otylia blushed, and Annie quickly poured the coffee. He drank it down and asked for another cup. "I think you've had enough, Anton," said Anna. "It's not good for your heart." "D'you see that, Josie?" He turned to her. "And it was Annie taught me how to drink coffee. I can still hear her: 'Here you are, Dvorak, black coffee. Why don't you stop that scribbling and try to drum up some decent lessons instead. We need the money.' So I had to stop work on my symphony and listen to the artless plonking of genteel young ladies." "You had no objection to listening to the artless plonking of some *genteel* young ladies, Ton. Or have you forgotten?" she said, and he retorted with a laugh: "You're quite right, my dear sister-in-law. But when Anna here drove me to take on those lessons, I was married, wasn't I? Now she sings a different tune. 'Here's your black coffee, darling. Now write!' And I have to write like a slave." "Someone has to mind the family budget, Anton, especially when you'd rather daydream about the beautiful ladies of Brighton," said Annie. "Like a slave, Josie! And yet I'm essentially a very lazy man." "That's a sin, Ton," she said. "I know, that's why I don't resent it when Annie badgers me." "I didn't mean that," she said. "I meant it's a sin, because you're lying."

Annie, my down-to-earth younger sister. All the same, she has a sterling character, she's always been far nicer than me. If only Ton hadn't been so transparent! It's true, Annie never lets on how she's really feeling. Why, there she was, burning with love, yet still able to plan strategies like the wiliest marriage broker. I've never seen anything like it. But the iron is only iron discipline. The heart beneath that armour plating is the heart of my younger sister, who offered him a soggy stick of liquorice, and four years later said to me, "I'm in love, Jo. Up to my ears."

Once she came unannounced, having walked from the manor house to bring her sister a tea rose, and from outside she could hear the piano and Annie's lovely alto voice and she felt a slight twinge of regret. Annie was singing:

> Love steals upon us like a dream
> Of beauty, grace and light:
> And, dreamlike, slips away too soon,
> Back to the tomb's cold night.

She waited in front of the white house till the voice had finished. After a while, she went in. Annie was still sitting at the piano, staring at the notes on the music stand. When she heard the door creak, she stood up swiftly. The Countess gave her the rose and they went into the dining room, where the sounds of a struggle between little Tony and Otakar outside the window sent Annie running to investigate; the Countess turned quickly back into the music room and looked at the sheets of music. At the top, in Ton's handwriting, was written Ave Maria, and beneath it the sedate dedication, "To my dearest spouse". She stood quite still for a moment, frozen in memory, hearing not the Ave Maria but the passionate song that Annie had just been singing, hearing herself singing it when Ton, *so nervous, stuttering, had presented it to her in her father's piano room. She hurried back to the dining room, and when Annie came in, dragging two bloodied little sons to the sink in the kitchen, she was reading, with the most exquisite interest, a French novel.*

That was not a happy memory. She snatched the spyglass from the balustrade and raised it to her eye. The green, gold and blue countryside danced chaotically. Otylia walked into the field of vision. Yes, even at that distance she could tell that she had been crying, her eyes dark, and in her hands such a sorry little bouquet of water-lilies. Of course. A melancholy walk by Rusalka's pond. Suk must be quite the sadist. Ah, but such are the games played at that age.

"No, Ton, no! Someone will come and...."

Gently, she pushed him away. Though the chest beneath the faded waistcoat was swelling not only with passion but with the muscles of a butcher's apprentice, he immediately abandoned his hesitant attempt to embrace her.

"And play something. We can't sit here in silence."

He sat down at the keyboard and mechanically began to pick out a minuet. His large eyes were beautiful and she was confused and thought she had better abandon French farce and learn more about tragedy.

"Please, let's meet somewhere, Josephine. I'll cancel my lessons for tomorrow afternoon –"

"You can't do that, Ton. You need the money."

"What good is money to me?" *he said dramatically, as though he owned the entire stock exchange.* "You have no rehearsals tomorrow – I know that."

"I don't know, Ton," *she said.... She was almost caught in his net now. With an alacrity that surprised her, he tightened the net around her and stopped playing.*

"I'll wait for you in Stromovka Park, below the château, at three."

'I – I don't know, Ton. And play, for God's sake!"

Obediently he played, and Annie walked into the room. Her clever little sister's bright eyes missed nothing. The distracted teacher played something distractedly on the piano to the distracted pupil.

"It's past four, Mr. Dvorak," *said Annie matter-of-factly.*

"Really?" *He stopped playing, his ears red.* "We – that is, I...." *He turned to her.* "For next time, Miss Josephine, would you prepare this ... this...."

"I promise I'll be better, Mr. Dvorak." And she quickly gathered up the music. "Well, goodbye then, and – see you" – she encountered a fervent entreaty from the dark eyes – "tomorrow," she added. He wasn't supposed to come for a lesson until the day after, and Annie looked at her sharply but sat down at the piano, beside the flaming torch of love. He endeavoured to say something. Her smile was full of promise. God, why do I do it? – and she rushed out of the room.

"You weren't very good today, Josie," said her father reproachfully. "All thumbs. What happened? Is there something wrong?"

"Well, Kounic and I had an argument, Father. And I don't even remember why. The reason was so petty it's slipped my mind. And last evening at the theatre I forgot my lines, dried right up, and Mosna had to rescue me and then, twice in a row, I buried the point of a scene so badly that kind old Mosna had to scold me afterwards."

Kounic wasn't waiting for her after the performance, and she had to go home by cab.

Should I? Shouldn't I? I don't love him. I'm fond of him, the old bullfrog. I'm fond of them both, damn it. But fondness isn't love. Angrily she threw the powder-puff and the face in the mirror was enshrouded in a perfumed cloud of powder.

Should I flip a coin?

She heard the clock striking in her father's room. A quarter to three. I'll be at least half an hour late.

Well, if he loves me, he'll wait.

This little rendezvous is going to cost him a good deal. He'll miss three lessons. That's almost half a gulden.

The bell rang. Who the Devil?

The Devil ushered in the Count, repentant, bearing a large bouquet of red roses.

"Are you still angry, Josephine?"

"Constantly, since yesterday. Because of you, I was impossible on stage last night."

"It was my fault. I'm an idiot," said the highly educated Count.

"No, you are not. Actually, yesterday I had a migraine."

"Ah!" he said, and the bouquet dropped despondently. "I sincerely hope it's not bothering you today."

"The migraine? No."

"May I take the liberty of offering you a ride in my new carriage?" he said, not noticing her tone. "We could go for a drive, just to try it out. It's so beautiful out – perhaps to Chuchle?"

"Not to Chuchle, no! Let's drive to Stromovka Park," she said, readying the dagger for Othello's heart.

She smiled at this sad memory. How the sadness softens in rec-ollection. An odd alchemy.

And Othello stood at the intersection of two rows of white asters that lined the road; he wore a shiny but well-brushed Sunday suit and a gay June sun fell on a bouquet of red roses only slightly smaller than the Count's. The lost tuition fees, the vain expense! She felt a dreadful sense of shame for what she was doing. "Look, Miss Jose-phine! Storks!" The Count pointed towards the roof of the château. And so she drove past Othello with her face lifted towards the storks, and from the corner of her eye she saw the bouquet droop, fade and wilt. It was as if the theme had shot across the sky, a lightning flash, a command in crotchets and piercing quavers. She didn't hear it until much later, in the concert hall, but it had sounded first below the Stromovka château, in Othello's mind, and God knows, perhaps through some kind of telepathy, it echoed in her mind as well as she stared at the storks' nest and felt a stiffness in the back of her neck and a smile on her lips like the smiles worn by figurines in a wax museum. And when at last she found the courage to look round at him, he was out of sight beyond a curve in the road that was lined with white asters.

The next day, that terrible, terrible lesson.

"Please, Miss Josephine, play from the letter c right to da capo." He opened the score in front of her and she saw at once that his hands were trembling. At that moment, it seemed to her that she loved him.

She murdered the first five bars and stopped. She turned to him. The beautiful dark eyes were awash.

"Ton – "

"Why – why did you do it?"

She pulled a handkerchief from her sleeve, but he moved his head away. He wiped his eyes with the palms of his hands.

"I had to do it, Ton. It wouldn't have made sense."

He wiped away the tears once more and said, with plain and therefore terrible bitterness, "I know – the Count –"

"Ton! That's not it!"

Isn't it? It is and it isn't. He wept. He turned away from her in his grief.

"Ton," she said uncertainly. "My Ton...."

*His grief was far stronger than those Herculean shoulders. He
leaned forward and put his head into his hands.*

*She turned to the piano. Faintly, in pianissimo, she played the
fifth song in the cycle To the Esteemed Young Lady, Miss Josephine
Cermakova. She didn't sing the words, but in the mirror on the wall
she watched the shoulders gradually grow tranquil. She didn't sing,
but he knew the lyrics as well as she did:*

> *How fine and golden was the chain*
> *That linked our hearts and dreams;*
> *How quickly snapped, as grief and pain*
> *Usurped our lovely schemes.*

*He took his hands away from his face and sat up straight. That
red handkerchief. Then he turned to face her. His dear face was no
longer ridiculous to her. What she saw in it was not sadness, but
something worse. Tragedy. Dear, brave, strong, sweet Ton, had accepted – she saw it clearly – defeat.*

"I'll always be very fond of you, Ton."

"And I of you, Josephine."

She smiled at that memory. It was already a quarter of a century
ago. Otylia, with her sad bouquet, went into the white house. She
reappeared a while later in the doorway and a happy change had
taken place. Instead of the white water-lilies, she was carrying a
white jug. She wiped away her tears with her hand and started running, an exotic butterfly in her pink and blue dress from New York.

She disappeared into the village inn.

The Countess pointed her spyglass in that direction. Because she
was confined to her wicker chair, the powerful instrument was her
connection with the village, the countryside and her family during
the final months of her life.

*Anna came into the bedroom and said, "What did you do to him?
He looked like a corpse, and there was about as much life in him
too."*

*"Annie, you know," she said, "I – well, I simply told him that he
shouldn't think of me any more."*

*Her down-to-earth sister looked at her for a long time with her
grey eyes, eyes that saw into her soul.*

"Don't you love him?"

*"I'm very fond of him, but it's not love. That is, if I know what
love is at all. But I don't think it's that."*

"That's good," said Anna, *"because I've fallen in love."*

"Fallen in love?" She welcomed this diversion, and she played a small role from one of those light comedies where her charm and grace outweighed whatever she could not call up in depth. *"That's wonderful, Annie. Who's the victim?"*

"Me."

From the white house, fourteen-year-old Annie came out with Magda and six-year-old Aloisia. Aloisia was carrying a large red, white and blue beach-ball. They walked towards the woods, Annie as languid as a fairy. In two years, I'm sure, there will be yet another Othello here in the village.

She looked at the stork family. When will their shift be over? Open scissors against a sky that was starting to blush pink.

She swung the spyglass back to the white house. Doves were perching on the roof of the summer-house. Her sister came out leading Otakar and Tony by the ears. A pantomime of gestures, two brooms appeared, and the reluctant workers began sweeping the doorstoop. Anna went back into the house.

She turned the spyglass towards the church. The shadows were lengthening. The sun poured the honeyed light of evening over the white tower. It was five, time for Ton to set out. As he did every day. Her final days would have been incomplete without that, incompletely happy. She turned the spyglass back towards the summer-house.

And there he was.

Ton walked out into the golden sunlight, looked around the garden and set off.

He was coming towards her.

She smiled, remembering the happy moments in her life.

9   :C): A REPORT ON
THE MASTER'S CONDUCT

327 East Seventeenth Street
New York
April 12th, 1893

My dear sister,

Forgive me, dear Jo, for not having written for so long, especially since I hear you have been feeling poorly. I find it hard to write letters though. This city appals me and ever since Mr. Thurber took us to the Lower East Side in his carriage, I feel as though I were living in a nightmare. Mr. Thurber is the husband of Jeannette Thurber, the president of the Conservatory – the one who was so keen to get Anton to come here, and I must say she and Anton get along famously. My own relationship with her is cooler. She seems to think that were it not for me Anton would be less firm in money matters – in other words, she could get him to work more for less. And the Lord knows she's right about that, for had I not been so strict about money we might still be living in a single room and kitchen in Prague. Unfortunately Anton has confirmed Mrs. Thurber's opinion in this matter – not deliberately, of course, but he can be as trusting as a child, and Mrs. Thurber is a very shrewd and cunning lady and she saw this at once and proceeded to wind Anton around her little finger. What he did was tell her, in all innocence, about that business with his German publisher, Simrock. I don't know if you remember – it was some time ago. But the fact is, if it hadn't been for me, Simrock would still be paying Anton the same amount for the rights to publish one of his operas that he gives others for a vulgar popular song. We'd been married just two years, and Simrock offered Anton a paltry two thousand marks for his Symphony in B Major. I did what I could to persuade Anton to ask for at least three, but oh no, he couldn't ask that much, he said. Mr. Simrock would think he was an extortioner! The symphony had been easy to write, he said, and two thousand was more than fair. He even got quite angry with me. But I think I'm a better judge of what's good for him, so I stuck to my guns and he finally gave in and sat down and wrote Simrock asking for three thousand, otherwise he would offer the symphony to another publisher. But he was still so upset that he unintentionally wrote in an extra zero and in effect asked for thirty thousand marks! Fortunately I didn't notice the mistake so I was completely unaware of what had happened until a letter arrived from Simrock saying he couldn't give Anton thirty thousand marks but would ten thousand do? Anton nearly had a seizure and it was all I could do to persuade him simply to accept the ten thousand, which he deserved anyway, and go on composing. You can imagine *how* Anton told this story to Mrs. Thurber because he still feels guilty about it to this day. And she must have put two and two together and realized at once that he would probably settle for fifteen thousand dollars for heading her Conservatory instead of the twenty thousand we asked for. Of course we didn't get it. Simrock could certainly learn a thing or two from Jeannette Thurber.

Oh, she's a shrewd lady! She let it be known in the most blatant way that she had taken a liking to our Otylia, and gave her a magnificent gown for her birthday, from one of the most fashionable salons in New York. Then immediately afterwards, instead of the three thousand dollars she owes Anton by contract, she gave him only a thousand with profuse apologies about what she called her temporary financial difficulties. The dress must have cost her two hundred dollars at the most. And for that, she remained two thousand dollars in Anton's debt.

She gets her money from her husband who owns a wholesale grocery business, with a large number of retail stores all over the state of New York and elsewhere which he supplies with goods from his own factories. He strikes me as a man of great refinement and a real gentleman. His enterprises are run along truly unusual lines: he sells shares to his employees so they in fact become co-owners. Naturally this fascinates Anton, and I've heard him say that Mr. Thurber has a genuine understanding of the poor, and that wealthy industrialists back home should follow his example.

He's right, of course. Mr. Thurber, through his own industry and talent, has become one of the biggest millionaires in America today, and yet, like my good-natured Anton, he hasn't forgotten that he came from humble origins. Mr. Thurber has been leading a campaign against powerful financial interests who have set up what they call "trusts" – which as far as I can understand are enormous monopolies that control prices and sell their products dear, and of course ordinary people end up paying for it.

As a matter of fact, it was Mr. Thurber who suggested taking us to the Lower East Side so we could see "how the other half lives in New York," as he put it. Tony and Otylia and I seldom venture out of the apartment on Seventeenth Street, and if we do we never go farther than Washington Square and Fifth Avenue, which is not far away in a well-to-do part of Manhattan. Occasionally, we take in a concert at Carnegie Hall when Anton is directing, and sometimes Anton and I go to something he wants to hear. In all such places, as you might expect, we mingle with high society, though I should add the Americans have their own peculiar approach to concerts too, and there are some things we might profitably imitate in Prague. For example, concerts are usually repeated the following day for poor people, who in fact are relatively well off: tradesmen, small merchants, city clerks, domestic servants, in other words, people who have some steady means of support. So it wasn't until Mr. Thurber took us on that little tour that I encountered real poverty.

I have never seen such destitution and misery, Jo. The slums of Prague are practically paradise by comparison, if only because they cover such a small area. Here, you encounter block after block of three-, four- or five-storey tenement houses, all very much alike, with squalid exteriors. Mr. Thurber took us into several such dwellings, and I confess I felt faint. The stench is indescribable, the walls are covered with slime and filth, and the corridors and stairways are so permeated with grime as to defy washing. I was loath even to step inside, let alone touch anything with my bare hands, for some of the walls appeared to be running with a hideous discharge, as though covered with suppurating wounds. There are thousands upon thousands of such miserable dwellings, and countless people live and even work there. Seamstresses sew garments for the large houses of couture and you see these wretched women everywhere, burdened like camels with huge loads of work they are dragging off somewhere to be handed over. The dresses they carry are beautiful, while they themselves wear rags. Hunger stares from their faces and they all look old, though Mr. Thurber says that few live to be more than forty. And many have children with them, little girls who don't look any older than ten, coughing and sagging under those awful loads. I have never seen so many consumptives, so many children with legs like matchsticks, so many inebriated men. Mr. Thurber says the men are mostly seam-stresses' husbands who can't find work, and if they do manage to earn a few cents they spend it all on drink to forget their misery. Many of the women are drunk too, wailing raucous street songs in voices hoarse from too much drink. The streets are teeming with people day and night, and no wonder, for who would want to spend any time indoors in those conditions? Negroes, Italians, Irishmen, Jews – vendors draped in shoelaces so they look like weeping willows, little newsboys everywhere shouting out their wares, dirty-faced lit-tle urchins who should be in school but run loose in the streets instead and see everything that goes on. The most wretched of the wretched are the women of easy virtue. And everywhere, grog-shops, pot-houses, bars, saloons, all jammed up together, and pawnshop after pawnshop where Jews will lend a few cents for the most unimaginable items because they can always find buyers.

The dishonesty and corruption is everywhere! Imagine, little Tony stopped beside a boy selling balloons on the street and kind Mr. Thurber bought him one. Just as the vendor was handing it to Tony, a guttersnipe sidled up behind him and cut the strings holding the cluster of balloons to a stone, and ran off. The balloons flew away in a flash with no hope of catching them and the poor vendor began to weep heartrendingly. People who had seen the incident felt sorry for him and gave him money from what little they had, and I even saw several gentlemen stuffing dollar bills into his hat. And of course you know Anton, he was as pitifully distressed as the young vendor, and was just pulling out his wallet when Mr. Thurber stopped him. At first I couldn't fathom why, Mr. Thurber being such a philan-thropist, but Josie, the whole thing turned out to be a swindle. The vendor and the urchin with the knife were a team. They knew they would make more from human kindness than from selling all their balloons, and afterwards they would divide up the spoils somewhere around the corner. And since the Lower East Side is such an enormous place, Mr. Thurber says they can go on repeating their little trick for a year without anyone ever catching on.

New York is full of such enterprising scoundrels. The other day Anton came home in a gloomy mood, and when I asked him what the matter was he told me he'd met a poor old lady on Twenty-third Street who said someone had stolen her purse, and she asked him for five cents to get to the Forty-second Street Ferry – a long walk for someone her age. "And you gave her the five cents?" I said. "Annie, I gave her a whole twenty-five-cent piece," he replied sadly. "Never mind, Anton," I said. "She probably needed it and, besides, we won't miss a quarter." "It's not the quarter," he said, "it's human wickedness that bothers me." Well, Jo, today he told me he had met the same poor old lady standing in the same place, and she asked him the way to the ferry, and told him – can you guess? – someone had stolen her purse! "Well, I call that very cheeky indeed," I said. "The shameless – " but Anton didn't let me finish. "It's wickedness, Annie. A poor defenceless old soul robbed twice in a row – so what could I do but give her another quarter?"

I felt it was best not to explain what had really happened – it would have made him sadder still. I only told him not to stand around on street-corners gawking next time but to come straight home. I hope he took it to heart, otherwise the crafty old hag will turn him into a regular customer.

But he wouldn't be Anton if he didn't come up with some new surprise every day. We'd barely managed to drag him away from the balloon-seller when something else caught his fancy. A short distance away, standing on a street-corner, was a group of ragged young Negro men with mischief in their eyes. They were whistling. It sounded unpleasant to my ears but Anton was fascinated and soon nothing else existed for him except those layabouts. But Mr. Thurber winked at me and put his finger to his lips so I stopped too. Just then a short little fellow walked by carrying a stick three times as tall as he, strung with fresh pretzels. Otylia wanted one and I must confess they made my mouth water too. They smelled almost like pretzels from the Pauls' shop in Prague. So I bought two for the children and one for myself. Anton was off in his own private world, probably composing another symphony, from the look of him. I must admit the Negroes had a wide repertoire, and they were whistling in four-part harmony, but it still bothered me. Anton had his notebook out by this time and was writing the music down, and he couldn't tear himself away from them until a police officer appeared and they ran away. Then, as if waking from a dream, he looked around. I did too – and I noticed that little Tony was gone!

I felt as though my heart had been torn out. Riff-raff everywhere, Italians, Negroes, drunks, those horrible street women – so I caught Otylia by the hand and looked around. And to my great relief, there was Tony, running towards us and grinning from ear to ear.

But what a grin it was, Josie! At first I thought he was wearing a set of artificial teeth, the kind that people wear at masquerades. His teeth were literally glowing like – what shall I compare them to? Alabaster? Freshly whitened sheets? "Tony, what have you done to your teeth?" I cried. "A man cleaned them for me, Mama." By this time, Mr. Thurber had noticed what was going on. Tony pointed to a nasty-looking man on the corner with a ring in his ear, scrubbing away at the teeth of another little boy. Mr. Thurber said to me (he speaks excellent German, thank heaven), *"Wir müssen Wasser haben! Aber schnell!"* and he dragged us into a tiny little shop so narrow you could practically touch both walls at once and asked for drinking water, but to get it he had to order coffee for all of us. Then Mr. Thurber ordered Tony to rinse his mouth out until he told him it was enough. Of all the nasty and irresponsible things! That man was selling a miraculous tooth powder and demonstrating its powers on the street urchins who, as you can imagine, were only too eager to let him. Mr. Thurber said the powder contained some caustic substance and if Tony hadn't washed his mouth out quickly and thoroughly he might have ended up with a mouthful of miserable sores.

New York is like that, Jo. Is it any wonder I wake up at night worrying about the children? Or about Anton himself? He was so enchanted by those Negroes that he goes back to the Lower East Side whenever he can. Most of the time, he goes with Mr. Kovarik (who is still working out well as Anton's secretary, and now has a room in our apartment) or Mr. Huneker, but sometimes he's quite alone. And Mr. Huneker, I'm afraid, has a tendency to lead him astray. He's a hard-drinking man with a paunch like a beer-barrel. Adele Margulies told me that he once had enormous ambitions to be a concert pianist, and it was a bitter blow to him to realize he did not have the ability. So he has become something of a famous critic instead, and teaches at the Conservatory too. He and Anton went out together soon after we arrived and got so inebriated that the next day Anton fell asleep by the tunnel on Washington Heights where he goes to watch the locomotives. His fascination with trains hasn't abandoned him and, to tell you the truth, I'd be far happier if he'd stick to his locomotives and not go wandering about among Negroes and drunks.

But even train-watching isn't as safe here as it was in Prague. Once, when we'd been in New York about a fortnight, Anton announced he was going to watch trains and Otylia said she'd join him. She's just a child, of course, and doesn't worry about things the way I do, and she wants to see everything and go everywhere. I swear to goodness she'd even try to spend more time talking with Mr. Huneker if I let her. Of course I strictly forbid any such forwardness, because besides his liking for the bars, Mr. Huneker is known as a libertine and they say he's already brought misfortune upon several young ladies. He may have a stomach like a pot-bellied stove, but his tongue is in fine fettle. He's an artist when it comes to flattery, and I admit he can even be quite funny. Otylka has picked up a rather heavy-handed joke from him which she finds amusing, though I suppose everything is amusing to a fourteen-year-old. She has started calling her father "Divorceshack", which sounds almost like Dvorak. I leave it to you to judge how well it suits Anton, apart from its sound, I mean. Almost no one here knows how to pronounce the name properly, so Mr. Huneker has invented a number of nicknames, and that is one of them. Another is "Borax", which has become quite popular, I don't know why, but at least it appears to be used affectionately.

As I was saying, Otylia wanted to go with her father to watch trains. I knew she only wanted to get out of the house – she'd never expressed the slightest interest in trains in Prague – so I asked Mr. Kovarik if he wouldn't mind going along, otherwise I was afraid those two dreamers would get lost in New York. Alas, I was courting disaster, as you'll see at once. They were gone all afternoon, and when they returned, the sleeves of Anton's brand-new jacket were torn, he was in a foul mood and went and locked himself in his study, Otylia was all flushed and Mr. Kovarik scuttled away to his room as quickly as he could. Apparently they'd gone to Pennsylvania Station – a large railway terminus here – and Anton headed straight for the platforms. But a guard stopped him and asked for a ticket. With Mr. Kovarik's help, Anton explained that they merely wanted to look at the trains. The guard told them they needed platform tickets. Mr. Kovarik offered to buy them, but Anton said no – he may be willing to give to the poor, but he told the guard it was absurd to ask people to buy tickets when they weren't going anywhere. Yet Anton was unwilling to leave, so they loitered around outside the station, and then – Otylia told it best: "I don't know how it could have happened, Mama, but all at once, Papa was gone!" She says she doesn't know how, but I fear that our sweet little girl has developed a strong affection for Mr. Kovarik and apparently he for her. (I trust you'll keep that to yourself for the time being. I wouldn't want Mr. Suk to hear about it – I have my own plans in that direction.) Anyway, clearly they had eyes only for each other.

I believe her when she says they were alarmed. But what could they do? Otylia wanted to search the nearby streets, but she said Mr. Kovarik guessed right away that Anton had found another way into the station, so he bought platform tickets and they went in to look for him there. They searched for about an hour – in vain! They waited another hour in front of the station, unable to decide what to do next. Mr. Kovarik thought they should have the police look for him, and Otylia was about to agree. Then she saw him. "Mama, it was awful," she told me. "Suddenly, a policeman appeared at the gate holding Papa by the collar and sleeve, and he pushed him over to the guard who grabbed his other sleeve and they shoved him down the steps. I felt like curling up and dying. Papa fell down, and a crowd of people gathered and I didn't know which way to look. But Mr. Kovarik kept his head, of course, and he helped Papa to his feet and we hurried away."

It seems that while those two were off in their own world, Anton had gone reconnoitring. Around the corner he discovered they were making repairs to the station so he climbed over a wooden fence and made a beeline for the trains. But the station is enormous and naturally Otylia and Mr. Kovarik couldn't find him. When he'd seen his fill he wanted to come out the main passenger exit, but he noticed they were collecting cancelled tickets and so decided to leave the way he'd come in. And as he was scrambling over the fence, a policeman caught him and dragged him into an office where they discovered he had no ticket. What could he do? He tried to pay – and discovered a pickpocket had stolen his wallet. At least the officials realized he was a foreigner, not a tramp – since in his excitement he was scarcely able to squeeze out a comprehensible word in English – so they took pity on him and simply threw him unceremoniously out of the station.

Something good, however, has come of his embarrassing little adventure. Now, instead of going to look at trains, he goes down to inspect the ocean liners. You are allowed on board after they dock, so he's in seventh heaven. If only he wouldn't wander around the Lower East Side!

And Mr. Kovarik worries me. I have nothing against him, really. He's a decent enough young fellow, a good secretary and amanuensis for Anton, and an excellent violinist, and Anton had no trouble getting him a job at the Conservatory. And yet, Jo, I cannot encourage it. I cannot bear to think of Otylia staying here in this Babylon with people robbing and killing each other every day, and danger on every corner, when we are back in Prague. I'd die of fear for her safety.

And what's more, believe it or not, Anton likes it here. I was so afraid he'd be homesick. You know how he is: whenever he has to go to Vienna or Berlin for a fortnight, he can't wait to be home again. And now.... It's true, he occasionally reminisces about home, but what he misses most, I would say, is the rest of the children. By the time they arrive it will be almost eight months that we've been apart. Otherwise he has plenty of companions here. Almost every day he argues about Wagner with Mr. Anton Seidl, the conductor, in the Old Vienna Café, which is more Viennese than anything in Vienna. He goes to the Sokol Club in the Czech quarter, he's found pigeons in Central Park, even though he feels sorry for them since they're in cages. He can get cigars from all over the world, there is music everywhere you go, the students at the Conservatory are good and he has his own school orchestra. I don't know, sometimes I'm afraid he'll get a harebrained notion to emigrate here, at his age!

He's fascinated by funny little details. "Here everyone is 'Mr.', " he said to me recently. "And they don't call a doctor 'Herr Doctor', just 'Doctor', because an academic title is honour enough in itself and Americans don't recognize aristocracy. Here even the President himself is 'Mr. Tyler', not 'Your Excellency'. A magnificent country!" is Anton's conclusion. And now we're getting ready to spend the holidays in a village in the West where Mr. Kovarik comes from. And Anton can hardly wait. Apparently Spillville – that's the name of the village – was settled almost entirely by Czechs. I'm extremely worried about it myself. Originally, Anton wanted to go back to Bohemia and spend the holidays at home in Vysoka, but Mr. Kovarik persuaded him to change his mind. Now that we're in America, he says, we should see a genuine Czech country village here. At first, Anton hesitated. It's several days' journey by train, in a frontier state called Iowa, and for all I know there are still wild Indians roaming about. At least, that's what Sadie, our landlady's niece, tells me. But Mr. Kovarik never ceased singing praises of the place into Anton's ear, and in the end Anton must have decided the village was a kind of Bohemian heaven on the prairies, and succumbed to Mr. Kovarik's honeyed talk.

Of course, I know *why* he went to such lengths to persuade Anton to stay. What I don't know is how I'm going to keep a proper eye on that girl all that time.

And how shrewd that Thurber woman is! She has already sniffed out Anton's fascination with America, and has been planting suggestions in his ear about how indispensable he is, encouraging him to extend his contract, suggesting that he could establish an American national music here, but three years are hardly enough for that, and she turns her languid eyes on him and behaves altogether like a brazen American woman.

What's to be done? I must hope that Anton becomes wiser. I long for the rest of the children to arrive. That will turn Anton's thoughts to other things, and perhaps he will see that America is no place for the children to grow up. Tereza has been doing a sterling job looking after the children in Prague and Vysoka – and since she'll be coming over with them, perhaps she'll help me keep an eye on our young troublemaker in Spillville.

Give her a sisterly kiss – and take one for yourself, dearest Jo, and do write me your news. Tell me if your health has improved, and about Kounic. Is he good to you? I know he surely is.

I promise to be more diligent about writing you sooner next time.

Your loving sister,
Annie

10 :◯: CORPUS DELICTI

I'M TELLING YOU, it's God's own truth, Professor. Every day he was here, he'd get up with the chickens and by six he'd be sitting up there in the choir playing for the old biddies at morning mass. It's also true – or so they say – that he listened to the birds in the woods and put their songs into that there fiddle quartet of his. Almost like he stole the tune. No, course not, I don't really mean that. He could've written the music without no help from the birds, and Lord knows what that young daughter of his actually heard. Young Kovarik claimed she told him she'd heard it in the woods, the very same bird the Master heard. Course now, it might've happened the other way around. Maybe the bird was listening outside the Kovariks' window when they were practising the piece in their fiddle quartet with old Dvorak, and it picked up the tune and flew off and sang it in the woods. They say it must've been the same bird. But then it'd have to be some kind of parrot, and there's never been none of them around Spillville, not wild ones anyways. Young Kovarik says she actually pointed out the bird to him, the kind they call a scarlet tanager, but maybe she was just trying to make herself look interesting. She was a real peach, that one was, and even if she'd had a head full of piss-soaked straw – beg your pardon, Professor – nobody would have minded, least of all young Kovarik. What's that you say? An interesting what? Idiom? I don't know about that. Anyway, about the Dvorak girl, she had good looks *and* brains, which ain't always the case. I wouldn't be at all surprised if she heard that magic bird just so she could get herself attention from young Kovarik. So you can go right ahead and stick that bird in your book, Professor, as far as I'm concerned. In fact, why not stick in three more birds, so you can have her hearing the whole quartet? No law says you have to believe what you read, now

is there? But what I want to know is, are you going to write about
the shameless woman? You know, the one young Kovarik thought
was a Rusalka, a water nymph? Rosemary Vanderbilt? That's right,
old man Vanderbilt's niece or grandniece, or some such thing. Don't
tell me no one's told you about her? Well, you know some people
around here are afraid of getting a little dirt on old Dvorak's reputation with a lot of loose talk. Remind me to tell you about it later.
Anyway, the old maestro was a religious soul, very respectful of the
clergy. Whenever he saw the dog-collar, he became all saintly and
righteous. That's why he was so close to Father Bily, our parish priest.
That was fine as far as it went, but when there wasn't no collar in
sight, you'd be surprised! I mean they *say* what happened with the
water nymph and him was just an accident, and maybe it's true. But
it's a fact he spent an ungodly amount of time in the woods and
never took his wife with him. She stayed home and did the cooking.
Old Dvorak sure loved his food. And something else: you'd never
catch Father Bily going to Tony Kapinos's. That caused some friction
between the two of them. Father Bily was a sworn prohibitioner,
and he was so strict about booze he arranged it so whenever he held
mass, all the saloons in Spillville had to close so his congregation
couldn't hear the beer-drinkers singing. And he kicked up a terrible
stink about having the saloons too close to the church. When our
grandfathers built the church, you know, it was before the saloons.
They didn't figure people would go so far overboard with drink. If
they'd of known, they would've built their church somewhere else.
Trouble is, they'd probably have to go all the way to Fort Atkinson
now to get out of earshot.

So anyway, by the time old Dvorak came to Spillville we already
had eight saloons, spread out from one end of the village to the other.
Of course, back when they started putting up St. Wenceslaus, Spillville was barely five years old. Some architect in the old country
drew up the plans for them, so I guess they must have come up in
the world by then. They say it was modelled after St. Barbora's Cathedral in Kutna Hora. Couldn't tell you that – I come out from the
old country when I was five – but that's what they say. You couldn't
tell by looking at it, eh? Well, I guess maybe the fellow who drew
up the plans was a little wide of the mark, or maybe he took the old
men for a ride. But they sure as hell didn't skimp on the church,
Professor. They got old Barborka, the famous clockmaker over Iowa
City way, to build them a clock. He built about two hundred clocks

all over the States by the time he died. How much did they pay for
it? Don't bother to ask; it was a fortune. Master Barborka started off
making cuckoo clocks in the old country, but when he came to the
States he went big. He put the same rig into those tower clocks that
he used to put into his cuckoo clocks, but instead of a cuckoo, he
used bells. The Spillville Catholics really wrung their pockets dry for
them bells. They had the first one cast by the Van Dusen and Tight
Buckeye Bell Company, an old company over in Cincinnati. There's
a Latin inscription on the bell that's supposed to mean: "The generosity of many benefactors, for the glory and honour of God, built
the Church of St. Wenceslaus, patron saint of the Bohemians, in
Spillville, 1867." Well, wait till I tell you about those benefactors.
They say you're a Catholic, Professor, so you know as well as I do
that the Holy Church is nobody's fool and has no illusions about
people. They don't sell indulgences any more, but let me tell you it
wasn't a bad arrangement. As a matter of fact, that's how the Church
has always operated. Man is a vessel of sin, right? Some are minor
and praying will usually get you off the hook, but some are major,
and some are real whoppers. In Spillville we've had a couple of cases
like that, and if all they had to do was pray, they'd be on their knees
for half eternity. By 1874, a single bell wasn't enough to make up for
our sins any more, so a new work order went out to the Buckeye Bell
Company. Problem was, we thought that since it was our second
bell, a smaller one would do, so we ordered a death knell, you know,
a funeral bell. Well, it didn't do, and I'll tell you why in a minute.
Ten years later, we added a third bell – "for the greater glory of God
and the exaltation of the faithful" – and by that time, even the most
faithful were in dire need of a little exaltation, let me tell you.

What? You say I don't sound too religious? Well, Professor, I was
never much of a one for church, not like old Dvorak. But I'll admit
the thought of the Lord God kind of spooks me. After all, I'm ninety-
two. I haven't got more than twenty or thirty years left, right? It's
a sin to be as old as I am. So I'm starting to think of ways to buy my
way out of purgatory, or at least to save myself a thousand years or
so. That's why, at my age, I've stopped cussing, taking the Lord's
name in vain, you know. I only play cards on weekdays and I play
for matches, not for nickels, and certainly not for quarters, like we
used to when they were repairing the church. I was a young fellow
then, forty at the most. Did you know it was me who carved all the
altars? Once Father Bily caught me playing euchre with Othmar

Kramesh and Joe Swehla, right below the altar of the Holy Family, which wasn't finished yet. You should have heard the holy father. Pretty raw language for the House of the Lord! He took our cards away from us too and later I heard he was playing euchre with the Master at the Kovariks'. But that might just be evil tongues wagging.

Why were we so religious? Well, because we were such sinners, that's why. I can tell you, Professor, we were proper vessels. And if you can't guess what was in those vessels, then you're no Czech. Of course! Beer! A sin our fathers brought over from the old country. All the rest they learned after they got here. Wasn't long before they got a taste for whisky, too. So the secret's out. Sin Number One in Spillville was boozing. Over in Decorah, they even used to call us Swillville.

Just think about it: our forefathers came here in '54 with nothing but their bare hands. There was virgin soil here, the Indians still hunted deer and wild turkey – wonderful eating – and pigeons. Old Dvorak loved pigeons; that's what they all say about him. Of course, by the time he was here most of the big flocks were gone. Most of the early settlers arrived without a cent in their pockets. Back then, it took two thousand bucks to start a farm in Iowa: a quarter-section cost two hundred, your basic log cabin about three-fifty, a hundred for a pair of oxen and so on. And look around you: it all came from those bare hands and the little bit they earned on the long way here from the east coast, and that's hardly worth mentioning because all they could get was casual labour. Of course in those first few years they scarcely had what you'd call a roof over their heads, Professor, just branches. They'd dig a hole in the side of a hill, cover it with boughs – and skins, if they managed to shoot anything – and live in that. And five years later, in '59, they started building St. Wenceslaus. How's that for religious? And they didn't even have a decent grave-yard yet. Now there's a story.

One day, they stumbled on an Indian burial ground that belonged to the Winnebagos. The Winnebagos used to live here before the government shipped them farther west, to the Neutral Grounds, and those graves were all they left behind. Heathens, of course, but by and large our fathers had respect for the dead, even though they must have believed the Winnebagos was frying in hell. So they ploughed around the burial grounds, and the crops, when they came up, hid the graves. But after every harvest, there they'd be, just like before. Well, pretty soon they began dying themselves, and what were they going to do with their own dead? The Mikotas' little girl was the first one to die, scarcely a year after they arrived. She was about three and the poor parents didn't know where to bury her.

And that's when someone came up with that bad idea. Since there was no consecrated ground for miles around anyway, they thought, maybe those dead Winnebagos made the ground holy, in a way, just by being buried in it. Maybe the Lord had mercy on some of them. Maybe they were good heathens, as heathens go. Anyway, the upshot was they decided to bury the little girl alongside one of the Winnebagos. So they all gathered around one of the better-looking graves that maybe belonged to a medicine man or a chief, and they recited the prayers for the dead from the missal and then old Mikota, along with Klimesh and Tony Kapinos, started digging and, well, they got quite a surprise, Professor. There was this Winnebago, lying there with all his gear around him. He had two bows, something like fifty arrows, two pipes, some knives and a spare set of moccasins to go with the ones he was wearing. Things he'd need for the happy hunting grounds, Professor. The Winnebagos believed there's no lounging around in heaven, you have to scramble for your living just like you do here in this vale of tears.

Well, no one would've ever thought of taking anything from the grave, Professor, but the trouble was that lying on top of all that hunting gear was a bottle of whisky. I figure two things: either the Winnebagos believed it was going to be cold in the happy hunting grounds or, more likely, the chief liked the stuff.

As I imagine it, it must have been quite a surprise. Their prayers for the dead probably got cut a little short as they stood there staring at the whisky, even Mama Mikota, with the poor little dead girl in her arms wrapped in a goat skin, there being no time to make a coffin. Then Tony Kapinos sank to his knees, but not to pray, no sir, right there and then the Devil got him in his clutches. He leans over the open grave, snatches out the bottle and says this is no fit thing to lay an innocent child beside, and he flings the bottle into the bushes. Well, the people came to their senses and began rattling off the Lord's Prayer and then they laid the poor girl in the ground beside the bows and arrows and moccasins, covered her with earth and put up a cross.

You've got to remember, Professor, that there wasn't a distillery for miles around in those days, and besides, no one had any money to buy booze. Folks were still living, as I said, in those holes in the ground. And now, I don't suppose you'd have any trouble explaining why Tony Kapinos didn't show up in the fields until the next afternoon? No, I don't suppose you would.

And there you have Spillville's original sin, and I'm sad to say it wasn't their last. At night, when everyone should have been asleep, you'd sometimes hear the crunching of pickaxes, and every so often in the morning you'd see someone staggering out to the fields, barely able to walk, and he'd be useless for the rest of the day. By that time, the Devil really had them in his clutches.

Naturally, as long as the old men were slaving away on the virgin soil, they didn't have much time to think about what they owed the Lord. The first thing they all wanted to do was build their cabins and pay off their claims. Later, when the old men had a little more money to spare, the sin of intemperance spread and soon a fit of bad conscience came over Spillville and right along with it came a wave of religious fervour. When you think about it, Professor, what the Lord does He does well. If it wasn't for those bottles of whisky we might have waited another fifty years for the church.

But the sin of booze spread, and that's a fact. Can you imagine this? Things got so bad we actually had somebody die of delirium tremens. True, it was only a one-month-old baby, and they can't hold their liquor too well. What? You think I'm kidding, Professor? Well, I admit it does sound strange. But I figure the baby got it from its parents. I understand the mother drank a lot when she was in the family way and the baby got the worst of it. Things like that can happen, Professor. I've actually seen the death certificate with my own eyes. "Cause of death: Delirium Tremens."

Well, you may be right, Professor. There was no doctor – I mean a properly trained doctor – in Spillville at the time. Joe Spielman signed the death certificate. Sure, of course he was a farmer. A Swiss fellow, the first settler in Winneshiek County. Spillville got named after him. Used to be Spielville until the first postmaster spelled it wrong and the name stuck. Later, Spielman opened a brewery and a general store so he could afford a licence. That's right, a licence to practise medicine. I believe the going rate was ten bucks, but Spielman could afford it, and it brought him in that extra bacon.

Well, you know, that never occurred to me, you may be right. People died of strange diseases in those days, but you never hear of them any more. Like brain fever, or dropsy. Annie Lukesh died of the summer sickness. What's that? I haven't a notion.

To be fair, you'd have to admit that every once in a while, whisky served some good. Take the war. No, I'm not talking about the Great War, I was too old for that one, I mean our war, the Civil War. I fought in that one. It was butchery, Professor. I'll bet you've never seen nothing like it. Once, just when the battle of Fort Donelson was raging, my commander had me deliver a dispatch to a field hospital in a village called Willdoonick. So I show up on my horse – I was in the cavalry – and the village is all kind of dead, all the houses look empty, no people anywhere. I figured they'd have the Stars and Stripes flying over the hospital, but there wasn't a flag in sight. I found the hospital anyway, Professor, and do you know how? No, it wasn't the groans of the wounded. I was riding down the main street and suddenly, about two hundred yards ahead of me, I see a fellow in a window heave something out and disappear again. I go for a closer look, and I see this strange heap of stuff under the window, all white and red. And when I got closer – well, Professor, war toughens you up but it still made me feel queasy. It was a pile of human limbs. Arms and legs. They was amputating them inside. That's how I knew it was the hospital. And by this time I could hear the groaning as well, but less than you'd think. Why? Well, they got everyone who was ripe for amputation plastered on bourbon. At that time there was none of that – what do you call it – laughing gas. You might get a bit of ether, but in Willdoonick they preferred bourbon to ether. Lots of the sufferers belonged to the old Lincoln Rifles. A Bohemian outfit from Chicago, you know.

But I'm telling you, if I ever have to have an operation, God forbid, I'd never let them put me to sleep. I'd rather just get plastered. I can stand a little pain, and at least there'd be no danger of me getting buried alive. I'm not kidding, that actually happened in Spillville too. Matter of fact, old Dvorak was there when it happened. The girl, Mary Podrashka was her name, hadn't turned sixteen yet. And all she needed was a tooth out. They always used to do it just like that, with no laughing gas or anything. The blacksmith – it was young Spielman at the time – just pried under the tooth with a gouge kind of a thing, gave her a quick twist, the patient would yell bloody murder and the tooth was out. But the problem was the parents – Mary was their only daughter, otherwise they had all boys, eight or nine I believe, but after that unfortunate incident the good Lord gave them twin girls. But when this thing happened, Mary was the only girl they had, and when they heard about a dentist in Decorah who used laughing gas, they said why should she have to suffer, and they took her to Decorah. Well, the dentist put her to sleep, pulled the tooth out and of course it didn't hurt a bit. But when they brought her home she was still out cold. They told them she'd sleep it off overnight but next morning by Jesus she was dead, like a corpse, cold. Wasn't even breathing. Well, it was summertime, so they buried her right the next day. The Master played the organ at her funeral. Of course word spread fast and pretty soon there was even talk of it in Protivin and Decorah, and someone in Decorah said they'd been too quick, they should've let her alone for three days at least, because laughing gas can affect some people more than others and it can even put you out for a whole week. Anyway, about two days after the funeral, Tony Kapinos brought word of all the talk from Decorah. Well, by the living Jesus, you can just imagine the ruckus. Old Podrashka and his wife tore out to the cemetery – we had a proper one by then – and began to dig and sure enough, the girl had managed to loosen the lid of the coffin and lift it enough to get her hand out. Then she ran out of strength and died for real, poor thing.

That kind of thing can't happen to you during a hangover.

But whisky was the original sin, Professor, the big one. Otherwise, most of the sinning that went on was petty stuff, with beer. About the time we built the church, there were two breweries in Spillville – Frank Nockles owned one, and later on his dedication to our national drink cost him dear. The other belonged to Rothenberger. At first, the beer wasn't too good. They knew what to put in it and all but not how to make it. Still, they tried, and each spring when they knocked open the first barrel the whole village was there, wondering what they'd have to drink for the rest of the year. But they drank it regardless of whether it tasted like beer or horse piss. The worst stuff was converted to whisky, so nothing got wasted. What? Sure, of course it can be done. Never tasted it, eh? No, I couldn't really recommend it, Professor.

Trouble was, though, that in this country there were some people so saintly and righteous old Dvorak himself was a real pagan beside them. First they taught the Indians how to drink firewater and the poor buggers drank themselves to death, mostly. Then when they realized what they done, the same sons of bitches felt so guilty that to make up for it they swore they'd get the Indians back off the booze again. But where were the Indians? So they turn around and decide to reform the rest of us instead. In 1882 Iowa voted on Prohibition and danged if the prohibs didn't win! Of course there weren't as many Czechs then as there are now. Here in Spillville the drys only got ten per cent of the vote – you'll always find a few sell-outs in any crowd. As it turned out, we had the best anti-prohib vote in the county. But it didn't do any good, because like I said, the state as a whole went dry.

Well, you can imagine this was a real calamity for Spillville. By that time, we had two breweries and eight saloons and people were hopping mad. John Cizek, our second blacksmith, escaped the gallows by the skin of his teeth. When a prohib by the name of Carlos Osgood – he was a farmer from up north of Spillville – started bragging to Cizek about how he'd voted dry, Cizek let go of his horse's leg and flung a hammer at him so hard Osgood barely had time to duck. The hammer flew right across the street, went through the Kovariks' front window and put a hole in their piano. Of course Cizek had good reason to get so upset. One of them eight saloons belonged to him.

That law took effect July 4, and whether they chose that day as a way of doing penance or just to rub it in I don't know. I'd say they was rubbing it in. They knew very well that for us Czechs a national holiday without beer is more like a national funeral, but you can't beat the Czechs for crazy ideas, so in Spillville we decided to celebrate the Fourth of July a day early.

Well, there's been nothing like it in living memory. At the target shoot, no one could hit the glass balls with a shotgun. They put the greased pole up crooked so when the first fellow tried climbing up to get the sausage at the top, the pole fell over and dumped him into a big vat of tripe soup. Lucky for him it wasn't boiling yet. And in the hundred-yard dash for fat men – that was always the high point of every picnic – they were so shellacked by the time of the race that only two of 'em made it to the finish line, and one of 'em was on all fours.

To make a long story short, everybody had a whale of a time!

But that was where Tony Kapinos's tragedy began because the very same day, the third of July, he opened a saloon in Spillville just to show the drys what he thought of them. Tony Kapinos had a lot of spunk. You can count people like him in Czech history on your fingers. They make you feel proud to be Czech, as if most Czechs cared about national pride. They say we're a small nation and we can't afford it. But I tell you, Professor, that if we'd had more people like Tony Kapinos around after '48 when the Hapsburgs lowered the boom on us, or like that handful of Moravians at the Battle of White Mountain in 1618, it could have all been different, and we wouldn't be in America today.

On the other hand, it ain't so bad in America.

Well, for a while nothing much happened, Professor. Not a single saloon got closed down. Spillville's own constable, Frank Valenta, owned one himself. He was the one who finished the fat men's race on his hands and knees. Of course, Professor, those pious prohibs hatched into a fine batch of feathered snakes. How's this for slimy dealing: they said half the fine for selling booze would go to the weasel who turned anyone in. Can you believe public servants stooping that low?

Well, for a long time, no one in Spillville turned anyone in, not even the drys squealed. But there's a saying: where the Devil fears to tread, he sends a woman, and there was a couple of meddlesome old biddies in Decorah who hired some private snoops and these fellows began cellar-sniffing around the counties, trying to locate illegal operations. Things were quiet for quite a while, then suddenly the old hens laid charges against forty-eight saloons and nine breweries all at once. So we had a monster trial on our hands.

A lot of people almost ended up in the poorhouse. Frank Nockles got fined five hundred dollars, and that was a pile of money in those days. He went bankrupt and turned his brewery into a buttery to recoup, and he distilled rye there on the sly. He was a real outlaw, Professor. But that's nothing compared to what happened to Tony Kapinos.

Kapinos stood his ground. As I said, they never found a local informer in Spillville, and the old biddies in Decorah weren't exactly loaded, so they could only afford to send their cellar-smellers out every so often, so between times Tony always managed to get back on his feet. Of course with all his fines, he was barely scraping by. But he stuck to his colours.

That all happened that famous summer of '93 when old Dvorak himself came to Spillville. He used to sit around in Tony's saloon, refreshing himself with beer that Kapinos was smuggling in from Minneapolis, I believe it was. And he wrote the New World Symphony right here in Spillville, and don't you believe anyone who says he wrote it in New York before he came. New York just wants to steal Spillville's thunder. Well, all right, there's no law says you have to believe me. But don't you take his opera Rusalka away from us. He wrote that because of Rosemary Vanderbilt. What? Who's Josephine? I told you, her name was Rosemary. What a floozie! Don't worry, I'll tell you about her in good time. But whatever you want to believe, it's a fact that old Dvorak got Tony Kapinos out of one of his biggest jams, because all in all Dvorak had a head on him like a horse-trader. It's a real shame he never settled down here. He'd have had peace and quiet, a church handy, and a saloon, and he could have done well by all those daughters of his too, and a lot cheaper than in Europe, because there ain't dowries here. For the life of me I don't know what made him want to go back. Longing for the homeland, you say? Now tell me, Professor, what homeland? Why, at the time we were under the thumb of Vienna. That's why we rebelled in '48, and when it didn't work out, we left for America where there's no potentates. Well, that's true, they took our beer away from us. But as our great President Lincoln once said, you can hoodwink all of the people some of the time, and some people you can hoodwink all of the time, but you can't go on hoodwinking all of the people for ever. And as it turned out, the will of the people won out, and it's so wet now, Professor, that it almost makes you want to turn prohib, just to preserve your health.

And even then, they were no match for us. Do you know what a blind pig is? We had several blind pigs in Spillville. One was at the Rothenbergers'. Naturally, when they turned the brewery into a dance hall they went on brewing secretly. The most popular pig was John Voppe's operation under the Turkey River bridge. Voppe was a kind of jack-of-all-trades. Summers he was a lawyer in the court of arbitration, and winters he had himself locked up so he'd be sure of food and a warm place to sleep since he couldn't spend the nights in Tony Kapinos's barn any more when it got cold. He never earned much money, even at court, so he made a little extra chopping wood, helping with the harvest, collecting ticket money at the dances and so on. But mainly he operated the pig under the bridge over Turkey River. What's a pig? I was just coming to that. After sundown, Voppe would sit under the bridge, the customer would come, put his money on the edge, turn away and pretend to be gazing at the stars. When he turned around again, the money'd be gone and there was a bottle. Do you see? No? Well, you're from the old country and I guess the courts there still aren't too fair, even now. Here it's different. Here you have to prove in court that a crime was actually committed, right? You have to say: "He's the one who sold me the bottle. I saw him with my own eyes." American judges don't hold much with circumstantial evidence, and they don't expect anyone to perjure themselves. People here are believers and they take swearing on the Bible seriously. Now do you understand, Professor? That's why they call it a blind pig. Why pig? I couldn't tell you.

Well, to get back to Tony Kapinos, old Dvorak was playing euchre in Tony's saloon, in a foul mood he was because he was losing, and to top it off they ran out of beer. So Tony set out to Calmar for a new barrel the very same night. It was going on ten, the time old Dvorak usually went home, but he still had a thirst so he decided to wait for the barrel. About half-past ten, Kapinos showed up empty-handed, all hot and hell-roaring if you'll pardon my language, but old Dvorak said as much himself. What happened? Well, the old biddies over in Decorah, they'd hired another snoop and laid an ambush for Kapinos. He had the barrel in his wagon under sacks of beans and dried peas and suddenly this constable leaps out of the bushes and says he hears Kapinos is bootlegging and he's got a search warrant. Well, the constable knew exactly what he'd find, didn't he – he even had a wheelbarrow stashed in the bushes to take the barrel back to Decorah.

I'd rather not tell you, Professor, how old Dvorak carried on when he found out, or the words he used. Some people are touchy about strong language, and maybe you're one of them. Two days later Tony got a summons and the same evening they all got together in his saloon for a confab. Old Dvorak was still mad. Maybe that's how he got the idea. Some people think best when they're on the boil. Well, Tony followed Dvorak's advice and when he appeared before Judge Gibson in Decorah he asked for a trial by jury, which was unheard of in these parts because if you lost it was a lot more expensive. But he was within his rights, so the judge adjourned the case and we got together a jury in Spillville. Problem was, the Master wasn't from Spillville, but us Americans aren't petty-minded so we made him an honorary citizen and that was that. The judge wasn't a stickler for formalities and anyway he was a musician himself, played the cymbals in the Decorah band. To make a long story short, old Dvorak got to be one of the jury and they elected him foreman right off.

The barrel was entered as evidence and the judge asked Kapinos if this *corpus delicti* was his property. Kapinos said it was. And did it contain an alcoholic beverage? Kapinos said it didn't. And how do you explain the inscription on the barrel? asked the judge: "Comstock Brewery, Calmar". Back when it was still legal, Kapinos said, I used it for beer. Now I use it for molasses. The judge scowled and said: And you expect the jury to believe that, Mr. Kapinos? In the past ten years you have been found guilty of bootlegging thirty-three times. Kapinos said nothing, the judge looked at the jury, and old Dvorak shook his head and scowled as much as to say he wasn't about to be fooled by the likes of Kapinos, so the judge figured he had an open and shut case. And that's where he made his big mistake. "The jury may now retire," he said, and he pulled a big onion-shaped watch out of his vest and looked at it. It was four o'clock. He thought the jury would be done in five minutes, so he'd have time for a game of billiards before supper.

We stood up, and so did Dvorak, but instead of going straight out with us, he marched over to the barrel, tipped it on its side and started rolling it towards the door. Judge Gibson dropped his watch and it swung there on its gold chain. "Sir, where are you going with that barrel?" he said. Old Dvorak straightened up and said, "Your Honour, I was told that in American trials, the proof has got to be beyond all doubt. The jury intends to examine the contents of the barrel, to satisfy ourselves as to its contents." Of course he didn't say it quite that smooth, his English not being the best and what he learned in New York he probably forgot in Spillville, so I don't suppose Judge Gibson was any too sure what Dvorak was talking about. He just sat there with his watch dangling from his vest and watched him bend to it and roll the barrel into the jury room. And there, as the law requires, we locked ourselves in.

We sat round the barrel, Professor, and for the first few moments nobody said a word. There was a jug of water on the table and twelve glasses with blue cornflowers painted on them. Dvorak looked at them, then at us, and then said – of course he was speaking Czech now: "Shall we degust?"

Frank Valenta, who had about fifteen years of tapping beer behind him before he went over to the side of the law, got up, walked over to the barrel, drove in the wooden bung, put his arms around the barrel, lifted it up and, one by one, filled our glasses as we held them out. Old Dvorak was last. We waited to see what he would say. He lifted his glass to the light, then held it under his nose, and then he tasted it. We followed suit.

"Well?" he asked.

"Molasses," said Rothenberger.

"Apple juice," said Johnny Cizek.

"Beer," said Dvorak.

We all looked surprised and he explained, "As I understand it, the jury's opinion has to be unanimous. If we don't agree, then our verdict will have to be: innocent for want of proof."

We saw what he was driving at.

"I say it's buttermilk," said Casper Benesh.

"Not on your life," said Joe Strakosh. "It tastes like tea."

By this time we'd all drained our glasses, and the Master said, "Let us degust again. In my opinion, it's beer."

You see, Professor, even though the entire scheme was his idea, he couldn't bring himself to tell an out-and-out lie. He was too afraid of the Lord. And because he was shrewd as a Jesuit, he played it so that as far as the Church was concerned, he was pure as a lily. The rest of us, we took the sin upon ourselves.

"Goat's milk," said Rothenberger.

"Ginger ale," said Johnny Cizek.

"Camomile," said Casper Benesh.

"Beer," declared old Dvorak.

Well, after we'd been degusting the contents of the barrel for an hour and we still couldn't agree, Judge Gibson sent a message asking if the jury was still trying to make up its mind. It is, the Master informed him, but we haven't got a unanimous verdict yet.

I tell you, Professor, it was a real feat. That barrel would have lasted a week in Tony's saloon and we had to empty it in a single afternoon, right to the bottom, so there wouldn't be a drop of evidence left and the judge couldn't bring a charge of obstructing justice against us.

It took us three hours and twenty minutes. In the courtroom next door, the judge was all in a lather. And when the door finally opened, and Dvorak appeared, the red rays of the setting sun were already falling on the Stars and Stripes. He tried to step boldly into the courtroom, but he stumbled and had to steady himself on the dock, and we straggled out after him, like a procession of true Swillvilleites.

"Your Honour," said old Dvorak, addressing the judge in a ceremonious voice – and just then, if you'll pardon me for being so blunt, he let out a large burp. "Your Honour," he said, "the jury, after a careful examination of the barrel's contents, has been unable to come to a unanimous verdict. And since, in the meantime, the *corpus delicti* has run out, we have no choice but to – " and he burped again.

Judge Gibson stared at us as if he couldn't believe what he was hearing. When it looked like Dvorak wouldn't be able to go on, he said, "Do you mean to say, sir, that the verdict of the jury is.... "

"Innocent." And that was the final word in the worst case Tony Kapinos ever had to deal with.

Well, Professor, we drove old Dvorak back to Spillville in Rothenberger's buggy and his wife was already on the lookout. When she saw the Master, she said, "Thank God the children are already tucked in. If they ever saw their father so plastered.... "

She couldn't have put it any better, Professor.

But Tony Kapinos came to a bad end, Professor. After that famous victory he got cocky, and soon after the Dvoraks left Spillville, he was summonsed again. It was a losing battle but he kept on fighting until 1899, when they managed to convince Judge Gibson, without a jury this time, that in the preceding half year he'd received twelve hundred barrels of illicit beer. The judge gave him a choice – a thousand dollars or jail, one day for each three dollars and twenty-three cents of court costs. Tony couldn't afford the fine. He'd been struggling for sixteen years and he was broke and tired, and so, in the end, they finally got him behind bars.

Nope, that wasn't the end of it, not yet. You know what he did as soon as he got out? You'd never guess. No, he didn't hang himself. That wouldn't have been so bad. They say it's an easy death. You can't guess?

I'll tell you, then.

He went back.

Where? To the old country, of course. To Bohemia. With its absolute monarchy and its police informers and all that.

No, there was no prohibition in Bohemia, none at all, you could drink beer, and Kapinos took royal advantage of that. But now comes his terrible end, so listen close. He was so used to shooting off his mouth any way he wanted in Spillville that in one of those Prague saloons he said something insulting about the monarchy, and whatever it was, it must have been terrible, because they locked him up for four and a half years.

I don't know what ever became of him. At that point, like they say in books, Professor, he vanished without a trace.

11 :C): THE MYSTERY OF THE CADENZA

HE ASKED TO BE LEFT ALONE in the dressing room for half an hour, after the concert in The Hague. Nothing like this had ever happened to him. It wasn't stage fright; he knew what that was, had grown used to it, had learned to live with it. And anyway, that was all part of being a musician, just like the six hours of cello practice daily.

But this time, it was as though the concerto – especially the last movement, the Allegro – had reopened the wound of an old and bitter disappointment, all the more painful because he did not understand it. Face to face with Anton's art, he had always been humble. He had also put up with his rebuffs, and God knows that when it came to giving offence, the Master was master of them all. Others had been crushed by his insults. Once, in the Prague Conservatory, he had seen the plump, good-natured Nedbal literally stagger out of a classroom, the way drunken men do. It was past ten, he himself had just finished teaching and was walking back to the staff room, when Nedbal, heedless of where he was going, almost collapsed in his arms, tears streaming down his puffy cheeks. It was only in the staff room, after a glass of kümmel brandy – an act of intimacy otherwise anathema between student and teacher – that the dreadful truth had come out. "Mr. Wihan, I told – I told him," Nedbal had moaned, "that I had modelled my overture after Tannhäuser and he...." His voice had been smothered in sobs. "He what?" "He ... " and the young man had bitten his lip and said, almost inaudibly, "He said that what great spirits can accomplish cannot necessarily be accomplished by.... " "By whom? By you?" Nedbal had looked down: "By great asses." He had tried to console him as best he could – the Master was a short-tempered old man and he didn't really mean it. But try to convince an aspiring composer, full of doubts at the best of times, that he isn't really an ass, especially if the composer of The Requiem and The Jacobin says he is. Even a second glass of kümmel brandy was not much help. Half an hour later, Nedbal, his head down, had slunk out of the staff room as if his shoulders bore the great weight of the music that so eluded his skill.

But the door of Anton's office farther down the hall was ajar, and he noticed that as the miserable Nedbal walked by the Master slipped out behind him. A second later, an arm around the slumping shoulders of the young man was helping him bear up under the burden of his sorrow. He walked over to the staff-room window and a few moments later he saw the two men appear on the street below. Nedbal was still misery personified, but he was reaching with chalk-stained fingers into the proffered bag containing Anton's famous hibiscus fruit candies.

So throughout those years of friendship, those years of performing, both on the podiums of practically every town in Bohemia and in the glitter of large concert halls, throughout those long years of common service to the majesty of music, he, Hanousek Wihan, the Master's acolyte, had grown used to those volcanic eruptions. He knew they would always be followed by the hibiscus candies.

But that other time, Wihan remembered now, it had not been an ordinary, uncontrollable explosion, but rather as if Anton were charging him with the duty – after all those years, and as his closest friend – of knowing his dark secret. Not to speak of that secret, but to know it. He was baffled. Anton was clearly more than merely irritated at him for having asked if he might, in the traditional manner, include his own ad lib cadenza at the end of the concerto, and for then having defended it so stubbornly, even after he understood that it would have trivialized the superb B-Minor Cello Concerto which echoed with the alien distances of America and the Master's desperate love for the countryside of his childhood, by crowning it with a jester's cap of mere virtuosity. The moment he realized that he had forgotten proper humility before the majesty of the music and succumbed to the temptation to celebrate himself by replacing Anton's music with his own cadenza, he should have relented, retracted his request, done penance. He should have taken the score for his cadenza and the Master's smouldering cigar, put one against the other and, when his own vanity had caught fire, tossed it into the stove as a burnt offering. But though he had not done this, and though the cigar – perhaps the tenth that afternoon – had remained firmly clamped between the Master's lips, what happened afterwards should never have happened.

Yet he still recalled vividly how *right* his cadenza had seemed at the time – it had, after all, been appropriate; and such improvisation was blessed by the traditions of Mozart and other composers.

The three masterful ascending cello passages in the third movement seemed to him – in the kind of intoxication one feels when one is suddenly able to play a technically difficult passage with ease – to be a prelude preparing the way for the cello's final entry where it would at last dominate the work as he felt it should, though only as a primus inter pares, *a purely virtuoso solo voice, a voice celebrated for its own sake* – though now, of course, he realized it hadn't been the solo voice alone he had wanted, but the chance to show off his ability to finger those intricately difficult passages, full of thirds, sixths and octaves; *there, he felt, was the place to insert his cadenza. He knew that Anton was not especially fond of the cello, for he complained of its bellows and bleats, and no one had an ear for tone-colour like his. But he believed passionately that after Anton's triple assault on the summit, the instrument should have been freed from the discipline of the score and allowed to soar to those heights where the player casts off the physical limitations that impede less skilful fingers. Instead, in what seemed like a malicious joke, perhaps a reminder of his true feelings about the instrument, Anton had merely recapitulated preceding themes three times – for clarinet, violin, and tutti (the cello was allowed to trill briefly above them, to sing, yes – but not to soar triumphant in the voice of the soloist whose art, unlike the art of the composer, will, each time, die with him). No composer, not even his friend Anton who had spent years behind a music stand with the fingerboard of a viola in his hand, could ever write a cadenza the way the soloist could. And what followed was only a grand, almost humorous, brief and predictable finale by the trombones and trumpets, for the Master was fonder of those.*

So what had made Anton overcome his distaste for the cello enough to write the concerto in the first place? For an old friendship? Anton had told him he had dedicated it to him, and he – delighted to have a concerto dedicated to himself – in the euphoria, the understandable pleasure of receiving from a friend a unique gift that one had not dared to hope for (and such a gift can be neither bought nor procured), he did not think rationally, but instead believed himself to be the first cause of the composition, himself and those years of musical comradeship, the podiums shared in countless small towns and great cities. Furthermore, Anton had written only one other piece for the cello, the Concerto in A Major dedicated to his friend Ludvik Peer. But that was an early work, and could bear no comparison to the B-Minor Concerto, in which he could hear America and his friend's own maturity.

But his ecstasy had made him thoughtless – he was not really that naive. He knew there was often a difference between the substance of a piece and its dedication.

That's why he had hurried to Jecna Street with his cello, eager to let Anton hear the fifty-six bars he was so proud of, his own cadenza, fashioned to give to the concerto the kind of brilliant finale it deserved. The apogee of the performing arts is the ad libitum.

Breathlessly – and masterfully – he had played the cadenza for Anton, and the significance of a detail, of what he thought was a mechanical ritual, had escaped him: for he saw Anton take out a huge cigar in the middle of the cadenza and light it up and then, behind the cloud of thick smoke, he had seen the deep furrow darken between his eyes. He finished playing, and looked up at the smoke-shrouded face in expectation of praise, of acknowledgement. But he felt a tremor of fear as well, lest the offspring of his imagination clash with some unforeseeable whim on Anton's part. The face reassured him. He knew the signs of rage well: the darkening of the already dark complexion, the bulging of the already prominent eyes, the bristling of the already fierce beard. But no, the face was calm, almost sad. "Wihan," said the Master – and the cigar smoke emerging from his mouth seemed thicker and more voluminous than usual. "It's a joy to listen to you. Not even Paganini could have played like that." A thrill of joy went through him, but because he was not thinking, because he had been disarmed by joy, he failed to notice Anton's intonation. And then it came: "But Hanousek, we can't use it." The verdict cut him, sharp as a dagger. "Why not, Anton? Don't you like it?" Anton shook his head. "That's not the point. I like it. But – it can't be used in this piece."

"Why not?"

His students had told him Anton was seldom able to answer that question. "I don't know why not," he would always say, "but – no!" He thought in tones and harmonies, not in words, and tones cannot be translated into words.

This time, however, Anton didn't even answer with those familiar words that explained nothing. He said: "But surely you know, Hanousek!" He got up, sat down at the piano, played three bars, looked at him questioningly and then resumed playing. He should have noticed the striking way the Master again emphasized that little sentence, "But surely you know, Hanousek!", which begged to be understood. Was it disappointment that stopped his ears? Instead of listening to what Anton was playing, he started to argue back. "My cadenza is in the spirit of the work! It builds it up to the finale. If the concerto expresses a longing for home, the cadenza is a sobbing air of fulfilment!" Thus he had conceived it. "And it contains transformations of all the main motives, just like the bars that it replaces," he had cried. "They are virtuoso modifications, naturally, but they don't go against the style or the spirit of the concerto...." Anton said nothing. He merely kept on playing, over and over again, a melody that he in his anger and pain and disappointment did not listen to, and the cigar smoke rose to the ceiling like smoke from a burnt offering.

He became more excited. Anton's only response was to begin playing mezzoforte. He grasped the cello and started playing his cadenza again. The mezzoforte became forte. So he bowed his instrument with all his strength, while Anton thundered out the same melody until the greyish-blue column of smoke quivered, rising to the ceiling in an undulating haze.

As he remembered it now, his pain was suffused with shame. They had been like two musical clowns. As he played fortissimo, his fingers began missing notes, he stumbled, and suddenly, in the midst of this absurd ruckus in which the beauty of the concerto was totally lost, the door creaked open and the voice of Anton's wife said, "For the love of God, Anton, have you taken leave of your senses?" He stopped the cadenza abruptly, in the middle, his cello bleating unpleasantly. He was ashamed to play with Anna glaring uncomprehendingly at him. Anton swung round on the piano stool, looking as he usually did when surprised by something unpleasant, his beard jutting up at his wife like the tail of a tomcat poised for a fight. "And dinner is on the table, Anton," said Anna. "Come now, or it'll get cold."

Instead of getting up, Anton reached for his cigar and inhaled. His face grew dark. Then he exhaled the smoke with such vehemence towards his wife that she involuntarily drew back. "For the love of God, Annie, leave us alone!" Yes, it was a growl, like a tomcat spoiling for a fight. "Stick the dinner in the oven and leave us in peace!"

The woman stiffened, her eyebrows raised in astonishment; she pursed her lips, then spun around and closed the door firmly behind her, almost but not quite slamming it. Anton turned to him. "You will not play the cadenza."

His anger and disappointment overruled reason. "Either I play the cadenza or I don't play the concerto."

"You will play the concerto, but without the cadenza."

He stood up and shouted, "It's either-or, Anton."

He knew that only three days previously, Anton had given the secretary of the London Philharmonic Society an ultimatum of his own. Either they consented to an April date, and did not insist on the nineteenth of March when his friend Wihan had another engagement – in which case he would come to conduct the concerto in person – or, if they refused to consent to the change, neither Wihan nor Dvorak would come. In that case, Leo Stern would play the world première of the concerto, but without Dvorak.

Now he braced himself for one of those well-known explosions of Olympian wrath. But it did not come. Anton only placed the cigar in his mouth and inhaled so powerfully that it seemed to be transformed before his eyes into a column of ash. He paled and said in a quiet voice: "Hanousek, you will not play that cadenza. You cannot."

And again he was insensitive, this time to the nuance of meaning in the repetition, and he reacted in a way that was more typical of his friend. "Is that your final word, Anton?" he snapped. He failed even to notice that there was no anger in his friend's prematurely old man's eyes, only sadness, as deep as the tone of a viola.

"You cannot play it, Hanousek...."

Not even the sadness in the voice brought him to his senses. He pushed the cello into its case, got up and left without another word. To the abundant crop of offspring sitting around the table with a steaming tureen on it, from which came the smell of beef soup, he said coldly, "I bid you farewell," put his hat on his head, threw his cape over his arm and almost ran out of the flat.

Sitting alone in the dressing room, after the concert in The Hague, remembering that moment, he slowly, with great effort, managed to steady his shaken nerves. Tonight he had finally, and for the first time, played the B-Minor Cello Concerto, and the finale had so upset him that when he stood to take a bow, he felt certain his legs would collapse. His colleagues had respected his wish to be alone. For a long time, he sat in the silent dressing room. The muffled din of the departing audience had long since died away and the pain awakened by those tones was gradually subsiding. Suddenly, there was a knock on the door. Half an hour had gone by and he guessed that his colleagues – the knocking was discreet – had finally become bold enough to remind him they were going to the café to celebrate.

For him, it would be to forget. To drive out memories with wine. He stood up and shouted, "Coming!", then threw his cape over his shoulders and opened the door. Leo Stern was standing there.

His wound opened once more.

"I'm afraid I'm intruding," said Stern. "You wanted to rest."

"It's nothing, Mr. Stern," he said, without really being aware of what he was saying.

Stern hesitated. His face, with its long whiskers, looked nervous. But he entered the room. "I wanted to – shake your hand," he said. "As student to master. And perhaps.... "

He asked him to sit down.

Stern walked over to an armchair by a small table covered with sheet music. An open bottle of kümmel stood among the papers. Stern placed his top hat on the floor, but did not remove his cape. Looking into his eyes, he said, "Mr. Wihan, today, listening to you, I finally realized that he wrote the concerto for you to play. No, there can be no doubt about it. Today I found the courage to admit it – to myself."

"He wrote the concerto for anyone capable of playing it," he replied, and his wound throbbed.

Stern, however, was shaking his head. "Music like that is not for everyone who can merely play it. It is not an empty carriage that anyone at all can climb aboard and ride to fame. I once thought that myself. But I was wrong."

In Stern's deep Semitic eyes he saw the sadness that he felt himself. He did not reply.

"I wanted to offer you my apologies," said Stern.

"You have no reason to."

"Perhaps there are some – extenuating circumstances. But I do have reason to apologize. You know very well that you were to have played it at the première in London. I know it as well. I knew it then, too, and I shouldn't have accepted when it was offered to me – but at the time I thought the dedication of the concerto to you was merely a formality, that it did not concern the music itself. Today, I realize how foolish that was."

He was finally able to speak. "The Master was satisfied with how you played it."

Stern shook his head and smiled drily. "No, he wasn't. It was just that there was no one else to choose from."

"I read the reviews."

"But you didn't hear me play."

"No."

"He did." Now he laughed out loud. There was still self-deprecation in the laughter. "My dear Mr. Wihan, I can't delude myself any longer. You needn't be polite. I'd be happy if you would only understand me. It was my big chance. When Bayer offered it to me, I jumped at it. I was willing to do anything, even to behave with disregard towards you, towards the man for whom he wrote it in the first place."

"It was – " His voice failed him, he coughed and reached for the bottle of brandy. "It was his decision, not yours." He poured himself a glass.

Someone knocked. When he opened the door, it was Anton.

"May I come in?"

"Of course."

He entered, his bowler tipped jauntily on one side, as always. He took it off in the hall. They went into the study.

"Hanousek," he said. "On April the eleventh, we're performing the B-Minor Cello Concerto again in Prague – in the Rudolfinum. Will you play?"

But the rage within him had not yet cooled. "Without my cadenza?"

"Let's not start that again. You know very well you can't play it."

"I can play it. I don't know whether Stern can."

"Stern couldn't play it if his – " He stopped in time. "But you know what I mean."

"And you know what I mean."

"Hanousek! You're my closest friend. Stern played well in London. Even though some details here and there – well, yes, let's face it: I would like to have heard the whole concerto played differently. But one can't be too choosy and one has to be grateful to have found anyone at all to play it. But you – "

"The English reviewers liked it."

"The English don't love music, or even understand it very well, they merely respect it." He reached nervously into his pocket, pulled out a large cigar and lit it, inhaling intensely.

But it still hurt, terribly. A blow like that, after all those years of friendship. An insult. He still couldn't understand it.

"Hanousek! Play it for me! Please! As I wrote it."

Oh, it would be such a satisfaction! Stern must have truly botched it. Then too, he felt the longing, that special longing of an old cellist, the sensation that resides in the fingers and flows from there to the heart. It was such a beautiful concerto. Magnificent. There was not another – or lamentably few – like it in all the world of music, and who knew if there would ever be again.

"You know, I got the idea for it when I was listening to a cello concerto by a colleague of mine, Herbert. He taught the cello in Mrs. Thurber's school and I tell you, Hanousek, the man had written some fiendishly clever passages. He had the cello accompanied by three trombones! Well, that's the Americans for you. They can score a concerto for zither and steam whistle or some such bird-brained combination. But it wasn't a bad concerto. It stayed at the back of my mind for a while and then – you know, I didn't know which way to turn. I was dreadfully homesick for Vysoka, but then there was the music of America, not so much what was being composed as what you could hear all around you – and that magnificent land. But there's no place like home, is there? So I said to myself: what about my old friend Wihan? I certainly owe him something. I was always writing things at the behest of any concertmaster, not to mention publisher – and what about Wihan? I know, the damned cello grumbles in the lower registers and bleats in the upper, but the middle, Hanousek – why, it's the very embodiment of longing. Those instruments – you know, the English horn, the French horns, the cello – anyway, I sat down, the inspiration came, and I began to write. That was at my apartment on Seventeenth Street, in New York. The damned Negroes kept creeping into it but otherwise, in spirit, I was in Vysoka – with her. When I was in New York working on it, Hanousek, I was back home faster than any steamship could take me. But then, of course, no sooner had I actually got home – only a month later, to the day – than she was dead. I may be a miserable sinner but I know what fidelity is! I know, Hanousek. So you see, I sat down in Vysoka and rewrote the ending to the cello concerto. I wrote it for Josephine – in her memory – "

Anton had written it for him — and yet not for him alone. That much was now clear. And he, a sinner more miserable than pious old Anton, had finally to learn generosity of spirit.

"Very well, Anton, I'll play it for you, without my cadenza."

A joyous puff of smoke flew from the cigar.

But then, the next day and the third day, he was suddenly overcome with anxiety. It wasn't stage fright. He knew stage fright. This was anxiety. Pain.

"I'm sorry, Anton, but I can't do it. I'm not feeling well, and the time is too short. Let Stern come and do it."

Anton looked at him with his childlike eyes. "Still bearing a grudge, Hanousek? That's not nice, not between friends."

He began to be afraid of his own fear. To drive it out, he said sardonically: "It's not me. You're the one who's bearing a grudge, because you still won't let me play the cadenza, will you?"

"I can't."

"Then send a telegram to Stern."

They pasted corrections on all the posters in Prague, as they had in London. Stern, the one-time chemist, did what he could, and only the indestructible beauty of Anton's music saved the concerto.

"What's done is done," he said to Stern, waving his hand. But the pain remained inside him. "As you can see, I'm playing it now."

"And I'm glad you are. You have no idea how glad I am. He suffered too, you know. I don't only mean," and he laughed his dry laugh again, "that for three weeks he had to listen to me and drill me day after day, and all the while it must have been obvious that the best I could do would only be a shadow of what he actually wrote. Do you mind if I smoke?"

He shook his head, and as Stern reached for his cigar case and took out a large cigar, he poured himself another shot of kümmel. Absurdly, it occurred to him that he'd been doing this for thirty years, perhaps more. Whenever he felt miserable, whenever he felt good. But then, how many of Anton's beautiful woodwind harmonies had sailed out of the darkness of the spirit on waves of tobacco smoke?

Stern's thoughts seemed to have followed his. "I didn't know him then. I didn't know he was a slave to nicotine. At our first rehearsal, for the world première in London, I brought him a Havana cigar. One like this," and he held up an enormous roll of tobacco leaves, placed it in his mouth and struck a match. "And do you know what he said? Not 'Thank you, Mr. Stern,' but 'Only one?' And he wasn't joking. He was genuinely disappointed, like a child."

Despite the pain, Hanousek laughed.

"Next day, I made up for it. I came with a whole box. Twenty-five cigars. By the end of the day, there were only three left. It was my fault, I botched the piece rather badly. On the evening of the third day, I worked up my courage and announced that I was giving up. I said I would rather play the B-Minor than anything else in the world, but I couldn't have the murder of such a magnificent piece of music on my conscience. And do you know what he said? He actually paid me a compliment. 'Shut up, Stern,' he said. 'You're not murdering anything, you're just doing it some slight violence. The problem is you don't have it in your fingers just yet. It's still mostly in here,' and he pointed to his heart. And miserable as I was, my own heart gave a little leap. 'The fingers are a little skittish, as they might be after five glasses of slivovice, but they can be coerced. It would be far worse not to have it here,' and he pointed again to the left side of his vest. 'So just shut up about it, damn it, and play it again.' Then he sent his pretty daughter to the tobacconist's and we went on playing until the smoke grew so thick we could hardly see the notes."

Suddenly, Stern became serious. "I'm sorry. I didn't come here to tell you amusing anecdotes. It's just that whenever I remember him, I have to smile, though he tortured me like a Grand Inquisitor...."

Oddly enough, Stern's amusement did not bother him. It was as though the aroma of hibiscus candies had permeated the pain.

"I know he suffered because of your quarrel," Stern said. "He mentioned it several times during those three weeks. 'You can't understand it, Mr. Stern,' he told me. 'You're not from these parts. But Hanousek – the things he and I have been through together! He should have understood what I was trying to tell him. I'm not going to trumpet it to the world – I can only play it. All my life, I've been playing it, Mr. Stern.' 'What, Herr Doctor?' I ventured to ask. But I asked in vain. 'You won't know – and you needn't know, Mr. Stern. So let's try it again. From the beginning. And please, pay attention to the dynamics, and to those semitone descents. You know, they should sound like someone sighing....' He lit another cigar and I sighed and sighed, and indeed, I had good reason to."

He stopped, smothered the stump of his cigar in the ashtray and asked, "You don't mind if I ask what your quarrel was all about?"

He knew, even though the significance of the quarrel continued to elude him. But he did not tell Stern that.

"It was about the cadenza I wrote for it," he said. "It was as appropriate for that piece as – well, as a bull in a china shop. So you have nothing to apologize to me for. I deserved it. And you deserved to play the première. You didn't try to ruin his magnificent allegro with an exercise in *Fingergeläufigkeit.*"

"I didn't have to," said Stern gently. "I ruined it, even without the cadenza."

"He was satisfied."

"He's a kind person." Stern looked at him, in his eyes the wisdom of someone who has learned his limitations and is grateful to have been granted a share, at least, of glory within those limitations. "Do you know, Mr. Wihan, Wagner was a genius. A giant. But as far as I'm concerned, I would trade all of the Nibelungen, including Siegfried, for that single concerto."

"Anton, are you still angry?" he had asked him when, long afterwards, they had met in front of St. Ignatius's Church. In the meantime – after a long period when he couldn't bring himself to look at it – he had gone back to the score of the cello concerto. Note by note, he had reiterated those fateful forty-eight bars that he had wanted to replace with his cadenza. He had already done this once. When he had been rehearsing for the performance – which never took place – he had come up with several ideas of his own right in the first movement. At bars six and thirteen, he had suggested a figuration of sextuplets instead of Anton's sixteenth notes. Anton had liked the idea, had taken out his legendary eraser, rubbed his own version out energetically and rewritten it. This encouraged him and he suggested another change at bar fifteen. Here the eraser hesitated, Anton balked and they compromised. Anton's willingness to entertain changes was one of the reasons he was so surprised, and ultimately so infuriated, by his strong opposition to the cadenza in the third movement. It had, after all, been appropriate, been blessed by tradition. It was logical.

But later, when he studied the score that, in the end, Leo Stern had brought to life on the podium, he was no longer blinded by emotion and he could recognize easily what he had been unable to hear during the duet between the indignant piano and the angry cello in Anton's smoke-filled study. He saw that the brief violin solo in the section he had wanted to replace was a direct quotation from a song Anton had written years before. It was not a recapitulation of one of the concerto's main themes, like the preceding passage for clarinet. "No balm is there, no sweet relief For this poor smitten heart; For love denied is sad despair...."

He began again, played the entire cello part several times until he had figured that out as well. In the second part of the adagio, there was a paraphrase of the melody from the conclusion of the allegro. It was inconspicuous, melodically it fit the context perfectly, but it was unmistakably a paraphrase.

And so he knew why Anton had insisted the music remain untouched, for the sake of this melody, even though he did not understand why it was important to him. The melody meant something special to Anton. He was not in principle against making changes, but he had been adamantly opposed to any change in the allegro, in the last movement. Certainly not because the clarinets would have repeated the main theme, but because this would have eliminated the single repetition of a song that meant something to Anton. What it meant, he did not know. How blinded he had been. And Anton had tried so hard, in his own peculiar way, to reply to his "Why?" on the strings of the piano.

"I was never angry, Hanousek. But you simply couldn't have played that cadenza there. I'm sorry."

They both found this mutual apology humorous, and laughed. "You don't have to apologize."

"Nor do you."

They almost embraced each other. "And I'm going to play the concerto next January in The Hague."

"Without the cadenza?"

"You can rest assured: without the cadenza. And anyway, you'd still never allow it."

"You're right, I wouldn't," he said. He looked at the floor. "But you surely must know why not."

He knew, but he didn't understand.

And when at last he performed the concerto, he was filled with a nervousness he had never known before. As before, not stage fright. Pain. Anxiety. It took all his strength to finish the concerto and so he had asked his colleagues, who were setting off for a drink, to let him rest for half an hour afterwards. And now he said farewell to Stern, reassuring him that he bore him no grudge – which was true – and had never borne him one – a lie. It was a lie because when he had heard that Anton had written Burger, the day after their argument, to say he was willing to come to London on the nineteenth of March to conduct the world première of the cello concerto, it was the most intense blow to his pride since his student days, when they had chosen Petrik instead of him to play the solo at the graduation concert. And he still vividly remembered, after that letter to Burger, waiting in a wet Prague February snowstorm, watching them unload huge trunks covered with foreign stickers from a carriage, and seeing a tall Jew in a beaver-skin coat stride into the brightly lit hotel. He didn't know whether he regarded the interloper with hatred or with pain. It was something of both.

Stern took his leave with a cordial handshake. Perhaps he was unaware that the wound had not quite healed. "All the same, I'm a fortunate man, and now that I know we're friends, I feel all the more fortunate," he said. "How many failed chemists have the good luck to play the première performance of the greatest cello concerto of all time, and on top of it, under the baton of the Master himself?"

He watched him go, and the lights in the gilded corridor of the Hague concert hall turned in Stern's luxurious top hat.

A year or so later, he was to play the concerto in Paris under Mengelberg. He accepted, but was again crippled by apprehension. It was the same kind he had experienced in The Hague, but more intense this time. He knew now why he could not play the cadenza, but still did not understand why a song meant so much to Anton. He did not understand! He turned the engagement down.

Several times after that he declined to play the concerto, and ultimately stopped making solo appearances. He could not bring himself to. He did not understand.

The procession arrived at the National Theatre in Prague and halted. He was walking in the second row, right behind the relatives of the deceased. The widow wore a black veil and her face was invisible. From the ramp of the theatre came the sounds of Anton's Requiem Mass. Otylia, supported by her husband, sobbed inconsolably. He too felt he could not keep back his tears. Dear friend! Dear, dear Anton! Forgive me for not understanding!

Requiem aeternam dona ... Domine....

12   :C): I MUST NOT BE IMPERTINENT

"LOOK, IT'S BURNING!" Otylia called and she pointed into the distance, raising a sun-tanned arm, bare to just below the elbow, the skin smooth and soft. He longed to touch it, but lacked the courage.

He was glad, though, to be given a topic of conversation, for not only was he too shy to take the girl by the hand, but he found he couldn't think of a single thing to talk about.

They were standing on a treeless hilltop. Below them, across a wood that grew farther down the slope and stretched all the way to the meandering banks of the Turkey River, they could see the Spillville valley, fields of golden wheat, blue islands of wild asters, the red village rooftops and beyond that, the far side of the valley rising again to meet the sky. And yes, a low cloud of grey-blue smoke did indeed seem to be suspended over the rooftops.

The first time he had seen her – she was sitting at the kitchen table of the flat in Prague, writing, her eyes red from crying – he had felt the first stirring of a sensation most young men experience on encountering a miracle. The miracle had dark blonde hair tied at the back with a red ribbon, a round face and grey eyes. As they walked into the room, the Master asked sternly: "Are you finished, Otylia?"

"I have six more to do," replied the miracle in a high, child's voice.

"Let me see." The Master picked up the scribbler and examined her work. He couldn't resist looking over the Master's shoulder.

On the lined page, he read:

> *92. I must not be impertinent.*
> *93. I must not be impertinent.*
> *94. I must not be impertinent.*

"And what about that blotch there?" asked the Master.

"I'll do it over again."

"Never mind." The Master was gruff. *"I can see you've tried to be neat. And forget the last six: you've done enough."* Then, in a completely different tone of voice, *"And now, children, I've brought something for you."*

From a paper bag he took a bundle of liquorice sticks, and handed them out to the children who had crowded around him.

"Thank you, Father," said the miracle.

"This is Otylia, our eldest," said the Master, rather proudly. *"Ottie, this is Mr. Kovarik."* The miracle held out her hand to him and smiled, looking directly into his eyes. Her teeth were miraculously white.

"A fine-looking lass, eh, Redskin?" said the Master, praising his own opus. *"Would you believe she'll be only fourteen come June?"*

But miracles exist outside of time.

"Mr. Kovarik is from America. He's a student at the Prague conservatory, Ottie, and he'll be teaching your mother and me English over the holidays. If you behave, he'll teach you too."

"That's not a fire," he said, delighted to have something to talk about, afraid that the subject wouldn't last long. "That's a special kind of flower. It's growing on the hill above the village. I don't think there's a name for it in Czech" – they spoke in Czech since her English was still too uncertain for them to be able to carry on any kind of a conversation – "but in English it's called a pasque-flower. When the first settlers came to Iowa forty years ago, it looked like a prairie fire to them, too."

"But prairie fires sometimes do happen, don't they?"

"Of course they do. Especially during a hot summer like this one."

"And do they burn everything up?"

"Oh no. The farmers have learned how to control them. And the river can stop them too.... "

He didn't know what to say next, nor did he particularly want to talk about prairie fires, except perhaps symbolically. The miracle he had first encountered a year ago had a peculiar quality: it was lasting.

"I'm awfully hot," said Otylia, undoing a button at the neck of her dress. "Let's go wading in the river to cool off."

"I em eh gerl," she had said, and he corrected her pronunciation.

"I'm a girl."

He had joined the family in the country for the summer, and he and Otylia were sitting at a table under the linden tree. The Master was off on one of his afternoon rambles in the woods around Vysoka. The distant smell of moss and pine gum reached them faintly. The Master's wife was picking apricots in the orchard.

"And now, use the second person, Miss Otylia." He was a violinist, not a language teacher. "You are...."

"You air eh boy."

"Well, okay," he said. He wasn't exactly pleased at being called a boy at the age of twenty-three, but he reminded himself that so far the miracle had a rather poor vocabulary. "And now in the third person: He is a...."

"He is eh men," said Otylia, flashing a glance towards the summerhouse. Reluctantly, he looked too. Behind the decorative wooden lattice-work he could see the gloomy face of Josef Suk, the young violinist. He was supposed to be copying a score for the Master, who had locked the door on him, and he was clearly not doing this, for he sat staring sullenly towards the two of them under the linden tree.

A faintly malicious smile crossed Otylia's face, but she suppressed it quickly and said, "She is eh voomin. It is eh taibel."

"A table, a woman," he corrected her. He wanted to take the inkbottle from the table and hurl it against the lattice-work, where it would smash, ruining everything the amanuensis had done that day.

"What do you call me, Miss Otylia?" he said, strictly.

The grey eyes stared at him until his heart was gripped. But the eyes were unknowable.

"I am a – what, Miss Otylia?" he encouraged. "A...."

"Butcher?" she replied, uncertainly, and between her eyes a miraculous miniature of her father's furrow appeared.

"Teacher," he said, irritated. "I am a teacher and you are my – my what, Miss Otylia?"

"Girl," she said happily.

He let it stand. The delight spilled over him.

As they walked through the woods towards the Turkey River, he thought of their first meeting.

"Otylia, why did you have to – " He paused. "I hope you don't think I'm being too bold.... " In the year that had passed, the only sign of progress had been the fact that he no longer called her Miss Otylia.

"You're never too bold, at least not to me," she said pointedly.

"But I am," he said, and he realized how desperately timid he was.

"You could have fooled me," she replied. "What was it you wanted to ask?"

"Just a small thing. Do you remember the time we first met, when the Master invited me home?"

"Father? I've forgotten all about it."

It was as if she poked an open wound with a nail. Despondently, he continued. "You were writing out some lines for punishment: 'I must not be impertinent.' "

"I've had to do that hundreds of times. Father can be a real ogre when he wants."

"But what did you do to make him punish you?"

The furrow appeared again. "Let me see, that must have been when I wanted to go boating with Matej Brukner and my parents wouldn't let me."

"And were you impertinent to them?"

"Yes, I was."

"How?"

The furrow deepened. "How?" She thought for a moment. "I'm not telling."

"Why not?"

"You needn't know everything."

As if he knew anything. He knew nothing.

It was only a few weeks ago that he had arrived back in Spillville, proudly bringing with him Dvorak and the whole family to visit his home town for the summer. The first night, the miracle appeared in the doorway when they were playing a polka. He saw her from the podium of Rothenberger's large hall, above the heads of the spinning couples, the dark blonde hair, and again something happened to him that had never happened before: he lost the beat. Uncle Frank, his cornet still pressed to his lips, turned to him abruptly. He recovered at once but her unexpected presence made the song seem endless. Without being aware of it, he increased the tempo again and his uncle's cornet described another angry arc. If only she'd stay! If only she'd stay!

When the polka was finally over, he said urgently, "Uncle Frank, can you do without me for a while?"

Uncle Frank looked intently at him and then stared across the hall thick with smoke.

"I see," he said. "And what do you want us to play when you're gone? A polka? A reel?"

"Make it a slow waltz, Uncle Frank!" he called out, already pushing his way across the dance floor, through the perspiring crowd of men and women, straight towards her.

"Otylia! What are you doing here?"

"I've come to pick up some beer for Father and ... " – a blush appeared on her cheeks, he thought – "I wanted to hear you play. I've never heard you with a dance band before."

"Well, that's – " He didn't know what it was. "A surprise," he added weakly.

Uncle Frank started playing the Blue Danube Waltz and the floorboards creaked as the couples began to sway and spin to the music.

"May I?" he blurted out.

"I don't know," she said uneasily. "Father will get into a terrible snit if there's no head on his beer."

But she spread her arms, and the dress stretched tightly across her small breasts.

Shyly, he placed his arm around her waist, leaving more than a foot between the blue linen dress and his sweat-soaked shirt. But with his left hand he could feel her hot skin beneath the linen, crisscrossed by some kind of laces. Someone bumped him from behind.

"But just this one," she said. "I hate to think what he'll do to me if the foam is gone."

"He won't do anything," he said, unconvincingly. Someone else bumped into him from behind and he felt the softness of her breasts against his chest, but only for an instant. "I'll go home with you," he said fervently, "and tell him it was my fault."

"That's all I'd need!"

She danced like a – like a – he stepped on her shoe.

"Excuse me! I didn't mean to." What kind of nonsense am I babbling?

"You'll have to hold me tighter."

Imperceptibly, he increased the pressure around her waist. Again, he felt her breasts nudge his chest. This time he did not draw back. The conversation was over. They spun wordlessly to the rhythm of the waltz and the shuffling of the crowd.

As soon as the number was over, she said firmly that she must go home.

"I'll go with you," he said in the doorway.

"Don't you have to play?"

"No, I don't."

He followed her outside. The stairs led down the outside of the building, a stone construction with a wooden second storey added as an afterthought. The moon was suspended in the sky and the spire of St. Wenceslaus's Church rose over Spillville like a black cut-out against the shimmering stardust. The pungent aroma of manure and the smell of wild roses reached them on a breath of air. They hurried down the wooden steps. The strains of the polka, and the din of couples leaping and pounding in unison on the pinewood floor, were muted by the wooden walls of the dance hall.

They found themselves on the road. The dance-hall sounds grew fainter and old Voppe passed them, carrying a ladder. He was light-ing the kerosene streetlamps, and had strung a path of golden light along Main Street right to the brick house belonging to Schmidt, the tin-smith, where Otylia was living for the summer. Her shoes echoed along the brick sidewalk.

"You can't go all the way home with me," she said. "Father knows you're supposed to be playing tonight, and it's too early."

As usual, he could think of nothing to say. The shoes tapped on the sidewalk. A dog barked. The leather in his boots squeaked.

"Is your work going well?" she asked.

"What work?"

"Copying Father's symphony, what else?"

"I'm almost finished copying the Largo."

The thought of his work as her father's secretary brought with it a memory of the little summer-house in Vysoka with its decorative lattice-work, and that other lovestruck amanuensis locked inside it. "Are you writing to someone back home, Otylia?" he blurted.

Her eyes flashed silver in the moonlight. Under a streetlamp the silver was permutated into gold, then extinguished.

"Guess!" said the miracle.

His brain, like his tongue, felt paralysed. His boots creaked, and from the rooftop came the caterwauling of a lovelorn tomcat. They walked without speaking, followed by the cries of the night animals, the squeaking of his boots and, in the distance, the fading, rhythmic beat of stamping couples in the dance hall. A streetlamp illuminated the brick façade of the Schmidt home.

"Is it Josef Suk?"

Otylia stopped, smiled secretly and raised a finger to her lips. But suddenly the smile vanished and she cried, "Ohmygod!"

He was alarmed. "What's the matter?"

"The beer!"

And hitching her skirt above her ankles she turned and ran, leaving him to watch her slender calves flashing in the silver alchemy of the night.

He ran after her and they were soon back at Rothenberger's dance hall. Otylia looked around, then ran up to the seventh stair and lifted away a panel. The blind pig had functioned reliably. The jug was there. But the foam....

She stared aghast into the jug. Inside the dance hall, Uncle Frank's cornet sneered and slid into a reel and the floorboards shuddered under the dancers' wild feet.

She ran for home. He ran after her. "Otylia, I – "

"Leave me alone! It's all your fault."

"I'll explain it to your father."

"What is there to explain? The foam is gone and he'll know why if you try to explain anything to him."

"Why should he ...?"

They were standing in front of the house. She turned towards him. "Because he's not as dumb as you are." And she disappeared inside with the jug. He waited. A few moments later, he heard an explosion of Vesuvian rage.

Poor miracle. But he wasn't that dumb. He was only terribly shy.

On the branches of an elm tree, a scarlet tanager was hopping about excitedly and singing with such fury that it seemed, in fact, to be scolding someone or something.

Otylia grasped his hand and stared wide-eyed. "Ohmygod!"

He looked towards the clearing. She dropped to the grass and pulled him down with her. Carefully, he parted the bushes. There was the Master seated at a large stump with his sleeves rolled up, scribbling notes on a piece of paper, rubbing them out, writing again, almost in time to the rhythm of the scolding bird, all the while puffing on a large cigar. Beside him in the grass lay a summer jacket and, on top of it, a red rosary.

As he lay there his hips were touching Otylia's and he felt himself grow hot and stiff.

"Father's got an inspiration," she whispered. "A good thing he didn't see us. That would have been something."

"What would he do?"

"He'd give us what for."

"Why?"

Why in the name of heaven, he cried to himself, do I have to ask such stupid questions! Neither Otylia's mother nor father would have approved of her wandering in the woods with him, he knew that. He also knew that he was supposed to be copying out the symphony and that Otylia should have been with Emily Kapinos, embroidering pillows – but Emily could keep a secret and he could catch up with his work on the symphony later that night.

"Because we'd be interfering with his inspiration," she said with a trace of sarcasm. "Father's a little crazy, Joe, didn't you know?"

It was the first time she had called him by his first name. It intensified his passion. He tried desperately to recall what a priest from the Knights of the Cross had once advised him to do, when he had confessed lust for a fellow student at the Prague conservatory. He had seen the girl grasp her cello between her legs, although she was wearing a long skirt, and not even her abominable playing had been enough to drive his impure thoughts away. And so, surrounded by the yellow-green shadows of the woods, the smell of grass and wild sunflower blooms, the cry of an irate tanager and the sensuous soughing of the breeze in the high elms, he forced himself to recall the stench of the toilet that would seep through to the reading room of the Urbanek Publishing House in Prague.

Suddenly a hand snatched the Chicago Czech weekly away from him, a bushy beard appeared and a huge, friendly voice said: "Well now, Redskin, they tell me you can speak English."

He was so astonished that he replied involuntarily in that language: "That's right, sir."

The Master turned to face the group: Urbanek, Kaan, Prochazka, all present for their regular late afternoon chat about music. He had come here for a different purpose: Urbanek always had on hand a supply of contraband Czech-American newspapers secretly brought in from Paris because they could not be imported into Bohemia legally.

"Look at him!" said the Master. "A real American! He can speak English! Why didn't someone tell me before now?" He turned back to him and said slowly, in an English of sorts, "You shall teaching me. We shall go to America!"

On the way to the Dvoraks' apartment, the Master offered him an enormous cigar. "I don't smoke," he stammered.

"You don't smoke? Are you a man?"

It was not long before he began to doubt it himself, for when they arrived at the house he saw the Master's daughter copying out those lines about not being impertinent, and he was overcome by a sense of his own inadequacy.

That evening, as he sat over an untouched plate of potatoes and cottage cheese, his landlady, Mrs. Andrsova, scolded him. "Mr. Kovarik! We'll be sending you back to America as skinny as the skeleton out front." *Mrs. Andrsova was absolute mistress of a baroque tenement house with the marvellous, macabre name "At the Sign of the Golden Skeleton".* "Your mother will think we tried to starve you to death in Prague. Come on now, eat up and no excuses."

For a long time he sat over his plate of potatoes and dreamed about the girl writing out her lines.

It was no use. All thoughts led to....

"Ottie! You – you.... "

"You – you what?"

"You've never called me Joe before."

"And you've never called me Ottie," she said and flicked a ladybug off her nose.

Nearby, in the clearing, the Master's pencil snapped audibly. "Damn it!"

"You see?" remarked the miracle. "And if I so much as say 'gosh' at home, he raises the roof."

She was whispering through pink lips.

Her face was near his. His shyness died a glorious death.

They stopped kissing only when the Master's boots squeaked in the clearing. Through a gap in the bushes, they saw him get up, stretch, smile broadly and hum something to himself. He began to conduct with his hands while gazing up into the tree where the scarlet tanager was still scolding. He chuckled, and began whistling loudly along with the bird. It was like a duel in sound.

They were lying side by side and his arm was around her shoulder, but even in the ecstasy of the moment he wondered if he would be able to conceal his altogether visible passion if the Master were to start walking in their direction and found them. The Master, however, bent down, picked up his rosary, wound the beads around his fingers, then sank to his knees and turned his face to the heavens, to his God, radiant above the countryside. The red beads slipped

through his fingers, as bright in the sunlight as the berries of a mountain ash.

In the presence of such communion with the Author of the Ten
Commandments, and with his hand on the warm shoulder of the un-
derage miracle, he was overpowered by a sense of great sin. He
took his arm away. Everything was his fault. Desperately he tried
to recall the theme of the symphony, but it would not come to him.

"Joe … Josie," said the miracle, and then clapped her hand over
her mouth to suppress the sudden laughter that threatened to disturb
her father in his communion with his Creator.

"What's so funny?" he whispered.

"Nothing. It's just that you and my aunt have the same name."

"You mean the Countess?"

"Aunt Josie – Jo." And she giggled again.

He realized that speech could be a scherzo. A scherzo capriccioso.
So he took courage and said, "Do-si-do – "

"Around we go," said the miracle.

He couldn't think of another rhyme. So he just smiled at her. But
she closed her eyes and whispered, "Don't let me go," and held up
her face to be kissed.

Miracles cannot be gainsaid.

In the clearing, the Master stood up and slid the rosary into his
pocket. They froze. The notepaper disappeared into a second pocket
and, whistling loudly, he set off at a brisk pace in the opposite direction, leaving his pencil, broken into two pieces, on the stump.
The tanager, which had been silent for a while, protested indignantly.

They walked side by side through the forest, holding hands, and he
experienced a delight that not even music could give him. The golden,
early evening light was tinged with pale green, tanagers flitted through
the trees like living rubies. He thought he could hear the Master's
muted strings in the sighing of the elms.

"Father is a good man," she said, her voice sounding like a small
bell among the muted strings, "and he just can't tell a lie. Sometimes
he shouts and makes out he's a terrible tyrant. Like in Vysoka, remember? When he locked up Suk in the – " She stopped abruptly,

her cheeks suddenly the colour of the tanager. "I think I won't call you Joe any more. I think I might call you J.J."

"Why?"

"Because of – well, because your initials are J.J. – J.J. Kovarik."

A rabbit jumped out of the grass in front of them and bounded away in terror. Otylia was startled, then laughed. He squeezed her hand. She returned the pressure, and he felt emboldened.

"I want you to tell me why you were impertinent."

"I can't."

"Why not?"

"It's nasty."

"What's nasty about it?"

"Tattling on Father when he's such a nice man. I shouldn't have mentioned it in the first place."

"I don't understand," he said. "You say your father didn't do anything nasty, but it would be nasty to tell me what it was, is that it?"

"Well, yes. Because it would be – embarrassing."

"Why don't you tell me in English? Then it won't seem so embarrassing."

"Well all right," she said in less than miraculous English, "I wanted to go on boat – little boat."

"I wanted to go rowing," he said, pedantically.

"I wanted to go rowing with Matej Brukner and Father said, 'No!' and I said, 'I'm forty– ' "

"Fourteen."

"Fourteen. And Father said, 'That's little!' "

"You mean too young?"

"Yes, 'You are too young,' said Father. And I said.... " She broke off a blade of grass and began to chew on it. "Well – " and then she impatiently reverted to Czech. "I said that Mother was only twelve when he started courting her."

"What!"

"Well, he wasn't really *courting*," said Otylia. "So I suppose it was impertinent of me to say that. But he *did* start giving her piano lessons when she was only twelve. To her and Aunt Josie. Aunt Josie was sixteen at the time."

They came out of the woods. In the distance, they could see the Master striding resolutely towards the church.

13 :C): EXODUS

"WELL, MAESTRO DVORAK, what did I have? A wife an' six kids, that was all, the oldest a lad of twelve, then there was four girls, and the youngest boy was two. The first one, he was born before they abolished serfdom. I had a cottage my father left me, and one cow. A horse? No sir. And two acres of swampy ground. Not enough to make a livin' on, was it now, Maestro? But I'm sure you know what I'm talking about. You may be a world-famous composer an' all now, and we're lucky to have you visiting with us in Spillville for the summer, but I reckon your father had to do – what d'you call it – forced labour – am I right? And even when they finally freed the serfs in '48, I still had to work on the manor to make ends meet. After all, six hungry mouths to feed and times were hard. No sir, it wasn't easy. Then Tony Klimesh, he went off to America and two years later he wrote a letter back to the parish priest, said he was a real farmer over in the United States now, with a hundred acres all of his own. Now wasn't that somethin'? And back home in Kriz, he only had half an acre more'n me. Well, he said everything was going like a house on fire, the air just as fresh as it was in Kriz, wild game galore to fill his larder and no gamekeepers snoopin' about, lookin' for poachers. Tony, he said he'd settled in with a bunch of Bohemians and they'd called the place Spillville and it was in the state of Iowa. So the priest reads me the letter – well, you know, I could barely read or write – and it was a bad year, the harvest wasn't worth spit, looked like we might starve. So I says to myself, Franta Valenta, my boy, I says, this is it. If Tony Klimesh can do it, so can you. So I sold the cottage and the cow and the field, and I bought a cart and an old nag from the manor stables and we set off for America.

"Well, of course, the first thing was we had to get to Germany, to the sea. Hamburg was where most folks left from. So we packed a few pots and pans, flour, potatoes and the main thing was the feather comforters. Yes sir, real goose down. The wife, God rest her soul, she wouldn't leave without 'em, and I don't blame her. She spent most of her life puttin' those feathers together, started when she was still a little girl, for her hope chest, you know. Well, took us six weeks to get to Hamburg, by the time we got there it was fall and the cold rains'd set in. But we made it with nobody gettin' sick, so I sold the wagon and the old nag for cash on the line and – what did I get for her? A couple of cents, maybe. But the problem now was how to get on the boat.

"In those days they didn't have no – what d'you call 'em – schedules, nothin' like that. The captains just hung around port till they shipped a full load of cargo and passengers, so they never knew before they left where they'd be goin', and when they finally made up their minds, it was accordin' to the freight, not the passengers. So there we set, in Hamburg, Maestro, for three months, before we got a boat. That was early January, and she was called the Wenderman. I'll never forget her because by the Jesus we had some hard times on that boat. Of course, in the meantime I found work on the Hamburg docks so we had money for the tickets, at least. In those days, they charged twenty-five bucks per couple, and up to four kids for the same amount. The two extra kids cost another five and the money I made barely covered it, sir, with a few cents left over for the trip. Y'see, I figured once I got to America I'd make some more, buy us a horse and wagon and head up here to Spillville. Ha! I had no idea the distances over here.

"I don't suppose you know what them old freighters was like. You came over on an ocean liner. Well yes, they had ocean liners in those days too, only they were sailin' ships and even so, a ticket cost ten times as much as we paid for our old tub, if not more. Most folks just couldn't afford it. We had to settle for what we could get. Besides, as far as I know, ocean liners only take on people, but the Wenderman was at least thirty years old and was built to carry cargo, and maybe livestock, but not people. There weren't no cabins at all, not even those big cabins for more than one family. All in all there was about three hundred passengers, and all they did for us was build a bunch of triple-decker bunks down in the steerage – no straw, no mattresses, nothing. We slept on hard boards. The chests with our comforters were stowed away somewheres in the hold along with the cargo, and anyways, the bunks were too narrow for featherbeds. The kids slept three to a bed, me and the wife slept on another.

"I'm telling you, Maestro, the Wenderman creaked and groaned so bad she always seemed just on the point of crackin' up. And the smell! After a while, of course, you stopped payin' any notice, but later, when I was workin' as a stevedore in the United States, I could always tell a ship full of immigrants a mile away – by the stench! The whole way over, Maestro, nobody washed. In the first place there was nowhere to do it, and in the second place there was barely enough drinkin' water for two cups a day per head. Now you couldn't waste that for washing, could you? Far as latrines went, there was only one, a rickety little shack back near the stern, and it reeked like a manure pile back there. Only one toilet, Maestro, for three hundred people.

"Well, if we hadn't been at sea, that might've done. Trouble was, a lot of people came down with seasickness right away. Mostly they ran up on deck when they felt it coming, but some couldn't make it, and there was always somebody in the latrine, heaving their biscuits. And even worse, Maestro, when we ran into a storm, almost everybody got sick, but the deckhands locked both the hatches so nobody'd get washed overboard, and with them shut, it was dark as a coal-bin at midnight down there. A few candles, maybe, but they ran out pretty fast. It was awful down there, everyone terrified, the women shrieking and the children wailing, beside themselves with fear, people gettin' flung out their bunks, rollin' around on the floor, and I don't need to tell you what it was they was rollin' in because just about everybody was bein' sick all over the place. Young, old, no exceptions.

"I remember prayin' all night long but sometimes I was so scared I couldn't even muster a prayer, and to this day, Maestro, I don't know how we came through it without crackin' up. Mind you, some did.

"Anyways, when the storm was over the women would scrub down the floor with sea water, but of course there wasn't no soap and don't forget the old tub had probably carried thousands and thousands of people across already, all of them tossing their biscuits, so the smell of all that sick was soaked right into the wood.

"Most of the time, though, it didn't even take a storm. The food was so bad I swear a dog wouldn't look at it. Sea could be like glass and soon as the kids touched the food, they'd start bringin' up. Half-rotten salt pork, gave you such an awful thirst you could've drunk sea water. Mouldy beans, weevils in the flour and the women had to do all the cookin' on tiny little stoves on deck. They had to cook in shifts.

"Well, it was no surprise, Maestro, when people started dyin' like flies. I reckon one out of every five never made it to America and ended up gettin' tossed overboard in a sack. At first, the captain would always hold a little funeral service with prayers and we'd all join in, but pretty soon there was somebody passin' away practically every day and those of us that were left felt so rotten and miserable we could hardly crawl up on deck for the funeral. So finally the sailors, they'd just stuff the corpses in sacks, slide them overboard, and no one said prayers except maybe the family if they were still on their feet. And if anyone in the family was still alive.

"Two of our children died, Maestro. First little Antonia, she was six and she was so weak from throwin' up I expect she died of hunger. Then two-year-old Karel. No one knew what it was he died of because there was no doctor on the ship. Poor little creatures. When I think of them, floatin' out there in the middle of the ocean.... But I hear you've lost children yourself, Maestro, so you know how it feels.

"And that was mostly what drove people crazy. They'd set out for America with three, four kids and all of them poor little things would end up in the ocean, and sometimes the husband or wife too. There were times we had to tie a mother or father down to their beds so they wouldn't go rushin' up on deck and fling themselves overboard. When we landed, we had quite a number of orphans go ashore with us, so the families that were left kind of divvied them up. We took one little girl, Vendulka, but she died our first year in Spillville.

"Anyways, Maestro, I cursed the day the priest ever read me Tony Klimesh's letter. We should have stood at home, I says. We was dirt poor, that's a fact, but at least we was more or less safe. My conscience was eating me alive, and the wife, God rest her soul, was in the family way through all this, I forgot to mention that. I tell you, I begged the Lord for forgiveness. I says, you made up your mind too quick, without thinkin' of what might happen, I says, and now you've gone and killed those poor little kids. Imagine that, takin' them all off to the ends of the earth like that.

"Well, Maestro, today I see that in spite of everything I did the right thing. If we'd of stood at home and they'd of lived, where'd they be today? What kind of life would they have? The girls might've got married to tenant farmers. And the boys, they'd either be in the army, or stableboys with the Schwartzenbergs. But now just look how they turned out here. My oldest boy took over the farm, the youngest got his own business in California, Caroline married a farmer right here in Spillville and Betty, she was good at school, so the principal, Mr. Kovarik – I mean young Joseph here's father – got her into Normal School in Chicago and now she's teachin' school in Iowa City. And our youngest girl, Teresa, she married well too, husband's a Norwegian up in Decorah, where he runs a farm machinery business.

"Teresa, she was born at sea and the captain christened her. It happened just a couple of days before we landed, with God's help, in New Orleans. At first the captain was headin' for Boston, but we hit a terrible winter storm and got blown off course so we put in to Cuba and took on some cargo for New Orleans. Didn't matter to me, I just wanted to hit dry land quick, New Orleans, anywhere, it didn't matter as long as it was America. By the time we reached Cuba, we'd been at sea for three months! And we thought we'd be five or six weeks on the water at the most.

"Well, the Lord be praised, the trip from Cuba only took about seven days, the sea as smooth as a fish pond, the sky clear, not a cloud in sight. It was hot, but we took on fresh water in Cuba, had a proper wash there too – the first time in three months. The wife, God rest her, was delighted, the children stopped whining and three days later the wife's time came and she had Teresa. She was born on deck. The sailors set up this big tent on deck where they let women who were in the family way sleep, and the sea was calm so they let us passengers spend more time up in the fresh air. Except for the miserable wretches who were tied to their bunks below. When Teresa was born, I went for a walk on deck at night. I'll never forget it. The stars looked different from back home, but it was a beautiful sight just the same. And I says to myself, Franta, I says, it was the will of God made you make up your mind in such a hurry. Two of the children didn't make it, but they were innocent and they're in heaven for sure. And the Lord gave us a new little girl. Maestro, I stood there in the warm breeze – they call them trade winds – and I tried to picture myself walking through my own wheatfields and the wind making waves in the wheat like the sea in the moonlight and, well, Maestro, I've got a team of horses and two cows in the barn, pigs, everything I pictured came true, even more than I reckoned on. The only thing was, our troubles were far from over, but of course I didn't know that yet.

"Anyways, there we were, standing on dry ground again after more than three months on the ocean, and we had six kids again, though one of them was adopted, you might say, and I was so happy I could've danced right then and there. It was a pretty-looking harbour, sun was out, boats were getting loaded and unloaded, all by niggers – that was the first time in my life I ever seen a nigger, Maestro. And I said to myself, don't look like there's no shortage of work here, in a month or two we'll have enough saved up to join Tony Klimesh up in Iowa. But things often turn out different, don't they, Maestro? Like they say, man proposes, God disposes. We waited around for them to unload our chests from the Wenderman – the niggers did that too – an' I tell you I just wanted to go into the hold with them and dig out the baggage myself, but the sailors said no, so we had to wait. Suddenly I got this queer feelin' – what if our chests got lost? And as the niggers hauled out all the bundles and crates, my fears grew. By this time there was a huge pile of baggage on the pier, some passengers had already got theirs, but most of the stuff was the cargo from Cuba they carted off right away with teams of horses. Anyway, not to drag the story out, that evening there was several of us families still standin' there, the ship all unloaded, and our trunks was nowhere in sight.

"Well, I thought it would kill my wife, God rest her soul. We had a few pots and pans, the odd tool – I mean we'd lost more than that before and we'd always bounced back. But the comforters, Maestro, that my wife had put together feather by feather. All those years of work – gone.

"Well, the captain and one other sailor who knew German came and said when they were in Cuba they had to shift some of the cargo onto another boat to make room for the new stuff, and they said that boat would be along in two or three days. 'What's the ship?' I says and the German sailor says, 'The Bullshit.' Well, Maestro, I wouldn't fall for it today, of course, but tell me, how was I to know what 'bullshit' meant then? And they both seemed so willing to help out, and the captain wrote each family a – what d'you call it – a bill of lading saying that such-and-such a piece of cargo on the Bullshit belongs to So-and-so, and the sailor helped him get our names spelled right. Some of us couldn't read, Maestro, but I could make out the odd word, enough to know that my name, Frank Valenta – Frank, that's how they wrote it – was on the bill in black and white. It was a great weight off my mind, which goes to show you how stupid I was. Not the wife, though. She never believed a word they said and she cried and said we'd never see those comforters again. I thought she was wrong. What a fool I was!

"The next thing was getting a roof over our heads until the comforters arrived, but the Lord provided again. A German family, Catholics they were, put us up. They let us sleep in the shed, gave us a bit of straw and I told them I'd pay them when I made some money. Well, sir, I'll never forget that first night in New Orleans. You know how at night you're always letting things chase around in your head anyway, and I got to thinking maybe the captain was just talking through his hat. The wife, God rest her, was carryin' on in her sleep about those comforters and I couldn't get a wink, so I crawled out of the shed, the moon was like it was a few days before on the Wenderman, except I didn't feel like dancin' no more. So I went through that bill word by word, even managed to figure something out because I picked up the odd word on the way over from that German sailor. Well, of course the bill was real enough. My name was on it. But it didn't ease my mind any.

"So I never got a wink of sleep that night and early next mornin' I set out for the docks to look for work. Another beautiful day – I don't suppose they know what bad weather is down there – new ships come in the evenin' before, the place swarmin' with niggers, but I didn't feel much like singin'. I went from ship to ship, soundin' out their names just in case the Bullshit might have come in durin' the night, and at the same time lookin' around for somebody like a boss or a foreman to ask about work. Everywhere there was niggers slavin' away with crates and barrels, and haulin' these enormous bunches of green bananas, except I didn't know what they were, I'd never seen a banana before. Finally, I see this fellow looks like a boss – straw hat, white cotton three-piece suit, smoking a cigar – so I go up to him, whip off my hat and say, 'Work?' He looks me up and down – and I was thirty-one then, still built for hard work, and he must have seen I could do as much as the niggers. He never even takes the cigar out of his mouth, but kind of spits between his teeth, 'Twenny cents.' Well, Maestro, I went kind of weak in the knees. First them comforters, probably lost for good, and now he's offerin' me beggar's wages. The German sailor, he told me that in America they pay casual labour thirty-five cents, sometimes fifty, and if you're lucky and get work on the railroad you might even make a dollar a day. So I says, 'No, thirty-five.' And he grins through his cigar and hisses something I can't make out. 'No understand,' I said, and he makes this ugly face, points his finger, which is loaded down with flashy rings, at one of the niggers and he says, 'Twenny cents.' And he points to another one and says, 'Twenny cents.' And at a third and a fourth and a fifth, and each time he says, 'Twenny cents.' Finally he points to me and says, 'Twenny cents, unnerstand?' Well, Maestro, I felt like cryin'. Twenty cents for twelve hours' work! I was countin' on the wife soon being able to bring in a little herself – but twenty cents! And I had to make enough for passage on a river-boat up the Mississippi to Iowa, or at least as close as we could get. The German family said it would take us a year to get there by horse and wagon. I could've walked to Iowa if it hadn't been for the wife and kids, but you can't do it with a family of six. So I stuck to my guns: 'Thirty-five!' I says, but he just shrugs his shoulders and turns his back on me.

"Well, this took a little wind out of my sails, but I went on till I saw another fellow standin' by a boat. This one didn't have a cigar, but the way he was bossin' the niggers around I figured he was a foreman. So I goes up to him and the same thing happens: 'Work?' I says, and he stares me up and down like the first one and says exactly the same: 'Twenny cents!' By this time I could hardly squeeze out my 'Thirty-five' and this one didn't even bother explainin' – he just shows me his back and starts shoutin' at the niggers unloadin' bananas like slaves. Well, Maestro, what I didn't know at the time was they really was slaves. Their owners hired them out to businessmen at twenty cents a day. It was a good deal for them. The nigger didn't get nothing, only a few scraps of food. And if they had kids, the owners sold them and made extra. I found all this out later that night from those decent Germans. But I wandered about from boat to boat all day long and it was the same thing everywhere I went: twenty, sometimes twenty-five cents a day. And don't forget, Maestro, two potatoes cost a nickel, and they was askin' eleven bucks for a barrel of flour."

"And what became of the comforters?" asked Dvorak.

"Well, you know what 'bullshit' means in Czech, don't you?"

The Master didn't know, and turned to his secretary for help. Kovarik explained.

The Master's response earned him a hundred and thirty-seven years in purgatory.

14   :⁀: THE SNARING OF THE MASTER

ANTON RETURNED from the manor house at five. Drops of spring rain were trickling down his face, making it impossible to tell if he was crying. She knew he was. When he spoke, his voice faltered: "Anna, would you feed the pigeons for me today?" He had never asked her to do this before, and it meant things looked bleak indeed. He went to his room and, through a crack in the door, she saw him sitting at the piano, closed like a coffin, staring at a blank sheet of music paper in front of him that she knew he could not see.

What did he see? Jo's face, as she had seen it herself that morning, where the pitiless black angel had left his sign. To put it out of her mind, she tried to remember the face on a day twenty years ago, when Kounic had arrived, penitence personified, with a gigantic bouquet of red roses and Jo was powdering her nose in the bedroom, but not for Kounic. The Count's broad shoulders – she had observed him from behind – were almost too wide for the armchair in which he sat waiting. Then he stood up, because Jo had appeared in the doorway; there had been a different sign in her face then, pale with indecision. She knew what it meant, Kounic did not. Kounic was merely a lovesick fool, like Dvorak. She watched him through the lattice-work of the bead curtain that hung between the parlour and the dining room, and she heard Kounic say: "Are you still angry, Josephine?" And again, only she could see the sign, as the pallor of indecision gave way to determination. But she felt no relief, no triumph, no joy; she simply waited, because she knew, and her waiting had not been in vain. For God, in his great goodness, does not give so much happiness to one person – in such a flood of bliss, Anton's music might have been overwhelmed, swept away. And so, to preserve that great gift, He sent the good Count Kounic who guilelessly, and because he was in love, offered her beautiful, successful and shallow sister the apple of a countess's estate. Anna watched as she reached out, hesitant at first, then suddenly decisive, and snatched the apple: "Not to Chuchle, no. Let's drive to Stromovka," thus drawing her dagger to kill the dream and thus – as sometimes, though seldom, happens – to give it eternal life. For Anna knew – she had listened with her ear to the door the day before – that Dvorak would be waiting beneath the château in Stromovka Park, in his hands, no doubt, a bouquet of red roses that would wilt and wither, because flowers do not thrive on mortal sweat.

Watching from behind the curtain, she saw the shining new carriage with the carmine wheels, a white top hat up in front reflecting the sun, and as the carriage moved away the reflection leaped to a black top hat in the rear and swirled, and between those two dancing little suns sat her powdered sister, pale as death, and the Count, a strapping figure, his hands in white gloves that were also soaked with sweat. The carriage drove off, bearing the cruel, beneficent sentence of death.

She let the curtain fall, knowing now that the long work had begun. But God had given her a clear head and the unshakeable knowledge that she had been born for this lovesick fool with the great gift of music. She had known this the moment the stammering, blushing bumpkin – whose awkward professions of love she had once parodied for her sister – had suddenly seemed transformed, and she felt in her childish breasts a new sensation: the sensation of love.

She walked over to the mirror. So this, now, is the future Mrs. Dvorak. Not her sister, the fair Josephine, now all but a countess, always the fairest of all. No. This blonde, grey-eyed, attractive and ambitious girl, of whom he need never feel ashamed, strong as a horse, the woman who could give him a child for every note in the tonic solfa.

But it had been tough going. She tried at the beginning to be witty, not knowing that Anton did not understand wit. He was seated opposite her in the parlour, depressed by his double defeat. Depressed, but not crushed. She knew that only death could crush her Anton – for he was already hers, though he did not yet know it – and that death would not come soon, and when it did come it would be too late for not even the black angel could destroy him then. He was waiting until she finished a row of crocheting, for she had told him that were she to stop now, she would have to count the stitches, and that, she said, was tough going, deliberately using an expression that was inappropriate for the young daughter of a goldsmith's family; for his sake, she wanted to be different in some way from other daughters of such families. He waited patiently until she was done crocheting and he could begin the lesson. She finished the row and smoothed out the half-finished coverlet for him to admire.

He looked at her work without the slightest interest. But she had a plan.

"How do you like it?"

"It's fine," he said gloomily.

"Do you want me to make one for you?"

"But Miss Annie, you don't have to do that."

No, but I want to, my sweet Dvorak, she said to herself. He added, "I wouldn't have anywhere to put it. We only have the bare essentials."

"But you do have a pianoforte?"

"Yes, but it's not mine. It belongs to Anger. And it's a spinet."

"Then at least you can have your own coverlet on it."

"You're most kind, Miss Annie, but I can't –"

"And I'll even embroider your monogram on it," she decided.

"Well, that –"

Then she proceeded according to her plan. She laid the coverlet in her lap and looked into his eyes.

"Oh my!" she said. "I've just realized something. How curious!"

"What's that?" With about as much interest as if he were asking after a stepfather's great-aunt's health.

"It's a perfect fourth," she said, laughing straight into those big dark gypsy eyes with – at that moment – something of a St. Bernard about them.

"A perfect fourth?"

"Your monogram."

Naturally, he didn't understand.

" 'A' and 'D', don't you see?" she babbled. "A perfect fourth."

Finally. The lips that were bent into a tragic half-moon curled reluctantly in the opposite direction.

"You certainly have ideas, Miss Annie."

"Don't I?" she said. "You'd be surprised if you knew about the ones you don't know about."

That one made no impression. He merely smiled painfully, as though his stomach were aching. The lesson was a complete flop, though she had practised the sonata three days in a row, six hours a day until she could probably have played it backwards. She should have done so. Then, perhaps, the half-moon that hung tips down beneath his nose for the entire lesson might have been induced to curl upwards.

She was desperate to do something unusual to distract him.

When he was leaving, she told him to wait for a moment and ran off into the kitchen. Before starting her crocheting, she had spent a whole hour setting her blonde hair in ringlets at the back, because she knew the ringlets danced alluringly when she ran. She took a red apple from the kitchen basket and brought it back to the waiting St. Bernard.

"Here you are, Mr. Dvorak."

"An apple, Miss Annie? Why?"

No, he understood nothing at all.

"Just so you'll have something from me."

"Thank you," he said awkwardly, and took his leave.

She took up her position behind the curtain. He strode away, beneath his arm a scruffy briefcase which, she knew, held a partly completed composition – a dirge, no doubt – and in his left hand, a red apple. Like a king upon his throne.

Suddenly, he took a bite out of the apple.

She was delighted. Afterwards she felt like a real temptress.

That week Josephine came home with the news that Anton had resigned from the Provisional Theatre orchestra. "I feel guilty about it. After nine years...."

"You should be glad, Jo," Anna replied. "Anton has better things to do in this world than fritter his life away on the viola."

Josephine looked at her thoughtfully. "But what will he live on?"

"Behold the fowls of the air," she recited. "They sow not, neither do they reap, nor gather into barns, yet our heavenly Father feedeth them."

He fed him, but more like a stepfather. Josephine's lessons were cancelled without an explanation and Josephine made a point of always being absent when he came to teach Anna. She all but vanished from his sight. Not from his mind, of course. But Anna was patient. There was no hurry. She was only sixteen.

The coverlet with its fateful monogram appeared on Anger's spinet which, as Anton told her when she gave him her gift, was missing several strings in the middle registers so that he had to fill in the missing tones with his imagination.

"Sometimes I whistle them too," he added.

"I could never do that," she said admiringly, and she tried to play a chord without the tonic and complete it by whistling. She could whistle like a goose girl, but she feigned incompetence because it allowed her to pucker her lips at him. But he, who could whistle like a shepherd, merely decided to teach her how. So she sighed inwardly and displayed a miraculous talent. By the end of the lesson, they were whistling Eine Kleine Nachtmusik together in perfect two-part harmony.

Just then her father walked in.

As always, he spoke affably, but she saw in his eyes an incipient suspicion that threatened to mar her plan. "Mr. Dvorak, aren't we supposed to be teaching Annie to play the pianoforte?"

In an instant, Anton was the colour of a peony. "Certainly, Mr. Cermak. I was only – "

"Mr. Dvorak was teaching me the proper technique for phrasing in the flute, Papa," she said quickly.

"In the flute? Shouldn't you first of all be mastering the pianoforte, Annie?"

"But I'd love to learn how to play the flute too."

Papa's eyes slid from her to Anton, then back to her again. He smiled amiably. "Well, we'll see. If you still feel the same way by Christmas…. But in the meantime, Mr. Dvorak, perhaps we should be seeing to it that Annie learns the keyboard properly."

"Indeed, yes – Mr. Cermak…. "

That evening Papa said, "I hear Mr. Dvorak has resigned from the theatre orchestra. A rather thoughtless young man, Anna, thoughtless indeed. He's past thirty and must certainly be thinking of getting married. But how he expects to support a family on the strength of music lessons and composition, I'm sure I don't know."

That was Papa's way of saying he disapproved of her flirting with a musician. All the years this same musician had tried to win Jo's heart had escaped his notice, she thought angrily. Of course, Jo is an actress and she always knows how to handle Papa. Her anger got the better of her and she retorted, with an insincere laugh, "I doubt Mr. Dvorak will be getting married as quickly as all that."

"Perhaps not – but that won't prevent him from thinking about it," said Papa.

"First he'll have to amount to something. Otherwise no woman would marry him."

He looked at her inquisitively. "That's true, Anna, very true. Could you please hand me my drops? My heart is acting up again."

And he will amount to something. Something big, Papa, she said to herself. And half a year later the great Smetana himself conducted Anton's overture to the opera King and Collier. For a few days at least the half moon lay on its back.

He sent them five tickets. Papa couldn't go – his heart seemed able to act up on demand – and Jo had a performance that night.

"I'm going to give him a bouquet," she told her mother.

"Do you think it's appropriate?"

"He's my piano teacher. And it's his first big opportunity."

"He taught Josie as well," said her mother, for whom propriety was the chief law of nature.

"Let Annie give him a bouquet for both of us," said Josephine, coming to her aid. By now, Jo was a co-conspirator.

"In that case," said her mother, "we'll give him a bouquet from the whole Cermak family."

But Anna was the one to present it to him. White roses, and inside, a red apple fastened with a ribbon. This was not from the Cermak family. The Cermak family knew nothing about the apple.

"Have you eaten it yet?" she asked him during the lesson two days later.

"No, Miss Anna."

Oh, that was a setback.

"And what did you do with it?"

"Anger ate it that night."

Ah! Progress was slow.

But there was progress all the same. The little half-moon no longer lay on its belly and Jo still contrived, conscientiously, to be absent from home whenever Anton came to teach. His chamber music and songs appeared with increasing frequency on the programs of private recitals at the Neffs', the Porgeses', the Strosses'. He bought himself a new hat. Mrs. Munzarova, the seamstress, let her clients know that the young Dvorak would soon be the talk of the town.

Then he came for a lesson, and the half-moon was turned up at the corners.

"Have you won the lottery, Mr. Dvorak?"

"No, Miss Annie. You know I don't gamble. But Bendl liked my cantata. He said he'd do it right away."

She clapped. It wasn't a habit of hers, but she thought he might be intrigued by this expression of girlish delight. "Congratulations! I mean it, with all my heart."

"But the Hlahol Singers can't perform it."

"Why not?"

"It's a cantata for mixed choir. But the most important thing is, Bendl likes it. Someone will sing it for me someday."

She said nothing, so as not to give him any ideas. This is my great chance. And Jo must help me. "Kounic won't be pleased if he hears I'm plotting to help my former suitor," Josephine said. "On the other hand – I'm plotting to help his present admirer, so it's really none of Kounic's business." "Thanks, Jo," she said. And with this trump in her hand, she went to see Bendl.

"Hm, I'm not at all sure about this, Miss Cermakova," said the choirmaster. "Tradition is tradition. Hlahol has always been a male chorus – "

"And who else should perform Mr. Dvorak's work for him? You said yourself it was beautiful."

"Beautiful, yes. I would even go so far as to say it's brilliant. But tradition – "

" – is tradition. But this is the nineteenth century."

He laughed, and looked at her through narrowed eyes that seemed to read her thoughts.

"I can see you're rather fond of this cantata, young lady."

"That too," she said boldly, thus stopping him short.

He laughed appreciatively and said, "But perhaps the gentlemen will disapprove?"

"Gentlemen seldom disapprove of ladies."

"My, you have an answer for everything."

"I believe it would be an eternal shame for such a magnificent work to go unperformed."

He laughed, his eyes twinkling. For a long time he was silent, then at last he said, "Listening to you, Miss Anna, I see everything is in good hands."

Did he mean the cantata, or Dvorak? The crafty man! But both were in good hands – the cantata and Dvorak.

And so they rehearsed the Hymnus – The Heirs of the White Mountain. Jo managed to recruit two battalions of female singers from both Prague theatres and Anna brought in some of her friends from the better Prague families. Naturally, Prague was a-buzz with talk, and the talk wasn't exactly about the Hymnus but about how Annie Cermakova was carrying a torch for the rejected suitor of the beautiful Josephine who had taken it into her head to become a countess.

But Anna didn't care. Not a bit. Because now – he could scarcely avoid it – he walked her home every night from rehearsals. As she had foreseen, the gentlemen of the Hlahol had no objections whatsoever to the break with tradition.

The concert took place in March and, exactly as Mrs. Munzarova had prophesied, Anton became celebrated overnight. Even before the première, Ludevit Prochazka, who had heard the Hymnus in rehearsal, wrote a glowing report in Musical Reviews. She presented the article to her father and made certain he read it. As a result, his heart did not act up and the whole family, with Papa at the head, came to the concert. He was going, of course, as the proud father of a daughter who was singing with the first altos, but the stormy applause, she hoped, would reassure him that the young composer who was soon to be thirty-three was beginning to amount to something.

Perhaps he'll buy me that flute now, after all.

By an astutely engineered coincidence the Crocheting Circle – it did not exist, but Anton was unaware of this – changed its regular meeting day so that she had to go immediately after her piano lesson. Moreover they were able to walk most of the way together, since by a further coincidence the meetings were held only two blocks from the Fig Leaf, the building where Anton went to give lessons to the Neff daughters.

"Where do you go every week, Annie?" asked her father.

"For walks, Papa. It's spring – and it's so nice out."

"Alone?"

"Yes, but I always go part of the way with Mr. Dvorak. When he's finished here, he goes to teach at the Neffs'."

Because the Crocheting Circle did not exist, she could walk around the Neffs' house and be home in fifteen minutes. Papa could hardly object to a half-hour's stroll in broad daylight. And besides, Mr. Dvorak's star was rising.

It was indeed, but it was still tough going.

The spring passed uneventfully and summer came. One day, as she was walking back from the Crocheting Circle, her teacher was just coming out from the Neffs'. He was early. It was pure coincidence, but she grasped the opportunity at once.

"Mr. Dvorak, what a pleasant surprise! The circle finished early today. Come, let's go for a walk on Petrin Hill. It's so lovely out."

He did not appear to have seen through her ruse.

"I'd enjoy that, Miss Annie, but there is something I wanted to write – "

"You can always do that some other time. Look, the sun is shining."

"Well – it is lovely," he said. For the first time, she felt him within her grasp.

"I should say it is. So let's go now, before it sets. Just for an hour."

Their walks to the Neffs' were always duets, with the female voice strongly dominant. The hour on Petrin Hill was an aria for alto. It lasted for three hours, and ended with Anton's single remark, "Miss Annie, don't you think it's time you were going – home?"

Dusk was descending – irrevocably – on the bench shrouded in summer leaves.

"Not yet – Tony.... " She put all the feeling she could muster into his name and it seemed that it just might....

Anton uttered a sound that, in novels, is usually transcribed as "ahem".

"Isn't it getting rather – dark?"

"That's good," she said. Now, perhaps, at long last he would.... She looked into his eyes and held up her lips.

He swallowed.

And then, she finally got what she had worked so hard to get.

But it had been tough going.

"Annie! Where have you been? Father is half dead with worry!"

His heart had received an order, but naturally, Papa hadn't died.

She got a lecture. But it was somewhat obbligato. Anton's star was definitely on the rise, and she *was* eighteen. Later that night in the bedroom:

"So has Anton definitely swallowed the bait?"

"He has," she said happily and somewhat triumphantly.

"Thank God! I was afraid.... "

"Aren't you underestimating your sister, sister?"

Josephine grasped her hand. "Not in the least. But perhaps – you know – I underestimate the power of love."

They embraced. She felt sorry for her beautiful sister, who under-estimated the power of love because love had evaded her.

She was happy. Love suffereth long, yes. Love envieth not. Yes. Love beareth all things, endureth all things. Yes. Yes. Yes. Hopeth all things.

But she hadn't expected him not to come to the next lesson. He didn't even send her a note. She stood at her post by the window, the street swept clean of people, hot, empty.

"I say, is Mr. Dvorak ill?"

She shook her head and turned away, so that her father could not see her tears. The next day, her mother and father were planning a trip with the younger sisters to visit her married sister in Jicin. If only they were gone already.

Dvorak! You fool!

She got ready and left the house. She took up a position outside the greengrocer's shop, hidden by the awning that shaded the oranges in his window. At five minutes to five Dvorak appeared and hurried into the Neffs' house to teach the girls.

At six she was waiting outside.

He came out and for an instant it looked as though he was about to back into the house, like a turtle retreating into its shell. Then he realized he was trapped. He turned pale.

"Why didn't you come, Tony?"

"I – Miss Annie – I was afraid you would think.... "

"Why, Tony?" she implored again. Some people were coming towards them along the sidewalk. She put her arm through his and he didn't resist. The buildings they walked past were flooded with the rich, golden light of the late afternoon sun.

"Why didn't you come?" she said quietly, reproachfully.

"I was afraid.... "

"Of what? Surely you can't still be afraid of girls the way you were when you lived at the Duseks'?"

"No, it's not that, Annie. I was afraid you'd think I was taking advantage of.... since – since first your sister.... "

The dunderhead! But love thinketh no evil. No, no! "Shouldn't I be the one to worry about that?"

"Why, Annie? After all, you.... "

After all, I am the one taking advantage of the situation. Don't you understand?

She could see that he was beginning to understand, that he would soon see. So why do you think I took advantage of the situation? Why, my love?

A miracle occurred. He understood. "Annie, you mean you ...?"

"Haven't you recognized that yet?"

"Annie" – and the Adam's apple bobbed – "I – I'm.... "

"Are you fond of me?" she whispered, and pressed herself to him.

"I am." His voice caught. "I – " He fell silent as two pedestrians walked round the corner, a repulsive-looking woman leading a bratty little boy in a sailor suit. Anna clung to him, but less tightly now.

"You'll have to make the lesson up to me tomorrow," she said. "Papa was asking whether you were ill."

She thought quickly. This time tomorrow, her father would be on the train to Jicin, along with both her younger sisters and her mother. Jo was on tour in Pilsen. And Mary –

"Mary, how would you like to take the day off today?"

"But Miss – I was off the day before yesterday."

"There's nothing for you to do here. They're all away."

"Well, there's no denying I could put it to good use."

So could I.

When Anton arrived at four, Anna was alone in the apartment. He went straight to the piano and found it was locked. He turned to her with a puzzled look on his face and she said, "We're not going to play the piano today." She drew a deep breath. "We're just going to play, all right, Tony?"

"But – "

"No. No buts."

And then, gathering her courage, she did what she had read about in novels: she sat on his lap. He was strong and she was not yet nineteen. She put her arms around his neck and soon realized, at last, that he was no longer afraid of girls.

She had pulled the blinds down in the bedroom to make it dark. When he had finally slid his right arm from around her neck down to where she wanted it to be, she whispered in his ear, "Wait," slipped off his lap and led him into the semi-darkness. The day was overcast, the bedroom almost like night. He might no longer fear women, but he still hadn't learned what to do with them. "Wait," she whispered again. "I'll do it myself," and she unwound herself from his arms, which were now moving towards the hem of her skirt with the clear intention of continuing back up underneath. "You too." Then she pulled her dress over her head and stood before him in a white corset and knickers that ended just below her knees in lace frills and pink ribbons. In the half-light, she could see him tearing off his suit-coat, turning the sleeves inside out, doing battle with the stiff collar.

She tussled with the laces on her corset, but she had planned this beforehand and they didn't give her much trouble.

Anton tore the collar off.

They stood facing each other like the couple in paradise and he moved quickly to hold her.

She made a mistake. "Adam!" she whispered. "My little Adam."

He froze.

"Don't be afraid!" she whispered quickly. "It's not a sin."

He moved closer. She was aware that he knew very well it was a sin. But even the saints sin seven times a day, she thought. And anyway, sin did not frighten her.

They lay down on the bed. She knew very little, but something other than knowledge prompted her to take gentle hold of him and guide him to his proper place.

Did it hurt? Did it matter? It was all to show Anton, that great, handsome dunderhead with the God-given talent, that she loved him. Because even geniuses, it seemed, could only be made to see it in this somewhat ridiculous male fashion.

Next morning, the mourning banner of original sin, washed in the night with her own hands, hung on the balcony. Later, when she was taking the sheet back in, Mary came into the room and her mouth fell open.

Annie blushed and in her embarrassment stuck out her tongue at the maid.

"Miss!" Mary blurted out. And then: "Oh, but don't you worry. I won't breathe a word about this to the missus."

And she was happy. Happy, even though Anton nearly suffered a nervous collapse, because what he said convinced her that she was his and that he now thought of her in the same way.

"For the love of God, Annie," he said, "I can't support a family."

Kissing him, she replied, "Very well then, we'll live on dry bread."

He arrived, in accordance with the rules of etiquette, wearing a black suit and carrying a bouquet. Blessings were bestowed on them both, with Father conducting the formalities and Mother adding her obligatory tears to the occasion, for Anton's star was truly rising.

But they faced the problem of how to explain why the wedding should, if possible, be held at once. No satisfactory solution to this dilemma was found. Her father and mother could not be persuaded to forgo the customary reading of the banns, and once she nearly gave the whole thing away when her mother reacted to one of her urgent but unpersuasive arguments for an early wedding by saying, "Anna, for heaven's sake, get a grip on yourself. He's not about to get away. Surely you don't want people to think you *had* to get married?" She had blushed, but fortunately her mother was not wearing her glasses. At last, however, there was an official announcement: "Mr. & Mrs. Jan Jiri Cermak have the honour of announcing the marriage of their daughter Anna to Antonin, son of Mr. and Mrs. Frantisek Dvorak.... "

When their union was finally blessed by the church Anna was already five months pregnant, and she thanked God for the mercies of her anatomy that had so far kept her state practically invisible.

And then, exactly ten days after the wedding, Anton made a tragic blunder. He was discussing his prospects for the future with her father, and in his innocence – she was constantly amazed that he hadn't blurted out the truth long before, particularly at the moment when it seemed her father would delay the wedding until spring – he let slip the fatal phrase: " ... now that we're expecting a family – "

Ten days after the wedding!

"Did I hear you correctly, Antonin?" said Papa delightedly.

Anton turned red. Papa turned red. "Good Lord!" he shouted, as though he couldn't believe his ears. And then he said, "You bastard!" And then, a moment later, "My drops!"

The bastard didn't know where the drops were, and he had to ask the assistance of the equally flushed – what? Slut? Yes, that would be the word for it – slut.

"No one must know! No one!" Papa was purple. "Annie must go to Jicin and – "

It wasn't he who gave the order to his heart this time. It stopped of its own accord.

That night, Anton shuddered. "God will punish us for this, Annie. He will punish us terribly."

"It's not our fault," she said, trying to calm him. But she knew it was their fault. But how else ...?

"We should have waited until after the wedding," Anton moaned.

Tears burned her eyes. Papa, forgive me. Now you know why. If you'd let us get married at once, no one would ever have known. Papa! This way....

The birth of a healthy little boy in the fourth month is a rather unusual event.

But Anton was right. God did punish them. First Josephine, their second child, when she was only two days old. "What shall we call her, Annie?" he asked. She lay beside her in the bed, a tiny body of wrinkled skin and fragile bones. "She's our first daughter, Ton," she said. "Don't you know what we're going to call her?" "What?" And he gazed lovingly at the wailing little bundle of life. "Josephine, of course," she said. He turned to her, with his beautiful dark eyes, and pressed her hand. She understood, once and for all, that there was love enough for both her and her older sister.

But Josephine died the next day. God's punishment. And two years later, Otakar, that beautiful, first-born memory of the afternoon when she knew he was hers. And less than a week after that, his sister Rozarka. Then God took pity on the poor, repentant sinners –

– so for the three souls in heaven, we have six living bundles of worry, she thought. Aloisia, Otakar, Tony, Magda, Annie, and the greatest worry of all, Otylia, who left half her heart in Vysoka, half in Spillville, and now faces the same dilemma Jo once did.

She stopped feeding the pigeons who, suspecting nothing, cooed excitedly around her. One perched on her shoulder and tried to get at the grain in the sack – nature, ignorant of and ignoring what goes on in the world of people. She looked towards the manor house. Antonia, the old maid-servant, was coming up the road, pressing her apron to her eyes.

She stepped out to meet Antonia.

"The Countess.... "

She went into the house. She walked through the kitchen, into the dining room and quietly opened the door to the piano room. Anton was still sitting on the stool, bent over, his music paper untouched on the piano.

She went in. He raised his sad, sad eyes to meet hers.

"Tony.... "

Her eyes were hot with tears..

"Annie.... "

She put her arms around his big shoulders.

Josephine, her beautiful, unhappy sister, his first love, was no longer.

15 :(ʔ): MISS ROSIE TO HER SISTER MARINKA IN SKRCENA LHOTA

Sunday the 27th,
August, 1893,
Chicago

My dear Marinka,

This is going to be a very special letter because you will never guess,
dearest girl, what happened to me at the Chicago World's Fair. Well,
come to think of it maybe you don't even know who Dvorak is. I
sure didn't but when I heard that a Bohemian band was going to
play at the Festival Hall at noon, conducted by this Dvorak, I told
Jim – he's my fiancé – come on, I said, let's go hootchie-koochie.

But it wasn't that sort of band. There wasn't any dancing because
the hall was packed like a can of sardines. But I figure this Dvorak
must be some big name because as soon as he climbs up on the
bandstand there was such a hullabaloo of shouting and clapping and
cheers that it took at least five minutes before he got down to the
conducting business. So afterwards I ask a Bohemian gentleman (he'd
come in too for the Bohemian Day Rally and we had all the flags
out and the bands marching in the street, and I can't tell you how
exciting it was), anyways I asked him who this Dvorak fella is and
he says he's the most famous composer in the world, specially since
he's written all sorts of Slovak dances. I guess he started getting
famous after I come to America so I thought maybe you'd of heard
of him. Maybe back home he's something like that Sousa guy over
here – he's the most famous bandleader in the whole United States.

Well it's no particular matter if you know him or not, I want to tell you so you'll appreciate that I actually made his acquaintance. Not at the Festival Hall – I couldn't even get close to him there. Besides, I was worried about Jim. You know how the Irish are! It was a scorching hot Sunday and Jim got into the beer even before we got on the train to the fair, and as soon as we got there he switched to whisky, so I wouldn't of danced with him even if they'd let us because I had on my new white leather shoes.

Well, the band played one of those Slovak dances that made this Dvorak so famous. The dance was called the Gee, Major! – least that's what they told me. I never heard of the dance before and I know pretty well all the dances people in Chicago do, the polka, the mazurka, the jig, the waltz and even some of those nigger shuffles like the cakewalk or the bamboula. Our coachman taught me and he's a nigger himself, though he's whiter than the boss who's as red as a turnip because of all the port he drinks. Well, I can't see how anyone could of danced to that Gee, Major. After a while I got bored and Jim was crying for another drink so we pushed through the crowd to the bar, well, I mean the restaurant. I have to tell you there's all these powerful religious hoity-toities in the Senate and at first they got the World Fair shut down on Sundays because the ministers were afraid nobody'd show up for their old sermons. But the World Fair people didn't want to lose that Sunday business, because it's the only time most people can get out there. Me, I get every second Sunday off and if I snuck a day off during the week my boss would fire me for sure. So we had this big demonstration in our ward for the World Fair to stay open Sundays, mainly workers from the stockyards and some domestics. I went too. Our candidate for City Hall, Matthew B. Surrowey, he wrote a letter to our senator and they ended up letting the fair stay open on Sundays. But the ministers got revenge and forced them to close the bars at least, so on Sundays you can only get drinks in restaurants and that means you have to order food – a sandwich at least – each time you order a drink. Well, if the ministers thought this would keep the Fair dry on the Lord's Day they were wrong. The only difference was the restaurants made extra money on the food. When we left the Festival Hall – that was about one o'clock – Jim had sandwiches falling out of his pockets and by the time we finally left the restaurant he had another three. I had a few glasses of cider on account of it was so hot and I had to go to the ladies' room. Jim said he'd wait for me and the last I saw him that day he was walking – staggering would be more like it – over towards those chairs on wheels they had there. People call them gospel chariots because it's usually Bible students with summer jobs at the Fair who push them around like coolies. Anyway there were three enormous fat ladies waiting for a ride, about 250 pounds each, and all the pushers were pretending to be real interested in their Bibles or fixing something on their chairs. After those three ciders I was about to burst so I ran into the ladies' room and sure enough when I came back Jim was gone. I should of known better. Everybody knows the pushers like drunks because it gives them a chance to preach against the evils of booze while they're pushing them around.

Now, to tell you the truth, Marinka, I didn't exactly feel like weeping. I know Jim pretty well and I figured a few more drinks and I'd have to hire a gospel chariot for him anyway, and this way maybe the pusher might give him a discount for helping him get away from those fat ladies. The other three Bible thumpers weren't so lucky. I saw them about twenty yards off, pushing the gospel chariots with all that blubber stuffed into each one. They were bent forward like miners with those little carts in the coal mines, and they were sweating so hard they left footprints on the tile floor.

At first I was a bit worried about going around the World Fair all by myself. Some gentleman might of got the wrong idea. But luckily I ran into Zdenka Drbohlavova, so we decided to stick together and have some fun. You remember her, she's that carrot-top from Vypucena Lhota and now she's working as a maid in Cicero and she's changed her name to Denise Derby because nobody here can pronounce Drbohlavova. Most of them are too dumb to say Zdenka properly, and they called her Stinky. Well, Denise and I had quite a nice afternoon without Jim, thank you very much. There's lots to see at the World Fair. Some of it would be hard for you to believe! There are about six hundred pavilions, the Electricity Building, the Haiti Building, the Horticultural Building, the Woman's Building (unfortunately there's not a Man's Building), the U.S. Government Building and lots of others and they're made out of a kind of white marble they call plaster. Well, you've never seen marble like this in Europe, it's as bright as chalk, no comparison with that Carrara marble the Count built his summer-house out of in Lhota.

Or the art galleries! They show pictures there with naked women, completely naked, if you could believe it, without a stitch on. The only place you can see anything like it back home is the church, where they have Adam and Eve, but both of them are wearing fig leaves and Eve's got her arms crossed so you can't see a thing. Not here. Here they got no shame and show it all.

The Electricity Building was the very best! They showed Edison's phonograph and everyone could try it out. They put a sort of a funnel up to your mouth and you say whatever comes into your head and it comes out exactly like you said it. I mean the phonograph says it back to you. So you say, "How are you?" and the phonograph says, "How are you?", a bit like that trained raven the schoolmaster had back home, except it wasn't like the raven at all because no raven could do what this thing did. I thought I'd say something in Czech to see how they get around that one. So I said into the phonograph: "You old goat, what are you gawking at me for?" Well, I thought I'd faint. You know what that phonograph said to me? It said it right back, just like that. In Czech.

I guess that's America. Anything is possible here.

Well, if I had to tell you all the miracles we saw there I'd have to write a book and I haven't got time for that because in a little while I have to take a glass of grog up to the boss in bed. I don't enjoy that part of the job at all. He's a widower and every time I come near him he gets ideas and I have to slap his hand. Not that there's much danger. At his age, the worst he can do is put his hands where they got no business to be, and then I have to slap them away. But it's worse with his son, even though he never wants anything in bed. I mean drinks.

To make a long story short, we had the most fun of all on the Midway Plaisance. It's a kind of amusement park and it's about a mile long. We saw tigers riding on bicycles at Hagenbeck's and the Buffalo Bill Show and pygmys with enormous heads and right at the end, a Ferris wheel. The wheel is about a mile high. It's stood on its edge and it turns around and has these cabins hanging from it that hold about two hundred people each. It takes you so high up in the air you can see all Chicago down below and you can see New York on the horizon, but only when the weather is clear and that Sunday it wasn't. And wouldn't you know, we ran into Sam as soon as we got into one of the cabins.

Sam's the coachman I wrote you about who's whiter than our master, and still he's a nigger. It's a strange thing here in America. You don't have to be black to be a nigger. And it's not true that they won't let you into the fancy restaurants just because of the colour of your skin. You can be as white as Sam, and they still won't let you in. It's not your skin but your blood. Don't ask me how they can tell just from your blood if you're a nigger or not, that's asking me too much. Once I had to punch Sam in the nose because he was getting ideas and the blood that came out of his nose was the same colour as the blood that came out of the young boss's nose.

But Sam says he'd rather go to the joints where people of his own blood hang around, and since it was getting on night now, he took Denise and me to a joint on Ninetieth Street. He said some guy called Joplin, from Scotland, was going to drop in to play that night because he was in town for a couple of days to see the Fair, and also because his cousin was the bandleader in that joint. Sam says this Scots guy Joplin is the best piano man around.

It was a nice place, and some of the white folks, I reckon, were really white, even though it's hard to say. They had a dance floor in the middle and a small band with a singer who was black for sure, even though that doesn't necessarily mean she's a nigger. For all I know she could have been a black white person. A Czech girl has to think twice before getting married here, unless you know something about blood!

Most of the time the band played the cakewalk, sort of like those old folk dances back home. Well, as you know, I'm mad about dancing so almost as soon as we sat down we jumped up again and Sam and I hit the floor. Denise hit the floor too with one fellow who looked black but maybe he wasn't because she said his name was Polivka. I was real surprised because how could a nigger have a Czech name when there have never been any niggers in the old country? Well, it turned out this Polivka fella was from Texas, said his grandfather had a farm down there, but he couldn't speak Czech because his mom is a German. It turned out she wasn't his real mom, though, because he was a foundling. So that explained it, I guess. Whatever he was, when he danced with me afterwards he danced like a nigger for sure.

So we had lots of fun and then suddenly the band stopped, the bandleader tapped on his fiddle and announced that the guest for the evening had just arrived, and it was that Joplin. Well, Marinka, I was completely confused. He was black too, just as black as Polivka. And here were Sam and the bandleader saying he was a Scot. But he sure was a first class piano man. You should have heard him tickle the ivories. Why – he went striding up and down half the keyboard with his left hand and he never missed a note. And his music sure made you want to jump. I never heard music like that in my life before, not even from that Dvorak fella and he must be a lot more famous if they let him be bandleader in the Festival Hall and not just in some nigger joint on Ninetieth Street. Anyway that Gee, Major! of his wasn't much compared to the stuff the Scot was playing. It was called Mabel, Leave Greg, so it must have been sad though it sounded pretty happy to me.

And speak of the Devil! I look over Polivka's shoulders and there, standing beside the piano and scowling at the Scot's hands, is that Dvorak fella. That's what I call luck. So as soon as the piece was done, I powdered my nose and went right over to the table where the Dvorak fella was sitting. He had another nigger with him who was maybe white on account of his blood but hardly on account of his skin, but he was a dandy-looking boy, that's for sure.

I went up to Dvorak and I say, in Czech, "Good evening, Mr. Bandmaster. I'm so glad to see you here this evening."

He looked puzzled and said, "To whom do I have the honour of speaking, young lady?"

And I said in good Czech, "I am Miss Rosie A. Nowak from Winnetka, Illinois."

Well, he gets this huge wrinkle in the middle of his forehead. "Young lady, aren't you stretching my leg? I'd say you were straight from the old country. I can see it in your eyes."

"I'm from Winnetka, Illinois," I said, "but I was born in Skrcena Lhota in the old country."

"And what is your middle name? Anezka? Antonia?"

"Just 'A'."

"But how were you christened?"

"That's just it," I said. "I wasn't. That's why I only have a middle initial, not a whole name. But here it's fashionable to have a middle initial, so I gave myself one. 'A'."

I'm telling you all this so you'll know what kind of conversation I had with this Dvorak. Then Joplin began to tickle the ivories again and I asked the bandmaster if he'd like to dance. Well, he's at least fifty, you know, and so he said, "Why don't you take a spin with this young man here? He's a student of mine."

His student sure knew how to grab a girl. His name was Will Marion Cook (which it seems to me is a pretty strange middle name, for a man anyways, talking of middle names) but unluckily for me he lives in New York and just had a summer job in Chicago in the Haiti Building where everyone was a nigger. He said he brought Mr. Dvorak to this joint because he was interested in nigger music. I asked him, since he knew Dvorak did he know how to dance the Gee, Major!

He looked sort of puzzled and he said, "What?"

"It's some kind of dance," I said. "Your bandmaster played it today in the Festival Hall."

"Oh that! I'll show you," said Will, and he suddenly brightened up. But I tell you, dearest Marinka, this Will is a pretty dirty-minded fella and I won't even tell you what he did, but I nearly hit him in the schnozz. And I don't believe him either. Maybe they dance that way in Africa, but not in Slovakia.

Anyway, he turned out to be a pretty saucy fellow. When the Scot left the stand and the regular band and the singer came back, Dvorak asked Will if he would mind asking the singer to do a nigger love song. So Will went up and spoke to her and she smiled and announced that the next number was a special request for Mr. Dvorak, then she bowed in our direction – so I knew this Dvorak fella was really famous if even the floozies in joints like this knew who he was.

Here's what she sang:

> What's the matter, Papa, please don't stop!
> Don't you know I love it, and I want it up!
> I'm wild about that thing!
> Just give my bell a ring!
> Just press my button!
> I'm wild about that thing!

"Nice," said this Dvorak. "Very nice melody. Only could you explain, Will – I don't understand a word."

And just imagine what that saucy Will told him! He said the girl is telling her man he's gotta stop loving her, because her funeral bell is going to ring and she's wild with despair.

Will just sat there with a poker face while his bandmaster said, "I once wrote a ballad something like it, The Wedding Shirt. But in that song, it's the man who dies."

And the floozie went on singing:

> Hmmm, if you wanna satisfy my soul,
> C'mon and rock me with a steady roll!
> I'm wild about that thing!

Well, I have to say one thing. That Will certainly has an imagination. You'd never guess how he explained that. He said it meant, Fill my soul with happiness, and Dvorak interrupted him and said, "Is it a kind of spiritual?" and Will was saucy enough to say, "Exactly, except they don't sing this one in church."

Well, this was too much for me, dishing out all this applesauce to the most famous bandleader in the world just because he doesn't understand English. "Sir," I said, "he's trying to – how did you put it?"

"What?" he asked, and the floozie was just singing:

> C'mon, turn the lights down low!
> When you think you're ready
> Just say so, let's go!

And Will went even further this time: he said the lovers' lives were going out like a light and she's saying if he thinks it's time to go, then they'll go. To heaven, that is. And that's where the bandmaster kind of sat up and said, "She's not trying to persuade him to commit suicide, is she?"

So I said, really fast, "He's stretching your.... "

Something began to dawn on him.

"My leg?" he said.

"He sure is," I said. "It's not like that at all."

And that was when Will said he had to go wash his hands. (That's how people here say politely that they have to go to the toilet.) And it finally dawned on the bandmaster. "You mean it's not that kind of song at all?"

"It sure isn't."

"And what is it about?"

"It's not something you should be asking an unmarried girl to tell you."

"Why not?"

"I'd have to blush."

That wrinkle on his forehead appeared again, like someone hit him with an axe. He said, "Young lady, aren't you the one who's stretching my leg?"

I shook my head. "Cross my heart and hope to die if I'm telling you a lie," I said.

"Do you think you could sing a Czech song like that for me?"

I shook my head again and said, "But I could whistle one for you."

"Okay," said Mr. Dvorak. "Whistle one for me."

·

So I did. I whistled him that song the boys used to sing when they got soused. Marinka, I thought the bandmaster would have a conniption right there and then, his face got so dark.

I have to stop or my boss's grog will get cold. Maybe that wouldn't be so bad. Maybe he'd go mad and wouldn't get any ideas.

So, dear Marinka, please accept my warmest wishes and fondest memories from

Your affectionate sister
Rosie

P.S. (That's Latin, my boss says) Marinka, I'm adding another page. Please don't show this part to Father. Throw it in the fire when you're done. You know, there's one thing that puzzles me. Those hussies in the paintings looked like they were five years old. I don't mean above, I mean below. Maybe it's because the women who posed for the painter were Anglo-Saxon, and maybe Anglo-Saxon women don't have hair down there. Who knows? I don't for sure. I've never seen a naked Anglo-Saxon woman, except for Georgia, the boss's daughter, and she sure isn't hairless. But the boss's name is Cohen and I don't think Jews are Anglo-Saxons. At least not back home they aren't.

P.P.S. Don't show this to Father for sure, and throw it into the stove right away! That Will, who danced the Gee, Major! with me, he put both his hands on my bottom and rubbed me and tried to make me believe that was how you danced it. Maybe he thought I was born yesterday. I had to slap his hands, and like I said I pretty near hit him on the schnozz.

P.P.P.S. On second thought, throw this whole letter into the fire for SURE! Or Father will be scared I'll lose my virginity in Chicago.

Just between you and me, dearest girl, there's no need to worry about that. Not any more anyway. But they don't take that kind of thing so serious here, not like they do back in the old country.

16 :C): AN ENCOUNTER OF GENIUSES

Harper's Monthly

Hugh McGregor-Fitzpatrick reviews
AN ENCOUNTER OF GENIUSES
in the salon of
Mrs. Francis N. Thurber

EARLY IN 1893, or, to be precise, in the spring of that year, an encounter took place in New York City between two geniuses, the eminent Bohemian composer and musician Antonin Dvorak, and my teacher, the brilliant dramatic and conceptual artist Steele MacKaye, recently and sadly deceased. It was an encounter that promised to unite their forces, their dreams, their genius and their energy to lay the foundations for a new art form, to which Steele MacKaye gave a name that captures precisely its intellectual and conceptual essence: the Spectatorium.

The meeting between these two giant minds and tireless imaginations took place in the residence of Mr. Francis N. Thurber, whose spouse, Jeannette M. Thurber, was Antonin Dvorak's patron. Mrs. Thurber was also responsible for the first – albeit fleeting – encounter between the sensibility of Antonin Dvorak and the genius of Steele MacKaye, when she took the renowned composer to Madison Square Garden to witness a performance by the Buffalo Bill ensemble of which Steele MacKaye was the director.

In the grand conceptual plan of Steele MacKaye, the Buffalo Bill Wild West Show was intended to acquaint the American public with the mighty drama of American civilization. This is accomplished through a series of seven tableaux, the first of which was entitled The Primeval Forest of America before Its Discovery by the White Man, and so on until the seventh tableau, A Cyclone Is Born and Unleashes Its Fury in the Rocky Mountains, to which was later added an eighth tableau, Sitting Bull Defeats General Custer, in which the title role was played by Sitting Bull *in persona*, and thus, through a daring piece of casting by the director, Steele MacKaye, a unity of the truth of the imagination and the truth of reality, of reality and history, was achieved. The fact is that in the tableaux themselves one may observe the seminal idea of the Spectatorium, since the Buffalo Bill Wild West Show blended kinetic and visual drama into a unity. It achieved this remarkable effect by using the voice of a narrator located in a woodpecker's nest in the trunk of an enormous tree, greater than life size, which, being an original part of the Primeval Forest of America (Tableau One), symbolically recalled a past common to the other six, or rather seven, tableaux. The effect of actuality wedded to poetic vision was heightened by various ingenious devices designed and constructed by Steele MacKaye, such as his phenomenal wind machine, driven by a steam engine located outside Madison Square Garden which, for each performance, with the help of four gigantic six-foot fans, sent three wagonloads of dry leaves swirling through the settlers' camp in the Rocky Mountains (in the seventh tableau), all of which took place against a semicircular backdrop of the Rocky Mountains half a mile long and fifty feet high, the mountain in the foreground having been painted to create the illusion that it was larger than reality. But more than by any of these wonders, and even more than by the narrative itself, the Master of Music's attention was captivated by the peerless sharpshooter Miss Annie Oakley, particularly in the closing moments of her act when, on horseback and armed with two pistols, she shot, within ten seconds, thirty-three rainbow-coloured glass balls thrown into the air by Steele MacKaye's ball-tossing machine, against a background of an electric Union flag designed by Steele MacKaye with the use of his own patented Curtain of Light. Nevertheless, the spirit of Steele MacKaye so fecundated the creative potential of the Czech Master of Harmony that by the time of their historic encounter at the Thurber home his mind was already primed to receive the ideas of Steele MacKaye and a mutual infusion of their geniuses was made possible.

When Steele MacKaye entered the salon of the Thurber home that evening, he observed Mrs. Thurber leading the Master of Tones by the arm with the clear intention of presenting him to Mr. John Pierpont Morgan and his spouse, that most admirable patron of the dramatic arts. Like many giants of the creative imagination, Steele MacKaye was endowed with the ability to forget the faces of people he saw only very seldom or not at all, and he concluded that since Mrs. Thurber was leading the Master of Symphonies by the arm, she was his spouse. Therefore he bowed, took her hand, and kissed it with the words, "I bow to your beauty, Madame Dvorak." The slight embarrassment that ensued was resolved by Steele MacKaye who, having been informed of his mistake by Master Dvorak himself, who jokingly retorted, "This isn't my Mrs., this is my mistress," perhaps not fully aware of the nuances of the English word, replied with an equally ready wit, "Pardon me, Maestro, but a woman with the charms of Mrs. Thurber would be an adornment well deserved by your genius." And without further delay he set about acquainting the Master of Harmony with the revolutionary idea of the Spectatorium.

Rooted in that historic conversation, then, lie the beginnings of the great musical achievement of Dvorak's imagination in response to very definite instigations of Steele MacKaye's concept of art in the New World.

The occasion of this great aftermath arose from the intrinsic nature of that new form of art, evolved by Steele MacKaye from his dreams and labours of many years. From his intimate experience, in the theatre, with the compromises in fine art necessitated by the uncontrollable elements of the human actor in drama, Steele MacKaye had conceived a new theatre-synthesis that would eliminate not the human actor as yet, but his individual voice from the total harmony of elements in a grand-scale production.

Grasping the great composer by the lapels, Steele MacKaye unfolded his vision to the astonished genius. In his Spectatorium, the *dramatis personae* would neither speak, as in a drama, nor sing, as in an opera. Though essentially pantomimists, yet they were not conventional allegorical figures like Pierrot and Pierretta of the music-hall "Pantomimes". On the contrary, they became gigantic human personalities. To this end, the actor representing the hero would be enlarged by an enormous magnifying glass which would bring to life Steele MacKaye's vision. With the elimination of the actor's

voice, the aural components – choral and symphonic – would be
intensified and thus the *musical* elements would be on an equal
footing with the *visual*. Hence the need for collaboration with a
brilliant choral-symphonic composer.

Radiating intellectual harmony, both great men moved across the
salon, accompanied by Mrs. Thurber, who was attempting to offer
Steele MacKaye a drink while he, in the firm grip of his muse and
heedless of his surroundings, stared intently into the eyes of his equally
immortal and exceptional colleague, which were becoming ever more
filled with wonder.

Refusing the proffered refreshments, Steele MacKaye continued
his explication unabated. He was now, he said (since he lacked the
experience, if not the talent, for musical creation), looking *outside*
himself for a musical partner in his grand scheme for the Spectatorium.

Here Steele MacKaye fell silent, being justifiably convinced that
it was not necessary *expressio verbis* to actually pronounce the *name*
of the person he sought to draw into his plans. The company, by that
time profoundly fascinated by the burgeoning *entente* between the
two titans, one European and the other American, the likes of which
none of those present had ever yet witnessed and would doubtless
recall for the remainder of their sojourn on this earth, joined Mrs.
Thurber who, deeply moved and honoured by the historic event taking place beneath her roof, forgot herself entirely and drank both the
refreshing alcoholic beverages she had originally proffered to both
Steele MacKaye and Antonin Dvorak. Now, when Steele MacKaye
had eloquently left unfinished his final sentence, which, though un-
spoken, was clearly a direct invitation to Master Dvorak to collab-
orate on the Spectatorium, the silence in the room became absolute.
At that moment, the Czech Master of Music, astounded by the daring
of Steele MacKaye's vision and still backing away, brushed the back
of his frock-coat against a velvet drape over a birdcage that stood
against one wall between alabaster sculptures representing, appro-
priately, the Muses Erato and Euterpe, causing the drape to slide to
the floor. The Harz canary, hitherto asleep, was now aroused and in
the silence began singing a melody that, as it were, symbolically
expressed the jubilant consent of *nature itself* to the grandeur of this
moment of destiny. Steele MacKaye grasped the Master of Tones by
both hands and the great Bohemian, aglow with profound enthusiasm
for this epochal act of mutual creation, cast a glance full of creative

rapture at the representative of nature, now warbling his full-throated delight with the future entente, and sighed: "What an artist!"

Later, Steele MacKaye would, at every opportunity, declare that of all the many honours and distinctions bestowed upon him, he valued this accolade most highly of all.

17 :𝄢: THE SNARING OF THE COUNT

THEY WERE BEAUTIFUL RED ROSES – *three dozen sweet-smelling blooms, their stems in blue crêpe paper still bearing traces of his perspiring hand. Now they stood in a blue vase that Mary had set on the piano.*

"Would you be kind enough to wait in the salon, sir? Miss Josephine should be back any time now. It's been four hours since she and the family left."

He wanted to comply, to go into the next room, settle down in the plush chair, gaze at the oil portrait of Josephine on the wall, perhaps light up a cigar, and wait. He even hoped it would be a long wait, since waiting for Josephine was bliss because it always ended with the joy of seeing her face and merry eyes and hearing her "Good afternoon, sir!" if her father was with her; or, if her father was having a nap in his room: "I hope you haven't been waiting long, dear Vaclav. You have? Was it an awfully long time? You're not angry with me, are you?"

This time, however, he saw a handwritten score on the piano, and noticed the dedication: "To the Esteemed Young Lady, Miss Josephine Cermakova...."

"I'd rather wait here, Mary. I'll pass the time at the piano."

"As you wish, sir."

As soon as she left, he reached for the music. It was like touching a nettle. He did not yet realize that the sensation was jealousy.

He walked behind the coffin with the family of the deceased. In front of him walked Anna and her children, and the husbands of her children – Suk, Sobotka, Santrucek; and behind him the friends – Wihan, Kaan, Prochazka. They proceeded along the embankment of the Vltava towards Vysehrad and at intervals the May sunshine broke through the clouds and sparkled on the varnished coffin. Nine years before, Anton had walked next to him behind another coffin – it had also been in late May, but that day it had rained – and he had cried. But now his jealousy of Anton was long past. Only when they lowered the coffin into the grave did the tears flood his eyes.

The salon door opened and Josephine's little sister appeared. She curtsied.

"Are you waiting for Jo?"

He overcame the disquiet he felt. "Indeed I am, Annie."

"She had to go with Papa and Mama to the Srameks'. The alderman was given the last rites today."

"I know, Annie."

The girl ambled over to the piano, then noticed the roses. "Did you bring those?"

"I did."

"For Jo?"

"Yes."

"Jo says you're her suitor." She reached out for the roses and sniffed them. As she did so, she knocked the music off the piano. "They haven't much of a smell."

He bent over and gathered up the manuscript and though he didn't want to – after all, there was a signature beneath the flowery script – he asked: "Did Mr. Dvorak bring this for Miss Josephine?"

"Indeed," said the girl. "He doesn't bring her bouquets; he doesn't have the money. But he's her suitor too."

So here was verbal confirmation. He arranged the sheets on the piano stand and began to play. A quick surge of emotion, which he now realized was jealousy, threatened to overwhelm him. He made several mistakes right away.

"Play it properly," said the girl.

He started again, carefully. What a viper Josephine is! The child, in her childish voice, began to sing. What else could he do but accompany her? His anger mounted.

> *No balm is there, no sweet relief*
> *For this poor, smitten heart;*
> *For love denied is sad despair,*
> *And fortune's cruelest dart.*

That rascal of a composer! Musicians certainly know how to go about it: "I suffer! I weep! Have mercy on me!" they wail. And in this case Josephine has certainly had mercy. He shuddered with anger and made another mistake.

"Can't you play it properly?"

He smiled. The romantics had been popular at the time, and they were masters of the art of lamentation. They scarcely needed – and usually didn't have – a reason. But how could he have known, back then, that Anton had a real reason to lament?

He played and the girl sang quite prettily, with a child's blithe ignorance of the implication of the words:

> And on the stone these words inscribed:
> A broken heart here sleeps –

"You're a terrible player," said the child. "You need more practice."

"I'm sorry, Annie." When he lifted his hands off the keyboard, he saw they were trembling. "I promise to work on it."

The child was quick to notice the tremor. "Are you in love with Jo?"

"I'm – I'm extremely fond of her."

"So is Mr. Dvorak."

He smiled despite the funeral march, which called for gloom and high seriousness. And then the cloud of another memory of what happened almost a decade later darkened his face....

With trembling hands he held the letter, put it down on the table, picked it up again, carried it to the wastepaper basket, stopped, set it back down on the blotter, then picked it up and examined it again. He had stopped counting how often he had read it now. The letter consisted of a single sentence: "Dvorak was in Berlin last week."

Of course it belonged in the wastepaper basket. But that would not erase the sentence from his memory, nor would it alter the fact that Josephine too had been in Berlin last week. To attend the christening – so she said – of her god-daughter, the child of a colleague from the Weimar Theatre.

He was panic-stricken: Should I take steps to determine if there really was a christening? If she really has a new god-daughter? That was silly, of course she had. He had seen Hedvige's letter with his own eyes. But women are always doing each other favours, it's a vast conspiracy of the fickle, he cried out to himself – and immediately felt ashamed. He tore the letter in two and threw both pieces in the basket. He walked to the window. A cock pheasant was strut-

ting testily across the lawn and behind its back, in the opposite direction, ran a hen. *It's so silly, after all. Josephine loves me, she's always finding ways of showing it in the most passionate and intimate ways. Certainly, she did hesitate at first. What beautiful young lady with a suitor for each finger wouldn't hesitate? Cruelly, one after another, she mows them down, cuts her way through that battlefield until only two or three contenders remain, until finally the beauty herself must choose — and then it becomes serious. Josephine had made her choice. Because she was an actress, she had made it dramatically.* A drive lined with white asters, and only at the end of it did he realize the import of her command: *"Not to Chuchle, no! Let's drive to Stromovka Park!"* At the vanishing point of those two white rows stood a bouquet of red roses like the one Josephine held in her lap, and above them the desperate exclamation mark of a deep furrow. At the time he said nothing. But he knew.

He turned away from the window. The wastepaper basket caught his eye.

But who was Anton then, and who is he today?

I'm still a count. And a member of parliament. But parliament is crawling with counts. And how many Antons are there in the world?

A silly idea.

There are the nights, after all. Could her passion for me be feigned?

They played the funeral march at a terribly slow tempo, perhaps taking the beat from the swinging censers. The coffin was a black mirror reflecting the sun.

He had begun by sending roses to her dressing room. Then he waited at the corner of Florenc Square. A fresh bouquet of roses. He had her note in his pocket: "My dear Count, I thank you with all my heart for the beautiful flowers. With kind regards, Josephine Cermakova."

She appeared in a pink coat with a black fur lining, her hands in a black muff and a hat of black lambskin on her head. Beneath the hem of her coat, black lace-up boots trod elegantly in the white snow. He gathered his courage and, holding up the bouquet, walked towards her. He swept off his hat in the freezing air.

"Ah, it's you! How tall you are!"

It sounded to him like a line from Shakespeare. But perhaps she doesn't like me being such a Goliath? Subconsciously, he tried to make himself smaller.

"Why are you slouching?"

"I'm not slouching, Miss Cermakova."

"Now you've just straightened up." Her bright eyes mocked him. They seemed to be waiting for him to act.

"May I walk with you?"

"I'm going to a rehearsal."

"I know," he said, and blushed.

She laughed. *"Off we go then."*

He walked by her side and forgot about the roses. She walked beside him with dainty steps, and he tried vainly to adjust his giant stride to fit hers. The effect was comic and he gave up trying. On the other side of the bridge, people were feeding the gulls.

"Look! Gulls!" she said. *"Haven't you got a bun?"*

Unhappily, he replied that he hadn't.

She laughed. *"Ah well, they won't die of hunger."*

"I – don't suppose they will." He felt like a dunce.

A while later: *"Next time bring one."*

They had gone about a hundred yards before he realized the significance of her words. Quickly, he said, *"May I wait for you again?"*

"If it amuses you."

"Oh, indeed it does."

"But you don't seem to be enjoying yourself."

"I'm enjoying myself immensely, Miss Cermakova." I'm enjoying myself, yes. But what can I say to amuse her?

"Then why don't you say something?"

"I – I don't know."

"Well, let's not talk at all then."

How had Anton conversed with her? But he had been giving her piano lessons, so there was always something to talk about. She was so different from the other girls he'd known before her. Now, at the end of Anton's journey, he knew that there had been more to it than the charm of romance. All the girls before her had been silent and their silence had loosened his tongue. Josephine was never silent for long.

"Do you often send flowers to actresses?"

"Never!" he said, hurt. He was still clutching the forgotten bouquet.

"That's not true, strictly speaking."

"I swear it is!"

"I wonder who could have sent me those tea-roses last week?"

"That was me, Miss Cermakova. I thought – "

"I don't suppose you're lying, are you?"

"No!"

"Hmm," she said, laughing up at him. "So there you are. I do have an admirer."

"You certainly do, Miss Josephine."

Suddenly, they began to talk. Not about roses, only about horses, and he had no idea how in God's name they had got onto that, of all things. But however it was, he knew more about horses than he knew about flowers. Later it turned out that Josephine really was fond of horses.

He was crushed by his sadness. For nine years now, he had had nothing left of Josephine but a portrait he had moved to the manor house from the Cermaks' salon. Those sad, final years, when her happy heart slowly began to run down. Beginnings are always wonderful. Whatever she said, whatever she did, the slightest movement of her little finger, everything was a miracle. Everything was happiness. After more than a quarter of a century, his love came back to him from those snow-filled streets, from the peripatetic lecture on horses that flowed like a dream, like water, like nothing, like those eighteen happy years, like a day, squandered, half forgotten, the terrible destiny of everything living. Now it came back to him with pain, the painful knowledge that there is no going back –

Their walk was over almost before it started. By the stage door, he suddenly realized he was still holding the roses, as if he'd brought them only for his own pleasure.

"I took the liberty of bringing you some roses, Miss Josephine."

She saddened theatrically. "Oh, dear. I suppose that means I won't get any this evening."

Now at last it was his turn to laugh.

That evening, during the curtain call – it was one of Tyl's comedies, he didn't know which, paid no attention to the plot and knew only that she had played part of her role disguised as a man – he leaned far out over the rail of his box and, doubly excited by her costume, applauded and shouted "Bravo! Bravo!" and she held his enormous bouquet in her arms. A card attached to it read: "I will wait again. I will always wait. Your K."

And he waited. Oh how he waited.

And how terrible endings always are. Every raising of an eyelid, every movement of the bony hand, no more, no more, never more....

He waited. More than an hour. Anna quickly became bored with the conversation and with his poor showing on the piano and went off somewhere into the depths of the large apartment, to its mysterious chambers, for in there somewhere was her room with all its secrets, and he went into the salon and sat down in the plush chair, drawing deeply on his cigar, and stared at a finger of sunshine moving slowly across the oil painting, and he could not get the ominous piece of music out of his mind. Finally a knock came on the door. Mary went to open it. In walked the master of the house, his wife, an older sister and, at last, the goddess. In a white dress with red roses.

"Ah, Count Kounic! Your humble servant." The old goldsmith's voice. "Please excuse us. We sent you a note, but the messenger found you out. I'm sure you'll understand: an old friend was on his death-bed, and there was no time to lose – " Josephine merely smiled and lowered her lids as though the sun were in her eyes, but it had another, serpent-like quality, and she swept away the cigar smoke with her fan. For all his great love, greater than yesterday, he caught himself hating her.

"My, but you're a heavy smoker," she said afterwards, when her parents had left them alone in the music room, though of course they were right next door in the salon. He didn't reply, but with his finger on the handwritten score, he asked with passionate indifference, "Did your music teacher dedicate this to you, Miss Josephine?"

"Are you jealous, sir?" She was disarmingly direct.

He was getting ready to declare, with a disdainful laugh, how ridiculous and absurd such a question was, when her serpent eyes caught his again. He deflated. The eyes compelled him to tell the truth; and no sooner had he answered than he understood too that Josephine continually compelled him to abandon the convention of telling easy lies, of pussy-footing around unpleasant truths. "Yes," he said, "I'm jealous."

"How sweet," she replied.

"It's not sweet for me, Miss Josephine."

"I mean, it's sweet that you're so fond of me. If you weren't, you'd never have noticed that score."

"I love you!"

"I know."

"What about him?" And he nodded his head towards the piano.

She looked at the score, placed a white hand in a white sleeve on the keyboard and played a few notes. Later, at home, he would play them over many times. The melody had burned itself into his memory.

"Mr. Dvorak?" she said, pensively.

"Yes, Mr. Dvorak."

"Well," she said, "what would your guess be?"

Anger and jealousy combined in a fervent plea: "But what about you, Josephine?"

She looked towards the window, and it seemed to him that across her face, framed by the dark hair, there passed a fleeting shadow of melancholy. Once more she looked into his eyes. "Can you write songs?"

"No, I can't," he replied. "I can't match him in that."

"But if you could, would you write me music like this?" She sat down at the piano and made it echo with those heavenly sounds.

"I would," he said. "It's like my own soul speaking."

"That's because you're jealous. But did you feel that way before you saw this score?"

He recalled how in the early afternoon he had rushed to the goldsmith's house, where miracles were commonplace.

"Well, no," he admitted. "But now...."

"And yet he wrote it, you see?"

He hadn't said what he wanted to say. Absurdly, he thought of his old tutor, Ferdinand Schultz, who had told him with admiration about the Socratic method. He understood. Rather than saying anything further, he reached for the delicate hand lying in the white lap among the red roses. "Josephine...."

The little hand, with some power, returned his grasp and the goddess stood up cheerfully. "But come now, let's go next door. It's almost five. Father will be serving Eierkognak and he always gives me a sip."

She led him by the hand to the door, but before they opened it, she put her lips to his ear and whispered, "He thinks the theatre is full of teetotallers."

She laughed, her white teeth very close to his eyes. For the first time, he stole a kiss from her. That is, he thought he'd stolen it.

The rock of Vysehrad towered above the river like a huge tombstone. Clouds now covered the sun. It started to rain. The funeral march seemed to drag on for ever. A flock of ravens took to the air above the rock.

What if, right from the beginning, it had all been just serpent's wiles?

Nonsense. All those years! And nights. He lifted his foot and drove it into the wastepaper basket. What bastard could have sent me this packet of poison?

The birds wheeled in the air above the procession, their shadows flashing across the black mirror. The deep tones of the helicons echoed the grief –

He waited, as he had promised in his note, but it was a mutinous wait. He was never completely reconciled to the idea. Nor was his mutiny of any avail, for it merely led to unlovely arguments, fol-lowed by new bouquets, kisses to make up and: "Please try to un-derstand, Vaclav dear, I'm an actress. I have no desire to become a housewife at twenty-one."

"You will be a countess."

"Then a housecountess. And by the time I'm twenty-five, I'll have a dozen little counts and countesses clinging to my skirts."

"It's too late to accomplish that before you're twenty-five, Josie."

"How do you know? With my luck they'll all be triplets."

"Is your luck really so bad, Josie?"

She frowned. "You know what Neruda wrote about me? And of all the critics, I respect him most."

"He said you were beautiful and charming. That's entirely true – and you're a great champion of truth, aren't you?"

"And is the rest of what he wrote true too, Vaclav? Do you believe that too?"

"Not in the least!"

"I'm not so sure. In any case, I have to show them that I am an actress. I must!"

But everyone wanted to see her in light comedies – the audience, the critics, her admirers, and therefore the directors as well.

Then he learned the amusing news. He burst out laughing.

"That's not nice, Vaclav," she scolded.

"I think it's funny."

"Count, that's not a bit nice!" She was genuinely angry.

But he still found it funny. That cheeky, innocent girl. The little sister. "Play it properly. You should practise more." Of course, she was sixteen years old now. Still, he had to stifle his laughter.

"I'm very happy about it," intoned the goddess. "They're an ideal pair, Anton with his head in the clouds and Annie with our father's acumen. Anton has no idea what a bonanza he's found." She stopped, still playing somewhat testily with a ringlet of black hair. "Of course the question is, will they get married? I hope they do."

He no longer laughed, but shared her hope, though for different reasons. It was with a sense of relief, therefore, that he sat in a covered carriage near Florenc Square where he could see the entrance to St. Peter's and watch the wedding party leave the church through a modest gathering of guests. Prochazka, Kaan, several faces that he had seen in the orchestra from his box seat, the eldest sister who had come in from Jicin with her husband, the mother and father. The groom wore a conventional smile: the bride, unconventionally, was not weeping, and everything was just as it should be. He nodded to the coachman and off they set for Weimar, where the goddess was just starting a new engagement. A good excuse for not attending the wedding of her favourite sister, heiress to the second of her many admirers. He sighed with relief, lit a cigar and watched the Prague streets, in a cheerful rainfall, gradually become fields, gentle hills, the melancholy countryside rising to the Ore Mountains.

The mournful rain, the mournful procession, the mournful tones of the tuba, the mournful river.

And she waited too, knowing that she was dying. Waiting for Ton to appear once more, as he had during the past holidays, walking along the pathway to the manor house where she sat on the terrace, with a small bottle of pills on the balustrade in front of her breaking the rays of the evening sun into the seven colours of a hopeless rainbow. His wise wife Josephine, who had cured him of the follies of jealousy, who had taught him the secrets of a love that does not exclude love and is fulfilled by love.

And Ton did come, but by that time she could no longer sit on the terrace. She was all but lost in the wide bed beneath the silken arch of a dark blue canopy. Ton made only one more visit to the manor house. And then she was no more.

His eyes burned. The sun once again appeared among the tattered clouds. The black coffin shone in the May sunshine. He saw Otylia in front of him, crying. Anton had cried then too. He had stumbled along beside him like a sick child, heedless of worldly proprieties. Naturally people had talked. Romance? The good Lord himself knows whether it stopped at that, my dear. Speak no ill of the dead, but – the poor Count! Ridiculous. How ridiculous it was. He felt a warm trickle down his cheek, and he wiped it away with his finger. The coffin shimmered like a black diamond.

And one sad evening in an empty manor house, on an empty terrace, on an early evening in June sunshine shortly after she had died, Anton and Wihan came to visit him; music does not offend mourning. They rehearsed a new concerto, Anton at the piano, Wihan on cello. Wihan's magic cello. Tragic melodies, one after another, his inexhaustible richness. The music touched heaven by virtue of its peasant's faith, a faith that he himself, alas, did not and could not have – a faith that Josephine was. Even after death. "Wait, Wihan, I have to rewrite that last movement a little," said Anton, tearful old Anton, gathering up the score.

He didn't understand why, afterwards, Anton insisted that a cellist come all the way from England to perform the concerto. But the glory of the B-Minor Cello Concerto had shone through the foreigner's interpretation even though he had never stood in early evening on the terrace, now bereft of its little lighthouse, the glass vial that split the sun's rays into the colours of vain hope. And he, perhaps only he – and Anton, of course, sitting in the box with him at the Albert Hall – could hear the traces of her loveliness in the final bars, in the sobbing swell of the lovely cello, the lovely melody, and he saw her in her peignoir, seated at the piano and singing: "No balm is there, no sweet relief, for this poor smitten heart...."

But he had once been consumed by jealousy, a jealousy implanted in his soul by that vicious letter.

"Josephine – I hear Anton was in Berlin too?"

She stopped playing. "Yes, he was."

He couldn't resist sarcasm, cheap as an evening tabloid. "Was he there for the christening?"

"What would Anton be doing at Hedvige's christening? He was there to see Joachim. Joachim was performing his new sextet."

"Were you at Joachim's too?"

"No. I didn't meet Anton until the following day, in a café. Then he took the evening train to Prague."

Was it so innocent? Or was she merely a clever tactician who knew that to deny it would have been a mistake because everything could be checked?

It's all so foolish. After all, I'm not going to write to Berlin to find out if there really was a christening, a baby girl, a godmother from Prague –

And yet once more he spoke like an evening tabloid. "Well, it certainly was a coincidence, wasn't it? Why didn't you tell me about it before this?"

He heard the false intonation in his own voice.

"Vaclav! I thought there were no misunderstandings between us about that. I'm fond of Anton, I always have been and I always will be. And I love you. You're my husband."

He blushed, feeling the full depths of his folly exposed. "But why didn't you tell me you met Anton there, Josie?" *he said dejectedly.*

"And who told you, Vaclav?"

Embarrassed, he told her about the letter he had trampled in the wastepaper basket.

She sighed. "I'm sorry, Vaclav, please forgive me. I didn't want you to fuss over it, but of course I should have told you – I'm such a fool."

"I'm the fool, Josie."

She embraced him, and laughed. "What if we're both right?"

There were traces of her loveliness everywhere in the wide landscape of Anton's music. The coffin, like a black diamond.... *Hardly a year ago. Anton looked very old. Death, which nine years earlier had settled mercilessly on the terrace of the manor house, had now, like a ghastly hairdresser, transformed his wild mane into wretched strands of straight grey hair, and like a mean beautician, had turned his wrathful features into the face of an apoplectic old man. He sat in the box, decrepit, surrounded by the splendour of his music that welled up, as always, from improbable sources. Her loveliness, a bitter memory melted down in the sorcerer's cauldron of talent into the loveliness of reconciliation – the last trace of a victorious afternoon and a bitter defeat –* "White asters bloomed along the path and everywhere around it...."

A bright day in May, the black, triumphal coffin of the Assumption. Suddenly, he felt Anton's old-fashioned faith, closed inside the sarcophagus, reaching out to him through the shades of Schopenhauer, Spencer, Feuerbach, Darwin, the shadows of those dark names taught to him by Schultz, his tutor. Josephine is. Everything lovely persists *in saecula saeculorum*. Only what is bad, foolish, wrongheaded, ugly has no duration after death.

The unhappy exclamation mark above that enormous bouquet, purchased beyond his means, at the very end of two rows of asters. "Waste no time, my lad, hurry to your love" – he recited to the rhythm of the funeral music the lyrics from Rusalka, Anton's opera about unrequited love – "soon you'll grow to be a man – "

I waited, I waited over a decade, but I rebelled, he thought. *She was sitting in front of the mirror in the dressing room when all at once she said, "Count! This is dreadful!"*

"What?" "Count" no longer meant only that she was angry; it also meant that something unpleasant had happened but, because she never cried, that she wished to shrug it off with humour.

"I've got a wrinkle!"

He leaned over her shoulder and looked in the mirror.

"You see? Here it is." And she pointed.

He couldn't see anything, but he said cunningly, "My word, yes, I see it too. And I know what it means."

"I know what it means too."

"What do you think I think it means?"

He encountered her eyes in the mirror. There was a slight uncertainty in them.

"What ugly thoughts are running through your mind, Count?"

"My thoughts are not ugly. Far from it."

She took a powder puff from the table and began drowning the wrinkle in powder. "I don't know of any nice thoughts one could have on seeing a wrinkle."

"I do."

"Tell me, Count. And don't lie to me!"

"I think the wrinkle means a definite end to my period of waiting."

"Hmm," she said, in a cloud of powder. She leaned close to the mirror to examine the result. "Hmm," she said again. "You may well be right."

His happiness took all the strength out of his legs, and he sank into the position recommended in the book Courtship and Marriage: Precepts for Young Gentlemen.

The tones of Anton's Requiem rose over the open grave as the coffin was slowly lowered in its golden sling and the light of the brilliant black diamond was extinguished in the shadow of the earth. He looked at Anna and her six children standing on the other side of the grave. They were all crying. But the tones of the Requiem denied the eternity of mourning and sang of the eternity of the beauty that is left behind, and of those who were beautiful on this brief pilgrimage. Traces of loveliness remained through all the endless countryside of his music. Traces of a loveliness whose name is Josephine, who is, as Anton is.

When the soprano began to sing Rusalka's great aria on the darkened stage, where a white stage moon hung among the blue treetops, somewhere in the chambers of ancient memory an afternoon piano picked out a melody, a melody imprinted on his soul by an age-old gust of youthful jealousy, and love, magnified by grief, poured from his heart and drenched his body and soul despite the space of forty years.... It was the same melody, sweetly beautiful, that he had first read on the piano in Josephine's salon, there at the beginning and the end, the alpha and omega of a brief life, for – he looked at the grey, dark-skinned old man in the box beside him – Anton's days were coming to an end....

The coffin reached the end of its journey.

How foolish he had been. But he couldn't have been otherwise. *Anna, no longer an impudent child, but a sixteen-year-old Miss Annie, toying with a white parasol on the corner of Spalena Street and saying, "Mr. Dvorak is teaching just me now; Jo doesn't have time for lessons."*

But he was caught in uncertainty, for Josephine, though she was twenty-one, had merely laughed when he brought up the subject of marriage in her dressing room. "Come now, Count, this is hardly the time. What would all my other admirers say? Don't be such a selfish one. They'd stop coming to see me perform, and if that happens I'll be thrown out of the theatre." "I'm being serious, Josephine." Still she had laughed, then laughter subsided to a smile. "Seriously, then. Don't we still have plenty of time, Vaclav? Do you really want to stick your head in the horse-collar when you're barely twenty-two?" "I do," he had declared stubbornly. "But I can't have that on my conscience," she had said – a line from one of her French comedies. "Horse-collars are hard to get off."

He looked hard at the little sister as she made her carefully phrased announcement, twirling her parasol with deliberate indifference.

"Is that a fact, Miss Annie?"

Anna nodded. She lifted her blunt little nose in the air. "Are you still jealous?"

"No, but – "

"You have absolutely no reason to be," she said. At the time, he had no idea why she sounded so sure of herself. When he learned why soon afterwards he couldn't help laughing, and Josephine said, "That's not nice, Vaclav!" But he only said: "I just hope you're right."

Anna frowned up at him from under the parasol. "If you're really fond of Jo, how can you think any wrong of her?"

"I don't – " and he stopped. I really don't think any wrong of her, it's just that because I'm so fond of her, certain things cross my mind.

"Jo's not that kind of person," Anna said, frowning and twirling her parasol. "She doesn't deserve your jealousy." He was ashamed.

The weeping Otylia bent down, a lump of earth struck the coffin now lying in the earth's embrace. Otylia hid her face on her husband's shoulder. The falling lumps of earth gradually came round to him, then he too bent over. He felt the dampness of the earth, as though he were touching the end of the brief pilgrimage. But it flowed into eternity, leaving behind those traces of beauty he had so often perceived as wounding thorns before he gained wisdom, before the wise Josephine taught him with her entire life.

How joyfully his carriage clattered through the evening streets of Weimar! Past Goethe's house, past people on their evening promenade savouring a late Indian summer, past the theatre and along avenues that led to the quarter of large residences. The wedding he had watched from a distance with such anxiety and such relief was far behind him, in Bohemia. They slowed down, he looked for the address and at last the coachman halted the horses. An expansive villa clothed in bare ivy vines, bright windows half open to the mild evening. The carriage halted, the rattling of the wheels ceased. In the dying light, he could hear the lovely voice singing a melody that had been burned into his soul – and his joy was transformed into the grief of knowing, which he did not yet understand was false knowing, a foolish mistake.

> Love steals upon us like a dream
> Of beauty, grace and light:
> And, dreamlike, slips away too soon....

He sat in the carriage, rigid. The lovely voice was like a blow from a fist. The driver was discreetly silent. Long after the song was over, he finally gave the order to drive back to the hotel. Next morning, after a night spent first in wakefulness, then in the sleep of the dead, tortured by nightmares, he had calmed down somewhat. At nine, he rang at the door of the villa. Josephine came straight into his arms.

"Is Annie safely married?"

He confirmed that she was.

"Oh, dear Vaclav, you have no idea how glad I am."

She kissed him passionately, more passionately than ever before.

Oddly enough – and later he saw the wisdom in it – he felt as he had when he saw the bouquet of roses, a blood-red spot at the vanishing point of two rows of white asters, and understood the significance of the order: "Not to Chuchle, no!"

He drove off in the coach alone, the funeral over. There was still sadness in him, but it no longer oppressed him. He ordered the driver to take him to Vysoka. Soon they were driving through the countryside with its long, narrow, brown fields where the green spring crop was just beginning to push through. On the narrow road through the fields, the coach resounded with the wooden harmony of wheels and frame, the leather roof drumming in the wind like a kettledrum. A lark hung over the fields. Then, in the distance, the red tower of the church in Trebsko where he and Josephine had made a vow of their love, and then the village, with the white façade of the manor house. *She sat on the terrace in a wicker chair, the pill bottle splitting the sunlight into the seven colours of the rainbow. He stood inside the French doors with pain in his heart and looked at her black hair, carefully groomed as usual, gathered in its gold hair-clasp, and in it, thin strands of silver.* Now, rolling homewards in the coach, the pain was gone: Josephine sat on the terrace, young and beautiful, and along the road from the village strode a big man carrying an enormous bouquet of red roses.

He opened the French doors and walked out onto the terrace. Together, he and his wife greeted Anton.

18 :꒰꒱: A CONTROVERSY OVER BRAHMS

"BRAHMS, MASTER?" Jim Huneker's voice thundered through the staff clubroom. "You say Brahms is generous?"

"He sent Clara Schumann fifteen thousand gulden. And he offered me – "

Adele stopped listening and turned to the glass wall that separated the staff clubroom from the corridor.... Jim is only venting his anger against Dvorak because he botched the fingering in the Totentanz a short while ago and made a fool of himself in front of that new pupil of his, Arabella Van Fossen. He's still smarting from that little incident, for all his reputation as a music critic and teacher. What a rake! Or perhaps he still dreams of being a concert pianist. But it's about time he realized he's no Liszt. He could never hope to have a fingerspan of more than ten keys on the piano. Still, it's astonishing how ambition makes one stupid – imagine the clever Jim, like some fame-hungry aspirant from the sticks, having the superciliary tendon between his ring and little finger severed so he'd have a span like the good Abbé! Anyway, he certainly shouldn't torment old Borax now just because Arabella Van Fossen sneered at him.

She looked down the corridor and her mood sank to zero. Monsieur Senac had just dashed out of the gymnasium door with a naked rapier and after him pranced a bevy of female students in fencing outfits – clearly exploiting a pedagogical occasion to show off their legs to the admiring eyes of their colleagues. Naturally, Laura Collins was right behind Senac, and in the doorway of the orchestra rehearsal hall stood Will Marion, preening his moustache like a tomcat. Bitterly she had to admit that Collins' legs were for showing off, even to a connoisseur like Will Marion.

That's enough, Margulies! she reprimanded herself. Surely you never expected a summer romance in Central Europe to survive a trans-Atlantic voyage and almost two academic years.

Or course not, but it still makes me boil.

Will Marion had already turned to Collins and was buzzing something into her ear. Buzz away, you miserable bum. She turned away from the glass, caught sight of Jim's handsome, patrician features, the long Roman nose and prominent chin, and the Master's frowning face. The end of a heartfelt statement reached her: " – such a noble man!"

"And Clara Schumann paid him back right away with a piano concert. And what did she play? Guess, Master! Take five guesses!"

"I *know* she played Brahms. But he tried to stop her concert from taking place. I've heard – "

"Tried, and failed."

"That's not true, Mr. Huneker."

"What? You mean he persuaded her not to go ahead with it?"

As a little girl, mad about music, she had stood with her nose against the wide glass window of the Heinrichshof Café, where the massive genius with the St. Nicholas beard dozed over his afternoon mocha for the Viennese to admire, a living monument to himself. Brahms was generous to the famous and the wealthy: today, she was no longer impressed by the renown he had enjoyed in Vienna. She saw him clearly now: kind to the always popular children in the Prater Gardens, considerate to those whose consideration he needed and to the influential critics.

Collins is standing there with such studied formality, her highly visible legs esthetically crossed, while Will Marion wriggles about almost like Monsieur Senac who, as everyone at the Conservatory knows, is the female half of an inseparable male couple. Dear Maestro, supposing that instead of silly little arguments you were to use your butcher's fist? Jim has a chin that was made for an uppercut from the heart. Doesn't he realize that the state grants the Master received with Brahms's support – whatever the elder composer's motivations – broke the chains of poverty that bound him to endless hours of listening to young ladies plonking away on the pianoforte?

" ' ... then perhaps you might take a rather more critical look at the notes themselves, the lead voices and so on,' " the Master quoted. "Isn't that kindly put? Someone else might have written to me, 'You make mistakes only a schoolboy could make!' And I did make such

mistakes, Mr. Huneker. A wagonload of excessive notes, a whole
wagonload. But Brahms was so kind, so.... " At this point the Master's
English failed him, and English, unfortunately, was Jim's strong
point. Collins loped off after the retreating fencers, Will stroked his
oft-stroked moustache once again. His trousers revealed a well-
remembered swelling.

Now, now, Margulies. After all, you knew from the beginning....
But you can know everything – it still won't help –

" – and Brahms played the accompaniment so fortissimo, Master,
that he was actually pounding the keys as though trying to demolish
the piano. The racket completely drowned out poor Gaushacker on
the cello. When they had finished, Gaushacker whispered to Brahms,
'Johann, you were too loud. I couldn't even hear myself play.' And
do you know what your kind friend Brahms replied?"

She wondered whether the Master at this point understood a word
of Jim's angry tirade. Blooming now with the deep, rose red of an
impending brain stroke, he had almost certainly lost the thread of
Jim's argument. She knew what Brahms had told the wretched cellist:
"You're a fortunate man, Joseph," he had said. All of Vienna had
laughed at the remark.

– and I mustn't nurture such a primitive anger against Will Marion.

She ran her mind quickly over what she remembered of their common past to find something, some memory, that might rekindle her
fondness for the Moor. But, she thought, he is as counterfeit as his
middle name. Marion. He wasn't a Marion at all, that was his mother's name. He was a rather unpoetic Mercer. Collins disappeared into
the women's dressing room. A Mercer. Named after his father's friend,
the first black American diplomat and congressman. Mercer had once
tried to throttle with his own hands the author of a thin book, for
his blasphemous criticism of the young Will's virtuosity, but in the
end the black leader had disgusted Will.

*The bell on the castle tower rolling down the hill, the city re-
verberating like a giant celesta. The lust in Will's eyes gave way to
aggressive defiance.* "I felt like vomiting. There he stood on the
podium, my father's friend, the great race leader, bragging publicly
that he had inherited his lovely hair, his tiny feet and his delicate
hands from his white ancestors. Him! My namesake and patron, Adele!
But I sure didn't inherit this bushy, wiry hair of mine from any white
ancestor. And look at my feet – " *He raised them up off the bed, and
in the moonlight they did look enormous.* "So I went home and

shouted at my mother, 'You've named me after the wrong man! I won't be Mercer any more! From now on, my name is Will Marion! If Marion's good enough for you, it suits me fine."

He had christened himself at the font of historical anger. She smiled inwardly, in spite of herself. And perhaps he chases those white girls – Collins, Van Fossen, Geraldine – those blonde fräuleins, more out of revenge than lust. He's not really counterfeit. It's just that he's too young for me, when he's surrounded by eighteen-year-olds in fencing tights – *"Aren't you in love?" Jeannette had a fine nose. "I am," she had said impudently. "With Mr. Dvorak. You may forget his face, but have you noticed the figure he cuts?" "I noticed that back in Cambridge," said Jeannette. "The best-filled frock coat of the evening. But I'm afraid, Adele, that you'll get nowhere. Cerberus keeps a close eye on him." "What if you were to try, Jeannette? I have the impression he fancies you." Jeannette laughed. "Perhaps, but he hasn't made any advances." Thus she had adroitly averted Jeannette's attention, but she was still annoyed that her infatuation was so obvious. Of course, Jeannette had an exceptionally keen nose.*

" ... not at all. I have never read Schopenhauer," she heard the Master say in response to another of Huneker's snide remarks. "I never had a proper education, Mr. Huneker. And yet something I have in my head. Where else does such a gift come from, if not from God?"

"And where did Brahms get his from?"

"Brahms says he does not believe in God. But that is not the main thing. What is important is that the spirit speaks in his music."

"Would the Vatican approve of such theology?"

She turned around and, like a little girl, pressed her nose against the glass divider. The corridor was empty now. The clock on the wall showed that it was past five. From the open door of the orchestra rehearsal hall she could hear the enchanting voice of Will's violin. "Here my singing, hear my pleading, Borne across the night...." She closed her eyes and fought back an onslaught of anger. Doggedly she called to mind his tale of a black snake in a small boy's bed, how they both – the boy and the snake – had been terrified of one another that night at Grandpa Lewis's place, *everyone in bed except his fifteen-year-old cousin Renée who was taking a bath in a tub in the kitchen, and he shot into the room, his eyes wide, terror in his face: A snake! There's a snake in my bed! Renée forgot her nakedness, climbed out of the tub, knelt on the floor and held the terrified little head to her full, soft, dripping breasts and his fear was banished. When both of them realized what condition they were in, she whispered, "Go back to your room. I'll be right there." And she came, in a thin cotton nightgown, smelling of soap. The Devil had taken care of the snake, which had clearly burrowed into the earth in terror. "And we just about became man and wife!" he said, grinning. "Will, how could you!" she had said, shocked. "Don't forget, Adele, that less than ten years had gone by since the abolition of slavery, and many of the old customs – some of which, like this one, were not necessarily bad – still persisted. All a man and a woman had to say to each other was, 'You're my man!' and 'You're my woman.' And they were each other's."*

"For how long?" she asked.

Will stretched out blissfully. A cool breeze came in through the window, bringing with it the faint smell of smoke; the yellow moon slid behind a tower.

"Oh, as long as one of them wasn't sold," said Will drily. "But in our case the marriage never got rolling. The noble savage had already been spoiled by the white man's wisdom, and this particular noble savage was only – well, let's say twelve – so his understanding of the white man's wisdom was that of a child. I was just about to take her beautiful breasts in my hands when an inner voice scolded me: 'Close relatives must not marry.' 'Close relatives must not marry, Renée,' I muttered, the breasts retreated and I watched as they vanished from my life. 'You're right, Willie,' she whispered. She slipped out of the bed, and the snake which had been peeking out through a hole in the floor quickly withdrew his head; the flimsy nightgown moved across a beam of moonlight and she was gone. And I lay in bed and wondered how close a second cousin who was the step-daughter of my mother's stepsister was."

She laughed. *"And did you come to any conclusions?"*

"I did, but by that time it was too late. The next day, the last thing Renée wanted was to be reminded of what had happened, and the day after that Grandpa Lewis gave up trying to whip me into shape and put me on the train with those cigars and the kid with the sign."

"What became of Renée?"

He grimaced and looked at her with something she couldn't decipher in his eyes.

"Do you really want to know?"

"Yes, I do."

"Shortly after that she had an idiot child by her half-wit uncle. The child died when it was a week old and Renée died a month later."

"Now the woods are cool and quiet, come, my heart's delight," sang the violin.

Her nose against the glass felt cold. She turned back to the room.

"Eleonore von Breuning." Jim was counting on his fingers. "Giulietta Guicciardi. Baroness Ertmann. Fanni del Rio, Nanette Streicher, Theresa Malfatti – "

"I know that, I know that," shouted Dvorak. "But he wrote the Ninth – "

"And can't you hear the sexual passion in that, Dr. Dvorak? Music is the most sensual of all the arts. It reveals to us the hidden secrets of sex.... "

The Master's eyes opened wide. He was about to speak, but something seemed to stop him.

"When I listen to *your* compositions, Dr. Dvorak, I hear.... " And Jim slyly left the rest unsaid.

"What do you hear?" Dvorak barked.

"Well – not quite what I hear in Brahms."

The Master swallowed. She thought he seemed relieved – as if his soul were still safe from Jim's prying eyes. His voice trembled as he replied. "Brahms is a friend and protector of Clara Schumann. He thought – "

"It's not Clara Schumann I have in mind in this case."

"He is a high-minded and noble man. You have no right – "

Not what he hears in Brahms? The pale face, sad dark eyes with their hint of loss and death; the framework of the soul – "Now the whisp'ring leaves protect us, From the moon on high...."

"They say – Brahms is a striking figure, as you know – they say he can sometimes be observed in the light of the moon, quietly negotiating with the ladies of the night on the Mariahilferstrasse – "

"I don't believe it!"

"No? Why? As a boy he performed with his father in the notorious red-light quarter of Hamburg.... "

You're on the wrong track, Jim. Such lusts are not revealed in the music of the Master from Vysoka. Perhaps – she looked around through the glass wall, the corridor filled with the sensual sound of the violin

– "Fear no sound of traitor footstep, Fear no curious eye ... " perhaps in Will's music. When his people were slaves love could not be a matter of duration, only of intensity: for so long they were not masters of their time, only of single nights, of a few brief months –

And why are you still fiddling and not running after Collins, you miserable bum?

As if to answer her imperious question, he came swiftly out of the rehearsal hall, his violin under his arm, and strode off towards the dressing rooms. She felt irritated.

"Say no evil about anyone? Is that truly your philosophy in life?" Jim's voice rang with triumph over an easy prey. "Let me remind you of another Brahms *bon mot*, then. 'In dealing with Bruckner, one deals not with a body of compositions, but with a series of frauds.' Does that seem kind to you? A kind thing to say about a great organist and composer?"

"In a weak moment – he's only human, after all – "

"Yes. And in weak moments, he fears competition."

She interrupted him. "Then why did he not fear Dr. Dvorak, Jim?"

Both men looked at her.

"He had nothing to fear from me," said the Master.

She smiled at him and turned to Jim. "Didn't you say he curried favour with the powerful, the famous, the rich – "

"Bruckner is none of those, *chérie*."

" – and the talented?"

He glared at her. *In the Church of St. Stephen, she had heard angels singing in an organ like the Matterhorn. She was fifteen. "That's Anton Bruckner," her father told her, and they listened. The pipes were divided into seven ranks and seven heavenly lines of counterpoint mounted the steps of God's throne in complex, seven-part harmony. When it was over, a small man in baggy trousers that left his ankles exposed, and with the countenance of a denizen of the taverns – which he was – crawled out from behind the organ console. He bowed deeply to one of the burghers: "Your humble servant, Herr Provincial Councillor!" The dignitary nodded non-committally. From his rendezvous with the angels, the little man headed towards The Boar, where he immersed himself in Pilsener beer and surfaced only to tell her, as she sat admiringly beside him, a magnificent reminiscence that made her feel ill. In a coffin still reeking of damp earth lay a skeleton with scraps of decayed clothing clinging to it and swatches of long, grey hair sticking to the skull. Around it health officials, white smocks over their frock coats, were gravely measuring the skull. The little man with the face of a tavern habitué pushed his way in among them and reached out to touch the skull, whereupon four pairs of medical hands went out to restrain him. So he addressed the skull instead: "Do you see that, my dear Beethoven? Were you still alive, you would have let me touch you, would you not? But these gentlemen won't allow it." He bent over the coffin as though to kiss the skull with its strips of skin still clinging to it, when something shiny fell from his eye. Then they dragged him away. "When I got home, I realized that one of the lenses from my pince-nez was missing. The glass, Mr. Margulies, had fallen into his coffin. Now just imagine that among his dear bones there now lies a lens from my spectacles." She felt ill and asked to be excused. When she returned, he was reminiscing to her father, over a plate of pork, dumplings and boiled cabbage, about other adventures. "They laid it out, Mr. Margulies, on a table covered with black cloth. It was a beautiful yellow, almost golden. And then they let me touch it. With these very hands, Mr. Margulies" – and over the steaming meat, the man spread two hands like garden spades (but spades that had moved choirs of angels into song) – "with these very hands, I picked it up, Miss Margulies," he said, turning to her, "and laid it in the coffin. These hands" – and he held them out, absurdly, like a priest over the Eucharist – "these hands held the skull of the immortal Schubert." Again, she felt ill, and had to leave quickly. When she returned, the little man had placed his enormous hands on his own skull, almost completely bald save for a wreath of grey hair that had been trimmed short. "This hair," he said grandly, while his pork and dumplings grew cold, "was cut last Wednesday by Herr Schnappauf himself, barber to the great Wagner." He brought his hands down, looked about at his table companions with childlike eyes, noticed the pork and fell to eating with gusto. Suddenly she was aware of how the incense of a country church permeated the sophisticated harmonies of that angelic organ music, and how the village inn vibrated in the rhythms of those deep flutes. Bruckner and Dvorak: two strange servants of the Lord.*

" – because Brahms was jealous. They offered Bruckner a professorship at the university and passed him by. Nothing like it had ever happened to him before. And why?"

She pulled herself away from the hopelessly empty corridor on the other side of the glass wall, walked across the clubroom and looked out the window. A horse-drawn tram packed with passengers was moving down the street, and the sky over Stuyvesant Park was growing red. The street, too, was hopelessly empty, except for the sidewalk opposite, where Arabella Van Fossen stood in a bright spring dress, a sheaf of music under her arm. Van Fossen's landau was just pulling up beside her and a footman in a white top hat jumped lightly to the ground from the back seat. She turned around. Jim didn't know when to stop. She felt anguish for the Master, floundering helplessly in a foreign language in which he was unable to defend his benefactor.

He sat crushed, trapped in the impotence of language, while the carping piano teacher completed his revenge on the Master's gods because Van Fossen had not delivered herself up to him on the satin upholstery of her carriage, attended by a discreet footman.

" – because Brahms has everything: money, fame, position, the support of those head arbiters of taste, the critics. He wants for only one thing, Doctor. Talent! They may butter him up all they want, but entrust students to a clever imitator like him? Without talent, a man may be a good charlatan, but never a good teacher."

Her heart went out to the devastated Master. But suddenly light flared in the dark eyes. Not a kindly light. An unexpected light. Like his – and Bruckner's – famous modulations.

"Is that what you say?" he asked. "Without talent a man *cannot* be a good teacher?"

"He certainly cannot." Huneker raised his prominent chin.

"How is it then," said the strange barrel-organ of a voice, this defenceless child, "that you *are* a good teacher, Mr. Huneker?"

19 :C): TROUBLE IN HANNIBAL

"WASN'T LONG BEFORE I found a real job with a blacksmith and the wife, God rest her, made a few extra cents – the kind German lady we'd found room with let her use her wash-tubs so she could do other people's laundry at home. Wasn't much of it, was a lot of competition from the niggers, the nigger women who were free, I mean who wasn't slaves. But we scrimped and in January I had enough saved for a steamboat ticket and some extra cash just in case. I reckoned I'd go to Iowa first, sniff things out, take a claim, then go back to New Orleans, pick up the wife and the six kids. Well, it was a long trip. But I says to myself, Frank Valenta – I'd given up on Franta, 'cause folks had trouble gettin' their tongue around it – I says, this is it, you've come this far and you've no choice now but to go on. The steamboats only went as far as Dubuque, and after that, you were on your own. But I reckoned we could all be in Iowa in time for the spring sowing.

"In those days, Maestro, the passengers, those that travelled on the lower deck, had to help load fuel at every stop. Back then there was still sternwheelers on the river, and they burned big logs. Once, when we was loadin' up at Hannibal, the local niggers began singin' along with the work. Well you know, Maestro, I couldn't follow them yet – they're pretty hard to follow anyways – but they was nice songs, made the work a whole lot easier. So I thought, why not, I can sing too, I was in a good mood, I could see the end of our troubles, so I started singin' one of our old songs, the one about the bagpipes playing. And all of a sudden this young fellow who was hangin' around, shabby clothes, looked like he couldn't find work, he comes up to me and says, Are you Czech? And I says, Yes I am. You too?

"Maestro, turns out the poor bugger was someone called Johnny Jaros from Pisek, back in the old country, just turned sixteen and he'd got himself into a mess of trouble. The whole family'd been in America for five years, settled in Sumner Township where they'd a farm, and Frank and his dad had gone to St. Louis for some tools or somethin'. They stopped in Hannibal on the way back, and young Jaros wanted to take a gander at the town but he got waylaid by a gang of thieves who cracked him on the head, took everything he had and chucked him in the bushes. A search party from the boat couldn't find him, the captain wouldn't hold the boat up for more than an hour, so when Johnny came to, the steamboat was gone and so was his father. I tell you, Maestro, I felt sorry for the kid. He looked hungry, his clothes was a mess, and he was a sorry sight all round. When he found out I was goin' to Dubuque and on up to Iowa, he said, 'Countryman, Sumner Township is on the way. If you lend me some money so I can go with you, my dad will pay you back, maybe give you a reward or even bankroll you to get you started. We ain't short of money, the harvest was good last year' – and then he starts tellin' me about all the pigs and cows they had, two teams of horses, and right away I could just picture myself, farming all over again. Well, to cut a long story short, I lent him the money and we went to Dubuque together.

"At the next stop, when we were loadin' on the fuel, Johnny sets to with a gusto, grabs the biggest log he can find, gives her a heave up and suddenly boom! he's down and out like a light. We tried bringin' him round, finally the foreman pours a drop or two of bourbon down his throat, and that seemed to work because he comes to and says, 'Oh, Lordy, what's to become of me? I can't even lift a log without passin' out. Been like this ever since those bastards conked me on the bean and put me out for four hours. Oh, Lordy, how'll I hold down a job? What am I gonna do? What good is a cripple on a farm?' Anyways, he carries on like that for a while, Maestro, and before you know it, he's bawlin' like a woman, so the foreman, man called Sammy Clemens from Hannibal, took pity on him and give him the rest of the bourbon to get him movin' again.

"Well, that got him back on his feet and at the next town he sets to again. So I says to him, Johnny, you stay on board, we'll do your share for you, but no, he says, he feels fine again. He grabs the biggest log, gives her a heave, drops her, wobbles around a bit, then he flops down on the ground, shakes his head and starts wailin' again. Oh, Lord, he says, I'm gonna end up a beggar.

"So Clemens give him another drink of bourbon but he wouldn't let him have the whole bottle this time. Well, from then on, all the way to Dubuque, Johnny just sat on a railing of the lower deck at every port and watched us slavin' away loadin' the firewood, the tears rollin' down his cheeks like silver nuggets. Mary, Mother of Jesus, he'd wail, what's to become of me, I'll have to go beggin' for a livin'. At night, though, he'd never stop flappin' the air about how many cows they had, how many calves these cows had, all about their baby pigs and heifers and their pure-bred bull and how they had forty beehives and made their own honey wine and I don't know what all. There we were, lyin' on the open deck, wrapped up in burlap sacks because the nights were getting colder the farther north we went, the engine throbbin' and the paddle-wheel sloshing, and I could already see my farm and how I'd soon have money for a pocket-watch of my own, maybe even a silver one.

"Well, we got off at Dubuque and made our way overland to Sumner Township. We slept over with farmers, sometimes they fed us but mostly we had to buy our own food. Johnny had no money, so of course I had to stake him again. But I wasn't worried because after all, he had this rich father, the trip went fast, and a few days later we climbed to the top of a hill and there, down below us, was Sumner Township.

"Well, Maestro, I'll tell you it was a real shock. The whole township was burned out, couple of buildings left standin' here and there, the place a wasteland and one of those ruins was their farm.

"I thought Johnny was about to crack up. He tore at his hair, flopped down on the ground and started shoutin' that it was those red devils, the Kickapoos. Said they always threatened to take revenge because all this land once belonged to them, so this was their revenge. Holy Mary, he wails, on top of all my other troubles, now I'm an orphan. What've I ever done to deserve this kind of punishment?

"Well, I don't mind admittin' I felt scared too.

"When he calmed down a bit, he said there might still be hope his father and mother and brothers and sisters might of managed to save their skins. Course they'd lost everything, he said, but he had to find out if they was still alive. Maybe they'd made it to Calmar. So let's go to Calmar, I says, and find out. I wasn't too happy, as you can imagine, Maestro, because even if them poor folks was still alive, they'd hardly be able to pay me back, never mind stake me to a farm. But Johnny didn't think that was such a good idea, said it was dangerous around Calmar what with Kickapoos maybe still pokin' about in the woods, and he couldn't let me risk my skin and have me on his conscience after all I'd done for him. He said he had nothing to lose so he'd go to Calmar himself and he told me to take the long way round to the south, and when I got to Creek Point to head north-west and that would bring me to Spillville two days late at the most, but the main thing was it was safe. He'd come to Spill-ville after me, he said, and if he found his father alive and if his father had managed to save some property, he'd bring me a bit of money to make up part of what he owed me.

"So we split up. He set off north towards Calmar at a brisk clip, all doubled over so he'd be hard for any Indians to spot, and I headed south.

"I tell you, Maestro, I started to get that sinkin' feelin' all over again, sorry I'd ever paid any mind to Tony Klimesh's letter what the priest read me back home in Bohemia. After all we'd been through, to have some Kickapoos do me in – by the Jesus, maybe I should of stayed back home, never mind wretched poverty. East, west, home's best, that's what they say.

"But then, all of a sudden, I started gettin' ideas. Home's best, eh? If you call that best, it must be worse than hell itself everywhere else. So as I'm walking along, Maestro, the worm of doubt starts gnawin' away at me. I got thinkin' about that captain told us our featherbeds would be comin' on the good ship Bullshit, and a couple of other small swindles like it that we'd run into on our journey. Then it hit me. This fellow Johnny didn't look like too much of a cripple. His only problem was as soon as he set hands on work, he'd pass out like a soft-skinned little duchess. So I starts walkin' slower and slower and suddenly I realize what a damn fool I've been. That burned-out property couldn't of been no big farm with two teams of horses and all them cows and pigs, and I sure as hell never saw no beehives neither. Well, I kept slowin' down until finally I stopped. This Johnny may have fainted dead away like a delicate little lady but as soon as Clemens stuck the bottle of bourbon in his snoot he bounced back like a duchess after smelling-salts, and after that he drank like a Dutchman. So I turned right around and started headin' north to Calmar fast as I could travel.

"I arrived early in the evenin', stopped at the first farm and asked the farmer if he knew someone called Jaros. Man was Norwegian, but he spoke a touch of German. *Ja*, he said, he'd be one of the new ones, just came this year. there's a bunch of claims up at the north end, Jaros'll be the very last one.

"Well, by this time I was expectin' the worst. I went to the top end of the concession and everywhere you looked up there on the claims there was just shacks, not even a decent cabin let alone a farm. All newcomers. No time nor money to build a decent cabin yet. So I head for the shack on the last claim, and guess who comes waltzin' out, Maestro? Of course, it was Johnny. Soon as he laid eyes on me – well no, he didn't pass out, not this time. Turned around and lit out for the bush and was gone in a flash.

"So I go into the shack and the family's just havin' supper. They're eatin' gruel. The farmer's a great big hulkin' fellow, his wife's big enough for two and there's seven or eight kids. Your name Jaros? I ask. I am, he says. What brings you here? I've come to tell you, I says, that you've got quite the son. He's sure going to make his way in this world. And the farmer frowns and says, What's the miserable little bastard done now?

"He knew his own offspring well, Maestro. When I told him the whole story, he brought his fist down on the table and swore – well, sir, I wouldn't want to repeat it. Hard work has always had a bad odour for that one, he says. He's as strong as an ox but he's got two left hands. But he's a crafty one, so say I. He could pull a calf out of a barren cow. A calf? A trained monkey is more like it, says Jaros. And that's about the only thing would suit him, the scoundrel. Travellin' around the fairs with a trained monkey. But if he ever shows his nose around here again, I'll beat him within an inch of his life, I'll tear him in two and rip each half into three pieces!

"Anyway, sir, this Jaros was on the same boat as me. Didn't have no money neither, had to scrimp and save for the trip, and when they got to Hannibal they didn't have enough for them all to go so they left Frank behind. He was almost sixteen and clever, so they let him look after himself and come on to Calmar later. He had a map on a piece of paper showed him how to get from Dubuque to Calmar. One of the farmers on the boat drew it up for him. And that burned-out farmstead was there on the map too, Maestro, but it was three years old. Well, I already told you how he managed to look after himself – he was one hell of a smart operator.

"So I had to forget about the money he owed me. But Jaros took me to the saw mill where I got me a job and stayed there till the next fall. Meantime I took that claim in Spillville and by fall I had enough money saved to go back to New Orleans for the wife, God rest her, and the children. And the next spring, Maestro, I sowed my crops in Spillville."

Old Man Valenta fell silent, watching Kovarik and Dvorak out of bleary eyes.

"Did you ever run into that swindler again?" asked Kovarik.

"Not personally," the old man laughed craftily. "But Maestro, you have."

"Me?" Dvorak was perplexed.

"Yes, sure have. When you were in Chicago for the Bohemian Day rally. He owns the hotel you stayed in. I kept tabs on him, see, just to know. And in the parade, they say he carried the biggest flag. He's a big fellow, with a huge paunch." The old man chuckled. "Just like I told Jaros – his son would make his way in this world."

20 :C): FRANCIS AND JEANNETTE

FRANCIS PUT DOWN the seven-year-old glossy magazine, with McGregor-Fitzpatrick's remarkable account of their party, and looked at his wife who sat reading a score in the armchair on the other side of the hearth, then at the cage where their canary slept under a velvet cover. The eccentric Steele MacKaye had, on that evening, provided the only moment when he and Jeannette were able to put business worries out of their minds.

"I don't understand," she had said that morning, before the party. "Doesn't the government have gold?"

"The reserves have dropped below the acceptable minimum. It's caused a panic on Wall Street and some of the banks have stopped honouring cheques – mine included, unfortunately. Our situation is critical, but not hopeless."

She had looked at him over the Meissen cup from which she was drinking coffee.

"Are we going to be poor?" she had asked quietly.

"Not poor, exactly, but – " He had wanted to tell her that he would no longer be able to afford ventures like the American Opera Company, hundreds of thousands of unrecoverable dollars invested in magnificent but unknown American singers – unfortunately still unknown, because he loved his wife and wanted her dreams to succeed. She reminded him, not in what she achieved but in what she tried to achieve, of the hero of his favourite novel. Now, seven years later, he reached into the shelf where he kept the few books he owned and took out a thin, well-read volume, opened it at a place marked by a silken book mark and read: "That was originally what I had loved him for: that at a period when our native land was nude and crude and provincial, when the famous 'atmosphere' it is supposed

to lack was not even missed, when literature was lonely there and art and form almost impossible, he had found means to live and write like one of the first; to be free and general and not at all afraid." Jeannette was living almost a hundred years after Jeffrey Aspern, yet was not her native land, if not nude exactly, still crude and provincial? In its profligate expeditions to the old continent to bring back forgeries of Rubens? In its extravagant admiration of overseas giants, only some of whom were genuinely larger than average yet whom audiences in the Diamond Horseshoe would prefer over old Theodore Thomas at the drop of a hat? He set the book aside and returned to the magazine, where the confused student of that domestic giant Steele MacKaye had reviewed their party – climaxed by the Master of Tones' premature flight. He turned the page and read in another article: "We in America are still like babes in the wood, afflicted by a pious respect for Europe. Dvorak lives in Prague and we trip over each other to get to Prague to study under him. So we bring him to New York and lo! again, we rush back to study under any second-rate teacher in Europe."

" – but it'll be some time before you're able to hire another Dvorak, Jenny," he had said, finishing the sentence whose middle he had swallowed. He took a drink of his coffee, as the moneyed world tumbled in panic around them.

He had survived that collapse of the market in 1893. The problems had been sorted out. It hadn't been easy. It hadn't been easy at all for the firm he had spent his lifetime building up, which had gone under in the panic. And it certainly hadn't been easy for Jeannette. In the titanic clashes on Wall Street, the tiny craft of his co-operative ventures had come apart at the seams, while the monopolies he had challenged remained afloat. Yet he had done them some damage. He had struck a blow against the Vanderbilts, the Goulds and their arrogant power. The Interstate Commerce Commission, which remained and continued to watch over their shoulders, was a result of his long years of campaigning. He looked at his wife, who was reading a score old Borax had sent her from Prague. Borax had never held her personally responsible for any of the financial difficulties and clearly he still thought of her. Some of his letters, of course – but even the uncomprehending Borax knew, in the depths of his soul, what Jeannette's first concern was, and knew that for her, just as for him, money was merely a means to a more important end. Her concern was this country, which promised no one happiness on a platter, merely the right to pursue happiness freely. As he had, all the way from a small, rocky, barely subsistence-level farm in Delaware, to New York. In forty years, he had acquired this house, this beautiful and erudite woman and a firm owned co-operatively by his employees and customers, not in deference to some Utopian vision like the ones embodied in the Brook Farm community, but so that they too would have a better chance of realizing their own American dream.

He looked at Jeannette. The flames in the fireplace played on the smooth skin of her face as she read the score. *She had come to him and set a letter on his table. It was something she never did, so it must be serious. Half a year had passed since that breakfast when he had told her a second Dvorak was out of the question for a time, and now here she was struggling to keep the first one as well.*

"Read that, Francis," she said. "Isn't it rather – unkind of him?"

That was the harshest euphemism that his distinguished wife was capable of uttering. It must have been serious indeed. He turned to read the letter:

327 East Seventeenth Street,
New York,
November 20, 1894

Dear Mrs. Thurber,

I have waited patiently, but circumstances now compel me to inform you that I can wait no longer.

Allow me to recapitulate:

On January 25 of this year, my Prague bank informed me that the cheque for $7500 representing the second half of my salary for the school year of 1892-93 was not covered by sufficient funds. I informed you of this at once and, as well, of the fact that for almost two months, you had owed me a part of the salary I should have received on December 1, 1893.

On March 17, that is, after a delay of several weeks, I received a letter from you in which you promised to pay me a part of the instalments owing for 1893-94 to the end of April, and the remainder as far as possible before my departure for Europe in May. At the same time, you offered me a cheque to compensate for the one that was not covered, which was payable after October 15, including 6% interest on the unpaid portion.

In my letter of April 4, I protested against such a procedure and wrote that, painful though it might be, I would have to make the whole business public if I were not paid what was owed me by contract.

Subsequently, on April 20, you sent me $2000 and therefore not only did I take no further steps, but on April 28 I signed a contract for the 1894-95 school year, despite the previous experience, which suggested I might not be able to rely on prompt payment.

On May 15, I received $1000 from you.

On August 26, when I was in Vysoka, you wrote me that a part of the $7500 owing me could not be paid until October 8, but it would be paid then and the remainder on October 16. On the basis of this assurance, my wife and I and my son returned to America. I left the rest of my children in Prague this time because I was uncertain whether you would be able to fulfil your promises concerning the benefits due to me, and afraid lest the situation that arose this spring, when we were nearly left without money for food and accommodation, repeat itself.

In the belief that such a situation would not recur, I honoured my side of the contract and came.

Now, I regret to inform you today that of the $7500 owing – which should have been transferred to my Prague account in two payments, on the 8th and the 16th of October – not a single dollar has yet been paid.

This fact compels me to inform you that if your debt is not paid in full by the 30th of this month, I will be forced to take the matter to the daily press.

> With respect,
> Yours,
> Antonin Dvorak

There was a postscript:

Dear Mrs. Thurber, I assure you that this letter is not accompanied by feelings other than the MOST PROFOUND REGRET. I have always admired – AND I SHALL NEVER CEASE TO ADMIRE – your devotion to music and the American nation. I will always remember with delight the time I have spent with you in the Conservatory which *you love so well and which I consider to be – thanks to you – one of the best schools in the world. I am also aware that your husband has suffered great financial losses and that the irregularities in the payment of my salary are not the result of any unwillingness to honour the terms of the contract. I myself am not concerned with worldly comforts, and if it were for me alone to say, I would gladly work for you for room and board, like a student. But I have a wife and a large family for whom I bear responsibility. Please understand, therefore, that it is this circumstance, and this circumstance alone, that compels me to request the payment of the portions owing, at least in part.*

Your always devoted servant,
A.D.

He looked up at his wife. She was composed, but he noticed that she held a crumpled handkerchief tightly in her hand.

"It would seem, Jeannette," he said, "that this Master of yours has a dual personality. He writes the letter like Mr. Hyde, and the postscript like Dr. Jekyll."

She laughed at that. "Did you also notice that the postscript is written in a different ink? The same kind that we have in the inkwells at the school." Even when she was unhappy, she was as astute as ever.

"So he wrote the postscript in his office, whereas he wrote the letter ...?"

"At home."

"Dictated to him by Mrs. Hyde?"

She frowned. "Yes. Of course, I can hardly blame her. Six children – "

"And a husband exposed daily to you, Jenny?"

"Do you know, not long ago he actually noticed I was wearing a new brooch." She sighed theatrically. "But probably the only reason he noticed was because the treble clef on it was backwards." She looked at him seriously. "But Francis, we must find a way to pay him."

"We will." He tried to sound reassuring. "Our account has gained a little weight – not much, mind you, but a little."

Gratefully, he saw her eyes light up, something that had been all too rare over the past two years. He recalled the moment a streak of *silver had appeared in her chestnut-brown hair. She was terrified for the future of the Conservatory and had not yet fully recovered from the American Opera Company débâcle, from the fact that those two years of delight (and it was a delight, for him as well) and worry (that too) had cost two hundred thousand dollars. At the time he had been able to afford it, and it was Jeannette he felt sorry for, not the loss of his money. But she had felt terribly guilty, which was why she had tried so doggedly, months later, to pump the money to found the Conservatory – two hundred thousand, to be precise – out of Uncle Sam. She had argued that conservatories in Europe were subsidized by governments, the aristocracy and a wealthy church. And still they gave her quite a drubbing. "Political heresy, thoroughly foreign to the American system." And even: "an expression of deeply un-American thinking." That hurt her the most. But she didn't give up. And when he joined her, Master Dvorak, like a faithful parrot, wrote articles supporting her, but they pounced on him too. As long as he stood upon the podium, they honoured him. But when he spoke out he became a European who, through no fault of his own, didn't understand the principles on which this country is based. And as Jeannette, in private, tore her hair out trying to balance her books and juggle her figures, her devoted servant Dvorak heroically faced the domestic tirades of his eloquent – at least in her mother tongue – spouse. While his children wept for hunger. He smiled ironically. Dvorak was devoted to Jeannette – and who would not be? – to her devotion to the phantom of an American music that seemed to resist being born. So devoted, in fact, that in addition to articles, he wrote an American symphony – a truly American symphony, if only in the sense that the most beautiful melody in it became a hit. Not long ago, he had heard it blaring forth from one of the new calliopes on Coney Island.*

He looked at Jenny. In her head, framed by the flames of the fireplace, she was undoubtedly hearing the music of Borax's oft-revised score.

Everyone had come to the party. They suppressed their distaste for the radical hostess, or at least their wives did. At the time, there hadn't been a lady in the city who wasn't eager to meet the exotic Czech master. And so, pensively, he had watched as the sparkling golden tiaras and diamond tie-pins followed trance-like after the booming Steele MacKaye and the retreating Dvorak. Like the great Steele, they belonged – despite their wealth, now drawn from the four corners of the world; despite their private theatres, where the great opera stars performed for their personal amusement; despite their boxes at the Met and their lunches on horseback at the Jockey Club, where the horses munched oats served on the same silver plates from which they swallowed their caviar; despite all this Amphitryon-like excess – they belonged to the naked, crude and provincial America of Henry James's Jeffrey Aspern. All night long they had shivered, like children in the cold of the sea, on a squadron of steamboats drawn up in two rows, waiting for the ship bearing the great Adelina Patti back from her European tour. Bands hired at great expense were ready on deck to greet the divine beauty with a medley of her most famous arias. But the lookout on Fire Island fell asleep and Patti's ship passed unnoticed at night through the gauntlet of slumbering boats and arrived unheralded in New York harbour in the morning. She was insulted. While eight steamboats, fueled by the rage of powerful men awakened from wine-dark slumber, searched up and down the Atlantic far from shore, panic-stricken lest Patti had been shipwrecked, the diva herself left New York for her country seat and threw out the reporters. Like children. And so, like children in a deep forest, they had advanced behind the symbolic figure of Steele MacKaye towards the cage that held the sleeping canary.

"Do you really think the worst is over, Frank?"

"Mrs. Hyde can relax and Dr. Jekyll will be free once more to write his own letters."

She kissed him.

And in that other long-ago summer....

Perhaps it is time I kissed her. He closed his eyes and did it. Cool, girlish lips, and from her bosom arose an exotic smell, a perfume from Paris, no doubt. She let him kiss her for a while, then gently pushed him away. He opened his eyes. Dark brown pupils danced before him like tiny goblins.

"Ça, c'est bon, mon chéri!" *she said happily and he realized the depth of his happiness and the abyss of his ignorance. A month before, she had returned from Paris where she had seen the première of Gounod's Romeo and Juliet, and before that, the Wagner festival in Bayreuth. He, meanwhile, had been in his office trying to determine whether it made economic sense to build his own coffee-roasting plants and whether he had enough credit to establish a canning factory.*

"Jeannette, all I have to offer you now is – "

" – is yourself, chéri. I think that will do."

From where they sat in the summer-house, they could hear the sounds of Mr. Meyers's violin coming through the open window of her house.

"I can't even play a musical instrument."

"That doesn't matter. You'll learn. You could play the Jew's harp." She brushed her lips against his, stood up and ran into the house. He walked slowly after her. Her father was standing in the salon playing something from a sheet of music on the music stand.

"Papa," said Jeannette impatiently, "we want to talk to you."

Mr. Meyers set his violin down on top of the piano. "What is it?" Behind him on the wall, like a blue halo, shone plates made of Copenhagen porcelain. He plucked up his courage and asked.

"It's your risk, young man," said Mr. Meyers. "And knowing Jenny as I do, it's likely to be a considerable risk." And he went to the liquor cabinet for aquavit.

Thirty-three years ago. Now all three children were grown up, and his retail grocery business had gone under. True, he still had a lucrative law office on Broadway, and all his old associations had survived and gone on struggling for the right to pursue happiness. Yes, and there was even the Onteora Club in the Catskills, his refuge from the worries that make up this life. When they had opened it up, they had held a memorable party for friends and neighbours alike, and the Director of the National Conservatory had rolled up his sleeves and played second fiddle to the carpenter Donnelly.

"Dr. Dvorak," Francis had said joshingly. "You could make a living playing in cabarets. Why bother losing your temper over Jenny's thick-skulled students? I have all kinds of connections. Nothing would be easier than to arrange a string of nightclub engagements, a different place every night. That way, you'd at least get to know New York. As it is, you spend all your time sitting in Seventeenth Street – that is, when you're not getting yourself thrown out of Penn Station."

The Director of the National Conservatory laughed loudly. "That was some scandal, was it not, Mr. Thurber? But I'd love to play in those clubs. Only someone must go with me, so I won't go astray. Your wife, perhaps?"

"Would you let me, Francis?" asked Jeannette.

"I'd go with you. We'd make a trio."

"But, chéri, you don't play a musical instrument."

"Chérie, don't you remember?"

She shook her head.

"The Jew's harp!"

"What is a Jew's harp?" the Director of the National Conservatory had asked with interest.

"In your next symphony, you must write a solo passage for a Jew's harp – if you want it to be a truly American symphony," he had replied.

It turned out that carpenter Donnelly had a Jew's harp in his pocket. He joined the band, the Director of the National Conservatory rolled his sleeves up once more and they played while Mrs. Vanderbilt and Farmer Jensen trod a measure together.

And of course, above all they still had the Conservatory. That faith, that hope, that love.

His wife looked up from the score that old Borax had sent her from Prague. Her eyes were moist, as they had been once before over the Master's letter.

"What is it, Jenny?"

"This opera is magnificent. Rusalka, he has called it. It's about a water nymph who gives up immortality to marry a human prince, and he leaves her for a mortal woman. It's very beautiful. But –" and she sighed again, "I had hoped he would write an opera based on Hiawatha. Perhaps he would have, if he'd stayed."

"He was too old when he came over," he said.

"But he liked it here."

"He'd never have got used to it. Unless of course you could have found him husbands for all four daughters. How old was young Belmont then? I have the feeling he might have done for the eldest."

"Otylia had a young man here," she said after a while, looking again at the score. "But her mother didn't like him."

The flames in the fireplace brightened, the fire was dying out. Red light on hair that was now almost completely silver.

"Rusalka," she sighed again. "But it was America that inspired him to write this, all the same."

"Isn't that just wishful thinking, Jenny?"

She shook her head. "No, he told me about it. This opera is all woven out of moonlight and a shimmering river. It's about a beautiful water nymph – a Rusalka – a fickle prince who hides in the bushes to watch her and the kind but helpless waterman of European fairy-tales who is her faithful friend and protector. It's clearly all a reflection, an image, of what he told me he saw in that village in Iowa."

"Come on, Jenny! There may be water nymphs in America, but there are no princes. And certainly no watermen!"

Jeannette smiled. "Yes and no, *chéri*. You're right, there was no prince in Spillville. But as he told it to me, there *was* a water nymph who was a kind of princess. An American one. And there was a full moon, and even a waterman – although this one was black and apparently he crooned an air by Dvorak's favourite American composer, Stephen Collins Foster...." Jeannette put the score aside. "Well, so it's an opera called Rusalka, not Hiawatha, after all. And nothing can be done about it now. He won't come back. Adele told me she saw in his eyes, when she visited him that time five years ago to try to persuade him to come back here – it was soon after Josephine, his sister-in-law, died – " She stopped. A log fell apart in the fireplace, the last flame flickered and died in a cascade of sparks.

"What did she see, Jenny?"

"That he was getting ready to die," said Jeannette.

21 :☾: MOON OVER TURKEY RIVER

THE BUGGY WAS PALE BLUE, the horses white, and on the box seat was a driver with a face the colour of coal, dressed in a pale blue livery. The driver sang while a young lady, sitting with her legs mannishly crossed on the velvet seat, swung her white shoe in time to the rhythm. Her legs, in white stockings, were daringly exposed beneath her white muslin summer dress. A yellow straw hat with a pale blue ribbon was perched on golden hair. They stopped in front of Tony Kapinos's tavern and the young lady looked haughtily around the village. Old men were just gathering at the bar to dip the sun, which was dropping towards the horizon, in contraband ale. The black man in livery jumped down from the box seat and went inside.

"Who's that?" asked Otylia.

"Probably Miss Rosemary Vanderbilt," J.J. said. "I heard she was visiting Mr. Belgrave. That's her uncle. He has a summer place near Decorah."

"Who's Rosemary Vanderbilt?"

"Her grandfather owns the railways."

The black man emerged from the tavern with a large tankard and handed it to the girl. She removed her straw hat, put the tankard to her lips and the pewter bottom rose quickly to the sky, now turning a deep pink. He watched, fascinated. The girl had emptied the tankard like a backwoodsman.

"Do you like her?" said Otylia, standing next to him.

"No," he reassured her quickly. "But she can sure drink."

"What's so wonderful about that?" said Otylia, and reached for the empty pewter jug he was carrying for her. "And let's get going, so we can be home before Father gets back from fishing."

As they were entering the tavern, they collided with the driver who was returning the tankard. Politely, he let them go first.

When they got home, the Master was still out fishing. On her mother's orders, Otylia carried the jug of beer to the basement to keep it cool for him. It was dark there, and she had to carry a candle too. Unfortunately the jug occupied only one of her hands, so there was no reason for Kovarik to become her light-bearer.

Time dragged on. There was no sign of the Master, although it was well past the dinner hour. Anna became anxious. "I hope nothing's happened to him," she said. "He said he'd be home by seven at the latest and it's a quarter past eight."

"I'm hungry," announced five-year-old Aloisia.

"Probably the fish are biting and he can't tear himself away," Kovarik said. "There's good trout fishing in those deep spots upstream."

"But he hardly ever goes fishing. What if he fell out of the boat and drowned?"

"Father can swim," said Tony.

"I'm hungry," said Aloisia.

"But not in his clothes," said Magda. "And with his shoes on."

"Perhaps he stopped for a beer on the way home," said Otylia hopefully. "I could go to meet him – "

"When Father says he'll be home at seven," said Anna, "he's home at seven."

"As long as he doesn't stop to have a beer," said Magda.

Eight-year-old Otakar giggled.

"I'm hungry!" said Aloisia.

Their mother glanced uncertainly at the clock. "Perhaps we could start supper in the meantime."

"You know what, Mrs. Dvorak?" Kovarik suggested half an hour later. "How would it be if you were to start supper and I'll go and look for the Master."

"I want to go too," cried Otylia and Otakar together. Tony said nothing only because he had sprained his ankle that morning and had it bound in a starch bandage.

"You're not going anywhere," Anna snapped "Perhaps it really would be best if you'd be kind enough to go and look for him, Mr. Kovarik."

"I'll go with him, Mother," said Otylia.

"No, Otylia. Mr. Kovarik will go by himself."

"But what if something really has happened to Father? Then one of us could stay with him while the other ran for help."

The Prentiss Ingraham dime novels about Buffalo Bill that Otylia had devoured since her arrival in America were proving useful now. Anna hesitated.

"Perhaps Miss Otylia is right," Kovarik said. "I think it would be best if someone were to go with me, just in case."

Anna looked at him questioningly, seemed to waver and then finally made her decision. "Magda! You will go with Mr. Kovarik."

He understood perfectly well what this meant. The logical choice would have been Otylia, who was the eldest. But Magda protested. "Mama, I'd be afraid."

"What would there be to be afraid of – with Mr. Kovarik?"

"But Mr. Kovarik would rather go with Otylia," said Otakar brightly. "They go everywhere together."

"That's not true," objected Otylia.

"It is so," said Tony, from his sofa.

"Magda will go," ordered Anna.

And so he knew that his miraculous secret, although still miraculous, was a secret no longer.

But there were only three days left of the holiday in Spillville.

First they checked Klimesh's tavern, then Tony Kapinos's. The old men were there as they were every evening, dipping the sun in contraband beer, but the Master was not helping them out. They left the tavern and walked towards the church. Above it hung a full August moon, as white as milk and bright enough to cast their two shadows on the road, one long, one short.

"Are we going past the cemetery?" asked Magda.

"That's the shortest way."

"But it's haunted."

"No it's not. Give me your hand."

She gave it to him. He felt her trembling. He led her quickly past the graveyard where cast-iron crosses glittered in the moonlight, standing on the rising slope like a crowd of luminous skeletons while the weeping willows waved and nodded above them. Bitterly, he reflected that he could be walking here with Otylia instead of leading a terrified child by the hand.

They passed the cemetery and walked through the trees lining the banks of the Turkey River.

"You and Otylia go out walking hand in hand," said the child. "I saw you."

"No we don't," he said. "You're just making that up."

"I'm not. You were holding hands on Farmer's Hill and you were kissing, too."

He felt a hot rush of panic. He had not thought they might be at the mercy of witnesses hidden away in the bushes. This witness's word might be unreliable, but no chances would be taken – she would be believed.

"I won't tell on you, though," said Magda. He breathed a sigh of relief. "But you'll have to give me a nickel for ice-cream."

"And what if I don't?"

"Then I'll tell on you."

"Wouldn't you be ashamed to do a thing like that?"

"No I wouldn't. What you're doing is naughty, and if I tell on you, Otylia will get a licking."

"No she won't. She's big now."

"Then Mama won't let her out and you won't be able to hold hands with her any more."

"Okay. I'll give you a nickel tomorrow morning."

"No, I want it right now."

He stopped. The fair-haired Magda glowered up at him. The moon's twin shimmered on the surface of the river.

"This is blackmail," he said.

"No it isn't," said the child, " 'cause it's true."

He took the money out of his pocket and put it in her hand. It shone like the moon's little brother.

"Okay, now I won't tell on you," said the child. But his relief gave way to annoyance at once, for the child added, "but you'll have to give me another nickel tomorrow, or I'll tell on you the day after tomorrow."

The little extortionist! Fortunately, in three days she'd have no more opportunity to squeeze him. He would just have to put up with it until then. At a nickel a day, it amounted to fifteen cents. It was a price he could afford.

"Very well, you'll have your nickel tomorrow, Magda. But it's not nice of you."

"Neither is kissing."

"It is," he said. "And anyway, why aren't you afraid? Back home, you said you would be afraid."

"I'm only afraid in the graveyard, not in the woods."

They were walking along the river, illuminated by the moon and its reflection in the water. There was a monotonous concert of night insects chittering in the treetops. An owl hooted.

As the river widened, inlets began to appear in the folds of the riverbank. A silver fish leaped into the air, flashed in the moonlight and slipped back into the water. A bat flitted through the air. They could see a light among the trees on the other side of the river. They began walking faster. A horse whinnied.

"Magda, shh," he warned her, pointing to the light. Across the river they could now see a fire with two figures beside it. When they moved closer, they could make out two white horses against the background of the dark bushes. Then he recognized them. The pale blue buggy. Two hours ago, the beauty from Chicago had sat on the seat while the black man in livery had gone into Kapinos's for beer.

They stopped, concealed by the bushes, and looked across the river. The young lady in the white dress was biting into a chicken leg. There was a small spit over the fire, and the man, in his white lace shirt, was turning it. On the spit, lit by the flames, was the golden-brown torso of a chicken. The straw hat with the blue ribbon lay in the grass a short distance away, a banjo beside it. The inlaid mother-of-pearl on its fingerboard sparkled with the colours of the rainbow.

He looked at Magda. The child's eyes, wide in amazement, stared across the river at this fairytale banquet. There was silver thread woven into the girl's wide skirt and she too sparkled, as though scattered with diamonds. She had pulled the skirt up to her knees. Beneath it, they had a glimpse of pale lace on her knickers. And she was barefoot.

He looked at the straw hat. Yes, beside it in the grass a pair of white shoes had been casually tossed, and beside them lay a crumpled white pile.

"Are they going to kiss?" whispered the child.

"No," he said. "And even if they do, you won't be able to make any money out of them, Magda. There's no one you can tattle to."

Magda's brow wrinkled and she said, "They're up to naughty things."

The beauty stood up and threw the half-eaten leg into the fire. She stretched, said something to the man who took the rest of the chicken off the spit. She lifted up her skirts and, stepping gingerly through the grass, she began walking upstream. Her head became a coolly glowing torch.

Intoxicated, Kovarik stepped forward and silently followed the beautiful phantom's pilgrimage. Sometimes she was hidden by the bushes and leaves and he could see only the sparkling diamonds. Sometimes she reappeared, a white shadow floating along with her on the water.

The child padded silently behind him. The river widened and they came to a spot where the current had worn away inlets on both sides of the stream. The water was like glass. The girl stopped. They stopped too. The bank on their side of the river was higher and below them, growing thickly along the edge, was a row of bushes. The child whispered, "She's a Rusalka! A water nymph!"

He caught his breath. The girl across the river unlaced her bodice and before he knew it she had lifted the skirt over her head, slipped out of it and stood there in nothing but white knee-length knickers and a summer corset, bright in the darkness. She struggled for a moment, and that too fell away to reveal something he had never before seen in his life. She was milk-white, moulded into rounded shapes by the moon-shadows, her breasts rising to nipples as dark in the moonlight as the heart of a black-eyed susan.

"Jeepers!" said Magda.

Then a white cloud settled onto the grass and beside it stood a living, alabaster Aphrodite, her hands searching for something in the fire on her head, and down below, another, lesser fire gleamed between two curved whitenesses. He couldn't take his eyes off her.

"Don't look at her," whispered the child, "or I'll tell on you."

He was flushed with excitement and said nothing.

"I'll tell them you were looking at something naughty."

"Shut up," he whispered. "I'll give you a quarter."

Silence, and then: "Will you give me two?"

"Yes," he said angrily.

From downstream they could hear a banjo playing. A pleasant baritone voice sang, "I dream of Jeannie with the bright golden hair...."

The girl let her hands drop and the gleaming hair spread down over her shoulders. She stepped up to the water and put her toe in to test it. It must have been warm as the night. Even the moonlight seemed to warm the river with an amorous heat. Cautiously, she stepped into the water.

On their side of the river, beyond the low bushes below them, something creaked. Looking towards the sound, he could barely distinguish the outline of a small rowboat and, in it, someone's dark silhouette. The moonlight fell on the head, the wild whiskers, the hair in disarray.

The Master!

He looked quickly across the stream and saw the Rusalka up to her waist in the water. "Borne like a vapour on the summer air; I see her tripping where the bright streams play...."

The Master's head turned in profile towards the velvet baritone. He doesn't see; he only hears, he thought. He himself saw. The Rusalka was slowly lowering herself into the water, the water rising to meet the black-eyed susans. Finally, all that remained on the water was a burning waterlily.

Suddenly the child saw too and shrieked, "Papa!"

The Master started, looked around and then saw.

There was a splashing of water near the other bank, and another voice shrieked: "John! John! There's a Peeping Tom here. Come quickly!"

"Happy as the dai – " The song stopped abruptly. Branches snapped as a large body plunged towards the river. In the rowboat, the Master grasped the oars, leaned into them too abruptly and caught a crab. There was a thud and the Master vanished. In the clearing across the river the lace shirt flashed in the moonlight. The black driver looked around while the Rusalka, modestly submerged up to her neck in the water, screamed her lungs out.

The Master sat up in the boat and grasped the oars again. The boat set off down the current.

"I see you, you bastard! Wait till I get my hands on you."

The driver rushed down to the water and waded into it with long strides, then disappeared.

"I – " the Master, still rowing, called to the Rusalka, "I was fishing. I fell asleep. I heard the song but I didn't see anything!"

A dark head bobbed up from under the water. "Help!" Then it vanished again.

The Master stopped rowing. The Rusalka fell silent, and instead, from the waterlily, came a sincere, "Oh, damn it, John."

What was he to do? He didn't know – nor did the Master, kneeling helplessly in the rowboat carrying him languidly down the stream. The lily still burned on the water.

There was a sudden splash. "Help!" And the driver vanished again beneath the ripples.

He made up his mind. He jumped up, yanked off his boots, threw off his jacket, forced his way through the bushes and jumped into the water. As he did so, he caught sight of the Master turning the rowboat around and pointing it towards the spot where the driver had once more managed to get his head above the water and bubble, "Hulp!" The waterlily was silent. On the other bank, a child was yelling – this time, probably from fear.

He reached the driver. Strong hands gripped him about the waist and pulled him under the water. Fortunately, the Master arrived just in time for him to grasp the gunwale, and another strong pair of hands grabbed him under the arms. The driver surfaced, saw the boat and needed no instructions. The Master began rowing again, with J.J. and the servant in tow. Soon he felt the river bottom under his feet. The man let go of the boat, walked a few steps towards the bank, his enormous torso emerging from the churning water. He turned around menacingly. A few steps away, the waterlily was subdued. The driver raised an enormous fist. The Master leaned abruptly into the oars, and the prow caught J.J. in the nose.

"I wasn't watching," called the Master in the direction of the fire on the water. "I was fishing, I fell sleep, then I heard a song – "

"You come back here," came the driver's booming voice. "And make it snappy! Or else – "

"Oh, let him go, John," came a voice from the water. "Just go away, mister, please."

"Do what she says, Master," he whispered from the water behind him.

"I am not guilty," said the Master.

"Please, Master, let's go. We have to pick up Magda."

Magda was still standing on the other bank, whimpering. They put her in the boat and set off downstream. He looked around. The man was standing on the riverbank and from the water an imperious white arm lifted, pointing. The man turned and ran back towards the fire.

A bend in the river hid the water nymph from view.

In the end, Magda's silence cost him three dollars.

. . .

The Master himself did not pay anything. In fact, he made a profit. Next morning, when he was sitting at the piano, a melody came to him from the vast distances of the woefully short human life; it shimmered in the moonlight, the beautiful dream of Jeannie danced round it, the melody floated above the glass surface of Turkey River....

The Master opened the notebook with AMERICAN MOTIFS written on it in large, guileless letters, which had once elicited a smile from Mrs. Thurber. He thought for a moment, then wrote in the same guileless script: "Rusalka's Song", and began to jot down notes in the brisk tempo of inspiration.

22 :('): IN THE CATSKILLS

SUMMER. THE ELM LEAVES GREEN, the sky blue and high, two small white clouds floating above a mountain with twin peaks.... What is it called? Oh, Lord, I am old. I forget the names of the people and things closest to me, though I do remember that Dvorak noticed the strange mountain almost as soon as he arrived and asked that question I don't know the answer to any more.... She had known then, but before she could reply Maurice Strathotte, who was usually silent and deep, mumbled something off-colour but precise, for the mountain did actually look like the virgin breasts of a Gargantuan female reclining amorously in the undulating landscape of the Catskills. Fortunately Dvorak did not understand what Maurice had said. She had scorched Strathotte with a withering glance, his dark skin had grown even darker and those had been his last words until he asked Otylia to dance.

So long ago. Fifty-two years. Half a century, and the world altered beyond recognition, left stunned in the wake of yet another world war. And what does one become at the age of ninety-five? A useless vessel of memories. To what end?

Dvorak would have replied: God knows – life is a gift, and it is inappropriate to question it. The aroma of spruce drifted up from the woods, the song of a bird. Her sense of smell and her hearing were still serviceable. So were her eyes.... Yes, life is a gift. Automobiles growling in the village below. There were no such sounds here then. There wasn't even a village. Only the lonely mountain farmsteads, the road, the carriages slowly climbing upward and the horses steaming in the early spring morning. The smell of horses. The wonderful smell of horses. When was the last time I experienced that?

When did I last hear the sounds of beautiful New York? The clatter of the carriages, leather straps squeaking under the hansoms' light wooden frames, the Mozartian strains of the street bands, the bugles, the euphoniums, the whistling of locomotives on the El, drunken Irish women singing their lungs out, Italian organ grinders. And beneath it all, the clippity-clop of many hoofs.

She saw him standing by the open window, listening, the note-book he always carried with him in his hand, with AMERICAN MO-TIFS *written on it in large, guileless letters.*

A steamship hooted from the East River.

"The Prince Wilhelm is leaving for Europe today," he said wistfully, in his heavily accented English, over the open notebook. "The Hamburg American Line". He wrote something down. "We've been in America a month."

"Don't you like it here?"

"I do." He turned again to listen to the polyphony of New York, breathing in magnificent Indian-summer air through the open window. "I can't hear anything like this at home. But at home...."

She gave him her most appealing look. "You ought to try putting those new sounds into music," she said, "before you leave."

He sighed. "I have three years to do that," he replied, with such undisguised directness that it made her laugh.

"Seeing you sad makes me feel guilty. Are you cursing me in your mind for having tied you down like this?"

"No, Mrs. Thurber," he said seriously. "I'm most grateful to you. We'd never have had the chance to see America otherwise. My wife and Otylia were so much looking forward to it. If it hadn't been for that, I might have stayed at home, and I can see now how foolish that would have been."

"Are they enjoying it here?"

"Otylia yes, very much. She says she's not a bit homesick. She says she likes Americans."

She smiled. Americans? Like young Joseph J. Kovarik? Outside the window, high above Strathotte's buxom mountain, a straight white line moved across the sky, as though God himself were tracing it on the firmament. But it was only the vapour trail from an airplane flying south to New York. She looked at the wall, where sunlight from the window fell on some faded photographs. An old lady's treasures, she thought. But when she looked at the largest one, a group portrait of some people standing in front of a clapboard wall, she didn't feel like an old lady. At the time she hadn't been. She'd been forty-two. A memory.

I was four years older than his wife. And once that bizarre genius, Steele MacKaye, mistook me for Mrs. Dvorak and he complimented him on his beautiful young spouse.... Again, she had to smile. A plump woman with the face of a butcher's wife.... There I go, being catty about her again. It was doing her an injustice. But I can't help it – I think he deserved a more beautiful wife. She looked at the picture of Dvorak – the one that always reminded her of Mr. Micawber. Did he really look like a Cruikshank illustration? It was something about his face perhaps. She looked at the rather homely dandy in the photograph, his hat tilted rakishly to one side, his hands thrust into the pockets of his suitcoat, standing straight and tall, his strong legs in fashionably tapered trousers. And surrounded by all that elegance, the face of one of Dickens's comic old men. But he had been only fifty-one at the time. Mr. Micawber.

In the depths of his soul, he was a dandy. She smiled. His shirtfronts were always the brightest green or red. Adele once said that had he been endowed with Jim Huneker's self-serving, man-about-town disposition, he could have become a dictator of fashion in America. As it was, his ties did become the rage. After the première of the New World Symphony, New York blossomed with green cravats, as if it were St. Patrick's Day. And there were homburgs *à la* Dvorak, even cufflinks *à la* Dvorak, pure fantasy on the part of some entrepreneur because – she remembered them well – his were the most ordinary square ones cut from deer horn. And the beard *à la* Dvorak offered by Italian barbers? All one had to do was stop looking after any beard and there it was.

Lovingly, she examined the photographs she had studied a thousand times already. Say what you will, it's Dickens come to life. The boy in the miniature derby, Tony Dvorak, looking as though he has just stepped out of David Copperfield, his arms hanging straight down at his sides, relaxed and motionless for the long exposure; Sadie Siebert towering over him like a lanky Little Dorrit, and Mrs. Siebert looking proprietory, the owner of the house on Seventeenth Street – or was she only the owner's sister? I don't remember any more.

And Otylia. "She's not a bit homesick." Why should she have been, when there in the same picture, oblivious of the camera, was the dashing Joseph Kovarik, devouring her shamelessly with his eyes? Gentle Otylia, looking so meek and mild – little minx too! – wearing that country jacket they brought her to the New World in. Not a single photograph does her justice. She was so pretty – a charming young girl with a round, Slavic face, an inheritance, perhaps, from Attila the Hun.

She suddenly felt depressed by the sadness of time long past. She turned and took a record down from a shelf to the left of her rocking-chair, then set it on her gramophone. Poor Otylia. Dead at twenty-seven. The treacherous heart. At fifty-two, it had cut down her tyrannical grandfather; at forty-six, the beautiful Josephine; and Otylia, scarcely a year after Mr. Micawber himself.

She placed the needle on the record. When did Will Marion bring me this? Shortly before the war? Or during the war? In any case, it was only a few years ago. His beautiful – and, alas, former – wife had just been a hit in Porgy and Bess. Before the war then. Will's music had long since gone out of fashion, but Will himself had not. He had a wide-eyed young girl with him, young enough to be someone's granddaughter though she was certainly not his granddaughter. "Mrs. Thurber," he said – there was a faint lilt of the South in his voice – "if you listen to this, you'll see how Huneker's worst fears have been confirmed!"

Emilio Caceres. Playing Dvorak's Humoresque, as swing. "Listen to that!" Will made a face. "The Spaniard has just turned your Master's deathless melody into nigger music! *Quel outrage!*" And he rolled his eyes in mock indignation. Will always made fun of everything because he took everything seriously. She wondered how he and his Southern Syncopated Orchestra had played Humoresque. We don't play jazz! It's not an Original Dixieland Band! she could hear him protest twenty years ago, in rising exasperation. We play serious music, inspired by authentic folk melodies. Just as the Master ordered. But who paid any attention to Will? And there was that saxophonist he had playing for him. The one from New Orleans. He had a French name – it certainly wasn't Anglo-Saxon: Becher? Bechet? Yes, that was it. Bechet. He never quite managed to play serious music on the saxophone, no matter how much Will insisted. But he made beautiful sounds, and in the end they took him more seriously than they took Will, for all his large orchestra and his syncopated Humoresque. Huneker's terrible vision had come to pass. Jim had been right. They called Bechet's howling on the saxophone music.

"In America, I've been haunted by this melody. I don't know where it came from," and the Master began to whistle.

I may well be the only one who knows where the melody came from. She looked out the window at that bosom-like mountain, shaped by the Creator in an unguarded moment. The Master had not understood Maurice's remarks, and Maurice, under her severe glance, had not enlarged upon them until the moment he said: "May I have this dance?"

She enjoyed thinking back on that housewarming party. May of '93. The cottage, a rustic structure of logs with dormer windows, and a whimsical sign *"Hic terminus"* over the door, was completed and inside everything was ready as she had planned it. Poor Francis, so good-natured and generous, had carried the entire load without flinching. But his sister and her friends from New York couldn't understand why the house was full of masons and carpenters, men who had worked on the place, and their wives and girlfriends too, all in their Sunday best. They wondered what Farmer Jensen, a homesteader from down the valley, was doing jigging among those dignified Fifth Avenue ladies, spattering the new pine floor with gobs of yellow tobacco juice despite the new Tiffany spittoon she had installed especially for him. They were astonished when she started off the dancing with the master mason, whose collar was too tight and whose face was as purple as a berry. And why, they asked themselves, did she not bring in the Kneisel Quartet to christen the house with decent music, instead of this raucous rabble of mountain fiddlers?

In the end, however, even her Fifth Avenue friends surrendered to the fresh lumber smell of their splendid new cottage in the Catskills. Mrs. O'Neill-Russell was persuaded to allow Dvorak, who was not a good dancer, to trample over the shoes she had bought at Altman's. And towards the end, perhaps under the influence of the moonshine Farmer Jensen had brought in a wooden barrel, Mrs. O'Neill-Russell even danced with the master mason, who by this time had discarded not only his starched collar, but his jacket and waistcoat as well, and was dancing a jig with his braces showing and his sleeves rolled up, never once stepping on her shoes.

By that time the Master was no longer dancing. He sat on the improvised podium – constructed of wooden planks resting on barrels – and sawed the catgut. He played second fiddle, because the renowned virtuoso Donnelly, a carpenter from Tannersville, was playing lead and the Master couldn't keep up with his flourishes, so he merely followed with verve, his waistcoat undone and his sleeves rolled up like the others, like Stockwell on the dulcimer beside him and Steinbrunner behind him on the bass.

And out on the dance floor, Maurice Strathotte was spinning Otylia around in her muslin dress.

How nice it is – how nice it was – for young ladies to have more than ône admirer. How nice it was to have an admirer who was not a lover. Never to have a lover, but a flock of admirers instead – perhaps the Lord wanted to make it up to Otylia for the brevity of her life. Maurice Strathotte was undoubtedly an admirer. Nothing more, but nothing less either. And at the time, she had only twelve more years to live.

Not another half-century, like me. That day, Adele had a migraine (that was our euphemism for our regular monthly difficulties) and – how did Strathotte happen to be there? I can't remember. He was just there.

He sat next to Otylia at the piano, in Adele's usual place. She left them alone and they began playing a four-handed Chopin. When she came back a half-hour later she heard, through the open door, something that was not Chopin at all, but Huneker's horror of horrors, what he had once told her was not music, but pure rhythm, emerging from the dubious and never delectable realm of ragtime.

She stopped and listened. After all, Otylia took lessons from Adele to learn how to play Chopin, not to have her black admirer fill her ears with the music of the speakeasies. She listened to the untamed sounds, the erratic march of the left hand, the ragged syncopation in the right, triplet piled on triplet....

The rag abruptly came to an end. She heard Otylia say, in her stumbling, accented English, "Papa would like that."

And Maurice's reply: "Well now, I'm not so sure about that...."

"Yes," said Otylia. "He likes trains."

Maurice, not comprehending: "Trains?"

"Yes...."

Again, she heard something that sounded like ragtime, an artless imitation, but with the same rhythm. And Otylia speaking over the music: "Just like the clacking of the train on the tracks...."

It went on for a while. Then silence. Given what she imagined was taking place, the silence was eloquent. Then eloquent words from Otylia's mouth: "No, Maurice! Wait! Play something else!" Dissonance from the keyboard, as though someone were forcing someone else's hand away, "Please, play something!"

The response an annoyed "What?"
"You're black, play some black music."
"I've already played you some."
"Something even blacker, Maurice. Use only black keys."
Silence. Then a somewhat unsteady beginning. That ragged rhythm
again in the right hand, those bouncing chords in the left. Maurice:
"This is called Rag in O Major: O For Otylia."

It was the melody that later haunted the Master. Not all of it,
only a beginning. The motif began in F-sharp, then Maurice embellished the theme with little flourishes while stubbornly main-
taining the rhythm of the railroad in the left hand. Otylia clapped.
"How do you think your father would like this?" Maurice said.

"I don't think he'd approve at all," she said in a firm voice, entering the room. The train crashed to a halt, the rhythm of the wheels
ceased. Otylia turned towards her and she saw that the girl at least
had the grace to blush.

For the next half-hour, she sat in the piano salon while the two
of them played four-handed Chopin pieces, a virtuous effort but full
of blunders.

When Otylia had gone and she sat down at her writing desk
by the window, she heard the girl on the sidewalk below, whistling
– a country habit inherited, no doubt, from her father – that indestructible melody which not even the new century, with its gramo-
phones and radios, would erase from memory. It was an easily
recognizable modification of Maurice's *Rag in O Major.*

Emilio Caceres. Humoresque really swung. Swing was no problem
in Dvorak's music. I hear it everywhere, but especially in his Humoresque in F Major. Gershwin might have written that himself. I
can hear it in his American Suite too. The jigs and reels spun by
Donnelly the carpenter and embroidered by the Master's second
fiddle, syncopation for syncopation, the diminished sevenths.

A shadow was filling the valley but the twin peaks were still visible
above it, tanned golden by the rays of the setting sun. One more day
gone by. One more night.

It is evening. A glorious evening, the climax, in fact, of my own
life, not the Master's. What did I actually accomplish? I aroused Mrs.
Micawber's unselfish acquisitiveness and I opened a window for the
Master onto a New York street, where the pandemonium of internal
combustion engines was years away and the cab-horse hoofs still
clattered over the cobblestones in time to Italian tarantellas under-

scored by girls from the Lower East Side – girls who sang in raucous Celtic voices long before raucous voices became the fashion.

It was unfortunate that Francis was hit by the stock-market panic in '93. It would have to happen to him – a generous man, a crusader. He who turned his eloquent pen against the likes of Belmont, Morgan, Vanderbilt. Those men, of course, survived the crash unscathed, while poor Francis went back to school to become a lawyer, successful again at fifty-five. But it shortened his life. He might still be here. Not today, perhaps, but he might have lived to see – what? The collapse of my Conservatory? Let's say, to see how thoroughly black music has penetrated American life.

A memory of a gala evening. The première of his new American symphony. Otylia was like a butterfly in a gown from Worth, a gift from me on her fifteenth birthday. A sweet décolletage with a white rose – the rose of death – the slender, inimitable line of a young girl's body, the stitching skilfully camouflaged so as not to disturb the smoothness of the dress – Worth's trademark. "You'll spoil her, Mrs. Thurber," said the Master gruffly, but his eyes glowed and he gazed at his lovely daughter like a child at his first toy. "If you'd given her a doll, but –" Otylia's response was indignant: "A doll! Father!" And on her left sat one jealous admirer, white – her father's American secretary – and on her right another admirer, black – her father's best student, Maurice. That was just fine. That was as it should be. She had little more than a decade to live.

Like a white rose sitting in a prominent box in the Diamond Horseshoe. But all the opera glasses were trained on her father, an imposing figure in a frock coat. That evening, his moustache was trimmed and his hair was even slicked back. Then the opera glasses passed over Francis and settled on the white rose.

I had a new dress then too, she recalled. Heavenly blue damask, a deep neckline with masses of lace front and back. It had a lot of brocade – in a chrysanthemum-leaf design – on a delicate blue background. Pearls wreathed the clasps, which bore the cross of St. Jacques. And the damask skirt, too, was decorated with great garlands of pearl and crystal. She sighed.

Yes, and moving on from the white rose, the opera glasses, like insect feelers, lifted to examine my décolletage of white tulle and Venetian lace and then, as if on command, turned back to the podium as the conductor, Maestro Anton Seidl, strode proudly up to take his place in front of the orchestra. The lorgnettes had ignored Mrs. Micawber in her black velvet dress, stretched too tightly over her ample bosom. Seidl tossed his head, pushed his hair from his eyes with his left hand, presented his Gothic face to the orchestra, raised his baton –

And the greatest forty minutes of my life began. The major semi-circles described by the baton, the full, unerring harmony of the deep strings – God knows why he loved them so deep – the slow adagio descending to the velvet encounter with the clarinet in its lowest register, the resounding bassoons, then the profound mystery, suddenly broken by the lonesome call of the French horns in unison, a prefiguration of the magnificent air in the second movement, the call of beauty above the broad distances of our beautiful continent.

She always loved the exposition. To her, it seemed to contain him entirely, the gruff, good-natured man inciting the bass viols to play with more power, longing for eight bass viols instead of just four – "But who will pay for it?" she had heard him sigh unhappily in Cambridge, and had made a mental note for Francis – transcribing his bass parts four times for the conclusion of that prairie song, the wild, bristling bard whose spirit was a concord of deeply tuned violas and double basses, the genius of village brass bands, though she had never heard them, the unison of the horns, the reminder: "Learn to play brass instruments. If all we have are violinists, what will we write?" – and then, no sooner had the variations of the first theme died away, the theme which in later years, during the jazz era, reminded her of the great sound of Kansas City, than it was resumed by the horns and underscored by deep viola and cello tones, a brief, expressive, perfect Kansas riff, then to the strings in unison and then in fortissimo modulations, and finally, to the trombones. The full majesty of their sonorous depths and aggressive dynamics blared out until at last the flutes picked up the famous theme – America –

She reached into her shelves again and took another record out. Tommy Dorsey's Swing Low. Will had brought her this one too. The sounds now emerging from her gramophone were quite different – a deep harmony of saxophones. God knows why he never used them. He must have heard them in military marching bands at least, and Richard Strauss and Bizet had used them. Instrumentation was his greatest resource and he was utterly unafraid to use whatever occurred to him: bass clarinets, double bassoons, tambourines and tom-toms. Like his Wild Dove, or his Water-Goblin. She smiled. Or the Largo in A Major for flute, violin, viola and – triangle. He was unafraid of any instruments in any combination. Then why were there no saxophones? She wished now that she had asked him. Was it because Bizet had been a godless man obsessed with Eros and Richard Strauss had sinned against the canons of his masters?

Still, she wondered why. As she listened to Dorsey, she wondered – would the Master have liked this music? She was convinced he would have. He emerged, in her mind, from the evening shadow above the valley, fiddling vigorously beneath the stars beside the carpenter Donnelly, attentive to Catskill flourishes that were certainly fresh to his ears, his sleeves rolled up, the toes of his shoes with their New York shine tapping out the rhythm while his daughter swirls a jig with the young Strathotte. "When I hear Sousa's band, more than anything else I feel like joining in and marching down Broadway with him. Good brass music, that's the stuff for me!" *Doctor honoris causa*, the Director of the National Conservatory. An ancient argument with old Seidl over Nietzsche in the Old Vienna Café. "What my feet demand of music, most of all, is the ecstasy of a good walk, of steps, of dancing, Herr Seidl!" And this man, so full of the music of the heart and of its vital powers and, to be sure, of an unsentimental sadness, this is the man they called an epigone of Wagner! When the Master was still just an apprentice, you could hear Wagnerian harmony everywhere. But when he became a master himself? How quick he was to dispose of the influence, to sweep it aside! How he broke down the walls of that gloomy prison cell where melodies died of starvation! How far back he went to recapture the old spirit of music, abandoning Wagner completely and accepting Nietzsche: *We can understand where modern music – Wagnerian music – is headed if we compare it to the sensations of a person walking into the sea. Gradually the ground beneath his feet disappears, and at last he places himself at the mercy or displeasure of the raging elements: he must swim. The old music, with its swinging rhythm, serious or fiery, first slow, then rapid, required us to do something quite different: we had to dance.*

"Mrs. Thurber," Will had said then, as they were listening to the record he had just brought, the swinging, smearing music of Tommy Dorsey, "if he hadn't been so fond of his pork and dumplings and beer, he might have lived to see this era – and where would George Gershwin have been then?" And Will bounded to the piano, played the well-known introduction to Rhapsody in Blue and, with a glissando executed with bar-room finesse with the back of his finger, swept into the famous clarinet theme. "And anyway, it was Ruby Goldmark who taught Gershwin how to do it," he said, "and Goldmark always sat in the front row in Borax's class. And where would the great Duke himself be without Dvorak, Mrs. Thurber?" he grinned. He jumped up from the piano and pulled out another of the records he'd brought. "Listen carefully, my dear Mrs. Thurber. This is Come Sunday!" He sat down on the tabouret and crossed his legs, and his dapper shoe was tapping out the rhythm even before the music began. The deep saxophones sounded like Dorsey's in Swing Low – but was it like Dorsey? What, in fact, was it like? "Listen! Do you hear that? The same harmonic rhythm," Will said excitedly. "The Duke and I were pretty close, Mrs. Thurber. He named his boy after our Mercer, – mine and Abbie's, the Devil take her straight to heaven. I even gave him a couple of lessons, mostly in taxis on the way from Broadway to Harlem. But then, who ever got their best lessons at school? Most of it was nuggets of wisdom from the Master, because you could see the Duke's orchestra was just crying out for it. Do you hear that? Harry Carney? Tricky Sam Nanton?" He listened for a moment. "And this is what's come out of it. Johnny Hodges!" and with dreamy feeling: "Black, beige and blue.... " She listened. The alto broke away from the clutch of saxes. Yes! That too was a call. Not from the vast distances of the prairie. From the depths of Harlem – from the martyrdom of the spirit –

She shook her head. She had to return to the confluence of the sources, to the great New World Symphony itself. Outside the window now, only the very tips of the peaks shone a bright gold, and above them the fresh white light of Venus. Her record of the symphony was worn out. I must have my grandson LeGrand bring me a new one. She put the needle on the track for the second movement.

Those deep tones again, still those deep tones. Those long, extended half-notes sustained by exhaled breath, descending in harmony to the bottom of their registers, the vibrato still perceptible, softly, mysteriously, in pianissimo to the tragic, leathery rumble of the timpani on D flat. At the première, instead of watching Seidl at this point, she had looked at the woodwinds and the brass. She had always been thrilled by the sight of people producing such magnificent sounds – for beauty, for mystery, for the otherwise unattainable delight of the soul – sending tiny, ethereal waves into the nerves, the muscles, the heart. That delight was visible in the faces of the men blowing absurdly into hollow wood, sputtering softly through pursed lips into brass. The paradox of saliva, moist breath and trembling reeds becoming immaterial sweetness, a harmony of wood pervaded by the call of the forest, the ocean. This, more than anything else, saddened her for the blind. And she remembered an inconspicuous little man who sat at the edge of the brass section, beside the bass trombonist, and when Seidl raised his baton placed an enormous tuba on his lap, almost vanishing behind it. She kept her eyes on the tuba. They played the fifth bar, the mysterious melody passed to the bass strings and she caught a glimpse of the little man's face behind his tuba. There was no doubt about it, he was grinning towards their box. Perplexed, she glanced at the Master, and his unusually well-trimmed moustache seemed to be bristling with pleasure. The English horn began playing its immortal hymn to the pentatonic scale.

She listened. Outside, night modestly covered the golden peaks. Venus glowed fresh and bright in the brocade sky over the Catskills. The record spun. Theme and counter-theme, pyrotechnics of colour, the thundering of a kindly ruler over the empire of music. Who had said it? "A grotesque Indian waltz in the scherzo is suddenly followed by the sounds of a country inn where Schubert might well have gone to drink beer."

Lord, thought Jeannette, but isn't that America? Her own father and his amateur friends, evening after evening, struggling with the music of Copenhagen in a house on Thirty-third Street, in New York City? A Dane, an Irishman and a Portuguese, three dedicated string players, paying their homage to Haydn above the rumble of the El trains.

The English horn resumed the main theme again; she closed her eyes and saw Otylia sitting in the box between the two rivals. She saw the little man waiting tensely behind his tuba for his second entry into history, and generous, self-effacing Francis sitting behind her in the box. She saw the Master, his face furrowed in a frown, comparing what he heard with what he would like to hear, but good-naturedly accepting what he could hear. And another of his students, Harvey Loomis, aware of nothing but the music –

– Loomis had once told her how the Master strode into the classroom one morning, his fly unbuttoned, clearly in a foul mood. They were huddled over their desks, waiting for the storm to break. But they were wrong. He marched straight to the piano, played five slow bars of close-textured chords and then, in that booming voice, his veins swollen like cords in his neck, he sang wordlessly, his entire body labouring to deliver the melody in a wild scat, furious yet gentle. They sat up. The Master turned to them. "Isn't that magnificent music?" In his eyes, a triumphal joy. "You are the first to hear it. It's for my new symphony – but it's not symphonic music." He noticed that Laura Collins was staring at his fly, did it up without the slightest embarrassment and cried out, "No, it certainly isn't!" And he kicked the piano-stool with his lace-up boots, spinning it around three times.

The music was swelling to a climax. She saw the little man grinning behind his instrument again and thought he might even, if it were possible, have waved – then the violins on high D flat – then silence. The mysterious conclusion of a profound secret: the deep four-note chord of the double-basses. The echo of prehistory.

The little man climbed onto a chair with his tuba. The auditorium, sparkling with gold and diamonds, rose to its feet, hands echoing approval. Even the Master stood up. He bowed, the applause increased, and with each bow he moved backwards towards the exit. Francis opened the door for him. The Master backed into the corridor, but the applause continued from fortissimo to double fortissimo, and there were shouts and cries of "Bravo!" until, like a film run backwards, the Master bowed his way step by step back into the box, where he stood at the railing for a long time, acknowledging the applause.

She put the record back in the shelf, took a bottle of gin from the liquor cabinet next to it and poured it into a glass along with some tonic. She placed a cigarette in a long holder. The room was almost dark except for a dull light from the moon high over the mountain. She didn't turn the light on. The night breeze carried with it the smell of pine needles and pitch, and the honking of a car somewhere on the road below. The red light of a passenger plane moved silently across the sky among the glassy stars. An owl hooted.

America. It was already in him. What if he had remained here? What if he had managed to overcome the weight and pull of Europe? What if he had been younger, with no family, with the courage to risk adventure? She sighed. And then, what if Francis had not been hit by the stock-market crash? Too many what-ifs.

She lit the cigarette. The smoke, irradiated by the moonlight, curled to the ceiling. Perhaps in this case, too, money had been the source of the problem, the reason he had never returned to America. She smiled at the memory of Otylia in her white birthday gown. And that inept Kovarik! Had Otylia remained here, the Master might never have returned to Europe with his wife and his other children. Such a division would have split the magnetic attraction of his offspring, with the stronger half firmly entrenched in America. Why, when she stood before him in that charming gown, he was transfixed....

She came, looking pale in a black skirt that reached her slender ankles, black lace-up shoes, a navy middy and, held primly under her arm, a black music case with a golden lyre on the cover. But once again Adele was away with a migraine, and so she invited her instead to have tea in her boudoir, and – What was it like in ... where was it you went? Spillville? How was it? Nice, she murmured, taking a bite of cake, and a desperate, thwarted love stared out of her eyes and echoed from every brief syllable she uttered.

"Did you have good weather?"

"Yes, we did."

"I heard you went to Chicago, to the World's Fair."

"Yes, we did."

"What was that like?"

"Nice."

The girl said it as though her father had died in Chicago. And yet, as she had learned from her scouts, he had merely become somewhat tipsy in the company of a scandalously young countrywoman of rather dubious repute – and in some sleazy Negro dive, too.

"Didn't you go anywhere else?"

"Omaha."

"Did they invite your father there?"

"Yes."

Goodness, what else was there to ask? The comedienne had become, over the summer, monosyllabic.

"And – what did you do there all summer?"

"Nothing."

She drank her chocolate, took a bite of her doughnut and looked at the girl.

"Otylia," she said, "no fibs now. You fell in love out there, didn't you?"

She exhaled the smoke, and caught herself smiling at a memory now fifty years old. Her new blouse, direct from Paris, had become wet as Otylia wept out her secret. The hat with the rumpled wreath of blue cornflowers lay forgotten on the tabouret.

She reached into the shelf, took out another record, put it on the gramophone and placed the tone arm at the beginning of the fifth cut. The American Suite, with its energetic, syncopated rhythm. Almost certainly, he would have liked jazz. It wouldn't have taken much. Suppose that Will Cook, Ruby Goldmark and Maurice Strathotte had sat in the orchestra instead of the musicians of the Czech Philharmonic. He wrote this American Suite right after his great symphony – not even a month had passed, then this. She isn't wrong: The fifth movement is the most American, perhaps more American than anything else he ever wrote. Again, only she knows – and perhaps some other old-timers – that the Indians danced to this in Madison Square Garden for Buffalo Bill. An energetic Indian gavotte, and they even tinkled on something, though it wasn't a triangle. Iron Tail, Good Horse, Holy Bear, Sam Stabber, Loud Thunder, Iron Cloud. She wasn't entirely convinced, but Mark Twain, whom she regarded highly, wrote that Buffalo Bill's spectacles were wholly free of sham and insincerity and that the shows matched his own memories of his youth on the frontier. So she had taken the Master to Madison Square Garden with Otylia, and the even, galloping rhythm, the melody sung in an unknown language by rough voices, dominated by the high voices of the three squaws, Jennie Spotted Horse, Mary Kills Enemy and White Cow, had remained in her memory. And not just in *her* memory. It was there in The American Suite.

What might he have written had he stayed here and lived to see the age of the saxophone? Woulds, ifs and supposes. All pointless dreaming, though interesting none the less. But as much as he would have liked to, Francis couldn't shake loose enough money to satisfy Mrs. Micawber. So once again, she failed.

She removed the cigarette butt from the holder and stubbed it out. The Indian finale of The American Suite. Once the Master had stared at a portrait of Sitting Bull. What humiliation! "Did he really appear in a circus? The man who defeated Custer? He let them boo him because he killed Custer?" "Yes," she replied. "Of course he was paid, and he was given exclusive rights to sell photographs of himself. He made a few thousand that way." He shook his head. "Well, that's America. But in the end, they cheated and killed him just the same?" "Yes," she said, "because he really *had* killed Custer. It wasn't just part of the show." And he shook his head, as though he knew but could not understand.

She rang for Estelle.... To put it simply, I failed. In the end, nothing I tried to do really worked out, she said to herself, but without bitterness. She remembered – "The influence of Dvorak's American compositions has been evil," Jim Huneker had written. "Ragtime is the popular pabulum now. And ragtime is only rhythmic motion, not music." She smiled. She knew Jim had been right. She was glad.

When Estelle had gone and the wooden ticking of the cuckoo clock on the wall was putting her to sleep, she remembered another of Huneker's *bons mots*. She hoped he was right about that, too. But from the distance of her ninety-five years, almost an eternity, it did not seem important to her. "Mrs. Thurber," Jim had written, "has achieved more through her failures than most people achieve through their successes." She fell asleep.

When she woke up the next day, there was the Master sitting next to her bed in a waistcoat, with his sleeves rolled up, and he was playing a saxophone.

23 :( ): THE SNARING OF OTYLIA

IT RAINED ALL THE WAY. It was a refreshing but melancholy May-time rain. Otylia looked at the small greening fields, at the neatly groomed woodlots, dark in the rain, at the gloomy rivers. The train rattled over bridges, swaying to the rhythm of the buffers. With her nose pressed against the window-glass, she heard in that rhythm the Rag in Otylia Major. Afterwards she had wept on Mrs. Thurber's blue, perfumed blouse. She leaned back into the seat. Her father, sitting opposite her in the compartment, embraced the damp countryside with his vision, and in his dark brown eyes the telegraph poles, the birch trees along the track, the poplars, swam backwards. She closed her eyes, felt the burning tears, wiped them away with a handkerchief and sat there in her private darkness for a long, long time. When she opened her eyes again they were passing the first houses on the outskirts of Prague, and her father cried, "There's Vysehrad." They crossed a long bridge, steel beams flickering light and dark, and emerged into the shadow of the city streets, sliding at last into the deep gloom of the vaulted terminus, the train slowing down, half-darkness, Father opening the window, slower, slower. Then shouting. Hurray! Welcome! The sounds of an orchestra. An enormous crowd on the platform. She stood up and over her father's shoulder saw a large beribboned bouquet held high by a girl in folk costume so they could read the inscription: WELCOME HOME! The high, dirty, smoke-stained glass roof admitted a brownish light that lent to the white faces beneath the black top hats and bowlers the pallor of corpses. She glanced from one to the other – Bendl, Picka, Chvala, Cech, Kaan, Anger – but where was he? Where was Josef Suk? Until at last she saw him, standing at the outer edge of the welcoming committee: the small black moustache, the pale forehead under the brim of his bowler, the black eyes.

The orchestra, the babble of welcoming cries, the embracing, the kissing. A kiss from Bendl, from Kaan, she didn't know who was squeezing her hand, everyone embraced Father, Mother, Magda, little Ota daringly gave a kiss to the girl in the folk costume and she recognized her – Lida, the Prochazkas' daughter. She saw her mother beckon Suk, heard her call him, felt herself pushed towards him. Magda was given a bouquet by a boy in plus-fours.

Suddenly they were facing each other. His face was blank, his eyes stared past her. He bowed but did not offer his hand, leaving her own hand hanging in the air. She let it drop quickly, awkwardly. "Welcome, Miss Dvorak," he said. His voice was cold, like frost. It made her feel stupid and wretched, and when he repeated the same greeting to Magda he managed to make it sound more cordial. Then he greeted her mother, his face vanishing for a moment behind hers as she planted a kiss on his cheek. Turning to greet Kaan, her mother threw her a questioning glance. Otylia clasped her hands quickly in front of her and then Prochazka was offering his hand: "Welcome home, Miss Otylia!" White teeth, delight in the smile. She looked around to see where he was. He had retreated to the background.

They were riding in an open landau through streets lined with crowds. Jezdecka Street was jammed with people and the carriage was forced to stop. "Hurray! Hurray!" Father stood up in his new green vest from Macy's·and bowed in all directions. She was also wearing a new travelling outfit, from Worth, picked out for her by Jeannette. It was beige silesia with shiny gold watteau in both front and back and a beige capote. And he probably hadn't even noticed. The carriage began to move again. And then they were home.

A gala dinner with Bendl, Kaan, and him. Her mother sat him beside her, but he never glanced at her or spoke a word to her and she had to endure Anna's constant, questioning glances.

Did he know the thing she had done? There couldn't be any doubt. But who could have told him?

At the head of the table, Father was talking and talking. She wasn't listening, she merely heard his strong voice: " ... a whole ox, right in the middle of the square, with the horns still on it, wrapped up in an American flag! They'd roasted it on a spit – they call it a barbecue. And a fellow with a knife that looked more like a sword cut off swaths of meat and passed them out to the voters with slices of bread. The ox was donated by Tammany Hall. They fix the elections – " "How'd they do it, Anton?" And he, meanwhile, cut his smoked meat into tiny pieces and ate them one by one, staring motionlessly at her father as he told his stories, not a glance for her, not even out of the corner of his eye. She poked at her food and felt sick at heart, very young, very foolish.

"J.J., you can't always be traipsing after me like a puppy."

"What's wrong with that – even if your parents noticed?"

"They mustn't notice. Mother doesn't like it here in America."

"That's too bad. But I don't see the connection."

"Because I'd catch it from her!"

"Just because I'm following you around like a puppy?"

"Of course. She would be scared."

"Scared? Of what?"

"Can't you guess?" asked Otylia, then sighed deeply. "You really can't?"

"Doesn't she like me?"

"She doesn't like America."

"But I'm Czech."

"You're an American Czech."

Otylia conscientiously gave the rug hanging on the rod a thwack.

"I'm a pure-blooded Czech," he said. "My mother's neither an American nor a German, nor is my – "

"That's all very well, but you live in America. And you have a job in New York. Mother's terrified of New York."

"But we're in Spillville now! There's no Lower East Side here. And the Master likes American Czechs!"

She stopped beating the rug and turned to him. "Of course you're absolutely right, you American," she said coldly and her nose went up in the air. Then she said archly, "Looking at it now, I see she doesn't really have much to worry about after all."

"But we're not doing anything – bad," he said, dejectedly.

"We aren't, are we?" said Otylia. For a while she said nothing and it seemed to him that she began beating the carpet with increased energy. Then she said, in a very cold voice, "So you can go right on playing the puppy-dog, if you want, since clearly it's only for the holidays. I thought you cared about me but clearly you don't, so after the holidays I'll be gone, out of sight. Obviously I needn't have worried about Mother worrying – "

"Otylia!" he interrupted. "You mean – you'd marry me?"

Otylia sighed. "Well, it would be nice if you'd ask me, at least. But that's what I've been trying to tell you. Mother would never let me stay in America – so what could we do about it anyway?"

That question provoked an old-fashioned idea in his mind. And that idea was the beginning of his bitter fall.

Not a glance from Suk.

And Father is prattling on. " ... in the Seventh Regional Armory. Impossible to listen to. It's not a proper concert hall, more like a huge drill hall where they used to store cannon. And now imagine the place with ten thousand people in it and above them – not in front of them, above them – on steep risers, like in an amphitheatre, you have a two-hundred-and-fifty-piece orchestra and twelve hundred singers. And right up at the top there's an organ, and along the sides and at the back of the hall, three brass bands. Well, when they all began to play at once, it turned into a great big jumble of sound. It would have driven Berlioz crazy, but it was a tremendous success. Well, that's what Americans are like. These monster concerts were started by someone called Gilmore. We had a tuba player in our orchestra, a very good musician, who was always telling me stories...."

She finally got her courage up. "Josef?"

Nothing. He merely swallowed a piece of smoked meat and continued staring at her father.

She touched his sleeve. He half turned his head towards her. Angry eyes in a blank face. She smiled at him, but not even the smile evoked a response.

"How have you been, Joe?"

"Marvellous." A slap in the face. As though she were a stranger. He turned his face away and began to follow the chatter at the other end of the table with theatrical absorption.

He must know. But how could he have found out? Mother wouldn't have written to him about it, would she? Or did Father let something drop in a letter home? But Father doesn't know anything about it.

The supper dragged on. Afterwards, they drank coffee in the sitting room. She carried the coffee pot from guest to guest, and when she got to him she deliberately spilled some on his trousers.

"Oh goodness! How clumsy of me. Come into the kitchen, Joe. You've got to wash that out with water right away, before it dries."

He got up and followed her without a word. It annoyed her to see her mother watching her approvingly.

In the kitchen: "I think my hands were shaking."

Nothing. She knelt down in front of him and began to wipe away the stain with a rag soaked in water. He stood above her like a pillar of salt.

"I guess it's because I haven't seen you for such a long time, Joe."

The pillar of salt said nothing. Anger began to seep through her confusion. What if he did find something out? That's no reason for him to torment me like this. I'm good enough at doing that myself. She stood up and looked him in the eye.

"I was nervous, do you understand?"

His lips seemed sewn tight.

"I mean because we haven't seen each other for so long."

Finally, he made a sound. It sounded like a snort.

"Joe! Who's been telling you stories?"

The pillar of salt spoke. Bitterly. "Stories?"

So that's it. All I had to do was be direct. "I mean what have people been telling you?"

At last he spoke an entire sentence. "No one has told me anything, Miss Otylia."

"Miss Otylia?"

"Miss Dvorak."

Better still.

"If no one's told you anything, why are you ignoring me?"

"What is there to tell?"

"You used to be my friend. You used to tell me how much you liked me. I don't know what to think any more." She stopped. "What about, 'You look pretty in that dress'?" She spread the beautiful silesian skirt out for him.

"I'm sure others have told you as much, Miss Dvorak."

"Don't 'Miss Dvorak' me any more. Joe. I have – " she wanted to say "missed you" but felt a sudden stab of conscience, and a hot wave of shame made her blush. But it wasn't really a lie. She did miss him – afterwards, in the cold loneliness of New York, with Mother, like a prison warden, escorting her on the short trips between the Conservatory and the house on Seventeenth Street; in the bleak days of her discontent the whole story with J.J. turned into a nightmare and she yearned for the security of Vysoka, where Joe was copying scores for her father. But then, there had been that magic honey-smelling hot summer on the slopes that appeared to be on fire – and sweet J.J. – oh, what a sinner I am! And poor Joe, why – there is a tear in his eye –

He reached quickly into his pocket and pulled out a piece of lined paper, thrust it into her hand and said, "Here, Otylia, read this." Then he turned and ran out of the kitchen.

An anonymous letter? But who in Spillville knew about Joe? She blushed again. I mean this Joe, the one in Vysoka. She walked over to the kitchen table, sat down and spread the paper out in front of her. For a few moments, she couldn't bring herself to concentrate on what was on it. She rubbed her eyes. The letter, written in a childish hand:

Dear Lida,

We are back in New York now, we had a nice time this summer in Spillville, Iowa. Now it is time to start school again. This year I am in grade four but I should be in grade five but because of my English they put me in grade four. Magda is in grade seven and Anna is in grade eight and Ota has the whooping cough so he is still at home and Aloisia caught it from him. Otylia is taking piano lessons from Miss Margulies at the Conservatory and Mama goes with her to the lessons because in Spillville she was kissing with Mr. Kovarik all the time and Mama found out about it and –

Lida Prochazkova! That little viper! And waiting so innocently for them at the train station in her folk costume! Without finishing the letter, Otylia stuck it in her bosom, wretched and uncertain. When she returned from the kitchen, he was gone. He had said his farewells and walked out. All she had left was her mother's strict glance and her father's voice enthusiastically regaling his guests....

She was uncertain, but she went anyway.

A hot day in August, the buckboard bouncing along through the Iowa cornfields and beyond, in the distance, the silver, meandering Turkey River. Behind her, on the luggage rack, rested her small suitcase. What am I getting into?

"J.J., I'm afraid."

He began to soothe her, but she sensed that he too was feeling uneasy, though he ought to be happy. He merely cracked his whip furiously over the mare's flanks and made a heroic effort to put on a carefree smile.

"What if my parents throw us out, J.J.?"

"They won't. You'll see. They love you, don't they?"

"But if I do this to them? And this priest isn't even a Catholic."

"But that – I mean, that doesn't make any difference," he said uncertainly. "It's still legal."

"It will certainly make a difference to Father."

Yet here she was, going along with it. *Should I tell him to turn around?* They rode along between two rows of elm trees, and at the top of the hill a village appeared in the distance.

"We'll soon be there, Otylia."

In the blue sky above the village stood a grand temple of white cloud and rising above that loomed a dark and threatening cathedral – a black thunderhead heralding a storm. *Lord, forgive me, for I know not – or rather, I know but I can't help myself.* Those secret matters projected themselves into the black and white symbols in the sky. *He will rent a room, a bed, in the dark, Lord – and it won't be a sin. Not that sin. But what about the commandment to honour thy father – and thy mother....*

"There! That's the church."

The buckboard turned off the road onto a rutted track that wound through the fields. It began bouncing so violently that she had to hold tightly to the tiny rail around the seat. They were approaching a small wooden church. Once it had been white, but now only patches of the original paint remained and the exposed wood was weathered grey with age. The steeple had no bell and leaned precariously to one side. Lush, long grass was growing around the church, forcing its way up between the wooden steps leading to the front door. A goat with an enormous udder grazed in the grass. Beside the church stood a dilapidated structure, more like a shanty than a house. A broken wooden railing surrounded the rickety porch, the windows were filthy and in one of them a yellowed newspaper was taped over a broken pane of glass. A dog that looked part German shepherd and part St. Bernard lay on the porch, and when J.J. brought the mare to a halt, the dog pulled itself wearily to its feet and regarded them with bleary eyes, a long tongue lolling out of its mouth. In a small garden beside the house an old black man, naked to the waist and wearing only a pair of patched trousers, was hoeing tomatoes. It was hot.

She couldn't bring herself to move. J.J. jumped nimbly down from the seat, trying hard to appear nonchalant, like an amateur actor. He held out his hand; she stood up, slipped on the foot-step and fell *into his arms. He caught her. He was strong. For a moment, she felt safe. For a painfully brief moment.*

They walked together towards the shanty. The black man ignored them. The dog sniffed at J.J.'s crotch and J.J. pushed it away and knocked on the door. They waited there in the stifling heat. Not a blade of grass moved. The black thunderhead beyond the white temple of cloud was bigger now. J.J. knocked again. They waited.

"Perhaps he's not home," she whispered hopefully.

"But he knows we're coming."

"Maybe he had to go somewhere."

J.J. pushed against the door. It was unlocked, and opened slowly. They stepped inside. The musty, suffocating stench of an unventilated, unswept, unwashed, irredeemably squalid hovel assailed their nostrils. It was a single room, a pot-bellied stove in one corner with a tarnished copper kettle on it, and a wooden table in the middle, covered with dirty plates, cups and pots caked with dried food. An empty bottle lay on the floor, covered with dust. Items of clothing hung from a row of nails driven into the wall. Against the back wall, on a filthy bed, lay a man in trousers and a jersey. He had several days of grey stubble on his chin, his mouth hung open and from it came a rasping, nasal snore. The bed, missing a leg, was supported by two flat stones and a thick book. Beside the bed was a bottle half full of something.

She pressed close to J.J: "Is that him?"

He squeezed her hand. "But he has a licence. He showed it to me."

She looked around. She hadn't imagined it. this way. She had pictured a country church, like their own church in Trebsko, or St. Wenceslaus in Spillville, the priest in a freshly washed white alb and a green cope....

But this one is a Protestant, of course. What was the name of his church, anyway? She couldn't remember. She looked at the revolting minister sprawled in the bed. On his jersey was a large greasy food spot.

"Reverend Jones?" said J.J.

The snoring subsided but the man did not move. "Reverend Jones?"

No response. J.J. approached the man and shook him lightly. He opened his eyes. They were as bleary as those of his dog on the porch.

"It's me, Kovarik," said J.J. "Kovarik. Don't you remember? I was here yesterday."

The man struggled into a sitting position, and swung a pair of bare feet to the floor. He reeked of whisky; she recognized the smell from Rothenberger's.

"Yesterday?"

"Yes. It was about – about this...."

Then the minister noticed her. He rubbed his forehead and ran his eyes over her. "You got three dollars?" he said to J.J.

"Yes, I do."

"And a witness?"

"You promised to look after that."

"Yeah, but it'll cost you another dollar."

"I'll pay you," said J.J. The man stood up and looked at her again. His face wrinkled in a rough smile, revealing a few yellowed teeth. She shuddered.

"Is the young – ah, lady – eighteen?"

"And – and a half," J.J. stammered.

"Well, well," said the minister, showing his yellow teeth again. "How'd you like to go over, wait in the church? I'll just toss on my gown and go get the witness."

J.J. took her by the arm. The man stretched out his hand towards him, palm uppermost.

"Payment in advance."

J.J. let go of her, reached into his pocket and pulled out a wallet. He counted four dollars into the waiting hand.

"Plus a dollar for the marriage certificate."

J.J. handed him another dollar. They turned and walked towards the door. Once more J.J. took her by the arm. In the doorway, she turned around and saw the minister taking a drink from the bottle of liquid that looked like urine.

Outside she turned to him: "J.J., please – let's get out of here right now."

"It's too late, Otylia. They'll be looking for us already."

"Then we'll say that – that we got lost in the woods or something."

"They wouldn't believe us."

"J.J., he's – he's such an awful person! Awful!"

"But he's got a licence."

"But we can't let someone like him marry us!"

*He pulled her towards the ramshackle church. But she could feel that
he too was hesitating. "It will only take a moment and then – by evening we'll be in Dubuque," he said. "We'll stay in the Red Rose Hotel.
You'll like it there, believe me. It's clean and – and tomorrow...."*

*Better not think about tomorrow. Tomorrow would be terrible.
What if they drive us out of the house? What if Father has a heart
attack? She didn't even want to think about the impending ceremony. She clung instead to the vision of a clean Red Rose Hotel, the
vision of a porcelain jug in a porcelain washbowl, the vision of
darkness – they say it hurts, but J.J....*

*The white temple of cloud had almost vanished in the blackness
of the approaching storm. Sheet lightning flashed silently in the
depths of the enormous black thunderhead like a portent. She hesitated but J.J. held her firmly. They climbed the four rickety stairs
and he opened the door. Inside there were six decrepit-looking pews
and on a small platform at the front stood a table with a lectern for
the Bible. The dog lay on the table, asleep, its long pink tongue
dangling over the edge. As they walked towards the front their foot-
steps made the floorboards creak, but the dog didn't even lift its
head, merely cocked a worried eyebrow. At the other end of its body
a scrawny tail wagged a weary greeting.*

*They sat down in the front row near the dog, and she noticed that
yellowed newspapers covered the lectern. A buzzing fly hovered above
them. The dog sighed tiredly and twitched its eyebrows.*

"J.J., couldn't you – "

"What?"

*"Couldn't you get that dog off the table? It's really supposed to
be like an altar, isn't it? Animals don't belong in a church."*

He hesitated.

"Please, J.J.!"

*He got up and pushed at the dog, which licked his hand, laid its
head back on the table and sighed contentedly. J.J. walked around
the table and grasped the animal by the hind legs. Rays of light from
the afternoon sun slanted through the window and fell directly on
the table. J.J. tugged and the dog, without even opening its eyes,
hooked its front paws over the edge of the table. J.J. pulled, and the
table moved backwards. The dog barked in a deep, hoarse voice.*

*A door squeaked and the minister stepped into the church through
a side entrance. He was wearing a dingy black gown, and a cross*

made from some gold-coloured metal dangled on a chain around his neck. Behind him came the black man who had been hoeing the tomatoes. He was barefoot and wearing the same ragged linen trousers as before, but now his bare torso was covered with a thread-bare dress jacket. He also wore a clip-on tie fastened to a yellowed, vulcanized collar.

"Out, Frolick!" called the minister. The startled dog scrambled to its feet, jumped off the table and scurried out of the church. She looked around. The sanctuary resembled a pillaged warehouse. Over by one wall lay a broken pew. Nearby was a metal barrel. A barrel in a church? She looked up and saw that directly above the barrel there was a hole in the roof the size of a human head. A blue sky shone through.

Then blackness covered the hole and the sunlight beyond the window went out. Large drops of rain began beating on the windows. Several panes were broken or missing.

"All right, come on up here and let's get it over with," said the man in the gown.

They got up, she stood beside J.J. in front of the lectern on the table. The minister began to speak in an unnatural singsong.

"Dear brother and sister in Christ, we are gathered together in the house of the Lord in order that, before me, by the power invested in me by God and the state of Iowa, you may be joined together in the bonds of holy – "

"Reverend!" croaked the black man in a stage whisper.

"What is it, Tom?"

"You ain't got no Bible."

Only now did the man in the gown notice the yellowing news-papers on the lectern. "Damn it! Where is it?"

"You used it to prop up your bed," whispered the old Negro hoarsely.

The man wiped his forehead. "Right you are, Tom. Go and get it, would you?"

He turned to them. "You can sit down for a while if you want." They returned to the pew. The minister gathered the newspapers from the lectern, glancing at them rapidly as he did so. Outside, the rising wind whistled through the cracks in the clap-board walls. It grew darker. Water began trickling through the hole in the roof and dropping with a metallic clamour into the barrel. The reverend removed a cigar butt and matches from his pocket, struck a match on the sole of his shoe and lit the cigar. He stared

at them for a moment sadly and then gazed up at the hole in
the roof.

"Have to get her fixed," he said. "But not till after the harvest. I
can't get up on the roof any more, never mind Tom." He looked at
J.J. and blew a smoke ring the way her father would. She watched
it. The halo of smoke rose, expanded and began to thin out. "Don't
suppose you could get up there to fix her yourself, could you? You're
young. I got a ladder...."

"Well," said J.J. "We don't have much time."

"It won't take but five minutes. I've got the boards, all it needs
is to nail up two or three – "

"Okay," said J.J. "I'll do it."

The old Negro appeared in the doorway. He was drenched and he
held the Bible against his naked body under the dress jacket. He put
the Bible on the lectern.

"Much obliged," said the minister. There was a crash of thunder
and a streak of lightning lit the darkness outside the window.

"Well, let's get down to it."

They got up and went back to the table. Once more, the man
assumed an unnatural singsong. "Dear brother and sister in Christ,
we are gathered here together in the house of the Lord –

"Miss Otylia Dvorak, do you take this man, Joseph J. Kovarik, to
be your lawful wedded husband – " Yes, she said in spirit. For better
or for worse. It will be worse when we tell my parents tomorrow.
But they won't drive us out of the house. Father will roar like a tiger,
but he's good and kind at heart and things will smooth out again.
I only hope it doesn't give him a heart attack – "till death do you
part?"

Otylia opened her mouth.

"Otylia!"

A gust of wind blew through the church. The minister stared past
her, over her shoulder. She turned around.

"Dear God! Mother!"

J.J. jumped to one side as though he were going to bolt. Then he
controlled himself and turned too.

Into the church marched Anna, an open umbrella over her head.

"Well, well," Otylia heard the minister say philosophically. Then
a muted slap as he closed the Bible.

Her mother grabbed her by the hand. "Come with me, child! And
we'll sort this out tomorrow, Mr. Kovarik." Her voice was as cold

*as steel. Then she dragged her out of the church into the rain. The
wind turned the umbrella inside out and in a few seconds they were
soaked to the skin. A black buggy stood in the drive. Old Frank
Valenta sat on the driver's seat with a hood over his head.*

And then they were inside.

*"Father knows nothing about all this," said her mother icily, as
the buggy started off. "I left him a message saying we'd gone on a
visit to Protivin. But you're in for it, young lady!"*

*The buggy rattled out of the drive through the field and onto the
road. Old Valenta whipped the horse. It was all happening too quickly.
Her head was spinning.*

*"And you can thank your guardian angel this Reverend Jones is
such a drunkard. If he hadn't talked about you two in the tavern in
Protivin last night, and spread the news, this madness would be
irreversible by now!"*

*Madness? She turned around and through the little isinglass win-
dow she saw a heart-rending sight. Right behind the buggy trotted
the mare, and on the buckboard, with nothing to protect him from
the weather, sat a sad-looking creature in his Sunday best, glistening
as though he had just stepped out of the river like the legendary
waterman.*

The family left Prague for the summer home in Vysoka. She hoped
Suk would be in Vysoka. He wasn't. As soon as they arrived, they
had to go to the church to offer thanks for their safe return from
America. Her father sat at the organ and frowned. The wheezing
instrument hissed and snorted. The stops didn't work properly. "A
thousand times we thank Thee ..." he sang in his thundering voice.
He sounded almost angry, and at suppertime he said, "You know
what I'm going to do, Anna? It's all very well to thank the Lord, but
it's not enough. Certainly not for watching over us all that time in
America. I'm going to buy a new organ for our church. Why, I'm
ashamed of what we have – they have a better organ over there in
Spillville. What do you think, Anna?"

"How much does a new organ cost?"

But yes, Otylia thought, He did watch over us in Spillville. And
if Father knew, he'd probably build a whole new church....

· · ·

Week after week went by, and Suk stayed away. They said he was on tour with his newly formed quartet. But couldn't he have found at least a few days free? Even an hour? Clearly, he was angry at her.

She walked out onto the terrace of the manor house. Inside, behind the French doors, Aunt Josie was playing the Ständchen. And what about poor J.J. away over there in America? Oh, unfaithful sinner. Doubly unfaithful. Sweet Mary, what shall I do?

She wrote Suk a brief note. Just a sentence. "Joe, please don't be angry with me. Your Otylia." She hesitated over it for a long time, then tore it up and wrote: "Dear Joe, please don't be angry with me. Otylia."

She didn't send it until three days later. Then she waited. The days grew shorter and it rained a lot. Father was busy revising his new opera, Dimitri, and was in a foul mood. The pigeons came down with some kind of illness. So she spent most of her time at the manor house playing four-handed piano pieces with Aunt Josie. And still a reply did not come. Once she burst into tears in the middle of a piece. Josie said, "Don't worry, Otylia. He'll come back."

"Do you know about it?"

"It hasn't been hard to guess. He used to be virtually a member of the family and since your return he hasn't even put in an appearance."

"But do you know about – about what happened in America?"

She told her about it. It was evening. A weary sun shone through the french doors.

"And I'm fond of them both, but – oh, it's terrible, Aunt Josie. I'm so confused!"

She wept on Josephine's bosom as she had once cried on Jeannette's.

"I was confused in much the same way, once," said her aunt. "Don't cry, Otylia. You'll get over it. And everything will turn out well."

"It won't," she wept. "How could it?"

"I was also fond of two men at once."

"Which two?" she asked in tears, curious in spite of herself.

"Well, Kounic and – and another man."

"But you loved Kounic more. You married him."

"I don't know myself whether I loved Kounic more, but yes, I married him."

"And who was the other man?"

Josephine was silent for a long time. The sun outside the window sank below the horizon. "It's not important," she said. "I married Kounic because I loved him."

"So you didn't love the other man?"

"I loved him too."

"Then how did you sort it out? Why Kounic?"

Josephine was silent again. The fit of weeping had passed. Otylia took out her handkerchief and blew into it.

"How did you decide, Aunt Josie?" she asked urgently.

Josephine laughed. "I tossed a coin, Otylia. It came out tails. And I've never regretted it." She was silent again. "And I don't think the other man ever did, either."

"I'm sure that's not true, Aunt Josie."

"Maybe it's not," said her aunt.

Just before she left New York, they had met unexpectedly in the corridor of the Conservatory. It broke her heart. He still looked like the legendary waterman. Not wet, just desperate and unhappy, and they were both nervous.

"I'll come to Bohemia, Ottie," he said.

"You'll come in vain, J.J."

"Why? You'll soon be of legal age – "

"No. You'd better forget about me. My parents will never let me marry you now – and...." She didn't tell him about her dream. How she would wake up at night not knowing whether it had been real or not. She dreamed they had buried her, that she was already dead. The gas lamps on Seventeenth Street were outside the window, Magda was breathing beside her in bed. Why should I die? But somehow the idea had got into her head, perhaps because her father cried over Kounic's letter. When he left for the Conservatory, she had slipped into his study and read the letter. Aunt Josie ill. Not much hope. That night she had first dreamed she was dead. They were carrying her in a coffin, her father was weeping –

"Won't you wait for me, Otylia?"

"I don't know. Oh God, here comes my mother!"

He started, ran quickly down the corridor and vanished around the corner. Her mother was marching towards her.

"I saw you, Otylia. Remember what you promised?"

"Yes, Mother."

And together they set off home again. A journey under guard, the short journey from the Conservatory to 327 East Seventeenth Street. House arrest.

The Spillville miracle sat in a corner of the piano room and watched them floundering about in the music, unable to get anywhere. "By heaven!" said the Master. "What's this I've written? I can't even play it myself. My friend, wouldn't you like to play first violin instead of me?"

"That wouldn't be proper, Master," said J.J.'s father, though old Kovarik was a better violinist than the author of the quartet.

"Or you, young man? But the trouble is, I can't play the cello."

"Nor can I," he said. Moreover, the cello had dried out, he'd had to dig it out from under piles of junk in the attic, it slipped hopelessly out of tune when you played it, giving the notes a kind of permanent glissando.

"It's all those cussed years on the viola. Ann, how about trading your viola for my violin?" said the Master to J.J.'s sister.

Ann, however, liked to tease the Master, so she replied in English. "You stay on the first fiddle, Master. If we traded, we'd have a first-class viola, but the violin" – and she paused – "would sound like, how do they say? – like drawing a horse-tail over the entrails of a cat."

"Aha. Of course," said the Master. "Okay, once more from the letter F."

They started again, sailed smoothly for a while, then floundered and sank again, at precisely the same spot.

"It's that confounded bird!"

"Which bird, Master?"

"The red one. Can't you hear it?" and instead of playing the part on the violin, the Master whistled.

"Once more from the letter F. If I can't play it now, I'm going to hang up my hat."

He couldn't play it. He didn't hang up his hat.

The months passed and no answer came from Suk. On the other hand, the organ did arrive. It cost eight hundred gulden. Anna examined it thoughtfully as the workers unloaded it, piece by piece, off the wagons. Dvorak glowed and he worked for three days, from morning till evening, helping to assemble the instrument. But he didn't play it himself. It was tested by an organ master, register by register, pedals, keyboards. It was ready on September seventh, a day before Dvorak's birthday.

Suk's quartet was on a concert tour in Vienna.

On the morning of her father's birthday, when she got into the dress that Jeannette had helped her choose in New York, she found she had lost weight. The dress hung loosely on her, as though she were a clothes tree.

Her sister had grown plump. Little Anna couldn't do up the buttons of her dress around the waist and it took all her strength to lace herself into a borrowed corset.

"I eat too much," said Anna. "I'm always stuffing myself. Living in the country doesn't suit me." She looked at her sister. "How do you do it? You're a regular skeleton."

It's easy, Anna. All you have to do is fall in love with two men at once. The best possible way to reduce. And you can stuff yourself all you want; the only problem is, you feel more like dying.

It was raining. They drove to the church in the Kounics' coach. They all sat in the front row except Magda, who went to the choir with Dvorak because she was going to sing a solo. One of his American students had written words to the Largo of the New World Symphony and sent them as a gift for his birthday. Dvorak sat down at the organ, glowing so that it seemed he might outshine the countless candles that flickered throughout the church.

And when he touched the keyboards and stepped on the pedals, the new organ thundered into life, magnificent, sonorous, like a large orchestra. The priest, in his golden vestments, emerged from the sacristy accompanied by six altar boys.

Oh Lord, forgive me! I've caused a lot of pain. In a week Father will go back to America, and only Mother and Ota will go with him this time. J.J. isn't at the Conservatory any longer. He's going to play in the New York Philharmonic. But I know why he left the Conservatory. And Joe is touring himself to death with his quartet....

Introibo ad altare Dei....

Ad Deum qui laetificat juventutem meam....

... and I'll be left looking after the children in Prague. Will the quartet ever give a concert in Prague? Surely it will. But what good will that do me? He won't come to visit me anyway.

Judica me, Deus, et discerne causam meam....

Help me out of my distress, Lord! I shall write J.J. No, I won't write him – he'd come over here to see me. And what then? What would I do?

Father's fingers on the keyboards. He plays like the Lord God Himself. He's probably happier now than when he had to take all those bows in New York. He's all aglow up there in the choir, just as Jeannette was all aglow then at the Met.

Emitte lucem tuam et veritatem tuam....

Quare tristis es, anima mea, et quare conturbas me?

Why are you troubled, my soul? Why indeed? You know, Lord. And outside it's raining, raining. And the quartet is on tour. Father doesn't stop playing even when the organ should be silent; he plays on, pianissimo.

Deus, tu conversus vivificabis nos.

Ostende nobis, Domine, misericordiam tuam.

Have mercy on me, Lord. *Mea culpa, mea culpa, mea maxima culpa.*

Exaudi orationem meam.

Et clamor meus ad te veniat.

My cry goes up to Thee, oh Lord. I, an unfaithful woman, an adultress – well, almost. Which one do I truly care about? How can I know?

Clamor meus ad te veniat!

Cold air washed over her. Someone had opened the side door to the church. She looked over and felt herself go very still.

O, Deus, Deus, tu laetificas juventutem meam!

In the doorway stood another waterman, his sad gypsy eyes black but full of hope, glistening as though he had just stepped out of the river.

Joy! Joy!

And Suk sat beside her, her hand in his hand, wet but warm. Father thundered on the organ, rising to full volume, and then quietly, while Madga's lovely alto voice, still childish, sang their father's Largo –

"Going home, going home, I'm a-going home," sang Magda. "Going home, going home, to where I belong!"

Aunt Josie was right.

Joy! Joy!

. . .

"For the love of God! If it isn't Kovarik! Mother! Children! Come here, all of you! The Redskin is here!" The Master rejoiced. He was terribly aged, his complexion darker than ever. He jumped up from his erasers, grasped his hand – he still possessed his strength – and dragged him out of the summer-house into the garden. "Mother! Otylia! Children!"

His wife was not as glad to see him. She came slowly out to meet him, coolly offered him her hand and said pointedly, "What could possibly have brought you all the way out here, Mr. Kovarik?"

"What a question, Mother! He came to see his old friends after all these years."

One old friend had just appeared around the corner of the house, with Suk beside her. Suk too was less than enthusiastic. Otylia's face, however, shone as it had in the woods near Spillville. She left Suk to his own devices and ran to greet him.

"J.J.!" It was an ardent, girlish welcome. Unfortunately, they weren't alone.

"You look wonderful, Miss Otylia," he said sincerely, and felt miserable.

"You've come just at the right time," the Master declared, and then caught himself. "Should we let the cat out of the bag, Mother?"

Anna shrugged her shoulders. Suk sauntered up and offered his hand. "How do you do?" Which meant: what the devil are you doing here?

"As you wish, Anton," said his wife.

Suk bent over, pulled a stalk of timothy from the grass and began chewing it. For a moment, he thought Suk was going to offer him one too.

"We're celebrating an engagement, Redskin!" announced the Master joyously.

Later, as they walked together through the woods to the pond, the Master said, "Believe it or not, it took me completely by surprise. You know what they say – it's always darkest right under the lamp post. You see, I still thought of Otylia as a child." The Master chuckled. "I'm quite the father, wouldn't you say, Redskin? Here they are, wandering around under my nose, hand in hand, and I can't see for the fog."

You're quite the father, Master, he thought. What a shame Otylia also has quite the mother.

"But she's eighteen, after all, and I predict a glorious future for Suk. My wife was very pleased about it – you know, I think she rather expected it to happen all along. True enough, I didn't want her to marry a musician – they're mostly wretchedly poor – but Suk doesn't look as though he'll end up that way, and since they're fond of each other...."

And Suk was like a watchdog. But the good Lord stepped in and chose, as his agent, the father who was blind to what went on under the lamp post.

"Why should he go with you, Josef?" said the Master. "He's come all this way from America to visit his old friends, and you want to drag him off to Prague? In the middle of summer?"

"He must have friends in Prague as well," grumbled Suk.

"But my best friends are right here in Vysoka," J.J. said, astonished at his own audacity.

"And he'll have plenty of time for Prague. Now, it's time to be on your way if you don't want to miss your train."

He mentally blessed the Prague concertmaster who had sent an urgent telegram to Suk asking his help with a score. He also blessed the Master who refused to go to the station with them because he had a deadline to meet.

At the station, Suk kissed Otylia demonstratively, swung up onto the back platform of the last car and, from there, glared at them both. He had seen the same look in those black eyes four years ago, from behind the lattice-work of the summer-house.

He stood neutrally to one side, displeased with the way Otylia waved and continued to wave until only the smoke was visible. When that too dissipated, Otylia turned around and he helped her into the gig. She glanced at him, and the look in her eyes was uncertain and heart-rending.

He cracked the whip over the horse. They drove in silence for some time along the narrow road winding among the fields, golden ribbons of rye, red ribbons of poppy blooms, past dark green wedges of woodlots, the wooden harmony of the gig accompanying the clop-clopping like an Indian drum.

"It wouldn't have worked out, J.J.," Otylia said quietly at last.

"Of course not," he said bitterly; "Mother doesn't like America."

They were silent again, clippity-clippity-clop, clippity-clop, like that little Kickapoo drum when, three long years ago, they had struggled to play the Master's new string quartet.

"If I had asked you to move to Prague –"

"But you didn't ask me, Otylia."

"No, I didn't." He turned towards her and saw the profile of his Spillville miracle, as miraculous as ever. "But I was miserable, J.J.! I cried so hard I soaked Mrs. Thurber's blouse."

"You didn't tell me about it, though."

"It was impossible, J.J. They wouldn't let me see you."

Clop-clop, clop-clop, a lark's song suspended in the blue sky. Clop-clop-clop along the road through the fields.

"Out of sight, out of mind," he said to her reproachfully. "When you were in America, you put Suk out of your mind. And as soon as you get back –"

"I haven't forgotten you, J.J. I'm equally fond of both of you. Perhaps it's a sin, but it's true."

"It is a sin. Because it's a lie. If you were equally fond of both of us...." What should she do in such a circumstance? He didn't know.

"I like you both equally well," said Otylia, "but I'm not about to enter a cloister. So I came up with a different solution."

"You chose the one you were fondest of," he said bitterly.

"I'm equally fond of you both," she insisted.

They reached the top of a white hill; the church appeared, the white rectangular shape of the manor house and, a short distance below it, the Master's house. A warm summer breeze caressed them.

"I was on the other side of the ocean –"

"The ocean had nothing to do with it," said Otylia. "I made up my mind quite fairly."

He smiled bitterly. "Fairly?"

"There was only one thing I could do, J.J. I tried to be fair. I tossed a florin."

"What?" he shouted, startling the horse so that the gig lurched.

"I tossed a florin," she repeated, gravely. "You were heads, and it came up tails."

Many years later his cheerful wife said, "She was quite a wise girl, this Otylia of yours. I'd never have thought of that. In her place I'd have let it eat away at me and finally I'd have run off to the Klondike and started carrying on with the gold-diggers just to forget."

"You didn't have the same problem," he said.

"How do you know? Maybe I tossed a silver dollar for you, too."
He frowned. "Really, Jarmila?"

She ruffled his hair and laughed. "But mine came up tails too and it brought me good luck," she said, kissing him. "There's a trick to flipping a silver dollar so it always comes up tails."

His happiness flowed over him. From out of the past stepped Otylia, but she was only a phantom, only the morning mist on a meadow flooded with sunlight. A trace of loveliness.

"TEN!" SANG THE BARMAN and a glass topped with white foam came sliding down the black marble counter towards the little man. The clock showed ten minutes to midnight.

"Right you are," said the little man. "Don't believe me if you don't want to. It wasn't at a rehearsal. It was because of the tuba –" with a habitual gesture, he reached behind him to where his instrument was perched on a bar stool, looking vaguely like Huneker in the dim light. Huneker had joined them this time, and was sitting on a stool next to the little man, drinking beer, "and because of his ears. The only thing is, it wasn't a tuba, it was a sousaphone."

"You're just making this up again, old man," said the violinist next to Huneker.

"How could I be making it up when I'm senile already?" said the little man. "I don't think any more, I just blow my horn." He took a drink. "And I drink. But don't believe me if you don't want to."

"We don't, but we'd like to hear the story anyway," said Adele.

"In that case – begging your pardon, ma'am – screw you," said the little man. "The Master was a genius, and your skepticism is an insult to him. Not only that, he was an educated man. He knew pretty well everything there was to know. The trouble was he could hardly remember anything he knew. It wasn't that he was so old, he was only in his fifties, just that his brain hardened up on him. If you ask me, he was too fond of meat. Ever see him eat steak? A pleasure to watch, make a good ad for butchers. Of course if he'd eased up on the meat, he might still be with us today. Too much meat brings on strokes. And the Master could tuck away a four-pound steak at a sitting and, on top of that, get all upset because the dumplings were cold."

"Ugh!" said Zeckwer, the violinist. "Steak with dumplings?"

"He had strange tastes, right enough," admitted the little man. "And as I said before, it was through blowing my horn I met him. At the time I was playing a side gig with Fritz Meyer's marching band and we were doing a parade for some German athletic club and we were going past Fleischmann's Old Vienna Café – "

... when through the café's stained-glass windows came a melody, a thunderous, melodic, marching tempo. Dvorak's eyes left the book he was arguing about with Huneker and Seidl – Nietzsche's book on Wagner. The music grew louder. The melody was sprightly, simple but full of life and in it – "What's that? What is it?" – Huneker could hear nothing special. Perhaps only that above the tune, carried by the trumpets and clarinets, there spread a strange, sonorous, almost velvet thundering – and the director of the Conservatory ran out of the café without paying, as he had many times before, but this time without his hands over his ears.

Huneker ran out after him. Marching past the café was a band in green uniforms with gold cording. In front was a belted bandmaster carrying a shiny black baton with a brass ball at one end that rose and fell rhythmically with the music. At the back, behind the neat rows of caps, was an enormous, towering tuba pointed straight at the sky, as though deliberately fashioned to capture the spring rain drizzling gently down on the band and make a refreshing rainbow around it in the scattered evening sunlight. The velvet thunder was coming from that horn; it rolled over the caps, over the spectators, over the hordes of ragged boys who marched ahead of the bandmaster like a vanguard and formed an unruly line around the band. Dvorak, his eyes fixed on the fascinating horn, joined the line.

Huneker remained where he was, watching the director march smartly away, watching him retreat from the learned discussion.

"Eleven!" The barman's bright voice announced another round. The glass, set in motion by his experienced hand, swept along the marble, missing Adele Margulies's cognac by a hair, tickling Huneker's tankard, slowing down and coming reliably to rest in the little man's outstretched hand.

"Right you are," he said, lifting the glass to his lips. "And as we were marching past Fleischmann's Old Vienna Café, a man with wild hair came flying out the door, his eyes starting out of his head as though he'd just been given the heave-ho. The old man fell into the second column like a trooper, among those street-urchins playing along on kazoos. He strode along beside the last row where I was marching, as straight as a candle, like the gymnasts in tights behind us, and when I took a look at him I saw him staring at my sousaphone the way a calf looks at a new gate, as we used to say. Every time I played a pretty figure on the bass, his eyes would light up like a Christmas tree.''

The description was exact. *Huneker remembered how he had lost sight of the director's dishevelled head, bobbing up and down in the evening light along Broadway, Nietzsche forgotten, Seidl out of mind, both ears turned towards the magnificent booming sound emanating from somewhere in the heart of the marching band, blasting through the drizzle and holding the Master so spellbound that he stumbled and almost went sprawling as the band rounded the corner and disappeared.*

"When we had finished playing and were breaking up to go home, the man said to me, 'Listen, my good fellow, what kind of tuba is that? It has a magnificent sound. I've never heard anything like it before.' 'It's not a tuba, it's a sousaphone,' I said, and I explained it was invented by the bandmaster John Philip Sousa and had a better tone than the bombardon, the only problem being the rain got into it. And the fellow – ''

"You mean Mister Dvorak," said the violinist.

"Surely you've figured that out by now, Mr. Zeckwer?" and the little man sent the empty glass sliding down the marble towards the barman. "I'm telling you about the first time I met the Master, aren't I? Because of the tone colour, or timbre, as Mr. Huneker here would call it. Because, gentlemen – and my lady – wild as the Master was for meat, he'd drop it the moment he heard any sounds he thought were beautiful. And in my books, any man like that is an artist. Strike a well-stretched drum with a stick and he forgets all about the world, steaks included.''

"*What is it, Collins?" asked the Master. He had just acquainted them with his uncommon pedagogical intention, and an excited hum rippled the silence of the class.*

"*I don't know, sir," said the girl. "Do you think it's appropriate for ladies to go to such a place?"*

"*You'll be going there for study purposes," said the Master.*

"*To a minstrel show?" asked Zeckwer, esthete that he was.*

"*Don't turn up your nose at it, Zeckwer. Where do you think Haydn or Beethoven got their ideas from? Each other? If that were the case they'd be just like each other, wouldn't they?"*

"But minstrel songs? Why, they're not even genuine folk songs."

To their general astonishment, Harry T. Burleigh tried to discourage them from going. The Master stared at him in surprise.

"It costs an awful amount just to get in," said Burleigh. "Just to see us black folk. And besides, it's not a very good group."

"Have you heard them?" asked the Master.

Burleigh admitted he had.

"Very well. You don't have to go with us. I don't want you to pay twice."

"But what about the ladies, sir – " Laura Collins piped up.

"In this school you're not a lady, you're a student of music, by heaven," said the Master. "I'll stand in for your father. You can go on my arm."

And so, *led by the Master with the not unwilling Collins on his arm, they entered the smoke-filled tavern, occupied a table, ordered beer – juice for Laura Collins – and pulled out their cigars.*

The banjo, the violin and the bones started up and onto the stage ran the Hick and Sawyer Minstrels. Playing the bones was a man with an unusually thick coat of blacking on his face. Dvorak's attention was aroused; the furrow appeared between his brows.

" 'My friend,' he said to me," the little man went on. " 'You're through for the day, aren't you? Come and play me something in the park.' Well, I was through for the day and I saw he was burning to hear me. Never happened to me before. Who ever pays any attention to a tuba or a sousaphone? Sure, when someone can really play the violin, everyone just melts. Women shed tears over the French horn and the flute – some even manage to pass out. But the sousaphone? So we sat down on a bench in Stuyvesant Park and here was this geezer listening to me like I was playing the cello. The thing is," said the tuba player, looking round at his instrument sitting safely behind him on a stool, looking like the golem, "I could play that sousaphone. I was the first one outside Sousa's band to get one. We were sitting on a bench, it was already dark, the stars were coming out over the rooftops around Stuyvesant Park and I, ladies and gentlemen, played Schubert's Ständchen for the Master."

"You played what?"

"Don't believe me if you don't want to. Or better still – " and the little man looked round at the tuba again, "I'll play it for you now. You've never heard this before, Miss Margulies."

Before they could protest, the little man had nimbly stripped the golem of its case and was sitting with the gigantic, carefully polished horn on his lap. Then, in the half-light of the bar, the deep, enormous tone thundered. "Hear my singing, hear my pleading, Borne across the night...." Adele opened her mouth. The small man's chest concealed lungs like the bellows of a cathedral organ.

The minstrels completed their walkaround and the Master said, "Do you see him? The one with those rattles?"

"It's hard to see him," said Laura Collins stupidly. This made the Master angry. He took off his pince-nez and set them against her face. She pulled back.

"Go ahead, put them on. Take a look."

Naturally, Zeckwer too had seen what the Master saw, and like the others he kept silent. On stage, they started playing a juba. The one with the blackest face had his back to the audience.

"Do you see now, young lady?" said the Master sternly.

"Everything is blurry now," she said bravely.

"You've got a problem, woman. With or without glasses, you can't see a thing. Give them to me. Now, look at the one with his bottom to you. Where have you seen that backside before?"

Her eyes widened. She was obviously blushing. "I don't look at things like that."

At this point, the blackened performer was compelled to turn around. But now he raised his hands, so the instruments obscured his face. He moved them in time to the banjo.

"Look at him," said the Master. "He's a clever one. But he can't fool me."

Zeckwer went to the washroom with Loomis and Will Cook.

"Do you think he'll catch it?"

"Of course not," said Will. "He drags the rest of us here by the collar, so why should he give him a hard time?"

"We're here for study purposes."

"He's here to gain experience."

"Okay," said Zeckwer. "But someone who plays kettledrums in Mr. Dvořák's orchestra – "

"Nonsense," said Will. "Haven't you seen through him yet? He's just glad to be able to catch someone out. He can be infantile sometimes. But what does he ever do about it?"

"... Come, my love, my own...." The Ständchen was over, the glasses in the rack above the bar ceased their vibrating. The barman broke the silence: "Twelve!"

"I was rather moved myself," the little man said. He slipped his tuba back into its case and set it on the bar stool. "Lights started coming on in the windows around the square and I blew my heart out – well, there's nothing like a sousaphone. Not even Wagner's tuba sounds like that. It was," he added dreamily, "magnificent...." Adele sighed. The little man woke from his reverie. "And the Master says, 'My good man, since you've played so well, allow me to invite you for supper.' Well, I never turn down a free meal, so he dragged me, with my sousaphone, right across Manhattan over to First Avenue and Seventieth Street, into some Bohemian joint called the Sokol Hall. There was a kind of contest going on. But what a contest it was!"

"I'll bet it wasn't a dancing contest," said Huneker.

"You guessed it!" said the little man.

"Beer drinking!"

"Wide of the mark. They were all gorging themselves with dumplings. So we joined them – and I won second prize!"

"And did the Master win first prize?" asked Huneker.

"No – a notorious con man from Chicago called Jaros. He ate seventy-two. At least that's what he claimed."

"And how many did you have to eat to win second prize? Fifty? Don't give us that!"

"Fifty-one – and you don't have to believe me if you don't want to."

"*I can appreciate you covering up for another student,*" *said the Master, nodding his head approvingly, and then, suddenly changing registers, he bellowed,* "*but I don't like you lying to me. You know very well who that big fellow is!*"

"*We don't, Doctor,*" *said Will.*

"*You're the one to talk, Mr. Cook. And I suppose you don't know either, Miss Collins?*"

"*I can't see him, sir. My eyes are watering from the smoke.*" *The performance was over, the minstrels were taking their bows. The blackest of all was still holding his instruments in front of his face. Dvorak jumped up and moved swiftly off through the crowd. Backstage, the blackened man tried to escape, but there was nowhere to go.*

"I'm only filling in for someone, Master," he said defensively. *"They know me – "*

"What are you worried about, Mr. Burleigh? Don't you remember? I used to play in taverns myself when I was a boy."

"It's not you I'm afraid of, sir."

"Who then? Mrs. Thurber?"

Burleigh shook his head. *"I've been accepted into the choir of St. George's Cathedral. But some of the elders were against it. They said I'd turn it into a minstrel show. If word got out that I'm working here...."*

Word didn't get out.

The next day Huneker went into the Conservatory library and took a musical dictionary from the shelf. He found the entry and read: "BB-bass. The largest and deepest-toned instrument in the brass family, used in brass bands, with a range two octaves lower than a cornet. Usually in the shape of a baryton, it also exists in two other forms: the helicon, which has a circular shape and is carried over the shoulder, and the sousaphone, which has a large, widely flared bell pointing forward. It was constructed by the firm of G.C. Coon according to a design by John Philip Sousa in 1899...."

Huneker snapped the dictionary shut, laughing maliciously. Now I've got you, old man. 1899! A fine way to celebrate old Borax's devotion to the truth.

A week later they were sitting in the bar. When it was approaching midnight and the barman had sung out, "Twenty!", Huneker came out with his freshly gained knowledge and made a fool of himself.

Next morning, he returned humbly to the library, found the entry and read it to the end: "According to other sources, however, the first instrument made to Sousa's design was manufactured by J.W. Pepper in Philadelphia sometime around 1892. In this early version of the instrument, the bell was not directed forward over the player's head, but straight upwards, behind his back. The instrument's sound, therefore, went straight into the air, whence it dominated the entire band. Because of the bell's direction, this instrument was called 'the rain-catcher' by musicians."

25 :⁀: THE SPIDER, THE FLY, THE MASTER, THE BIRD, THE BUTTERFLY, GOD AND THE CAT

A FAT GREEN FLY settled on her plate. She drove it away with a fork, and because the man opposite her was silent now, concentrating entirely on his juicy sausage, she watched the fly buzz aimlessly around his grey hair, bump into the windowpane, down which large drops of heavy rain were streaming, and become tangled at last in a freshly spun spiderweb where it began to struggle for its life. The struggle was brief. From a hiding-place in the corner a large garden spider darted out and began wrapping the fly, still alive, in a silken shroud. Before long, it was a small, motionless bundle, a corpse bound in a white winding-sheet suspended in the middle of the web. The spider plunged its jaws into the little bundle and became quite still. Vital juices flowed from the bundle into the spider's enormous stomach.

Ochre-coloured juice squirted out of the sausage onto the man's green cravat, but he ignored it. All that beauty, she wondered; where did it come from?

A year before he had sat among his bees and his pigeons under the apple tree, looking more aged than when she had last seen him in New York. Beside him, his oldest daughter, slim, attractive, gazed beseechingly at her. Clearly the girl wanted to ask about something, but not in her father's presence. She knew what the question was. Jeannette had told her, and had given her instructions. "It was unfortunate that it didn't work out. Where the Devil fears to tread, he sends old Borax's wife," Jeannette had said, not in anger – Jeannette was never angry – but thoughtfully, like a businessman who has not yet closed a deal but is still hoping. "Unless – Kovarik hasn't given

up, has he? Why do you suppose he still comes to the Conservatory?"
"Because of your lovely eyes!" "J.J. was never one to admire my
eyes," said Jeannette. "He was enchanted by other eyes, wide-set
eyes like the father's. So who knows what may happen, Adele? All
may not be lost yet. For the school, it would mean...."

In theory it was not an impossible plan; in practice it was probably
a pipedream. Yet when she saw how Otylia had wilted, she felt that
there might be a chance after all.

"Mrs. Thurber is an American. She is very brave," Borax had said
then. "Look at all she's done to keep that school going. And I would
be very happy to see her succeed. I have great respect for her and – "
he hesitated, "and for her school as well. It has one of the best staffs
in the world. But it costs a lot, a lot indeed. I don't know. I don't
know, Miss Margulies. If she doesn't get the support of the Senate –
and now that her husband has lost so much money...."

"Jeannette will manage somehow," she said, and looked into the
eyes of Borax's hollow-cheeked daughter. "Jeannette can manage
anything."

"Well, I hope and pray she does," he said, leaning confidentially
towards her. "You know, I'd return at once. But she still owes me
three thousand dollars. If it was just for myself, I could be persuaded
to wait. But...." He fell silent. "You must understand. We have six
children...."

When Borax was out of hearing, she said to Otylia, "Kovarik sends
his warmest greetings. And he says he thinks of you a great deal."

The girl avoided her eyes and looked towards the manor house,
its french doors burning in the sunset. A motionless figure sat on the
terrace by the balustrade. She knew it was the woman with the lovely
hair. The Countess.

"I ..." said the girl in a small voice, "I think about him too –
sometimes...."

"He wants to come to see you."

Their eyes met once again. "Please, I don't think he should."

"Don't you want to see him again?"

She shook her head. "That's not the reason."

"Hm," she said. "Your father's amanuensis – he's not here, I see."

"He's on tour with his quartet."

"Oh, so he will be coming back," she said, disappointed. "Do you
know when?"

"Not really." The girl looked towards the white house from which her father was just emerging. "He hasn't been here in three months – not since we came back."

"Oh, I see," she replied, with relief.

"You know, don't you?" said the girl quickly.

"How would it be if we went in?" said Borax. "There's something I'd like to play for you – or perhaps I shouldn't. No, I think I will."

He finished eating his sausage while the juice dried on his cravat. The spider, motionless, still crouched over its prey. Drops of rain zigzagged down the large windowpane. Outside, a weather-beaten sign announced CESKE BUDEJOVICE – MAIN STATION. A train stood waiting on the tracks, dark in the rain. Figures passed back and forth, and a whistle blew.

"And what about my American boys? Are they doing well?" he asked. "What about Will Cook? Do you remember the first time he came here with you? They still remember him in Vysoka – not surprisingly. It was the first and last time a black man ever played for them."

Here was something to grasp. Now that Jeannette's match-making plans had failed, she had to clutch at every straw.

"I think he's done you proud, Master."

"You don't say! I'm glad to hear it."

The dark, expressive eyes were already covered with a watery film. For a moment, however, they flared with life again.

"They're going to do something of Will's on Broadway – a kind of, well, *eine Operette*," she said. "It's called Clorindy or The Origin of the Cakewalk. All the music, from start to finish, is inspired by black American dances."

"Aha!" said the old man.

"Exactly," she said. "You know, of all your students, Will had the most European training – four years with Joachim. But all it took was a single semester with you to – "

The old man laughed. "At least I've left something behind over there. You know, Miss Margulies" – and he grew sad again, fixing his eyes on her, the glow once more submerged in that unlovely watery stare – "I would love to go back. But – " and he leaned towards her across the table. The train outside shunted into motion and a jet of steam billowed against the window, "I'm afraid. For six months now I haven't written a thing."

"It's summer. You deserve a rest."

"I always wrote most in summer. In Vysoka. No, it's not that. I'm afraid."

"Of what, Master? You've already written so much...."

The eyes beneath that watery, twilight film turned towards the window. Shadowy reflections of the railway coaches moved under the water.

"It was the grace of God," he said dolefully. "Just look at it: I never went to school much, I never studied at a conservatory, and yet I've been given so much...."

So much beauty, she thought. These things have always astonished me. And what do we know about the sources of such beauty? Before leaving Vienna for Bohemia, she had been present when, over coffee, Sigmund Freud had talked on the subject of art. Such a thing would probably upset old Borax. So much beauty – and where did it come from?

They went into the piano room, he sat down at the keyboard and hesitated. But at last he began. They were his own inimitable, plaintive modulations, unexpected changes of key, on and on, and when he had gone too far – how had Mason put it? – he came back over the fence and went on in the opposite direction.

And yet something had gone out of what he played. Half-way through the theme, he stopped suddenly and slammed the piano shut. "I started writing that two weeks ago. Two weeks I've been slaving at it from the crack of dawn and – it's all wrong, Miss Margulies. Why, you can hear it yourself."

"It's – interesting," she said, but her voice betrayed the truth.

"You can't be serious. Fourteen days wasted on such a trifle. I must toss it out and start all over again. Twenty-five years ago, if this had happened to me – well, I wouldn't have been surprised. But today?" He looked around. "It terrifies me, Miss Margulies, it terrifies me."

"But surely it happens to everyone," she replied comfortingly. "Do you know how often Brahms rewrote his music?"

He wasn't listening to her. He gazed through the window at his apple tree, his hand still gripping the keyboard cover. "Music is a great gift," he said quietly. "I had that gift, to the full. But the giver may decide that one is no longer worthy of such a gift. He can take it back."

That evening she went for a walk with Otylia. The first day of September, the woods were changing into a palette of rusts and reds, and stubble fields cross-hatched the land sloping upwards to the sun, also rust-coloured, that crowned the rain-filled clouds. The manor-house windows were ablaze once more and the motionless figure of the Countess looked like a distant portrait set in a gold and russet painting of times gone by.

"Aunt Josie is very ill," said the girl.

"I've heard."

"They say she'll die soon."

"Perhaps it's not so serious."

"It is," she said. "I'm going to die too."

She had to laugh. Otylia, wrapped in her cape, looked towards the manor house, golden rust in her dark blonde hair, her lovely eyes reflecting the conflagration that surrounded the Countess on the terrace.

"One doesn't die from that," she said.

"Not from that, I know."

Ah, Jeannette. Your ridiculous plans. Even so, she forced herself to say, "Kovarik is coming."

"Oh, Lord!" sighed the girl. "It will cost him such a lot of money."

The Count came out onto the terrace. He leaned towards his wife. The Countess lifted her face to his and something flashed suddenly in her hair. A diamond. Like a soul. She stood up, and the Count led her away into the conflagration which parted as a servant opened the french doors.

"I see you've already made up your mind," she said, breaking the silence. "But what if Mr. Suk doesn't come back?"

"Don't say that!"

She sighed. Jeannette will be upset. "Well, you've made up your mind, then."

"No, I haven't. It's fate."

"Don't be silly. What has fate got to do with it? It's just that one day, you make up your mind."

"I didn't make up my mind."

"Do you mean to say that Kovarik still has a chance, then?"

The girl shook her head.

"So then you did choose, didn't you?" she said, annoyed by this girlish silliness.

"No, I didn't," said the girl. She looked towards the manor house and her eyes caught the conflagration. "I tossed a gold florin."

The spider completed its banquet, leaving an ugly, shrivelled little sack in the web. It began lowering itself to the ground on a thin thread.

"Please understand, Miss Margulies," said the old man intently. "I can't go back any more. I have no time to waste. My eyes have finally been opened. Now I know what I should do. But what about those lost years, the pointless work! Sometimes I despair – "

"How can you talk that way, Master?" she broke in, with more indignation than she intended. "It's ridiculous."

"If only it were," he said. Another train had pulled away from the platform; dusk had fallen and the windows of the coaches were lit. They had not yet turned the lights on in the restaurant. Something rubbed against her leg. A glistening black cat, a well-fed restaurant cat.

"It's so stupid!" she cried. "You've written nine symphonies, the Slavonic Dances, a lot of chamber music. And now a beautiful, magic cello concerto!"

"That one perhaps," he interrupted her. "That was written out of love."

"It was all out of love. Everything you touched, you – "

"I wrote a lot. Too much. First I had to support my family."

"But there's absolutely no way of knowing that from your works. You wrote the Slavonic Dances when you had to support your family, and who can tell? You can't hear it in the music at all. It's magnificent. Your whole world is in it. You are the only one who could write that way."

"Nice to listen to over a glass of beer, isn't that so?"

"Stop bringing Brahms into it," she said disdainfully. "Very well. He discovered you. He was good to you. He was always good to those he was afraid of. He knew he was no match for you."

She stopped. Will he get angry? Will he turn red? But he only shook his head sadly. "You're not being fair to him, Miss Margulies. Huneker wasn't either. You know, I've always been just a – I've enjoyed everything I've done. That may be the root of it. I always wrote a polka, or any silly trifle at all, with the same zest, the same delight, as I wrote an oratorio. I should have, like Brahms – "

"Yes. That's just it!" she said, irritated. "You have a gift from God. Like Mozart. Every minuet he composed with the same zest as he did the Jupiter Symphony. And it's there, in everything of yours, in every little polka. Something you'll not find anywhere in Brahms."

"You're being unfair to him, very unfair. He doesn't believe in God, but that doesn't mean...." The eyes, with their watery film, looked towards the window again. He nodded his head. He said, "Strange indeed are the ways of the Lord."

They are indeed, she thought, controlling her anger. She noticed that the cat had moved close to the wall and was observing something with interest. Above the cat's black nose, suspended by a slender thread, was the motionless spider, caught in the focus of those amber eyes.

"But I can't go back to New York," he said quietly. "I want to try something. I have this idea – it occurred to me" – the tragic expression on his face gave way to a half smile – "and you'd never guess where I got the idea."

"It must have been in Vysoka."

"As a matter of fact, it wasn't," he said, still smiling. "It was in Spillville."

She relaxed. Here, at least, was something to cheer Jeannette up.

"I once fell asleep fishing on the Turkey River and there was a full moon and I thought about the fairytale about that beautiful water nymph who sacrificed her immortality for love of a prince – " he checked himself, and wiped his teary eyes. "Well, the long and short of it is, I'll make an opera out of it."

The cat rose up on its hind legs, snatched the spider out of the air and ran off with it.

"Perhaps the good Lord – once more – for the last time...."

Wind lashed at the coach and large drops of rain drummed on the leather roof. The axles groaned. Over the countryside that had shone gold, green and blue when she had driven through it with Will, a mist now rolled, swirling in the gusts of wind. I hope Jeannette manages to raise the money, otherwise that old witch of his will never let him go. Unless, of course, Otylia tosses another coin and it comes up heads. But that's even less likely.

And him, with his unsuccessful, uncompleted composition. Divine intervention again? Nonsense. It's just old age creeping up on him. He's repeating himself. He's plagued with self-doubt. Quite normal. His wife will roast him up a side of pork, he'll eat his fill and out of that side of pork will emerge another Scherzo Capriccioso. Or wherever it comes from.

She stuck her head out of the window and cold drops lashed at her face. This countryside is bewitching even in a storm. Even in this autumn dance of the spirits. They were driving along a road lined on either side with poplars. The trees, bent over like giant bows, swayed above the coach. On a branch, pressed against the trunk of a poplar, she saw a raven. The rain came down harder. In the treetops, she could hear harmonious moaning, unheard modulations.

The magnificent mystery of sounds. Where do they come from? How?

She had some time to waste at the station but she didn't feel like going into the restaurant. The Vienna Express stood waiting on the platform and she told a porter to put her luggage in her compartment, then went for a walk. The rain was drumming down on the vaulted glass ceiling, yellowed with dirt, and the acrid smoke stung her nose. His locomotives. That silly, old, brilliant child. He had invited her to stay until the day after tomorrow; it was his fifty-third birthday and they were going to consecrate the new organ in the church. An organ from America for that good Lord of his. But she had to go to Vienna. She had promised Freud she would play at his Sunday soirée – and also promised to let him know if she succeeded in persuading Dvorak to return to America. He was intrigued by Dvorak's music. Last time he had asked her: "Have you noticed that you find the same motif in many of his compositions? And yet it is certainly not emphasized. He is such a wizard with melodies. Such rich powers of invention. If you transpose it to C major and forget about the different rhythms you get C-D-E-D-C. Boring, is it not? You'll find it in the Slavonic Dances, in the Symphony in D Minor, in the New World Symphony, and elsewhere as well." "And what does that mean, Doctor Freud?" "You can't say what it means. But it does point to some subconscious obsession. This country friend of yours isn't quite the happy man you've described to me, Miss Margulies."

The mystery of music. She strolled to the end of the platform and turned around, crossing the platform and walking back alongside the neighbouring train. A dispatcher stood next to it, ready to signal it off. People were clambering on board. A tall young man was running towards her. I know him from somewhere. A small moustache, close-set eyes.

"Mr Suk!"

He stopped.

"Do you remember me? Adele Margulies?"

"Ah, yes, of course." *He revealed a healthy set of teeth.* "What brings you to Prague, Miss Margulies?"

"As a matter of fact, I'm just leaving. Duty takes me to Vienna. And where are you going in such a hurry?"

He laughed. "To Vysoka. The Master is having a birthday."

The dispatcher blew his whistle and raised his signal baton.

"I'm sorry – but I mustn't miss my train!"

He jumped onto the step at the back of the last coach and the train started up. She waved to him, and he waved back until he was hidden by the smoke. I'm not very happy about this, Mr. Amanuensis. Because there goes Jeannette's last chance.

She stood in the open door of the Vienna Express. It was still raining. For a moment, the old man was veiled by the smoke of the locomotive. As the smoke cleared, he said, "Of course, Mrs. Thurber can use my name if she thinks it will help. But I really can't promise you I'll come. I would like to, but man proposes – "

"Come!" she said fervently. "America was a good experience for you, wasn't it?"

"It was," he nodded.

The train began to move. He took off his bowler, a halo of grey hair glowed around his ruddy head, the wind waved his wild beard. She heard him call out, "God be with you!"

And he stood there waving his hat until he vanished in the smoke and the distance.

26 :C): ON THE SHORES OF THE ATLANTIC

FOR THE SECOND TIME that day, the telephone rang. A real frenzy of interest. Sissieretta struggled to her feet and hobbled over to the window where the device was jangling unpleasantly on a small varnished table. Beyond the window, rain was pouring down onto the ocean from a bank of grey, low-hanging clouds, and waves were slapping bleakly, stubbornly, against the stone jetty. A white rowboat was tethered to the jetty, beating its white cloth buffers irregularly against the stone walls. She often wondered why she bothered having a telephone at all. This was only the third call in the last fourteen days. Two weeks ago, Dr. Lovecraft's receptionist had rung her to say that the doctor wanted to see her. This morning, Maurice had called to say he was in Providence for two days and would like to drop over. This was the third time it had rung.

"Jones," she said into the receiver.

"Long distance from New York."

Who was the last person to call her from New York? She couldn't remember. And when had it been? It must have been several years ago.

"Sissieretta?"

"Yes?"

"This is Jeannette!"

Jeannette who? "Yes?"

"Jeannette Thurber."

"Oh, Jeannette! Is it really you? I didn't recognize your voice. How are you?"

"I'm just fine, thanks, Sissieretta. I hope you're keeping well yourself."

"Yes," she said. So far, anyway. But as long as I can talk I'll say, Yes, I'm doing fine, thank you. Maybe my old friends will remember me now, though of course it's too late: generally speaking, Mrs. Jones, this type responds very well to radiation.... Generally speaking. And how lasting is the response? Well, I'm in no pain so far. But maybe I should have gone to a different doctor. Who knows if this one isn't a relative of the novelist? Skin and bones, a bare skull covered with the pink blemishes of depigmentation – nothing uglier can happen to me.

"I'm so glad to hear it," Jeannette was saying. "I'm calling about two things, Sissieretta. First of all – and I'm sure you'll be delighted to hear this – Langston Hughes wants to put together a concert of old-timers at the Cotton Club. Will Marion Cook, Harry Burleigh and Sterling Brown have all promised to come."

She never gives up. Why, she must be way past seventy by now. But Jeannette will never give up, not even on her death-bed.

And suddenly she remembered that time Jeannette had called from New York. More than ten years ago. Sometime during the war. Not long after, her Troubadours were ingloriously forced to close up shop. (Black Patti's Troubadours, she used to call them – in her vicious mood, when she could no longer bear the accolade they threw at her. No white singer would be fêted as a White Sissieretta.) At the time, Jeannette's voice had trembled with indignation. *"They turned you down, Sissieretta. If only poor Dvorak were still alive and here to help us. By myself I – well, the gentlemen from the Met have had their fill of me, I'm afraid." "It's not worth upsetting yourself over, Mrs. Thurber." "Of course it is! This is the twentieth century. If I'm not mistaken, we once fought a Civil War over the matter. But that was a long time ago, and the gentlemen from the Met have apparently forgotten." Then Jeannette levelled a devastating – and unjust – criticism against Signora Marinelli, who had not sought out the role for herself, Sissieretta was certain about that. On the other hand, Marinelli did not turn it down either, even though she knew that at Jeannette's urging they were considering Black Patti – her skin colour, after all, made her the logical choice for the role. She smiled bitterly. But Marinelli is a Mediterranean type, with a dark, olive-brown complexion: thus did the gentlemen from the Met justify their choice.*

" ... and Mr. Ellington wants to write something in the style of the second movement of the New World Symphony, the Largo. It's more because of me than anything else. Harry's going to let us have Dvorak's arrangement of Old Folks – "

"I don't sing any more, Mrs. Thurber."

Her voice hasn't aged. She's probably just as she always was.

"All you have to do is be there, Sissieretta. You don't have to perform. It's just in honour of the old days." Jeannette laughed her girlish laugh. "Kovarik is going to play Humoresque. That was Harry's idea. His grateful students want to pay a tribute to old Borax," and she laughed again. "This year is the twenty-fifth anniversary of his death. Harry is trying to get his whole class together. Fisher has promised, Collins too – "

"Maurice is here with me right now," she said.

"Strathotte?"

The cracked white rowboat, covered with a tarpaulin, bumped against the jetty, making dark, hollow sounds like a wooden drum. Maurice, who was sitting in an armchair, waved his hands in a gesture of rejection.

"My God!" Jeannette's joyous voice could be heard coming from the receiver. "And what's he doing?"

"He's teaching," she said, unable to repress a tone of irony. "At least that's what he does for a living. As for his vocation – well, you know what they say: many are called, few are chosen. I ended up teaching too, Mrs. Thurber. But I gave it up. I'll put Maurice on the line."

Maurice was still waving her off, but he could hear Jeannette's enthusiastic, insistent voice all the way across the dark room and he had to get up and take the receiver. She heard him say, "Good day, Mrs. Thurber," and then a flood of words in that youthful, indestructible voice poured from the receiver.

She watched the boat bobbing in the waves, butting the jetty like an angry ram. The rain had brought fog with it. The coast was beginning to resemble an illustration from a story by her doctor's namesake. She shuddered.

Mr. Dvorak put two fingers in his mouth and whistled like a loco-motive. Everyone in the orchestra looked up in astonishment and the music collapsed into confusion. She looked around. Jeannette had just entered the rehearsal hall and was walking across the room to a door on the other side. She was wearing Oxfords and a tweed suit, and her magnificent hair was coiled up into a chignon. Apparently she had not heard the unusual sound, for when Mr. Dvorak whistled again Jeannette looked around at him in astonishment. Just then, someone in the orchestra whistled back. Bailey, the clown. Several people around him burst out laughing. "Lachen Sie nicht!" roared Mr. Dvorak. And in a quieter voice, but still imperious, he said, "Mrs. Thurber, please, come over here. Here." Then he jumped nimbly off the dais and lunged like a tiger at Maurice, who was sitting among the first violins. "It wasn't me, Dr. Dvorak!" Maurice protested, but the conductor was already pulling him by the arm towards the flabbergasted president of the Conservatory. "Mrs. Thurber, I want you to meet the future American Dvorak!" "Hear, hear!" brayed Bailey, and then whistled again. Mr. Dvorak let go of Maurice, who scurried back to his place, rushed over to Bailey and an instant later was dragging him and his clarinet towards the door while Harry, in the background, began a dark, dramatic pianissimo roll on the kettledrums. Bailey was flung into the corridor against his will by a pair of strong arms, they heard a terrible racket – the clatter, perhaps, of a clarinetist tumbling down the stairs – the conductor came back into the room, strode over to the kettledrums and pounced quickly on Harry, who had stopped playing too late. Caught by the ear, he too went flying through the door. This time, no racket followed the expulsion. Mr. Dvorak walked back dusting off his hands, set a chair beside the dais for the astonished Jeannette, raised his baton and the orchestra began another run-through of Maurice's Plantation Dances.

Realizing almost at once that he had just banished the first clarinet and his only timpanist, Dvorak tapped the music stand angrily, jumped down from the dais again and ran out of the hall. Boldly, Jeannette announced, "Anyone who annoys Doctor Dvorak any further will have me to deal with." No one laughed, although the thought of having to deal with the soft-hearted Jeannette alarmed no one. Harry came meekly back into the hall and took up his position behind the kettledrums. They waited. "Meanwhile, Mr. Burleigh, you can tune up," said Jeannette. "Your bottom drum is at least a semi-tone too low." Harry energetically set about tightening the screws, as the door opened again to reveal Bailey, the conductor's hand leading him firmly by the collar. A lump was rising on Bailey's forehead, but his clarinet appeared to be intact. Mr. Dvorak mounted his dais with poise and the orchestra began a sprightly rendition of Maurice's dances.

I wonder if young Buster Bailey knows of his father's former glory, she thought. But of course, he must. All of Sissie's band knows it. Even when old Bailey was touring with the Troubadours, he was still bragging about his constant run-ins with the great Dvorak.

"No, I don't think so, Mrs. Thurber," she heard Maurice say. Then Jeannette spoke, then Maurice again. "Dvorak was a lot too generous," he said. "I believe he was just happy that someone had listened to his advice, at least, and tried to write music that way. Remember how some people turned their noses up at the idea? I think it got under his skin. That was why he overrated my piece."

Overrated? Dvorak certainly hadn't thought that. She looked at the small boat bumping against the buffer on the jetty. *She saw Mr. Dvorak in the front row, tapping the toe of his polished boots to the rhythm of Maurice's Bamboula while Maurice, at the podium, with a bad case of the jitters, was merely going through the motions of conducting the orchestra. Fortunately, it didn't need conducting. It was – on Mr. Dvorak's advice – their own music: syncopation, pentatonic scales, diminished sevenths. She was delighted with Maurice's success. The girls and boys in the choir nodded their heads to the beat as they did in church, and she caught herself tapping her toe as well. Quickly, she regained her self-control. But then she thought: Why not?*

Why indeed? she said, looking numbly at the stubborn little boat. She considered the years spent with the Troubadours, the boys capering about the stage to the rhythm of the bones and the banjo while she waited behind the scenes until the audience had had its fill of gawking at Black Sambos – made even blacker by soot – and she could remind them, for a while at least, that they were white and thus a cultured folk. Martha, Il Trovatore, Lucia and of course Sousa's El Capitán. They donned expressions of absorption and applauded her more loudly than her minstrels. Yet she would never be more than an exotic curiosity singing arias in the intervals between Black Sambo's gutter songs. She had never been cast in a real opera. "They turned you down, Sissieretta." "Listen to that!" they would cry in amazement. "Black as the ace of spades and she sings – almost – like Patti!"

Black Patti. Why not call Adelina Patti a White Sissieretta?

A shaft of pain in her stomach. Is this the cancer announcing itself, then? But the disease isn't in the stomach. Still, I suppose the pain will be everywhere. This is a different kind of pain, though. Far older than the pain Dr. Lovecraft is treating me for.

After Martha, after Il Trovatore, the black performers with banjos would rush out from the wings, rolling their eyes and flashing their teeth as the audience expected them to do. *She noticed that even white gentlemen in the front row, in frock coats and diamond-*

studded shirt-fronts, were tapping their toes like Mr. Dvorak, and she felt glad. And yet when the concert was over, they insulted Maurice just the same. Perhaps it was their way of taking revenge on Mr. Dvorak, who had refused to talk to the critics after the concert. "The work," they said, "could easily be adapted for performance at patriotic assemblies. Everyone in the choir kept time with their heads." Just in case anyone was tempted to take Maurice's Plantation Dances seriously. After all, they said, it was only a slightly more cultivated version of the minstrel show, a Negro Charakterstück. And Maurice had longed to have them recognize that his piece was at least a faint reflection of Mr. Dvorak's Slavonic Dances. He had tried so hard.

When the papers came out, Mr. Dvorak was in a rage. He had learned – probably from Will Marion – the word "shit", and that day he peppered his vocabulary with it repeatedly, even in front of Jeannette.

"I don't think I'd even want to, Mrs. Thurber," Maurice was saying into the telephone. "Now, after Gershwin, it would sound too – primitive. And besides, I don't have a copy of the score any more."

Jeannette's insistent chatter.

What was that woman's name? Ella? Ella something. Ella Sheppard. She used to play the piano for the Fisk Jubilee Singers and she had a daughter studying violin at the Conservatory. But at Maurice's concert, her daughter had sung in the choir. A tall, pretty girl with a head like a black' lamb's, nodding to the rhythm of Maurice's cakewalk, abandoning herself entirely to the music. She had introduced her mother to Mr. Dvorak at a rehearsal. He took the fragile lady by both hands and squeezed them so hard she winced. "The Fisk Jubilee Singers!" he thundered. "I am so sorry I missed you! I came to England two days after your last concert. But everyone there was still talking about it." Then he took them all to Fleischmann's, where everybody stared at them in astonishment, Dvorak in the company of three black women and the shy, silent Maurice. But it had probably never occurred to Mr. Dvorak that certain things were not done. They stood out in the Viennese café like his outrageous green tie against his cornflower blue vest. Mr. Huneker came over to their table with a tankard of beer and sat down to listen.

"But Gershwin does it far better, Mrs. Thurber," she heard Maurice say. "And as a matter of fact, he's a student of Dvorak's too, in a way. A second-generation student. Goldmark taught him – "

Dum-dum-dum went the boat against the jetty. Death knocking on my door. The indifferent sea, rolling, murky, wave upon wave, the water pitted with drops of rain.

That woman, Ella, bore the marks of smallpox on the brown skin of her still pretty face and her eyes were haunted like those of a long-suffering animal, though her statuesque, cheerful daughter, with full, ripe breasts in a tightly laced bodice, had the mischievous and happy certainty of freedom in her eyes. "My father lived in Nashville, Tennessee, Dr. Dvorak, and he bought himself for eighteen hundred dollars." "Bought himself?" Mr. Dvorak was astonished. "Yes. His owner, Dr. Wilmore, was a good man who didn't hold much with slavery so he let my father buy himself. My mother's master was not so kind, and his wife, Mrs. Jonesborough, was even worse. The Jonesboroughs had five daughters and something was always going on in the big house: social visits, balls, garden parties, picnics, birthday parties. There was always a raft of suitors and the household niggers had their hands full. Momma was beautiful. I only saw her twice, but I remember how beautiful she was. She could iron silk dresses and blouses better than any of the other girls. But she was beautiful, so she also had to work as a chambermaid. When the Jonesboroughs had guests in – and that was most of the time – Momma would pass around the refreshments. They gave her a black silk dress, a white apron and cap – at least that's what my daddy said. I never saw her like that. She had four other children after me, but they were all light-skinned. I was the only one she had with my Daddy." "What became of them, Ma?" asked her daughter. "I don't know, Lauretta. The Jonesboroughs owned the largest plantation in the county, and they had the most magnificent house as well, with statues they say came all the way from Italy and huge pictures on the walls, and all the domestic slaves were tall, good-looking and young. The Jonesboroughs had an aversion to anything ugly, so as soon as Momma was back on her feet after having me, she had to go back into the big house, and the little girls who didn't have to go to work yet looked after me in the cabin. Momma would come back late each night and leave for the big house before sunrise. Daddy lived in Nashville and he'd only met Momma briefly when the Jonesboroughs were up visiting Mr. Lattimer. Daddy hoped that in time he could save enough money to buy her. When I was about six months old Mr. Lattimer went on a return visit to the Jonesboroughs, and when he came back, he stopped by Daddy's workshop – my father made and repaired carriages – and told him I was dying of neglect. Mother couldn't look after me and he thought the Jonesboroughs might be willing to sell me to Daddy because it didn't look as though I'd live much longer. Mr. Lattimer was a good man. Daddy was making him a carriage, so he loaned him two hundred dollars in advance and let him go down to Mississippi before the carriage was done. Daddy went to the Jonesboroughs, paid three hundred and fifty dollars for me, and brought me back to Nashville. But since he worked from sunup to sundown he couldn't look after me properly either. So Mrs. Walker, a free Negro who did white folks' washing for them, took me in, and Daddy paid her something towards my upkeep. And as soon as he finished the coach for Mr. Lattimer and another one for the Reverend Mr. Higgins of the First Presbyterian Church in Nashville, he set off for Mississippi to buy my mother as well."

"Inflammatus et accensus," *Sissieretta could hear her own voice sing,* "per te, Virgo, sim defensus." *The girls, to her displeasure, nodded their heads even to the rhythm of Rossini, and she saw Mr. Dvorak at his podium, glowing as he always did when a piece was going well, the furrow between his eyebrows relaxed in the happiness of the moment,* "Fac me cruce custodiri, morte Christi premuniri", *and in the first row, his plump, round wife, her face too lit with a smile, and she imagined briefly how when the concert was over this woman would say to her,* "You really do sing almost like Patti!" *and she sang,* "Quando corpus morietur, fac ut animae donetur – "

"The bargain was struck, Daddy took Mother to Nashville, and the Jonesboroughs sent along an overseer who was to sign the bill of sale the following day before a notary public. Next morning, however, Mr. Jonesborough sent word that he had reconsidered; Mrs. Jonesborough and her daughters needed Momma, he said. So the overseer took her back to Mississippi and I remained with Mrs. Walker. But not for much longer." The rain was falling harder now and dirty brown foam was lashing the jetty, dum-dum-dum went the rowboat. Jeannette's voice was still chattering on the telephone, and Maurice's pantomime indicated that he was trying to wriggle out of it, that he would rather be sitting talking to her again.

"Maurice, oh Maurice, I'm so unhappy!" and her dark blonde head slumped to her hands and her hands to the keyboard, a cacophonic chord of girlish desperation. Maurice hoped that Mrs. Thurber couldn't hear it. He made a special effort to refrain from offering the girl

another lesson in ragtime, anything. "Why, Miss Otylia?" *he asked,*
already knowing the answer, because he had seen young Kovarik
wandering through the Conservatory corridors like a ghost, and how
the girl was now always accompanied to her piano lessons by her
plump mother who would then go off to watch the unusual sights
in Monsieur Senac's class, where young ladies in knickerbockers and
masks fought duels with the fleuret, before returning to take the pale
girl home to their apartment on Seventeenth Street. And he knew
because he too had wandered ghostlike through the corridors, though
he lacked the courage to say anything and merely sat at the piano
with her when Adele, who was too busy and frequently indisposed,
could not take the lesson. And he would watch the white fingers
with their mother-of-pearl nails beneath which Mozart, always sunny,
now wept for longing, and finally the dark blonde head slumping
on the white arms, the cacophonic discord of despair. "I knew all
along, Sissieretta, that I didn't stand a chance. She was a white girl,
a foreigner, the daughter of the famous Master and in love with his
secretary. But love knows neither hope nor despair; all that matters
is the love itself, and I was in love, Sissieretta. I never told her and
then later, the poor girl died. She was twenty-seven." *Dum-dum-*
dum of the little boat, the rain growing heavier, the end of the jetty
now invisible, shrouded in fog. "My father still had to do robota –
compulsory labour," *said Mr. Dvorak.* "When I was a little boy, I
sometimes went to help him. It was bad. But the things you've been
telling me, madame – and you say these people were good Christians?" *The diminutive lady nodded.* "Some of the slave-owners were
kind people," *she said, and her daughter looked at Sissieretta and*
rolled her eyes. Her mother noticed. "Oh yes, they were, Lauretta.
People can't be blamed for the circumstances they live in. And no
matter what they are, the circumstances will always show who is a
true Christian and who is not. The lawyer, Mr. Allen, secretly warned
my father. You know, when Daddy couldn't buy Momma, he married
again after a time and he bought his second wife for thirteen hundred
dollars. But they couldn't draw up her free papers in a slave state
and the nearest free state was Ohio, which was too far away. On top
of that, Daddy's health began to fail, he didn't complete some orders,
got into debt and couldn't afford to go to Ohio. But Mr. Allen secretly
informed him, through his own Negro manservant, that some creditors were intending to claim my stepmother against the debt, because back then, when a man bought a wife, she was his property

in the eyes of the law until she got documents stating that she was free. So Daddy's creditors could legally have confiscated her and auctioned her off like the rest of his property. That night Daddy took my stepmother far away from Nashville to a railway station in the woods, where no one would recognize her, and he sent her to Cincinnati by train. A few days later we went secretly to Cincinnati too, and he left everything to his creditors. And there he started all over again – ”

Huneker, who had been listening somewhat restlessly to Ella Sheppard's story, suddenly looked up. "Oh dear, it's Chopinzee!" he whispered. They looked around. A small man with wild eyes had walked into the café and was looking around cockily. He caught sight of the massive Huneker crouched behind his tankard. The little man crouched too, but it was more like the stance of a wrestler about to lunge. He stretched out an extraordinarily long arm pointed straight at Huneker. "Aha!" he cried. Everyone stopped and looked around. Huneker huddled down almost out of sight. "I see you, don't try to hide. So, the great music critic Mr. Huneker says de Pachmann plays his Chopin effeminately, does he? De Pachmann is the fairy of the piano whose Bach is worse than his bite? De Pachmann isn't what he once was, isn't that what you wrote, Huneker?" The man stormed over to a piano at the side of the restaurant. "Now you listen to this, Huneker. This is just for you. Listen carefully." He sat down and began to play, while the others stared at each other uncomprehendingly. The man's body wove strangely about but his eyes were fastened firmly on Huneker. What he played made little sense. It might have been Chopin, performed with a torrent of feeling and theatrical virtuosity – but if so it was a strange, unfamiliar Chopin. As he played, he talked in a loud voice: "Huneker, I'm playing you a very difficult composition – and I hope I'm playing it well." Several chords, and then: "Listen to my left hand. Pianissimo! Is it good? No? Yes! Ha-ha-ha! Liszt played it faster, but – ha-ha-ha! – Rubinstein was slower." An acrobatic flourish in the left hand, then the right, the piercing eyes never once looking at the keyboard but stabbing Huneker's face, which had now broken out in a sweat. The critic shuddered. "Ha-ha, Huneker! There used to be two great pianists in the world: Liszt and de Pachmann – and now, Liszt is dead. Joseffi tried to play it, Huneker, but it's far beyond his abilities, ha-ha! But I, Vladimir de Pachmann – the greatest interpreter of Chopin in the *world – oh yes, I know how, Huneker." The pianist writhed, his head a thicket of black hair tossed far back, but both hands were controlled, the diabolical fingers fell upon the keys with catlike gentleness, the eyes were anchored upon Huneker's face.*

"Something else, perhaps, Mrs. Thurber," said Maurice's voice into the sound of the rain beyond the window, into the roar of the increasingly turbulent Atlantic. "I have a few other pieces, better ones, I hope. Caprice Espagnol – " She pressed her forehead against the glass. It felt soothingly cool. Blackness was seeping into the fog; night was approaching, blackness. The glory of the Cotton Club. A belated souvenir. My life, my career, my mission. It can't be brought back to life; it's too late for that. The darkness is nearing, through the distant, Lovecraftian fog on the North Atlantic. *Mr. Dvorak seemed to be apologizing to Ella Sheppard: "And many of my countrymen fought against the South too, madame. That general – Sherman? Sherman. He had five of them in his bodyguard," he said in his approximate English, but then he continued, fluently: "Krch, Janovsky, Kapsa, Zinkule, Malek – "* The darkness was coming, dum-dum-dum. A gull flew out of the grey fog, something in its beak. Dum-dum. *"... and they even tried to take away our tongue – our Czech language. Three centuries of foreign rule. Everything but music – that they couldn't take from us."* Dum-dum-dum. The Atlantic boomed, Jeannette's warbling voice, dirty foam lashing the windowpanes. "Sissieretta," she heard Maurice say. "Please, can you explain it to her?" She reached for the telephone and heard Jeannette: "Try and persuade him, Sissieretta. He lives in New York, after all.... Sissieretta, are you there?" "I am, Mrs. Thurber." "Come. It will be magnificent! Cook, Kovarik, Fisher, Burleigh – " But I don't want to remember. What is life for? Dum-dum-dum. Like a ram against a wall. It won't get through, it won't. *A final, lightning arpeggio, and the little man stood up from the piano and grinned at them. "You're a great critic, Huneker, but you've never heard anything like that before. Only Vladimir de Pachmann can play like that." With an ominous chuckle, he walked over to their table. Ella Sheppard's pretty daughter edged closer to Dvorak. "How did you like that, Huneker?" Huneker stayed put but there was a quaver in his voice when he replied. "I never like any composition played backwards. Especially Chopin." The pianist clapped. "You're a bright man, Huneker, but you're still a skunk! For someone who can't even play the piano himself, you're a dirty, critical, son-of-a-bitching skunk!"* The gull vanished into the fog; I'll never know what it was bringing me in its beak, what message, what sign. *The plump woman came up to her and pressed her hand. Mrs. Dvorak. She waited for the well-worn insult, the well-intentioned comparison to Adelina Patti.* "Splendid, Miss! I too once sang the Inflammatus," *she said in scarcely understandable English, but sincerely.* "But not like you, not like you at all. You are" – here it comes – "better than Albani. She sang it for Anton in London. You have more feeling...." *A deep relief and joy.*

To end the program, they sang an arrangement by Mr. Dvorak. She didn't like the song, but it was expected from her, just as people expected somersaults from her Troubadours. She had to do it. Old folks at home on the old plantation. When you're old, you can even have fond memories of hell. Of those brief moments when the fires under the cauldron went out. "All de world am sad and dreary, ebrywhere I roam," wailed those silly little girls, that cute one in the first row, swinging her hips from left to right, "Oh! darkies how my heart grows weary...." *The heart. Heaviness of heart. But my heart won't be the death of me, not like Maurice's inaccessible white girl. It's the black night that will be the death of me, rolling in on me, dum, the kettledrum of the boat, dum-dum-dum. Harry Burleigh's remarkable velvet baritone:* "One little hut among de bushes, one dat I love.... "' *But Mr. Dvorak said,* "One day they'll appreciate what Stephen Foster's songs did for American music." *She didn't resent him for saying that. Dvorak knew nothing. Ella Sheppard did. Dvorak could only hear the sorrowful melody; the words, in that painful dialect, were beyond his grasp. She took the solo from Harry, her large, half-schooled lyrical soprano against the background of those wonderful, shrieking, swinging little girls, she was twenty-three and her voice sounded like a bell....* "All up and down de whole creation, sadly I roam," *and now Harry Burleigh will bring Dvorak's* arrangement to the Cotton Club, Ellington's saxophones will underlay it with their alluring honey – "When will I see de bees a-humming all round de comb?" – but Harry Carney, in the low register of his baritone, will burst through that honeycomb with his raw, grating tone, the bristles of ridicule will penetrate the honey, the melody remains, soaring and lyrical, but the black, earthbound saxophone will slaughter Foster's maudlin, sentimental lie. Harry Carney. And Johnny Hodges an octave above him. No one will know but me – Black Patti. Not even Jeannette. She laughed bitterly. "Okay,

Mrs. Thurber, I'll come. If I'm feeling all right. I'll let you go now, and see you at the Cotton Club." "*You smell like a toilet, Huneker.*" *Huneker rose to his feet. Suddenly, de Pachmann bent down, grabbed a tankard and, in a flash, hurled the golden liquid into the critic's face. De Pachmann lunged at Huneker, but before he could land a blow he found himself pinioned between two large waiters. Mr. Fleischmann, with his severe, partriarchal beard, approached. "Apologize to Mr. Huneker, Maestro, or I'll have to ask you to leave the establishment.*" *The virtuoso muttered: "Very well, I apologize. Let me go! I apologize!"* Mr. Fleischmann nodded his head, the waiters loosened their grip, the little man straightened his tie with dignity and in a tone of profound disgust said: "Skunk, I apologize to you."* And he wheeled about triumphantly. The door slammed.*

"You're right, Sissieretta," said Jeannette. "There is something else. Kovarik called today." Maurice put out his cigarette and looked at the clock. Don't go yet, Maurice. I'm all alone here. It's getting darker all the time. "*Mother would hide in the woods and my sister would take her food, but it was never long before they caught her. Once she was mauled by the dogs, and they always whipped her so hard she couldn't move. She wasn't pretty any more, so they sent her from the big house to work in the cotton fields. But she never stopped trying to escape and finally Mr. Jonesborough decided to sell her in New Orleans because she wasn't much good for anything any more. After the Civil War my father went looking for her, but her new masters had gone to the West Indies and taken her with them. I never saw her again.*"

The small pianist's hands rested in her lap. Dvorak pulled out his handkerchief and placed his left hand, white, freckled and hairy, around the delicate black shoulder. "Anna Dvorak is dead," she heard Jeannette say. "She outlived old Borax by twenty-five years, Sissieretta. There was never any love lost between us, but today – "

She stopped listening. Behind her, Maurice stood up. The sea outside the window lashed wildly against the stone jetty, the white patch of the boat and, beyond that, the black, black darkness.

What was it all for? she wondered.

The sea cried out to her like a wild animal.

Deo gratias!
September, 1980 – July, 1983
Toronto

A NOTE ABOUT THE AUTHOR

Josef Skvorecky was born in Bohemia, emigrated to Canada in 1968, and is now Professor of English at Erindale College, University of Toronto. He and his wife, the novelist Zdena Salivarova, run a Czech-language publishing house, Sixty-Eight Publishers, in Toronto. Skvorecky's novels include *The Cowards*, *Miss Silver's Past*, *The Bass Saxophone*, and *The Engineer of Human Souls*. He has also written many short stories and filmscripts, and is the winner of the 1980 Neustadt International Prize for Literature and the 1984 Governor General's Award in Canada.

A NOTE ON THE TYPE

The text of this book was film-set in Pilgrim. Originally called Bunyan, it was designed by the British artist Eric Gill (1882–1940) for a book published by the Limited Editions Club of New York and re-cut by Linotype (London) in the 1950's. In its general appearance, it resembles Gill's Joanna type.

Composed by Q Composition Inc., Canada

Printed and bound by Fairfield Graphics,
Fairfield, Pennsylvania

Designed by The Dragon's Eye Press